Soul Break Part One

ISBN: 978-0-9921977-4-2

First Edition 1 April 2016
Second Edition 10 July 2016

Cover Illustration © Lynel Coetzer 2016

www.lynelcoetzer.co.za

For my hero - my right hand, my left hand, my friend and wife Soreen.

0

<u>37 Days Before:</u>

Staring into the pitch black of the night with the haunting silence of the wide-open fields that surrounded him, he knew his hopes were not far from its reach to untouchable freedom.
Kneeling down among the tall grass enveloping the range of shadows and darkness, he could almost feel the hands of the night's eerie darkness touching his soul.
It was as though it was pulling him towards the ghostly silence that boomed from deep within the darkness, with an untold and sinister cry – whispers of a dark history and a future screaming to be told.
It was daunting; the darkness, the excitement, the fear, the thrill. Part of him felt as though it was destiny in the making, but more so something that destiny had already seen.
The cold of the night and all the spiraling emotions felt familiar. Shutting his eyes, he calmed his breathing in the hopes to control and regain a focus on his objective.

As he crept forward through the drying brush, his thoughts continued to gyrate and churn when the ever ominous hoot of an owl sounded somewhere within the distant brush of tall and eerie tree's and he stopped. Somewhere in the darkness something scared the bird and its wings clapped into the sky as it fled.
His heart hammered against his chest and throbbed inside his ears as he strained his wide eyes through the blackness above the tall grassy fields that now, bore in them only a loud calm. He closed his eyes again, heaving out a sigh of both relief and trepidation and continued to creep forward through the grass towards the undertaking that would resolve him of his self-loathing.
The month of February had left only a few weeks before the claws of autumn would dig into the air above the provinces of South Africa. The gentle airstreams that circled the land bore in it a shivery omen of the winter cold to come. There were sounds to the side, further ahead near the fence. He paused. Something was moving, walking slowly, one foot in front of the other. His eyes strained in the dark but the night was black and the light from the spot lights around the mine were not advancing his vision in the thick blackness of the veldt around him.

A few moments passed before he resumed his path forward. The range of seemingly endless grass fields around him had already begun to dry and wilt to its winter's beige and the daunting moon hung above the silent openness surrounding the abandoned old gold mine.

The entirety of the mining grounds near the colossal shaft tower was circled by an eight foot high perimeter fence. The bulk of which was steel chain link fencing which had rusted through the years, where palisade fencing was used around the office buildings predominantly. As he reached the chain link fence, he turned to look back towards the road where in the distance he could vaguely see the four cars standing in the darkness beneath giant willow trees - like ghosts in the faint glimmer of the moonlight. In front of him stood the metal shaft tower, looming up high in the darkness, lit only by the spot lights surrounding it. It was quiet the sight to be so near to something that seemed to have in it so much power and dominance over the land beneath it, waiting patiently for its giant headgears to arrive so it could begin churning out the rich reefs of gold beneath his feet.

At this distance he could no longer see the silhouettes of the others, but he knew they were looking back at him through their binoculars anxiously waiting for the big moment to arrive. Giving an arrogant grin into the night, he heaved a sigh, his heart still rampant against his chest as he stared down at the fuse chord in his hand. He knew that the breaking point was upon him, one shot to clamber out of the life he could no longer tolerate and into the pastures of esteem - yet the ever-conscious urge to drop the bundle of dry fuse still raged war inside of him.

Everything he had been taught, raised upon and believed to be good was about to be cast aside for a chance to leave behind scars that he believed he could outrun. He closed his eyes again, his entirety wishing him to proceed and simply forgive himself in the days that would follow – regardless of what would be.

As he scurried over the fencing he could finally see the giant pit beneath the shaft tower – it's gaping of darkness only a few feet away behind a ring of palisade fencing that would remain there until the cages were ready to be installed.

He stalled atop the fence, a leg on either side – staring at the giant pit of gloom, the haunting remnants of the old shaft. For the most part he knew it was wrong to be there now at such close point to the mine being reopened. He knew it was a risk the others probably never took, but he had to prove himself to them. He was a new version of him and couldn't let them know he was anything different.

There was another sound nearby, somewhere in the shadows around the shaft. He lowered beneath the radius of the spot lights but the night was still again. The daunting height of the metal tower felt as though it pressed on him, it was dominant and ominous in its own shadows created by the surrounding lights. The old shaft had in recent months become known as a chance to regain former glory to the surrounding towns, with a reopening ceremony to follow in the very next week. His hands gripped the fuse chord and looked back to the road, but the night's blackness had engulfed everything from site, including the silhouettes of the massive willow trees. He slowly began down the fence again, his clammy hand weakening his grip on the fence.

As he silently moved low to the ground towards the palisade fencing, the shaft's darkness felt overwhelming as though it had a force invisible to his eyes that clutched at him, drawing him closer and closer. At the palisade, he took great caution to avoid stabbing its sharp points into his flesh as he hoisted over the top. Time was now an enemy, he had to hurry before the security guards caught wind of his presence. But he was careful of his hands, his legs and black clothes to avoid any contact with the shards of metal sticking up into the sky above the fence.

Now, even more than before he had conjured up the will power and defiance to jump the fence, he felt the breath of the untouchable freedom fill his lungs as he took his first step away from the fence that secluded the world from the confines of the giant dark mine shaft.

He hurried closer towards the old entrance to the mine shaft, crossing quickly through the brightness of the security flood lights – making him a clear portrait to anyone watching.

He held his breath as he sunk to his knees beside the remnants of the base of the previous giant metal headgear. Weak from the adrenaline and fear - although he had barely used a portion of

3

energy he was panting breathlessly.

"Keep it together."

It was in that silent hiatus away from the night's sounds and darkness that he felt his disordered brain begin to make sense of the adrenaline's memorandum that ravaged through his body. The purpose of the palisade fence was to act as a secure boundary to keep enclosed the entire quarter where the mines old shaft sat waiting like a giant black mouth in the earth. And as his eyes hunted around the diffused portion of the mine he could feel the dark half of his soul take over and shove aside his logic and everything he knew was wrong.

Carefully taking step for step closer to the portion of thick cement that was the former shaft tower, he scanned the perimeter fence that they had told him would partner with mine security under strict instruction to keep trespassers away from the area where once the colossal headgears stood proudly, muscling the gold from the soul of the Earth. But now, on the other side of the fence a deafening silence screamed around the abandoned vicinity and he too felt a strange calm befall him as he neared the shafts portal wall, forward into the stream of light beaming down from the tall spot lights a few feet away.

With trembling hands he fumbled through the loosely bound fuses they had given to him, listening to his own loud heartbeat in prayer that this would be the road which would lead him in a clear escape from his life as a boy who felt trapped by his own heart and fears.

Carefully and silently, he stepped closer towards the waist high concrete segment of wall where soon the entrance to the cages would be, the very last space between his body and the menacingly dark shaft pit. The high metal tower continued to howl as the nights wind circled between its massive metal structures. Holding his breath he peeked over, down into the darkness that stemmed to the deep guts of the Earth and the wind hurdled up at him from the depths of the shaft like a phantom in a high pitched screech, reaching for him.

He gasped and stumbled backwards, hitting the ground on his backside with a bump as the stale odor from the deep hole twirled in the air around him. He closed his eyes, heaving breathlessly while also high on the dire need to not be who he was.

Whispers in his mind said *"Do it!"*

But he couldn't make out if it was his own demons or something far greater at play, luring him to his destiny.

He felt the butterflies swallow his insides as the intensity of the rush riddled through him as he stood up again and peered over the partition into the baleful hole - fenced from the world with no head gear to conceal the ferociousness of its glare upward to the heavens.

The strength of the darkness forced his already swirling mind to compel his eyes to gain control as they achingly surged through the severe gloom for just a hint of what it could hold in its dismal entrails. Just then a loud metal clunk tore through the silent night and he dropped down to the ground, cowering against the concrete partition, away from the surveillance lights. His ears pricked to the stillness that seemed to squeal so loudly in the chilled air, his wide frightened eyes searching desperately the darkness beyond the fence and each ominous shadow around him for a sign of security or other intruder. Nearby, something moved in the shadows across the giant black hole and he froze, kneeling down. The area was filled with sounds, creaks and groans. Everything around the shaft was new. He knew there couldn't be ghosts out there, that security would refuse to work if there were truly were malicious entities behind the strange screams of the night. He tried to stay focused and do what he had come to do – a chance at really breaking the rules his life so invoked on him. Again his heart beat echoed in his head, his breathing too and feeling like both were only causing him more threat, he held tight his breath and clenched shut his eyes.

He had made a definite identification of the danger in what he was doing, in where he was at that very moment in his existence and yet he felt it screaming throughout his body to not leave nor back down this close to breaking free of who he was day to day. He opened his eyes and released his breath to a quieter world, sure that the moment had past, and that he indeed was alone in the circling fence at the old shaft where security had no reason to suspect any intrusion.

He clenched the fuse in his fist again, confident that the ominous sounds were only the specters of the night haunting the remains of the old mine. Bravely, he stood up and with one hand lit one of the fuses. In that very split second of watching it spark and sizzle to life, he knew he was on the doorstep to a world of a new him and he tossed it outwards. The sparkling fuse flittered towards the centre of the dark hole as it crackled in the air. Its dim spark allowed enough light to uncover the massive red metal beams that structured the shafts walls, the light quickly fading to the deep black to which it fell. Fear stuck him like a blow to the chest, and he knew that there was no undoing what he had just done. Panicky, he turned again to scan the surroundings as he fumbled with shivering cold fingers to light more fuse.

"Hey! You!"
He spun around in alarm, almost tumbling over his feet as the security guard hurriedly began to scramble for key that would unlock the massive padlock on the gate.
"What are you doing over there? Don't move!"
In alarm, he tossed the sparsely-lit bundle of fuse down into the darkness, sparkling on its way down directly along the wall of the shaft as he made a bolt for the far side of the perimeter fence. The bewildered security guard flung open the gate - barking into his two way radio for assistance.
As he stumbled around the shreds of giant concrete and steel around the giant hole something ahead of him stood watching in the shadows, he could see something black in the blackness of the night and he jolt to a stop. "Stop!" the guard called again. He wanted to pause and investigate the sparkling litter he saw enter the pit, but instead rushed after the intruder who already began an unplanned jostling up the palisade.
As the reached the top of the palisade he very quickly searched the blackness before hurrying to clamber down.
The guard grabbed his baton from his belt clip, racing after the trespasser, "Stop! Jou bliksem!"
In the darkness of the shaft the bundle of old fuse chord flared up, exemplifying the magnitude of the shafts colossal walls and structural beams.
As he toppled over the very top of the palisade, the metal shard sliced against his chest, but with the guard battling up after him,

there was no time to stall or realize any pain.

He grappled to his feet against the struggle of legs weakened with fear, running towards the chain linked fence while his eyes stayed fixed on the guard attempting to scale the palisade after him.

"Stop you piece of shit!" the guard repeatedly warned as he rushed after him, swinging his baton at the intruder who was now at the top of the palisade fence.

The bundle of fuse lay on the red bulked beam, fusing its way before finally firing out a bright flare and lighting up the darkness within the shafts deep hole and the guard spun around in alarm. He looked first to the intruder who stalled frozen atop the fence, then back to the shaft where the strange glowing distortion grew from the blackness beneath the giant tower.

His mind, heart and body now pulsed in a disarray of fear previously unknown to him. From within the shaft a loud crack and whizz echoed through the night sky, the fuse chord had blown.

He hit the ground from atop the fence with a thud, barely seeing the guard rushing towards the shaft again before a force beneath him began to tremble and shake the earth.

He scrambled to his feet, another flare of light burst up and over the partition, his fear weakened body toppled down to the ground as the earth continued to roar and moan with tremors beneath him. With his body riddled from unqualified regret and horror, he scurried to his feet as the sound of security guards shouting from the far side of the fence dimmed to his hearing and he began to run as fast as his soul could carry him towards the road where the sound of the four cars screeching droned in the night as they sped off. To the far left in the emptiness of the field more lights sped off through the darkness and he kept on running. As fast as his wobbly legs could afford, his chest heaving as the fear and dread engulfed him. Darting across the tar, through the brush and continuing into the dark stretch of fields, he ran on. Knowing that getting away was the only chance he had of surviving what he had just done – the collapse of the E-Shaft.

Not knowing that he had just opened Pandora's Box of secrets that lay within the darkness below.

Chapter One:
Understanding 'Boy X'

As 21 year-old Kyle Evans sat watching the green fields and hills pass beyond the window in the rear seat of his families sedan, the itch with no cure began to nibble at his veins. It was a beckoning for his soul to break, pleading for a numbness, as it had ever since his 8th birthday when the darkness first clawed into his skin and began scratching towards his soul. His life was complex and chaotic. In essence, his soul was a maze of chaos and anarchy, and his thoughts and emotions a cavern of distortion and mayhem. Yet the picture of God's world outside his window, with such dainty notes of perfection made the search for redemption that his soul so sought cringe with a contemptuous lament.

The humidity inside the car refused to offer the greatest support or comfort and it added to his suffocation, making him feel caged – harder now with the move than before when he could remain caged up at his own freewill in more comfortable surroundings to overcome being everything he was.

The yearning for escape bubbled inside of him, almost unbearable now. Eight hours of road, eight hours to escape one life and attempt to start a new. Kyle realized it wasn't him, the itch had barely been a factor for a very long time but the overwhelming apprehension of the move was too much no matter how he tried to put his mind at ease. He wasn't ready to be emotionally strong enough.

The fear and depression added an overwhelming weight to his soul, making his insides cringe and squirm. As he sat at the window, staring into the world that swept by silently beyond the glass, he knew that he had to make himself change. He had the perfect opportunity now to step out of the darkness of a world he had come so deeply to know over the years, but his self-loathing was an acid to his thoughts, to his strength. Escape his past and with his family leave behind them a life of secrets, tragedy, darkness and shadows. This was the time for the Evan's family to regain their strength and rebuild their broken and exhausted souls, and as the world flew past his window Kyle Evans tried desperately to imagine himself without the blackness that bulked

over his heart, without the solid steel around his emotions, cutting him off from letting anyone in. His heart raced in nervousness.
I can't do this, I don't know how?
Inside he wanted to die more than anything, as it seemed to be the only way to escape the darkness that clung to him and for failing his attempts, he clenched his fists, scoffing at how pathetic his existence had become.

The events of his past were stored in a place within his substance where it lingered in obscurity and cold, where its shrieks and groans would echo through his mind and snake through his blood. His tortured and tormented past was there all the time abrading his soul and no treatment or therapy would remove it or subdue its force. Behind his eyes lay a vicious and cruel darkness.

By their home at the coast it was easier to try and free himself of the darkness that he willingly buried himself into but now the more the droning of the tires on the tar hummed around him, he wondered if in this new world they were heading to, it would be as simple to ease his ever self-hating soul. A soul that at only 21 years old already carried on it deep, awful fraught scars, besieged by anger, tormented by the never ending shame and self despise that devoured his heart daily. Beneath his clothes lay old scars stemming from that 8th birthday through every passing day until present, a reminder that he could never out run the darkness. Seeking absolution from a life of torture, deceit, and suffering – such self-loathing and inner despise had proven impossible to shake. The life he would - with this move - truly try to leave behind him despite the anger and rage boiling within his core, beneath his skin was the life he had felt ensnared into and confined to back in the small town of Salt Rock just north of Ballito and Shaka's Rock on the Dolphin Coast.

This was the perfect chance to escape the dark, leave behind pain and suffering and take small steps towards the light he had long forgotten. But he didn't know how to be the normal guy he'd always craved to be and the thought alone frightened him, made him feel weak and pathetic – adding to the darkness feeding inside of him. It had been that way since he looked up 13 years ago into the eyes behind the light, the day his life had been stolen from him. The last 'perfect' day he could remember before the life he found himself thrown into, and now trying desperately to forget. He looked to the peaceful sky above the flat and calm plateaus beyond his window and his mind travelled back to the first time I he was able to remember the life he lost.

◻◻◻

In the quiet dimly lit office of Doctor Naidu at Crown and Lake, he was able to speak again of the events that led him there and in the silent humidity of the car with the wheels droning beneath them he reviewed his past in the hopes that this future would free him of his torment.

"I remember it like it was yesterday. The colourful table cloths, the cake and the jumping castle standing in the back yard. My friends from school were running around with those cheap plastic water pistols. You know those little see-through ones from the cheapie stores? Mom and I went to get them the day before. Everything leading up to that moment was so exciting. I can remember the way I felt when I woke up that morning. I remember the smell of the house, mom had been up early to clean the house and the smell of the cookies and cupcakes she baked the night before still filled every room. Mom was a great baker…I think." He spoke softly.

"By the time everyone started to arrive, I was still struggling to overcome the aching in my belly from clearing out every bowl of icing, dough and cream from the night before. Didn't take long though and I forgot about it.

We were on the jumping castle long before dad even had a chance to plug it in! My gran and mother were still putting out the last of the streamers – lines of such colourful ones all along the fence and up between the house and gazebo. My mom she…she really did go through a lot of trouble to make my first party as spectacular as possible for me." He said pausing as the recollection grew vivid in his mind.

"There were colours all over, if not the hundreds of balloons then the streamers, table clothes and even the piñata was an assortment of colours. If I think about it hard enough I can still hear my friends giggling and being aloof all over the place."

A silence hung, his breathing still calm.

"These thoughts don't excite me! They bring that pretentious feeling of joy to my existence! No doctor, not me. I don't have anything but the feeling as my gut fills with nausea and my body tenses in anger! Anger I can…" he paused.

The room remained silent, the doctor not moving nor speaking, simply allowing him to set free his memories on his own accord.

"The afternoon sun was already on the horizon, I remember that golden orange glow of the skyline when my parents began to argue about the candles for my cake. It was always my favourite time of day. I was so tired of them arguing, when dad asked me to run up and get them I did it because this was the moment I had been waiting for all day - cake and presents."

He was quiet again, his breathing still calm as he sat there in the dimness talking softly from a portion of his soul so sad that it gave the doctor tears in her eyes – tears she had to control if she wanted him to continue.

"Mom put her hand on the side of my face before I went back into the house. She asked if I was happy and told me that I was her Mr Handsome. That simplest touch on my face kept me going, I felt it for a long time after…I don't know if she even knows that.

I remember rushing up the stairs as fast as my legs could carry me. I wanted to get back as soon as possible because until that moment it was the best day I have ever had. I went so fast, didn't even put on the lights or care about the fact that I still had some mud under my shoes. Every second that I wasn't outside with my friends, my balloons and my streamers was like an eternity. I remember very briefly thinking that my dad was spiteful for having left the candles upstairs in their bedroom because it cost more time. See I didn't want the party to end at all, and I knew it would. Eventually everyone would go home again, the yards colours would dissipate and the days would no longer be my special one. Crazy how easy a kid can get lost in being the centre of attention."

He paused, his hands gripped tightly together in his lap.

"Still now, despite all my frustration and anger and dire will to erase my history – I do not know why I first went to the window. I mean, the house was just about dark – those Maple trees or whatever they were kept the sunlight out on a good day. The party must have gone on longer than anyone anticipated because I remember just how dark it was on the horizon when I first took

the candles from mom's bedside table. Why I first stepped to the window, I don't think I'll ever know. Maybe it was because of the happiness coming from down stairs in the back yard that I just had to look. Maybe it's because I could hear mom and dad arguing about him still not having started the fire for the adults to eat their burgers. I honestly, without a doubt do not know why I stepped deeper into the room, away from the door. Maybe it was fate. The last thing I remember about my life before….was standing there with the candles and dad's lighter in my hand smiling down at the back yard thinking that it was a perfect day."
A silence hung again, the sun beginning to fade through the blinds as its glow touched his skin, his cheeks wet from the tears. The doctor watched him, fighting back her own tears as best she could.

Staring down into the back garden with a smile across his face and the candles to his birthday cake in his little hand, eight year old Kyle Evans was unaware that in the shadows behind him in the corner of his parents' bedroom stood a darkness that would consume his soul.
The eyes watched him standing there, his small frame just a silhouette against the dimming light fading behind the tall trees blocking their view of the ocean in the distance. It waited for hours just for him to be there where they needed him to be.
He turned away from the window, this time not as quickly as before. Instead he took slower steps, the lighter in his hand as though a torch to light his way out in a childlike adventure.
Then he saw it. There in the shadows beside the bedroom door in the corner of the small apartment room, the blackness of a figure.
He carefully moved closer towards the dark corner, knowing that everyone downstairs was waiting for him. As much as he wanted to make a dash for the door, he moved closer. The light of the small flame now revealing it, the eyes behind the light.
In the backseat, his fists clenched as the calm of this recollection escaped his soul and the truth of this memory poured from his thoughts.

Kyle's face portrayed on it such a calculation and innocence, yet his eyes were riddled in a pain and anguish, holding within them masses of agony and sorrow. He hated everything about himself because it was, to him, a lie.

At first glance his gorgeous face was structured at hiding his emotions and everything of his soul. His facial structure, eyes, faultless chin, full lips and perfect skin portrayed a wonderful being, remarkably handsome. But it was his eyes that glistened with the desperation and torment, begging for the soul once lost to be set free from the cages he had himself constructed, cages that had locked the person he could have been deep inside, banished from ever being normal or free to experience the simplest things of life.

It was this fact that he scorned the most about himself because the world saw something that was nothing more than a lie.

At first sight of Kyle Evans, his striking good looks and Greek god-like handsomeness subtly eluded the intensity of the boy the world would never know – making the world around him oblivious to the boy who died on his 8th birthday. A boy that was valiant and brave, filled with life and adventure had been murdered and replaced by a forgotten boy that bore in him such a charge of dangerous rage-fuelled intensity – beautiful chaos.

His long golden blond hair often hung free on the sides of his face, or tucked behind his ears on rare occasions when he did not want to hide from the world.

For obvious reasons to those only seeing his shell - Kyle Evans was an idol and the one thing that scared him more than anything else was the moment someone would see what lie beneath it all. He saw only filth and used everything possible to keep a strict distance from everyone around him, out of fear that they would uncover the real being behind the shell.

There had been no talking in the car since they left the garage in Volksrust more than an hour ago.

His mother Claire, in the front passenger seat, had nodded off to sleep and Edward, although fully focused on the road, had his mind all over the place, nervous and excited about his new job, but worried about how the family would react in a new town so far inland away from the only life they had known. The silence hadn't deterred him, in fact he welcomed the time to let his imagination picture together the life ahead of them all in Secunda. On the back seat next to Kyle lay his four and a half year old brother Bennie - slumped up against pillows fast asleep.

Seeing his little brother there, so innocent and with a full life to lead without knowing such darkness and suffering, Kyle felt the numbing cold graciously dissipate, a slight hopefulness filling his heart that at least his brother would know life, love, friendship and the simple things he had never known. As he softly caressed his brothers golden hair, he saw shining from within the little boy's heart a faint reflection of himself that he had long forgotten. It was the peacefulness of youth, and the innocence he had lost when all the guests were out in the back yard waiting to sing and eat cake on his 8th birthday. While he, the star of the day first became engulfed by the blackness that would tar his soul each day after, for an eternity of pain and heartache.

Stop thinking about it; let it go, bury it.

His thoughts screamed in his mind and he clenched his eyes shut, his soul to shattered to think of it, recall it or speak of it.

He clenched his fists and slumped back into the seat again, riddled again with frustration and self-contempt.

You can't protect Bennie, you failed piece of human shit!

What plagued him as he sat staring into the nothingness beyond the window was his failed attempts at ridding the world of his existence, because now at 21 he was faced with trying to be a grown up when he didn't want to be alive at all.

It was a hard road he'd been on, to reach the point where he was now en route to a new life with a chance to really leave behind everything in the shadows and attempt stepping into the world again.

But the thought of it all caused a craving to be numbed, and he grit his teeth, the angst more dire to quench the need for an escape. And his remedy was called V.

Stop thinking about it! Breathe! Remember your steps!

He tried to control his thoughts, clear his mind.

You have to stop hurting them all. Get a grip you piece of shit!
He sighed trying hard to shrug off the nausea and hatred he felt inside, for everything he had done to lose his purity and his hope, his innocence and his identity.

Looking back out the window at the lowveld plains stretching far into the distance and the tranquility of the world in that moment he felt a grin moving over his lips as the dark face inside laughed out loud, roaring in amusement at him for finding beauty in anything touching his eyes, his hands, his lips or his skin. He looked back down at little Bennie, then up at Edward and Claire in the front of the car, resigning himself to the silence, the self torment again, sordid and violently strained to keep forever in his soul the darkness he met on his 8th birthday, burning away at everything great he could ever be.

Kyle shut his eyes and lay back his head hoping that prayer would find life within his heart and escape from his lips, yet as it had in the years before, he could not find prayer inside himself. In defeat he turned his attention to what lay beyond the window of the wine red Toyota Fortuner, wondering what life now lay ahead of him in the inland Mpumalanga province and town of Secunda almost 580 kilometers away from his deranged history in Salt Rock.

Remember the steps. Remember the steps.
He couldn't imagine a new life away from Salt Rock where he could no longer run to the ocean and spend whatever time he could hiding away with only the water and sand to judge him.

The silence that paved way to his thoughts broke by the voice of his mother Claire who raised her head wearily, smiling to her husband Edward with a yawn, "Still not there yet?"

Edward turned to face her with a bright smile, "Not to far now, about an hour or so at the most." He answered as he lovingly tapped her leg.

Blonde, with short bob cut hair tucked in tightly behind her ears, Claire Evans was two years junior to her 46 year old second husband Edward whose balding brown hair and eyes naturally complimented his gentle graying age while her kind and patient face exposed her gentle courtesy and mothering human nature.

"I'm going to need a chiropractor if we don't get there soon."
Watching them relish each others trust, partnership and love, Kyle could not help but feel a moderate despise for both of them and

what they shared at that moment of looking at them from behind without them knowing. They smiled and seemed to enjoy a freedom, an existence he could not imagine despite how hard he had tried. It was the niceness, the smiles and all other normality that he could never truly muster – not with all the feelings of worthlessness and self despise writhing inside of him. And regardless of how hard he tried to find that normality, and he couldn't stand it – it was this in other people that drove him to want to linger in V.

Normal ceased to exist for him and at this juncture now, facing a fresh start he wondered if he would ever care for it either. In all degrees he preferred the blackness of his soul for it was all he knew how to be alive with and be comfortable in.

Since leaving Crown and Lake, he had gotten good at keeping others at a distance, safe from him and the blackness he smeared over the world. He'd growl and deliver a coldness to anyone trying to get close to him because he knew it would only be one of two outcomes – either he'd ruin or hurt them, or he'd suffer from the look in their eyes when they realized what filth lay behind his beautiful image.

The world to him was simply a place where good strived to conceal its wicked face by wearing a mask, the identical mask that made people turn their heads away when someone was being mugged or a child being pulled into a strangers car, the same mask that threw a blind eye over the suffering of street children, abuse and injustice. It was this very mask that made people observe and do nothing when something should indeed have be done that Kyle had painted black, welded up and used to keep barrier to the world so no one would ever peer in. And through everything he had endured since his 8th birthday, he had learned all about masks. Yet as much as he felt safe within the dark confines of his silence and tainted soul, the one thing he could never escape was the reality that every human soul has imbedded in the blueprint – feelings and emotions.

Failing to understand and control FEELING often made his inner rage uncontrollable, regardless of how much he would try. As he watched his mother lean over to kiss his stepfather on the cheek, a faint smile cracked on his face and he looked away, again exasperated by his subconscious attempts to be normal and enjoy the blissful fixations that were being alive.

Despite sometimes feeling despise or contempt to the way people were, especially Edward and Claire who were always in his world - he did want her to be happy with a man of Edward's caliber. Even in the loudest, harshest of arguments with him or her nothing would cause revulsion towards Edward or their marriage to each other. Kyle's hatred stemmed from deep inside of himself, at the weakness, the emotion and the life that he was - there was never any hatred for the world for his neither his problems nor his life, Kyle hated himself and as his thoughts ran across his consciousness he felt the urge rising again: V.

He knew he had to chase it from his mind and he looked to his little brother again. He heaved a deep sigh, trying hard to remind himself of the choice he made – to try find a way to live anyway he could to try and break away from the need to self destruct and eradicate every aspect of the missing years.

As he watched Bennie asleep so peacefully, he wondered how long it had been since he had shown the world his face without the many masks, unsure if he would ever be able to without his voice breaking and being to overwhelm to let it go from inside of him. Having missed almost his entire school career he was beneficial in terms of allowing his hair to grow long because it made him feel safely hidden from the world, from anyone trying to see past his eyes. And the years he spent finishing his education at home, meant never having to worry about people wanting near him. There were no friends, no girls, nothing but the walls of their house that he barely left. All that the world could see of whom and what Kyle Evans was, was the window to the depths of his soul through his captivating blue eyes. The dog style bands on his wrists that covered one of his suicide attempts and the paleness of his soft smooth skin hid a gorgeous young man with the handsomeness and body of a Greek god.

"We're about an hour or so away Kyle, you better try wake your brother up now or we'll have a gremlin on our hands when we're trying to unpack." Edward said, looking back in the rear-view mirror.

Kyle studied his step-fathers' eyes and warm smile, and it was in that moment he realized that it would be convoluted for his heart to begin beating now after years of lying numb and soullessness. He again grind his teeth and looked back out the window, wishing that he wouldn't succumb to admitting such a fate, to live a life of darkness, pain, anger, sadness and of depth never to be known by any other. He looked back down to his little brother and a smile cracked on his face, over time he hoped that choosing this life with his family would someday bring him to expose his face again. This conflict of reality and the pit of his heart and soul tore at him and he craved to outrun his fear – fearing the move, the life ahead and how he would ever grow old in peace without memories of the eyes…staring at him while the party waited his return, the eyes behind the light. He shut his eyes, forcing his mind to accept the choice he had made three days before…

○|○|○

Claire, exhausted from the packing and universal anxiety associated to moving house, wiped her forehead as she leaned up against the railing of the staircase and again called up to Kyle, insisting for him to carry the boxes down from his room as she had previously asked five times before.

"Kyle please can you bring your junk down stairs already? What are you doing up there?" she asked, her voice filled with worn-out frustration. As she turned back to the kitchen area, she heaved a breath that carried in it a prayer for her to overcome the severe angst and uncertainty towards their future and the move. Concern for Kyle was the overall cause of her almost constant nervousness and tentative emotions, yet this move was the first in 21 years - from the only place she ever called home since moving in with her first husband Jimmy when he bought the unit. She had, albeit in turbulent and trying times, grown to know and accustom herself with Salt Rock and the people of the coast. Moving now, not only to a new home but an entirely new location, far inland – Claire tried gravely to assert her trust in Edward. Packing the cutlery she and Edward had received as a wedding gift, she knew that it was nothing more than leaping from her comfort zone, yet the uncertainty of everything involved was over whelming, almost stampeding over her conscious mind. "I don't hear boxes coming down those stairs Kyle!" she called again, looking to her wrist watch anxiously, fully certain now that she would not have all the boxes ready before Edward and little

Bennie arrived home with take out. She sighed, trying desperately to trust her that her first born son, after everything, was back with her, that her little boy was home and safe.

Her son had vanished on the eve of his 8th birthday, and the eight years stolen from them had changed everything within her soul. She didn't know her son, couldn't understand him or who he was. Barely had any real insight into the events that transpired in his eight years away and now since his return he chose to keep himself secluded and have the true darkness of his soul locked within himself for no other to ever know. After months at the Crown and Lake Rehabilitation center, her son came home and via home schooling managed to finish his high school career. There were smiles and short lived chats, but who the young man was she couldn't figure out. She often wondered if his isolation from the world was harder to fathom than his disappearance.

For Claire the move to Secunda was a hope that she would see her son step out of the shadows. He had been withdrawn from the world since walking out of Crown and Lake, awkward and unsure of how to socialize or even leave the house. It had been hard on the family, even with all the time he remained confined inside his room, and she did not know him as she once did – he was almost willingly feral.

It was time to move on, to start over even this late in her life, in his life. She wanted nothing more than to reconnect with her old self, before everything. She shook her head and continued wrapping the white porcelain dishes, her mind still trying to comprehend leaving Kwa-Zulu Natal for Mpumalanga with Edward who had a great opportunity there with the role of mine captain to open one of the areas's long closed shafts. Since getting the job Edward had been flying between there and home and she longed for him even though he had just stepped out to collect their take-out diner. The money was far greater worth it and even she had interviews lined up, yet it was a big step for her, especially since Kyle had only just begun to loosen up after all this time. As though driven by a higher power, a war of positives drove into her heart, accompanied by her inner being screaming out inside her gut; *'enough is enough!'*

"Kyle, will you please start bringing down your stuff?" she called again as she walked towards the stairs, frustrated that he had unwillingly made such a great portion of her life a bewildering misery.

She was excited for him to get back into the world again, and break free of being confined to the house every hour of every day since leaving Crown and Lake. But it frightened her too because she did not trust him to survive without episode.

◉

Standing alone in the cold empty space that was his short lived bedroom, Kyle's eyes were welled with tears that without effort caressed down his cheeks. All the time he had missed within those walls, and how being back within home's security felt like existing on a planet far from the sun on the outskirts of the furthest solar system.

"I'll be down in a second!" he retaliated behind a broken voice. The boxes shoved up against the door caught his eyes in that brief second - the glimmer of the light on the blade of the utility knife laying atop of them - the knife he craved so badly to put through his chest with a vengeance to silence the screaming of his soul to be free of the darkness.

Yeah right you are pathetic!

With a sigh he turned his attention to the box he was finishing up, knowing that he would never again attempt taking his own life out of fear for the disappointment of another cowardly failure. The failure simply stoked the fire of an already burning self-disgust. The smoke from his cigarette felt oozing into his lungs as he held tight his breath, silently screaming at the hatred curdling inside of him derived from his weakness. Nicotine was not enough to cure the itch starting inside of him, but he had to remember and etch into his mind, like a constant and involuntary function of the unconscious mind, to live.

Since the night four years ago when his parents were called to the hospital in a neighboring province where he lay bruised and shattered, he was forced to retreat from the unfaltering V. Cigarettes were never going to remove his pain, this he knew. It would never satisfy any dire craving to end his life, turn into a monster unleashing his rage or control his inability to feel human. This he knew, but being back in the world again was an existence numb and cold – an undiscovered planet far away from the best lenses where excessive smoking, exercise and reading were the only tools to distract from the haunting screams inside his soul and the flash memories within.

His mother called again from down stairs, but he was trailing other thoughts in the distance of his dark and battered consciousness. Looking at the cigarette in his hands with V lurking in the shadows whispering his name, Kyle knew it was about to get extremely difficult for him to leave behind the little security he had grown accustomed to since his return after 8 years missing. It was everything that frightened him about the move, gnawing at his nerves and made packing very strenuous. It was the security of knowing that he had his Doctor at Crown and Lake – albeit moot for the purpose, he had the doctor to discuss certain things with. It was the security of knowing the streets of his town, when to step outside and where to avoid any human contact or interaction. He feared V and how its voice would grow louder and louder the more change kicked in. He feared the strangeness of a difference place, small town or not, there were monsters in the dark looking for him and he feared where these beasts would be hiding in plain sight.

He feared the thought that perhaps the move to Secunda was just the first rip in the layers of confinement he had created for himself and that soon he would again be ripped back into the dark place where every demon lurked for 8 years of his life.

Slowly, he closed the box and lifted it atop the other beside the door, ready to attempt the strenuous task of closing off his final moving box.

V – It was there in his thoughts, whispering and calling, snickering even. The darkness felt close again, his heart beat had not slow once the entire week. The growing anxiety and fear, the pain of the past catching up - this made him fill with self -disgust again, feeling weak and controllable.

When Kyle was found after 8 years, it was clear that he was shattered at first. Less than shell, he was wholly broken.

After weeks of enduring the with-drawl, it was clinically determined that he had formed a manner of Haphephobia causing him to avoid all forms of touch or invasion of space. The boy who flung off the hospital bed into his mother's arms would not again allow anyone near him. He had lost his smile, his charm. There was now just a hollow rage staring at them, engulfed in paranoia and remorse.

In the confines of the Crown and Lake Centre, he had no choice but to learn again how to communicate without verbally abusing or cussing. He had to overcome his paranoia, but the fear was never truly gone. Outside of the numerous forms of therapy and psychology he would remain engulfed in books, reading everything and anything he could; from the Britannica Encyclopedia's to Roald Dahl to the doctors study books. The words would block out the darkness and help with the addiction V had invoked. In Crown and Lake he would for the 2nd time attempt suicide by tying his sheets into a noose.

Five years later and here you stand, where to now?

In the time he had been released back into the world most knew as normal, Kyle had many opportunities to leave the house, run away from the pain in his mother's eyes and the questions everyone who knew the story of Boy X were desperate to ask. He had considered it numerous times to once again dissolve back into the only world he knew. A world where your eyes were open but everything was dark, where there was only fight or die. Behind his smiles at the dinner table he would eye the forks and knives, wondering if they would be enough to finish what he had tried twice before. Behind his voice lay the pain of memories, the flashbacks of a former world and he would wonder if death would even begin to free him from the torment and pain.

He barely left the house and when he did he would hide behind long hair or hoodies, afraid not only of being clutched by the eyes behind the light but of those who never forgot the nationwide story of Boy X. Rarely those who remembered or knew who he was would ask or speak to him, instead only threw puzzled and bemused glares at him and his family. He brought pain to the world he was forced to leave behind and he could never take that back.

◉

He looked to the panel beside the door where his mother and biological father Jimmy Kent had began recording his growth from 2 years old, certain flashes of an earlier childhood streamed through his mind and he winced at the memories, both the bad and the good. He had once tried to speak of the darkness, in the weeks leading up to his 20th birthday but those words were nothing different to those he chose to allow Doctor Naidu to hear. He stood drenched in rain in the hall way, shivering and scared from an attempt at running away and sparing them the burden. But Kyle stood there, aching to answer to Claire and her new husband Edward, ready to let go of the darkness, set it free off of him and dissolve it into the big world. He was ready to tell them what happened moments after he stepped through the doorway, ready to say it out loud the darkness that stood there waiting to consume him.

"What is it Kyle? What is going on?" He recalled his mother's words.

Do it Kyle! Say it! You have to say it!

No don't! You piece of shit! Do you really want them to know WHAT you are!

He closed his eyes, his hands clenched tightly at his sides as the water ran down his face, blending with his tears.

Do you want to tell her what you did? Knowing that she is happy and married? With a small child! Can you be so selfish to ruin her life because of you being who you are! You are worthless!

He opened his eyes and looked up into their eyes, their wild and worried eyes, so confused and alarmed, waiting for answers.

And no matter what you do, no matter what you say they will always look at you knowing that you are black!

Everything inside of him quivered, tremors shaking his very core, slowly cracking his already splintered soul. And again he took a deep breath, knowing that if he didn't say something soon they would grab him and force it out of him which would be harder to endure.

Filled with blackness, like a disease that will destroy everything you touch you piece of shit!

It was in that moment, standing in the doorway covered in rain, the storm outside raging, his mothers desperate eyes, the anguish in her voice, the troubled anticipation in Edwards eyes…

In that single moment, he chose to never allow it out, to keep the blackness on his own conscience, to endure the torment inside and run from anything looking to pull him from the depths of its grasp and destroy them as it did him. That which has been told will be all the world would hear from his lips, nothing more.

Turning away from the panel beside the door, he moved back to the window and looked out to the stars, taking another deep pull at the filter, his body wet with sweat and realizing he was in a stage of panic he quickly removed his shirt. The skyline in the distance held a promise of a life he knew he would never know; doubtful ever taste or touch. He held up the 5 year old cover of the national newspaper's cover page, on it the greyscale picture of an eight year old boy with a bright smile and the headline 'The Story of Boy X' – the byline reading 'A world in shock'.

He carefully fold the page and placed it back in the middle of the book by Plato entitled 'The Republic'.

Taking a pull of the smoke while looking at his reflection in the glass of his bedroom window, he could not escape his darkness each time he saw the scars that remained. He despised being a young adult without any idea of how to face the future and any courage to end the present. Regardless of the thousands of words read in all the books, Kyle would never know how to approach LIVING the way he understood physics or the branches of biology and science.

Tossing the cigarette bud out the window to the garden below, Kyle moved across the room towards the dumbbells – anything to eliminate his thoughts. Again his mother called from downstairs but he was lost already to the madness inside the darkness within him.

He had been in a different place since his 8th birthday and now he was still nowhere to be found. It was frustrating to him and one of the outlets was exercising. As he began to lift the 30kg barbell where he stood facing the world beyond his window, Kyle could not understand his mothers grace towards him, or even Edward and Bennie's patience. In the time it took him to complete his schooling at home he saw in the three of them something he had not witness or experienced in an eternity.

It was a union between the three of them of trust and grace, kindness and togetherness regardless of any flaws. He admired them all for their compassion towards him even after he had only stained their lives, he envied the way they could see the world through untainted eyes. Failing to understand the mechanics behind 'opening your heart' was the thing which frustrated him and made him remember how stained he was, unable to ever touch or kiss in fear of what chaos he would spread. Yet they, and the world around him, seemed to have this understanding of life and love so commonly.

Claire remembered him, her son and all he was before he went up to his room. But he barely remembered her and yet she was kind and patient with him and everything he had to go through since being found in the middle of the main road. Edward, a man she had met long after his disappearance loved him too and cared for him, cared to know him. And Bennie, his half-brother – a young boy who knows and understands nothing of who or what Boy X is about, is so adamant to love his big brother. It was heart breaking to him because he felt guilty about it all. Jimmy, his biological father had only seen him once since his return home, but to Kyle his father was nothing more than a vile and wicked snake that should have its head removed. The furtive knowledge of the past they shared was something that would remain a fleeting memory; he was someone Kyle would never want to see again. Of everything that would escape his lips to reveal the truth behind Boy X's story – Jimmy was not one of them for the sake of everything built before his disappearance.

The dumbbell rattled as he began to raise and drop it faster and faster, trying to remember his mother more clearly, but it was a difficult task. On the night he returned, he had felt the dire utmost need to be in his mothers' arms again, something he had not thought of at all for 8 years. But it was a need that was the last thing he could remember as his body fell through the night sky towards the city below. They told him in Crown and Lake that he had been found on the side of the main road with a punctured lung, broken ribs, numerous fractures on the Humerus and Tibia but that he had somehow managed to flung up to embrace her when she and Edward arrived to his bedside in the emergency room, and that he clung to her tightly for almost a full two minutes before losing consciousness. But he could not recall it. In dreams he would recall falling with the dark sky and stars fading as the wind past his body, but Kyle couldn't recall why or how he managed to be falling in the first place. It was repressed, as was many of the 2942 days in which he was gone.

He stood flexing the bar up and down from his waist to the top of his chest, wondering what it would take for him to ever feel such normality again, such a peace inside himself.

You won't feel it. You shouldn't! You don't deserve it after everything you've done.

He closed his eyes with a deep breath to silence the thoughts that haunted him. In the twelve months of rehab and constant probing by numerous therapists and psychiatrists, the escape was exercising. It forced away the craving for the numbness, it distracted him from his own guilt and the more he physically improved, the less the doctors felt the need to press him into sharing more of his story.

Intermittent explosive disorder with hypomanic and haphephobic dissociative and repressed bipolar episodes.

He grinned recalling the words on his file, and as he stood there in the dim bedroom about to leave behind everything that defined him – he felt remorse for the failed attempt at ending his own life, wishing in a silent beseech that he would find the will to do it right, right there in his room with the door shoved closed with boxes. He was thankful to his mother for not giving up on him, because he had long ago given up on himself. He was thankful to Edward for allowing him patience when all he did was ruin their lives each and every day. Agreeing to attend college was both brave and utterly stupid on his part, because he was not ready to leave his self confinement. He was not ready to be part of something more than the walls he had managed to put up since they found him in the hospital.

◉

"Kyle!" called Claire from the staircase, breathless and tired but with a harsh adamancy.

"One second ok!" responded Kyle shouting towards the door again as he placed the barbell back on the floor beside the rest of his gym equipment. He still hadn't reached a point inside his severely torn soul where he could focus on being a remotely normal human again, he was still just a torn and broken shell of a human being. Claire sighed, her heart so tender and lost to her son who had for so long carried such a violence and self-destruction in him. As she laid her head onto her arm that leaned her weary body against the banister, she made yet another wish to somehow to know why her son had turned to such darkness inside himself.

"Special delivery…" Edward said from behind her, the aroma of beef and cheeseburgers filling her gut with added appetite as he and little Bennie entered at the doorway. He had been flying between home and Secunda for the past three weeks as often as the mine budget could allow and finally he was home to move with them and the hour that he and Bennie had been gone was enough to make her physically crave his presence near her again.

"Daddy got burgers!" said little Bennie excitedly rushing the parcels past her to the kitchen.

"And just in time too." she smiled leaning in against Edward's chest as she wrapped her arms around him, "I'm about to keel over and never wake up!"

He laughed, "Well I'm home now, and I'll handle it for the rest of the night while you take a good soak in the bath."

"That's the best idea you've had in a very long time Ed, good luck getting Kyle to bring his stuff down though."

"Everything ok?" he asked with the usual caution to the subject.

"You know how he is about coming down, I just…I don't know…" she sighed heading into the kitchen to help her son with serving the burgers, "I just want this to all be over so we can wake up someday and just be happy. The haphephobia is killing, I just want to touch him and hold and…"

Edward smiled and placed his hands to the side of her face, softly kissing her lips, "I love you and I love that you love me enough to leave this entire history behind for a new start and together we will make this thing work. And eventually, in time Kyle will be home again, really home. Like Dr. Naidu said, we need to cut him some slack for awhile, at least until things are settled."

Claire shrugged her shoulders with a cynical sigh and fell against his chest again.

"Are you sure we can't just fly ourselves down?" he asked again with a desperation in his voice, "It's going to give us more time to unpack and enjoy the house before I start for good on Monday?"

"We've been through this, I don't want our things landing in Johannesburg and then I'll end up having to go through alone and…"

"I was teasing!" he said reassuringly as her voice began to squeal. She smiled and looked down.

"Talk to me…" Edward smiled again, "Get it out…"

"I think a big part of him wants the change, the chance to start over and forget about this place and everything that happened to him." Claire answered softly, "But he isn't going to fly Ed, he almost hit full panic attack at the mention of it."

He kissed her forehead, smelling her hair as he embraced her against his chest again.

"I know, I really was just teasing...sorry."

"Besides, I'm looking forward to us all just being together in the car for the trip." She smiled stepping away, "I'm hoping it's an opportunity to try and socialize, even if it is just mumble jumble."

"How did it go this morning, was everything alright?"

"She's positive about it, less anxious than I am that's for sure." She joked as she quickly returned to finish packing while he stood with her.

"Doctor Naidu is very confident in Doctor Morris and believes everything will be fine if we just stick to the routine visits. She also gave me a list of things we need to monitor - it's on the night stand. She speaks fondly of Dr. Morris in Secunda so she's certain she'll help Kyle adjust to the move."

"She is, really I got zero negative energy from her." Edward teased, "The force is strong with..."

"I really don't want to hear it..." she slapped his butt teasingly, "...I would have preferred to just meet her myself before we moved, would have made me feel better I suppose. Doctor Naidu also suggested I open up to Kyle and tell him how I feel about the move."

"He's doing good Claire bear." Edward said tugging her against his chest, "I believe he wants this change as much as we do."

She stepped back wiping her brow tiredly, "Because I think he feels pressured into it."

"Claire listen to me, Dr. Naidu said he was a hard book to open. Who knows if he ever will be the Kyle you knew, but the point is he is home now. Home again, where you can see he is safe and eating, he looks good. He's already gotten his rage under control, the nightmares have taken a serious drop. It's only a matter of time before he'll feel comfortable doing things normal people do. And maybe this move will help? Dr. Naidu thinks so and I'm sure Dr. Morris is going to be fine."

She fell into his arms, resting against his chest as he wrapped his arms around her. The smell of him, his warmth made her feel a security she desperately needed.

She smiled up at him, "I've been living in this shaded place for too long. We all have. It's time we move on from here. Dr. Geel agreed that I could not let my life stop because of him any longer. I'm exhausted, I'm drained."

"I will be right there when you talk to him." He said kissing her forehead.

"No." she said stepping back out from the warmth and safety of his arms, "I will do it alone, Dr. Geel said it is something I have to do as his mother. I have to let him know everything. I love you Edward."

He smiled - his heart pulp at her strength and courage in admiration for a woman so amazing that chose him to be hers for life. She managed a weak smile and nod turning to the packets on the counter, giving a warning in the direction of the lounge where Bennie was leaping from couch to couch.

"So, how are things at the mine? You never got to finish telling me earlier..." she said trying to add distraction to her thoughts and obsession with Kyle.

Edward heaved a sigh, having hoped to escape the chaos of the mine for at least one night.

"Well the cages and cranes are only expected to be delivered sometime in the morning." He explained as Bennie comfortably took his place, "But it's all very complicated down there right now. Almost nothing has arrived, so much of the equipment is still tied up at the other mines and it's chaos because no one saw this incident coming. The whole place is a swarm of police cars and union men." He said as Claire handed him some of the food as he seated himself at the small kitchenette.

"I saw it briefly on the news, they aren't saying its sabotage?" asked Claire biting into her burger as she sat down. Shrugging with a full mouth, Edward proceeded to answer amidst chewing and swallowing.

"Personally I doubt it, even McDonald can't see why anyone would deliberately cause so many problems to the shaft knowing that this reopening will bring the town back on the map. You know how the police are - slow with everything, so we are still waiting to hear what type of explosive was used. It just doesn't make any sense…yet in some ways it totally does!"

"How so?" Claire asked with wide curious eyes.

"Well because they waited for the shaft to be cleared and exposed."

She frowned, "Not a miner here Eddie, if you want me to Watson to your Sherlock then you're going to have to give me something work with here…"

He laughed - his entire soul had missed being near to her existence in all the weeks away.

"Well, normally when mines are closed down, not only are the towers blown down, every bit of property on the grounds would be torn down and dumped into the shaft before it gets flooded and ultimately covered up with sand. It's a way to try and return the land to its original state…"

"Everything?"

"Pretty much yes, the land is left vacant, unless certain buildings or quarters are used by other owners – hostels, lodgings or whatever…"

"That is unbelievable, I had no idea!"

"Well in Leslie's case, the old single quarters and mine buildings are now being used by private corporations just like that. Which is why we will be working from brand new buildings."

"So this reopening must cost a fortune!" she exclaimed in disbelief at the mere thought of the costs involved in removing all the 'junk' from within the mine shaft.

"Exactly, hence the pressure." He said with a heavy sigh.

"I gave Kyle his food in his room." Bennie exclaimed in passing, his mouth full of burger as he sat beside her.

Claire smiled and caressed his hair as Edward proceeded to continue.

"Nevertheless, regulations need to be met before the entire operation gets suspended indefinitely pending questions from the local counsel and Monday is going to be crazy! There is utter chaos on the mine Claire. Maybe I'm in over my head?"

"Private funding Ed, those corporations just want the gold in their pockets, anything coming in the way of that is going to scare their pants off. And obviously the mayor is pissed off because this is over his head, but surely he has something to gain out of this financially?"

Edward nod as he chewed the burger, still talking from behind a mouthful, "Everyone benefits! When the mine shut down, many people lost their jobs and had to leave the country as contractors just to find work. From what Amie told me, things pretty much went to shit for everyone in Brendan and Evander after the mines began shutting down. This doesn't happen to mines, some are never ever reopened. E Shaft is offering an entire community of neighboring towns the opportunity to see growth. And for the next 15 years there will be work again and people don't need to rely on fuel giants to bring home the bacon. It's all political at the end of the day, it's about control."

"Isn't everything?" she huffed sarcastically.

Claire shrugged, winking over to Bennie who looked up at them bedazzled and confused but with such inquisitiveness she could not help but feel the warmth of motherhood.

"Oh and Ed, you are not in over your head. You know that as much as I do. I know it's rough but honey…please don't doubt yourself. You're confidence is all you have going for you…." She teased with a flirty wink.

"**All** I have going for me?" he said grinning, his eyes glimmering with kinky thoughts. She pout her lips, "I'll let you know later…" He smiled and managed a weary nod, finishing his take-out as she head up stairs.

◉

Fifty five, fifty six, fifty seven…

Kyle counted his stomach crunches, pausing to the knock at his door.

"Kyle? Can I come in?" Claire asked softly. "Sure." He said rolling to his knees as he stood up towards the door as she carefully came in past the boxes.

"I've been calling you…"

"I know." He said reaching for his shirt to wipe his brow, "I'm sorry."

"I wanted to talk to you about the move." She said, her voice soft and cautious, "Rather get it out now than later."

He nod and moved back as she stepped towards him, his body clenching tight at the mere thought of her trying to touch him.

"Are you going to eat?" she asked looking at the burger on his bed. He glanced to it and managed a trying smile.

"Kyle I'm not going to lie to you." She said nervously, sitting on the edge of his bed. "I'm scared. Scared of you, scared of what you're going to do when we get there. Scared of what you are going through inside that you aren't telling me."

He froze awkwardly, surprised at her forwardness and nervous to her apprehension and uneasiness which was clearly showing.

She smiled up at him, "There are things I need to get out tonight Kyle, before I never get it out."

"I am trying." urged Kyle softly, looking away from her.

"I know you are."

"What more do you want from me?"

"I just want to talk to you." She said trying to remain without tears, "I want to be open with you and you with me, eventually."

Nodding, he moved to the window where the cool sea breeze from outside could cool his sweat covered torso.

"I want to say something to you but I'm scared of how it will make you feel."

"Say it." He urged, his eyes dark and saddened.

She heaved a deep breath, her voice vibrating with apprehension baring in it a truth that forced his attention. She held the tears in her eyes bravely as she felt the weight pushing at her chest.

Don't break Claire, get this out in the open.

"I want you to know that I am very proud of you."

He just about gasped, his thoughts forever blatant; *You are? Why?*

"You've come a long way from when you were home before…" she paused looking down at her trembling hands, "So please know that what I'm about to say is very difficult for me but at this moment, with the move in front of us and a whole new life waiting out there, I have to let you know what I feel."

He felt his stomach tightening, his racing heart pounding against his chest nervously as his mind raced to think of what he could have done, he had been isolated since leaving Crown & Lake.

"Kyle I…." she paused to catch her composure, "Myself, Ed and Bennie want you to be part of our family. Really be part of our family, as best you can. I don't want you to fake it, but please I need to know that you are not going to just keep everything in and self destruct. I cannot stress to you how afraid I am about this move. I feel guilty."

"Do not feel guilty."

"I'm afraid that we are putting to much strain on you, that you might…." She paused again, "I've just got you back, this time together, these years are nothing compared to what we've lost. I cannot, I will not watch you destroy yourself because if you do then - as selfish as this sounds – it's going to put me in a place where I cannot go. I don't know how to…anymore…"

Claire paused again, feeling a release by saying these words to him, a freeing that outweighed her guilt for the first time in years. "I've exhausted myself these past years to the point where I feel like I am going to break and dissolve."

Her voice broke as tears filled her eyes and the confusion and dilemma broke across her heart, "I don't know how to make you let me in, to let me love you. I don't know how to understand most of what happened. I try and I don't push, I realize that I'm selfish but please, I have to know that you will see Doctor Morris in Secunda, that you will try your best to speak to me if you need to and not just fall apart inside because I love you and I want you to be home, wherever we might go we are family and we all love you and want you to be part of us."

He wanted to speak but his chest was in agony, his voice stolen by the pain shining off of her, he felt choked. Claire paused, taking a deep breath to correct her trembling voice before she continued.

"Kyle, I don't blame myself for the way you are since you are home. I did at first, for a long time. But I don't anymore. I've always loved you with every fiber of my body, with my whole heart and soul. I've tried to be there for you but you wouldn't let me in, you chose to shut me out. You shut everyone out."

He looked out to the ocean in the distance, his heart wishing he had died instead of having to be the person he was, but he clenched his fists to force himself to hear her without the blackness inside screaming *WORTHLESS* in his mind, drowning over her voice.

"I know that I have been hurt enough over the years to last me an eternity. It's your right to shut me out, I understand the whole personal space thing, I truly do but in all these years that you are home I feel that you could try to be more open to us." She said wiping her tears with the back of her hand, "As much as I want to know why…or…what I am doing or have done as a mother to fail you…"

"No." said Kyle dropping swiftly to kneel in front of her, "I told you before…I've told you that none of this is you. This is me, this is only me!"

You worthless black soul! Look at what you've done!
Crying she looked up into his eyes, and she put her hands on his shoulders.

Touch had been something he had outlawed, denied, restricted and forbade because he never wanted the blackness of his soul that hid on his skin to ever pass onto another. ZERO PHYSICAL CONTACT! It was a very firm boundary, something he had not had control over since he woke up in the hospital. He tried to overcome it, but it was etched in his mind.

You are dirt! You are disease! Look at what you are! It's all because of you!

Sensing his body tighten in distress, she sat back wishing with all her soul she could fall into her sons arms and feel him hugging her, but she had to fight it. The thought frustrated her, fighting to remind herself not to touch him, her own son.

He slumped up to his feet again, heaving a deep, heavy breath filled with sorrow, "Please don't ask me questions I can't answer. I'm sorry for everything I've done to you, to Edward and Bennie. I just...I..."

He choked again, his heart beat so overwhelming that he felt his breath escaping him. "I don't want to hurt anyone, I just...I don't know what more to do."

She stood up to face him, wiping her cheeks in frustration.

"I don't expect a miracle Kyle, but you barely leave your room. We barely know you are here unless we drag you out. I don't want you to ever say you are sorry, nothing is your fault do you hear me? I don't ever want you to apologize. I just need you to know where I am coming from Kyle. The last thing I or anyone want for you is to have something pulling or pushing you back into that...place."

It's black inside of me mom, can't you see that I'm lost in it? I can't ever escape it.

His inner thoughts were screaming at him, the darkness inside of him was clawing at his soul, tearing it savagely as his self hatred raged for him to leap through the glass of his window head first, end the misery that was his existence and rid the world of a soul so tormented it should never be.

She continued, slowly trying hard to allow her words out without tears, without drifting from what needed to be said. "We are about to make a major change, for all of us. And just like you Kyle, I am

34

terrified of it. I want to break away and begin to live again but more than that I'm just terrified of all the what-if's."

There was a silence between them as she caught her breath again. "I do not know what to expect, I don't think I have for years, I just cannot watch what is left of my son shatter until there is nothing left of you."

"I…" he muttered before she cut him off.

"I've been patient and I've carried a very heavy weight for a very long time, I don't think I'll ever shake off everything. So you are not alone, I have my own heavy shoulders."

She has a point…

"Kyle you have to promise me that you will do your very best to start over, with us. Or if you feel you aren't ready to - speak now because I have to know where I stand with you, where we all stand going forward."

A flash memory scorched through his mind's eye – the red glare of V, naked and dazed - trying to walk down the long seemingly endless corridor, cold.

Kyle could feel something between them galvanizing the air, stirring the connection they shared from blood. He could feel that she was done, that everything she said had such a cold and honest relevance that if he had to show one more sign of the damage inside of him, he would be lost to the darkness forever without anyone to be there to pull him back. He looked away from her agonizing eyes, their glare to painful against his skin.

"These past four years I have tried to be everything I can be to you - a mother, a friend. Everything I could to understand, to be there for you and until that night when you ran away I didn't realize that I will probably never be let in again, that whatever you were was no longer my little boy." She said, her tears now running down her eyes.

Another red haze stung through his mind – a cage, loud metal clanging together and a buzz. His eyes covered in blood and his body aching as the metal rod slammed into his back again.

"So I'm leaving it up to you now, it's your choice to make. Leave this life behind and give it your best. I'm not saying this to hurt you or upset you. I'm saying this because the chance I am giving you, it's a chance for me too. It's a chance to have my son back, to see your beautiful smile again. To see you become a man I knew you could be the minute I cradled you in my arms for the first time. I'm giving myself the chance to get over the fact that I believed my son was dead."

Her voice broke as the rage left her lips and he put his hand out, touching her shoulder and shutting his eyes as they filled with tears. She cried into her hands and he wanted to hug her, pull her against his body and feel his mommy again, let her know that somewhere very deep below all the vile hatred, all the repugnant anger, all the depraved pain and nefarious torment – he was there. He was down there, far below it all, a version of the eight year old boy who didn't go upstairs that day of his party, who wasn't taken by the eyes behind the light.

In the seconds of silence as she tried in vain to control her sobbing, he thought of the first time he tried to take his life away from the world to ease the world's suffering, but failed. He thought of the many times he had been beaten close to death, but kept regaining his life. He thought of the struggles in Crown and Lake, the journey back to being where he was in that very moment and he stepped back. Staring at her in disbelief, the daunting realization that his devastated and worn out mother had bore a cross on her shoulders because of the raw filth that he was, and she was one of many who had been in contact with him that had been affected by the disease he had become since that night of his party. She looked up at him and he knew in that moment that her eyes touched his, if he wanted to seal in the darkness and confine them to himself without ever causing her any further suffering - he would need more than solitude, more than isolation and the occasional smile. To beat the darkness and keep it from ruining anyone else he would need to find redemption first. He knew it would take time that he could not leap into seeking redemption at its deepest end.

He looked down, his skin crawling.

In a way I did. I didn't know any better.

"There is so much broken inside of me." He said softly - his voice broke beneath the weight on his heart, "I realize what I've put you through and I do want try, I struggle sometimes. I'm scared of what you will think of me if…"

The red glare struck again, slicing through his inner eyes – tied to a link on the wall in grey room the size of a cell, a thick clear plastic covering the floors, he was dazed and numb – naked and crying – calling out "Hello?"

"Kyle…" Claire said standing up for their eyes to meet, "I have never thought a negative thing about you, not one time. I love you now as I did when you were a baby. I know you are afraid and uncertain, I really understand that but Kyle you don't ever need to be scared of me."

He looked down, her hands were clasped around his and for the first time in months he didn't feel the urge to withdraw. Noticing what she had unconsciously done, his mother let go of his hands and stepped away from him as the silence hung in his bedroom. Kyle looked at his hands, his mother's warmth escaping them and more than ever he wanted her to reach out for him and drape her arms around him, holding him tightly and remind him that everything would be alright, that together they could remove the stain of worthlessness on his skin, in his veins. But he knew it was his own to harbor.

"I want you to know that every day you were gone, everything inside me died day after day. And I knew I would not ever rest or know peace or happiness until I knew if you were dead or alive. When the hospital called me, I didn't believe them. I believed you were dead. I know it's all you've wanted for such a long time." She said - the sobbing starting again and he took a step closer towards her. He wanted to hold his mother again, but the black chaos on his soul kept reminding him that he was never to allow another to touch him – because he was nothing more than a sickening and worthless shell that would only poison everyone around him.

"I have done everything I could and right now Kyle, while you stand here in front of me I know that I can't do it again."

She wiped her eyes and stared coldly into his, and he felt it. Like an electric current, the only love he knew.

Look at what you have done! Like a disease! Look what you became; look at what a vile and putrid waste you are!

He closed his eyes, fighting off tears as another red glare tore through his soul – falling through the air – then grabbing a steel shard and charging in a scream forward, his body soaked in blood – falling, the air cold as the stars dwindled away.

Claire finally sighed as she won the battle over her sobbing, he jolt back to reality and turned to face her.

"Like I said…it's your choice now if you want to live or attempt being alive, with us." She said simply turning and heading out of

37

his room, leaving him with everything she had released from deep in her wounded heart.

A movement caught his eyes at the door and he went forward, propping out into the hallway where little Bennie stood quietly.

"I will always love you Kyle." He said with a long face, holding back his tears bravely, "Please chose to come with us."

Kyle sighed and closed his eyes as he felt tears building inside of him and he fought to destroy it because it too was not allowed. He did not deserve to cry or feel anything a normal person was entitled to so freely. He deserved nothing but cold and dark.

When he looked up again, Bennie was gone and he head back into his room, to swim in his broken thoughts. He turned to the plate on his bed and went to pick it up when another red flash recollection struck him; the eyes again, the eyes behind the light. He gasped and stumbled back, quickly turning for the door and then driving himself to head out from his bedroom.

It's over, you are home he chant to himself as he head down the stairs to join them at the table downstairs.

◻◻◻

The road from Salt Rock, KZN to Secunda in Mpumalanga seemed endless, the journey only allowing his thoughts to unravel in the silence of the car.

You're being so pathetic! Simply make it work!

"You excited?" asked Claire from the front, smiling to the man she had married almost 6 years after her first husband, Jimmy walked out on them for younger blood.

"I am. I'm happy." He nod with a sincere and excited smile, "Concerned about what this little investigation is going to mean for our schedule, but I'm still happy. Are you?"

Claire smiled and squeezed his hand in hers, "It feels like I can start to breathe."

Edward smiled and raised her hand to his lips, "I love you."

"I love you too." She said with a certainty she had never felt with her first husband. Taking a deep breath in a leap of faith to his own judgment, Edward looked back to Kyle in the rear view mirror and asked, "How are you feeling? You ok back there?"

Kyle looked up at his eyes in the mirror, knowing nothing else but to shut people out even if not intended and he nod, "I'm fine."

"Excited yet?"

Kyle didn't know how to respond and simply shrugged awkwardly trying a smile.

Claire turned to face him, "Beats flying doesn't it?"

A cold befell Kyle's skin at the mention of it - flying was not an option. The mere thought of it chilled him to the marrow – it put flash pieces of memory inside his mind of the night that he was found on the main road in Salt Rock, the falling, the air encompassing him. Flight meant being whisked away, there was too much of it in the eight years of being gone.

Kyle slumped low in the chair to escape his step fathers' eyes. There was so much of those eight years that were missing, repressed somewhere among the dark demons of his soul. The more he tried to recall the events that led to him falling through the night sky, the more the face inside laughed at him.

V – The toxic venom that both neutralized and energized. It was the obscurity of his life for over eight years, the mind warp that never left his system throughout that time – until the falling. Whenever he thought of that time, it was red, it was V. It made the world around him red, there was no other color, no other thought or ability but a dull redness. When V was coursing through his veins it was red, and most of his recollection was limited. V – Paralyzing the mind and body, while keeping it active and mobile. The darkness began to invoke anger inside of him again, secrets that ate away his soul like acid.

Claire smiled at Edward, squeezing his hand in hers knowing that he would never know how much she valued having him in her life. Leaving behind the home she and Jimmy started 23 years ago was equally as hard as it was exciting to be heading in a new, cleaner life direction with the man she honestly loved, their little son together and her son who broke her soul with pride and joy when he brought his boxes down to the truck. It felt to her as the highway sped beneath the car and as the vast openness of the terrain swung by that the six years of marriage to Jimmy Maritz, the years of struggling as a single parent and the last four were finally beginning to let go of her.

"This is going to be the best thing for us as a family." She said offering Edward a gentle and trusting smile.

The truth was; she was terrified that her hopes would be crushed. That the endless cycle of chaos would never leave.

She was craving good days, and could barely recall the last time any day was good from start to end. And as much joy as she could recall, it was far outweighed by the negative. There were good occasions, but no days with total joy, peace and goodness that lasted. Kyle's birth was the only day she could remember being totally overwhelmed with joy, which never ceased for a full seven days after bringing him home. Life was new to her and Jimmy, everything seemed good and peaceful. The house was quiet, Kyle was a quiet baby and the existence of their tiny baby gave her and Jimmy reason to be whole again. But it too faded and she vividly recalled it was on a Saturday, Jimmy drunk after watching the rugby at the local bar.

They would argue often after that day, it was the day that changed their lives forever and the day which ultimately destroyed both Jimmy and their marriage. She could very vaguely recall times when days were happy, but it didn't last. Even when she found out about her pregnancy with Bennie, they were overjoyed but it faded when she recalled her pregnancy with Kyle and had to accept that he was gone from her. And every day between was the same. She felt joy meeting Edward, falling in love with him and getting married to him. She felt joy holding Bennie in her arms and seeing him walk for the first time or say his first word, build his first puzzle. But eventually the fact remained: her son was missing, gone without a trace. Somehow joy never lasted despite how much she tried to accept that Kyle was dead, because his death was more final than never knowing. But it was there, a subconscious alarm in her mind that he was gone, he was taken from her and that would never truly go away. It would always lead her back to the last somewhat happy day - his 8th birthday.

It was an exciting morning. It was going to be the first actual party they could afford, with friends over and cake and balloons, a clown and even a jumping castle. She and Jimmy kept their distance most of the morning until the party started and they had no choice but to put on their game faces. They set up a gazebo and Jimmy arranged the jumping castle under the trees in the back yard. Kyle was in his element from the moment his eyes opened, he was running and helping them to set up the decorations. He was thrilled at the thought of having friends come over and see his party because Jimmy never allowed any sleep overs. It was the first time the kids from school would get the opportunity to see his room and his toys.

He jumped and played throughout the party, tearing open each gift like there was no remorse to each carefully wrapped parcel. It was a good day, seeing him so happy and even being happy because she and Jimmy had no choice but to be civil, albeit fake for only a few hours. But as with every other time, the day grew dark. Not only did the rain clouds cover the sky threatening to ruin the party, but an accident involving a street light nearby caused the power to cut. Jimmy eventually turned to sneaking in alcohol and Kyle felt embarrassed because his friends could no longer enjoy the jumping castle. Luckily the blowing of the candles and cutting the cake was kept for last, and it was the perfect distraction. But Kyle never came back outside, she just wanted him to bring her the lighter for the candles, but he never did. He only came back eight years after.

Edward's hand on her lap pulled back her train of thought and she turned to him.

"It's going to be good for us." He smiled with an assurance that calmed the chill inside her skin. She gripped his hand tightly in hers and kissed it.

"Kyle..." Came little Bennie's voice in a whisper beside him, "Can I ask you something?"

"Yeah sure?" he said nodding with a smile only his little brother provoked in him,

"If you don't want me to be happy, I won't be."

There it was again, their love and empathy which he couldn't understand, which brought warmth to his cold forgotten soul, the final light in his heart that had not yet faded to the darkness that he survived every day.

"I do want you to be happy." He said patting his little brother's head playfully, "Don't ever let anything make you unhappy. Don't let anything win that from you, alright?"

Bennie smiled and put his head down on his brother's leg to resume his nap. Kyle could remember a time, before his 8th birthday and before the eyes behind the light. A time when his father Jimmy was still at home, when all they would do is argue and fight. He remembered standing by the doorway watching his father, his predestined hero standing in the kitchen – both of them caught in the middle of a screaming match. When they realized Kyle was standing there, the yelling stopped and they turned away from each other. He recalled how he wanted to offer his father a kind gesture but instead was shoved out the way as Jimmy passed. Kyle clenched his teeth, softly rubbing his brother's hair trying to avoid thoughts of his father until he could make sense of the lies within his memories, sense of the madness that he couldn't be sure of. *Were there any good days since you came around?* He turned his attention beyond the window again.

The mine formerly known as Leslie Gold Mines had been closed for almost 12 years, most of the mines former land had either been broken down or sold to private investors or other companies. The small community of Brendan Village, that once thrived with mining families in the heydays of gold mining at Leslie Mine, was sold to private owners who then began letting out and selling the houses in the hopes that the 'village' as such would become something of a resort for those looking for solitude and peace within its confining fence. The mine itself was one of the last mines in the surrounding area to get shut down and to anyone who had lived during the time of its hey days could feel the ghosts of the past alive within the mine, the village and the roads leading to, from and around the area.

Of the hundred some houses, many were empty and the private owners did as much as they could to maintain the neat little town for prospective renters and buyers. Yet the village sat some 30 kilometers from the larger town of Secunda - where the SASOL Plantation boomed on the horizon and with Evander sitting between the two. Secunda had grown over the years with SASOL enlarging its work force, and what was once a medium town now stood as a city. For Kyle, this was a surprising revelation and a relief – the bigger the city the easier to hide. Edward had very quickly driven through Brendan Village, sharing in the stories he heard from one of the Village's former residents Amie Horn who had been an artisan on the mine for almost 30 years before losing his job with the shutdown.

What was meant to be a slow and courteous move had been spiraled into a hasty packing frenzy to cross the province lines in time for Edward to join the investigation into the mysterious threat made at the mine shaft the week before when the security on duty caught up with suspected foul play at the soon to be reopened E Shaft.

The Toyota Fortuner tore across the black tar towards the home that would now restrict his every thought, confine him from what he knew to be his purpose and his pain. Behind them followed the truck with the life from Jimmy his father, and the newer years with Edward Evans stepping in as a real man, a father and a husband - mindless memories and keepsakes and furniture items that meant nothing to him.

To Claire, the move was more than simply following the man she loved to a town that needed him it was the opportunity to escape. To flee from a life she had lived to its driest, whether the years spent with her first husband Jimmy whom she had married under rush of being pregnant with his child and the pretense of who he was, or the last years of fear, worry and guilt to Kyle's sudden drop into manic depression. Leaving Salt Rock behind, her job as a classifieds ads writer for the local newspaper and her life opened a new road of possibilities for her soul and for those she loved most. To Edward, heading up the reopening of Leslie Mine's E Shaft was merely just another segment to be added to his already well-esteemed curriculum vitae. His life was spent traveling from coal mine to diamond mine and now finally to a gold mine, waiting to find the right woman to settle down with and parent with, the woman he had found in Claire just four years ago in a chemist in Ballito, the woman who gave him a heart more profound than he could dream of and a little son of their own. Everything else simply felt like the life that he had been waiting to sacrifice everything for. It was a long road.

The Fortuner pulled up into the drive way of their new home just as the afternoon sun began its decent below the horizon. Little Bennie needed only a second to undo his safety harness and leap out of the car with excitement behind his father, while Kyle briefly took the moment to absorb what he saw through the windshield.

The house was a large four bedroom home, with a red standard tile roof and a twin garage. The front lawn was wide with decorative and well kept garden beds and in the centre of the lawn stood a tall palm tree, encompassed with green ferns. The yard was fenced off from the neighbors with white walls and a red palisade fence kept boundary to the road. The drive way was paved and the front porch was wide, leading to a large wood crafted door, and as Kyle studied what he saw he admired this place far better than the duplex they had lived in all his life.

Claire leaned back into the front smiling, "Aren't you going to come take a look?"

Sighing, he got out of the car and watched as his brother circled around Edward as they head across the front lawn, his little arms spread out at his sides like wings.

"Kyle! Kyle!" came Bennie's call as he dart around to his big brother with excitement shining bright through his eyes, "Look! Did you see? We have our own trees!"

Kyle smiled and nod as Bennie ran up beside his mother who made her way down the drive way towards the back yard.

"That's right." Laughed Edward looking to Kyle, "Not to bad huh?"

Kyle raised his eyebrows in silence to stubborn to admit that he too felt a slight enthusiasm for the new place, despite it being so far from the ocean.

"Cool!" said Bennie laughing and running around the back of the house as Claire and Edward took hands and followed behind him.

Kyle looked up to the sky as the darkness of night began to creep up along the horizon. Looking over his shoulder now at the houses lining the short street he realized that Secunda wasn't as small and as obnoxious as he had anticipated. In his mind it was a small one horse town where everyone would know them and there would be no escaping his past.

The truck's engine broke the silence as it rounded the corner into the street and Kyle put a cigarette between his lips.

The truck bumped to a stop on the edge of the driveway and Kyle head towards the front door, still reeling from the sense of repose the tobacco provided to his system when the movers began leaping from the truck.

"Waar kan ons begin uitpak?" came the voice of the man in the dark navy overall from behind him. Without a word, Kyle simply turned away – the easier way of avoiding contact was to ignore it completely.

"Please don't smoke inside Kyle, besides I thought you were trying to quit." Said Claire as Kyle stepped into the entrance hall.

"So did I…" He said looking up at her with the sternness on his face that seemed to be built into his persona.

"Kyle, come on!"

"Alright…" he said taking the cigarette from his mouth and motioning towards the front door.

"Thank you." She said managing a gentle smile over her nervousness in even attempting any type of reprimand to the boy who felt like the coldest stranger.

"Mevrou, in watter vertrek moet ons begin indra?" one of stocky men from the truck asked as he stepped into the doorway.

"I don't know…" she looked back to the mover, "Laat ek my man vra."

"Ask me what?" came Edward around the side now as well, with little Bennie up on his shoulders smiling with great joy.

"They want to know where to unpack our shit." Kyle said pushing the mover aside with a cold and blunt arrogance, heading towards the car.

Chapter Two:
Heir to millions, heart to none

Standing with her back towards her husband as he yelled angrily, 42-year-old Lynette McDonald stared out through the kitchen window to the back yard where the Maple tree's autumn leaves fell gracefully to the fading grass around the pool.

As her husband Raymond continued to belittle the values of marriage she realized that the torment of living as his wife for the past 20 years had truly reached the point where nothing could change the numbness she felt as his wife.

"We discussed this two, three years ago!" He ranted, his face red beneath his dark hair, "We agreed it was safe to keep the money invested! I don't need this bullshit Lynette!"

"Am I not allowed to be concerned?" she asked turning to him, her shoulder length hair hung in neatly cut layers of sun kissed blonde that flattered her naturally olive toned complexion that broke to her full red lips and blend of brown and green eyes.

The droning of his excuses fell almost deaf to her ears as she watched the light breaking through the tree in the back yard and she longed to erase the tall black haired man with murky green eyes from her history as he mumbled back and forth behind her with much irritation.

"I don't see you doing anything to contribute to this house!" he snarled, "Thank god Joel's tuition is paid, imagine we had that expense too!"

"No, thank Albert." She turned to him, "Your father is the only reason Joel can…"

"Are you threatening me?"

"What? No I just…"

"Don't you play that game with me Lynette! I'll lose it I swear to god! Whenever you mention my father's name it comes through like a threat and I swear…"

She wanted to scream and lunge forward at him with her fists, or anything capable of destroying his egotistical and narcissistic halo. The abusive marriage was a lie, it had been for years and since he took the job at the old mine, that seemingly dormant side to him sparked back to life again.

"It's not a threat!" she exclaimed loudly, "Jesus Ray, I just meant that we have to eventually acknowledge everything he has done for our son."

"Your son!" he screamed, his finger to her face and his face curdling blood red in anger. Her heart sunk and she looked back to the garden.

"Do not fuck with me Lynette, that's all I'm saying." He said heaving a sigh, trying in vain to control the urge to slam his fists into the refrigerator and let free the rage of his life that screamed at the facts he could not undo.

She continued stirring her lemon tea from the counter beside the sink, forgetting that she had even begun making it when he stormed down stairs.

He started up again, ranting and raving about everything driving him off the wall about her, Joel, the disaster at the mine, his father and everything else about his self indulgent life that made him so full of fury.

There was a part of her that owned up to her faults, her lies and deceptions. She knew it was her mistakes, her burden to carry throughout their marriage but there was a part of her that longed for the man she left the Netherlands with to return and make more effort to accept his choices. He too had his wrongs, many and the hardest part of his outbursts was trying to make sense of which side of their marriage scale tipped the most.

They had married after only two weeks of having met each other, and being pregnant with no other family; she had no choice but to accept his insensible proposal. It was never her choice to sneak into his life but the opportunity his family name could give her and her unborn child was something she could not overlook, despite not being ready to accept the rest of her life with him. The proposal was neither something he or she wanted, it was enforced by his morally strict mother Evelyn and father Albert McDonald. Their name carried in it multi millions from the success of their logistics and shipping company and its numerous sub companies.

Lynette knew 20 years ago that it was the safest option to stay with Raymond as his wife but never saw everything unfolding the way it had. Their return from Den Hoek was the mark of the final stretch, the years trapped by her own deceit in a loveless marriage and fronting as a loyal wife to a husband who continued to have numerous affairs, were near over and the finish line was on the horizon. Joel stood to inherit millions in trust funds the moment he'd graduate from college and his grandfather Albert would keep true to his word and legally employ him at the company. Everything she had to endure in the twenty year marriage to Raymond McDonald would pay off and she would then be free to leave - knowing that her son was taken care of for the rest of his life. It was a long road to reach this future and they had agreed to part the moment Albert was six foot under. Raymond could languish in his millions and she and Joel could leave and live their own lives. The conditions of the agreement twelve years ago were simple: Joel must never know and Albert will never find out. Each day as she opened her eyes to the life she was glued to, she reminded herself of that and since receiving word that Albert suffered a minor heart attack, she knew that as cruel as it was he would soon be gone and their lives could start.

"Are you even listening to me?" he snapped, his hand gripped her arm, "Are you ignoring me?"

"I hear you." She said adamantly, "Now get your hand off of me you are going to leave bruises again."

He shook his head with a menacing grin across his lips, "You are the reason we are in this mess and you stand there ignoring me?"

"Excuse me?"

"You heard me!" He screamed wiping the wetness from his mouth as his anger began to foam, "We had everything good in Hermanus – you messed it all up! You pathetic…"

"Have you lost your mind?"

"You did! You opened your little fucking mouth and pushed me!" The house moaned with their screams. The dark reason behind giving up their life in Cape Town, going to the Netherlands, moving inland to Secunda and everything else between was always something he would come back to. As they argued and screamed, she with her version and he with his, the truth was neither but it would never matter – their hate and distrust for each other was beyond any reasonable repair.

She knew he was battling to come to terms with the truth, more so than her affair. But when she suspected his infidelity, she had no idea what devastation she had created within him and the beast she saw only momentarily when the truth came out had been unleashed. The first beating took weeks to recover from emotionally, and although they were able to handle it quietly without Joel's involvement it never corrected the cause. When his assistant filed sexual harassment, everything became a different game. The argument became uncontrollable, it dragged Joel into the middle of it and would eventually force his father Albert to dive into their lives and disrupt the conditions of their agreement. When the truth about Raymond's physical abuse reached Albert McDonald in his New Zealand offices he quickly became involved in their lives and it made their own personal game very difficult to manage with him scrutinizing their lives.

He immediately fired and cut his son off claiming that 'Silver spoons do not enrich any person with the fundamental values of life and family.'

Lynette and Joel were whisked away from him and stayed at one of the family homes in Den Hoek, Western Netherlands.

Raymond scurried about trying to regain his footing.

It was a hard lesson for them all, to lose everything within his father's shadow and to start over again with the bare minimum.

"Support you?" she gasped, "Are you forgetting why we are here in the first place?"

"Is that what this is about?" he interrupted with a cold sneer, "You think I'm late because of another woman?"

She took a deep breath, frightened to set him off, "I just don't want you to do anything more to…"

"What Lynette? What exactly? You are so pathetic! So insecure!" he huffed turning his back on her with his arms at his sides, "I was at the mine! In case you haven't been paying attention, there's a little bit of a problem down there with the damn walls that collapsed! And yes there were woman there but they were either cops or share holders and secretaries! I have paper work coming out of my asshole! That is where I was!"

She nod and stepped around him towards the stove, her broccoli near burning due to the lack of water in the pot.

"I used to work late all the time when I was still at my father's company. Why now is it so hard to grasp the idea? I'm a busy man, not some common..."

Raymond paused, unsure of which noun to use when she spoke out. "Adulterer?"

The words barely left her lips and she felt her stomach sink.

He slammed his hand down on the nook, "Amazing!"

His fist was clenched tightly at his side, but she knew the look in his eyes. She knew where it was going, she had to create a diversion and bring him down before Joel arrived.

Having now the news of attempted sabotage at the shaft with the blasting agent ANFO, Raymond was close to losing control of his dark frustrations.

"I'm not trying to upset you, I'm your wife, have been for over twenty years Raymond." She smiled carefully, "Please calm down, and forget I said anything at all."

She spoke calmly to avoid his flip from switching to crazy.

"But you did say something Lynette, that's the problem. You think you have some kind of place in this house, in my life and you should know by now that you don't really - do you?"

She kept quiet, now adding water to the dinner pots.

"What is it you want?" he pressed, "A loving husband to walk through those doors and cherish you? A slut, a whore?"

"Don't you dare..." she warned, her finger now to his face.

"Or what?" he laughed, "You'll call my father?"

She dropped her hand, "Leave. Leave now before you regret it."

"No see... that's just it darling wife." His voice was dark as he leaned closer to her face, "You are the one who will regret it. Because if you fuck with me I will tell him."

A silence hung, their eyes staring and searching each others.

"No you won't." She said finally taking a step back, "You wouldn't risk it."

He laughed and stepped backwards, brushing his hand through his hair. She took a deep breath and resumed her work on dinner when he threw the entire eggs basket down to the ground off the table, then turned to the microwave and ripped it from the counter top. As the power cord tore out a spark snapped but in seconds it flew across the room into the counter near the back door.

"Stop!" she urged, "Please Raymond!"

Like the strike from a black mamba his flat hand sprung forward and slapped her cheek, toppling her against the counter and then stumbling to the ground aside the stove.

"Don't patronize me Lynette! Just don't!" He said in coldness as his one hand gripped the back of her neck while the other maintained tight fist in front of her face. As with the previous blow outs, the reality of his father's conditions stung and he sighed dropping his fist.

"That wasn't fair." He said with his voice rasp, "I realize how hard this must be for you too. I try and I try, I have been since we came back but…"

"It's not worth it." She said beneath her tears, "Is it. Not anymore. Not for a very long time."

She looked down and he got up to his feet again.

"I don't know." He said coldly, "We are living a lie to gain benefits from a stubborn old man who just won't die."

She remained quiet as he spoke, moving towards the sink where she wet her hand with cold water from the faucet and dabbed it to her cheek.

"What have we been doing to each other all these years?"

"The funny thing is…" said Lynette turning to him with tears in her eyes, "I grew to love you because you were a great father."

Raymond shook his head, unable to admit that he had too fallen in love with her, the child and the life they began to build before the drinking and affairs, before the explosive truth.

She looked down, her stomach knotting deep.

"Sometimes I actually find myself…"

"Don't do that. I don't want to hear it." He interrupted, "We ended long before Den Hoek, and again two years ago. It's over Lynette you know that."

His eyes were ice and dark, she felt her legs trembling, fear gripping each part of her as she stared into her eyes.

"Without me you are nothing so know your place. You forget it's only because of my family, my stupid, ignorant cunt of father's generosity that is keeping up this charade we are playing."

For months since returning from the Netherlands things were tranquil and almost good. But with the pressure mounting on Raymond's investment in the reopening of the old mine near by they were back to the usual abuse, drink and infidelities. And although the relationship he had tried to build with Joel diminished, it fortuitously never returned to its previous bad place. Lynette knew better than to allow Joel knowledge of Raymond's return to his former self and simply endured the disparaging daily duty of being stuck in her self designed hell. She knew it was all her fault, she allowed all of this to unfold by creating secrets and lies. The important thing was Joel and Raymond were able to co exist again since Den Hoek.

"So you never loved me?" she asked, "Or Joel?"

He pressed his fist against the side of her face, "I don't care about you! Or Joel, not really. You made me live a lie, you whore…"

"You are a drunk." She said braving another clout, "How could I tell you when you were never home, always drunk?"

He laughed shaking his head as he stepped back away from her, "We tried, we failed. I have my demons and you have yours. I don't have anything to give you anymore."

"I don't expect it from you anymore Raymond." She said giggling to spite him as she round to the other side of the table dividing them, "I am dead inside because you were the first to change, to break everything apart. But you are right, I kept my secrets and I lied to your face for ten years. But do you want to know something sweetheart? If you think for one second that when this is all over the money is going to bring you what you're looking for you are very, very delusional."

"Oh really?" he mocked back.

"You will die alone Raymond, because you can screw your way through a hundred assistants and buy your way into a thousand more beds, but no one will ever be able to love you."

The secret she kept, the lies she told and burden he had on him since he found out was breaking him. She could see it every day since the first time he had struck her, and now a small part of her enjoyed his torment.

He burst out laughing and clapping, "Wow, you must have practiced that because of all the bullshit between us in all these years that was by far the most convincing you've ever looked!"

She shook her head and a smile crossed her reddened face.

"Do you actually believe that?" he asked in amazement.

"I fell in love with you before you became a drunk, before you fell apart over your insecurities. I know who you really are beneath all this…this chaos. And my deceit may have crushed you and nudged you further down this disparaging road Raymond but you were already on this road. No one is ever going to see that part of you Raymond, all they will ever see is this shell of a man craving his mothers love and his fathers respect. A monster!"

His smile dropped and his face grew solemn to the truth he already knew deep down within his demons. A silence hung for a few moments between them, the smell from the blown electric point hanging in the air. His eyes looked down into the abyss of his heart where truth and lies, ambition and greed had fused into a monstrous being without a soul or path to anything more. Everything he had done, everything he had become was from his own demons and he had always known it regardless of how many times he would put the blame on her. Her words were new to his ears and rang throughout reality he fought his entire life to face. The sound of the front door closing sounded behind him and he hurried to his feet in alarm, rushing out of the kitchen.

"Dad?" frowned Joel as his two friends Rendani and Collin cautiously maneuvered into the house beside him.

"Hello boys!" he smirked hurriedly re-maneuvering his red fist beside him as he walked towards them.

Standing tall with a swimmer's build, short spiked golden brown hair and his mother's natural tan, Joel's dark lime green eyes searched his father's face as he strode towards them smiling with pretentious intention.

"What have you guys been up to? Is this your friend Bongani I've been hearing so much about?" asked Raymond offering the college swimmer a firm hand shake.

"Why are you home? Where's mom?" Joel asked over his friend's politeness, trying to look past him, his fighting spirit never truly yielding to the critic of his existence.

"Cleaning…" Raymond frowned grinning, "Why are you home since you don't live here anymore?"

Joel shook his head, it was his grin that gave him away and Joel hurried past him towards the kitchen. Raymond turned to the college boys shrugging, "Crazy like his mother that one."

"Mom what happened?" he asked hurrying to help her with the over turned chair while his father ushered the two boys outside in idle chit chat.

"Nothing, I'm fine." Said Lynette softly, avoiding looking to her son as he entered the kitchen, "It's alright it was just an accident."

"Where's Maria?" asked Joel worriedly as his father stepped up behind him to answer.

"Not that it's any of your business Joel but she wanted the day off, and knowing your mother you can imagine how easy that was."

"Mom!" said Joel loudly, causing Lynette to face him, the red print on her cheek glistening behind her blond locks. He turned to face his father shaking his head, the vile anger that had always tormented his soul boiling through his eyes as he stared up at his father. It had years since the last incident, he felt utterly confused and alarmed. Hurried Raymond turned and head back towards the front.

Joel shook his head as his mouth crimped in disgust, "It's happening again…"

"Joel…please…"

"I'm calling grand dad."

"Don't Joel, just go out there and let me deal with this ok?" she said trying to hide the shaking in her tone, "He'll bath and go to bed. When he wakes up it'll be fine. You know how he is when he's tired."

"Tired?" he gasped, "Mom he's drunk! He hit you!"

"Keep your voice down!" she snarled, "You don't understand, you weren't here. Trust me, just let this one go!"

"If you don't make the call I will."

She grabbed him by the arms, "We have to learn to handle things ourselves Joel, your grandfather is too old and sick to deal with this right now. I can handle this."

"You shouldn't have to!" he said shoving her hand away.

"Joel you don't understand! He's…." she paused as Raymond walked across the passage and head up the stairs.

"Please just, not now. You have people here and…"

"Sure whatever!" he snapped turning away, "I don't even care anyway, I don't have to remember? I have my life thanks to grandpa so you both just do whatever you want."

"Joel…!" she urged as he head to the front door.

"If he calls, I am not lying. I have no reason to."

The door slammed shut.

He stormed past his new friends down the driveway to his Range Rover Evoque – a gift from his grandfather on his 19th birthday. He had known all along that nothing would truly bring peace to the turmoil in his home, his life and inside his heart. He wanted to stand up, step up and roar, let the world and everyone in it hear his voice and know that he was to be taken seriously, that he was more than just a guy with a big allowance. Every day of his life he was Joel McDonald heir to millions and money on legs, nothing more than a door mat for everyone to use and abuse to their leisure. And the worst part of it was that he allowed it, often even welcomed it because it kept him from being cast aside as always being the new kid everywhere. He had lost himself and couldn't remember how to get back. He craved belonging and his natural self, he wanted to be Joel and liked as Joel, not simply because he carried the surname McDonald.

No one knew him, no one cared to – he had to survive and somehow became enveloped in this person he designed and it followed him directly to Seymore Academic College. He wanted to start the engine and speed away, leave behind the fake pretense of his life. But no matter how many mornings he woke up determined to stand up against the world, he found himself buckling and giving in to those who only enjoyed his company because he could afford to indulge them or for the girls, spoil them and be something beautiful on their arm. Inside he was burning with a hatred for his father, knowing that it was the fear he instilled in him that made him so easy to push over.

As he sat there watching from the corner of his eye as two fellow swimmers on the college team came walking towards the car, he wondered if he could ever be anybody that people were interested in despite the money, the looks, the swimming. He felt smothered, trapped in a circle that he did not know how to escape, a person who he fell into being since returning from the Netherlands. He did an inventory of the people he had encountered at the college. *Will anyone ever know me?* He thought in a sigh. To the many guys circling him since they arrived in Secunda, it was about the car he drove and the money carried in his name, his swimming ability and the big parties he'd pay for. None knowing anything more about him because he had no reason to trust anyone, they were all as fake as the smile on his face. To the girls, he was just another attractive swimmer for the Delta Capital fraternity, a guy with a rippled body and the ultra benefit of being rich enough to accommodate their material whims.

As he sat there, burning with embarrassment in front of his new friends, both 2nd year students highly popular within the circle, he tried to paste a mask over his face.

"Dude, you ok?" asked Rendani hoping in beside him as Collin slumped into the back.

"Let's hit the road Mac D! Maybe grab some beers on the way?"

Are you shitting me?

Laughing, Rendani tapped Joel's shoulder, "Not for the designated driver though!"

They laughed and Joel turned to face them, his face grim.

"Look guys I know we had plans, but right now I just don't think I'm up for it."

"No way dude, come on!" insisted Rendani, "Hook us up!"

"Yeah man, we have to go check out the stuff for trails tomorrow." Rendani added with his own annoyance.

I – said - NO.

"F.P.P." Rendani laughed shaking him from behind.

He wanted to scream and lash out, but there were only two characters to him - just as he had learnt and that reaction was still blocked by his terrible youth, his troubled and emotionless past.

"Fun! Pussy! Party!" Collin roared excitedly. Joel smiled shaking his head and turned the ignition, much to his passenger's merriment. Character one had been activated and he was adamant to erase any concern or care, it was how he structured it. It was time to party and spend and ultimately be whatever he needed to be because he knew there was no point in wanting to be anything more, or have anything more. It was his fate, signed and sealed.

As the journey began from Secunda to Pretoria, the speakers boomed and Collin and Rendani enjoyed some beers while engaging in conversation, leaving Joel with nothing more to really distract him from the pain and confusion he had always felt. He wanted to talk to them, but suddenly he couldn't. It was as though he had forgotten how to engage the persona he had created to ensure his survival.

Oh God why was I born to be so weak? Why? I'm really pitiful.

Just stand up to them, why live this lie? Weakling!
The weight would only ever crawl back at nights when he was
alone or in the silent moments where self reflection occurred
spontaneously.

He had gotten so good at pretending to be the guy he wasn't
because it saved him, it surrounded him with people and protected
him from the dangers of ever feeling as low as he had felt the day
he could have punched Aldert Vos and simply roared…

◖◯◖◯◖

At thirteen years old with hormones raging, starting high school
was more overwhelming than he anticipated. No longer was he
the king of the play ground as he had been in his last primary
school. Now he was a bottom feeder, a face among many
competitors to be the new 'it' kid. The grade 8 initiations were the
first time he had ever been subjected to ridicule and humiliation
outside of what Raymond would torment him with at home.

As a student of the elite Saint Vincent's Primary in Cape Town,
he integrated with everyone without even trying. Each student
was of wealth and there were no special clicks meant for only
selected few because each elite student was the select. From the
crowd, Joel stood out because he carried his pride boldly and
never felt the need to avoid anyone's eye contact. There were
standards at all times, everything had class and nothing was done
to censure status.

There was violence in his home, and more troublesome was the
secret his parents were trying to hide. He knew it was dark, he
knew it was dangerous because it caused their communication to
become explosive and uncontrollable.

Never before had anyone other than his father, bullied or picked
on him nor taunt at him until his first year in high school. And
while the initiation week endured at paint drying pace, Joel
shrunk down from king of the playground to a shy and timid
teenager so awkward in his own skin, suddenly so unsure of
himself and what kind of person he aspired to be. With the tension
growing at home, and his father's wrath often directed to him
more than before, he felt lost and unsure and by the end of the his

first week in the exclusive Newton high school, he found himself utterly outside of himself.

The twelfth graders would humiliate them by having them stand in lines and throw them full of eggs and flour, or wear their clothes on backwards. They would get them to leopard crawl race in front of the entire school or during recess debase them by making them perform mundane and humiliating duties that were often utterly pointless.

The grade twelve head boy was Wickus De Kock, blond and blue eyed egotistical maniac who always on his back obviously enjoying every minute of his torture. In South Africa, the McDonald's and De Kock's had always been feuding families, but it never before touched Joel's existence. At home he faced Raymond's arrogance and at school there was Wickus acting out vengeance for the tender that his family lost to Albert decades before.

Throughout the time he attended the school – Wickus would bully him, humiliate him and downright torment him.

Each time Joel wanted to send his knuckles to his face, but could not find it in him – just like each time his father bulldozed his self-esteem. An out of place teenager, awkward within his own skin, Joel was constantly out of place, like a butterfly in a tackle box full of worms and everyone around him couldn't wait for the fishing to begin. There were days when Wickus would cross lines and he felt that nothing could save him, or it was too late. Joel found himself filling with anger each day, an anger he couldn't vent. There was no will to vent or exercise, laugh or cry. Numbness befell him, and it was frustrating because he knew that he was able to scream, to retaliate, and to stand up for himself. But inside there was a broken switch and he couldn't figure out how to mend it and release himself from the cage of teen depression suddenly compounding the inner him.

As a result of Wickus and his actions, it became the norm throughout the school and everyday Joel found himself isolated and alone, often skipping classes to avoid further torture. He had no friends, no one who cared or dared to befriend him.

It followed him to Europe when he and his mother were obliged to live with Grandfather Albert. He had been so hopeful of change, to step into a different set of shoes, but being a foreigner he could barely find the laces.

The school was an elite private school catering only for the super-rich, hosting boys and girls in grand hostels from all over the globe. The only time Joel had ever stood firm since becoming a teenager was staying adamant to not live on the grounds.

The older teens kept to themselves on the east side of the campus, so there was never any risk of being bullied – in fact the school had a zero tolerance for it and in the first few months of attending Joel realized that students were more afraid of their elite parents than the school rules itself. Most taunts occurred outside the gates or in town, away from the school and never in the school uniform. His life was simplified and although he had certain relationships with kids on campus, he chose to keep to himself because he had learnt that there was no point in befriending anyone or building a life there if he would be whisked away again at anyone's whim.

Drika Ahrens was the girl, the event in his life that would be the turning to point in the type of person he would be going forward. Before her smile and the way her accent rolled out English that brought his blood to boil, Joel had only ever had the usual uncontrolled horny thoughts about girls, but Drika was his first real crush since puberty. She knew he liked her and he knew she felt the same because her teasing flirts, scribbled notes in the text books and occasional physical contact were typically and blatantly obvious. With his self-esteem in turmoil, Joel could never muster the courage to make anything of the situation, but Drika had strung him on long enough and didn't want to waste any more time on games.

◉

"I don't understand?" he said frowning in alarmed confusion. Joel hadn't yet begun swimming and his thin, scrawny body now trembled timidly as the heat of their near kiss escaped his veins. She laughed, flipping back her hair as she replied in Danish. The crowd of students gathered outside the school gate laughed. "Dacht je echt dat ze kon houden van 'n buitenlander?" Joel turned to face him, Aldert Lochte, who had spotted the victim the minute he saw Joel eyeing out his close friend weeks before.

"It was a game." Aldert said chuckling, "We have game with you."

Drika shook her head grinning, her eyes filled with pity and Joel felt the voice within him clearing its throat.

Aldert and his friend Schuyler had been behind them from the moment they left the doors, waiting for Drika to finally reveal their cruel prank.

"You bitch!" he said, his voice cold and hard.

Aldert stepped forward and pushed him, "Stuk strond! You don't call her that."

"Why would you do this to me?" he asked fighting back the tears of humiliation, "What have I ever done to you Drika?"

Heaving an icy sigh she grinned, "Easy target."

There were no words to explain everything he wanted to say, there was chaos traveling through his thoughts.

"You think you are American hustler no?" Aldert poked at him, "You think you can come here and take our girls?"

Turning to him in bemused surprise, unable to control anything out of pure alarm and sickening to their game.

"I'm South African you stupid fucking tulip!"

Aldert's bag hit the ground, he was ready to lay into Joel and while he rolled his sleeves Joel knew his fists would break every bone in his body.

"Vecht je varken!" Aldert snarled as he rolled his sleeves up the muscles of his arms.

"Aldert stop." Said Drika stepping up to Joel her gaze as icy as her demented grin, "He is not worth being kicked out again."

Joel's teeth clenched, he had never before wanted to ram his fist into the face of a girl as badly as that moment.

"You don't have to save me you... kwade teef." Said Joel glaring back into her eyes, "You wasted your time on messing me around, because truth be told..."

Alderts fist struck so hard that the one punch was enough to cripple him face down into the dirt. As blood ran from his mouth he got to his feet, the students around them laughing and hissing personal insults and remarks about his birth country.

The disdain within him had erupted throughout his body, as aching as it was from hitting the ground he wanted to exact his fury on them all, Drika most of all for the hurt and squalor by leading him on. It was the lowest moment of life. He couldn't fathom the lowness that engulfed him, swallowing his soul, his personality, everything he had been trying to hard to figure out. He felt the dirt inside his mouth, and began swirling it with blood and thick spit and as though without a split second of thought – he spat it directly into her face.

Alderts scream was the last thing he heard before everything went black and pain dispensed. His consciousness regained to the smell and taste of urine in his mouth as Aldert stood over him –the students screaming and teachers surrounding them trying to regain control of the situation.

It was the last day Joel had existed in the same hemisphere as his soul and since had chosen to always be the heir rather than the loser and simply dream about being the real him in between.

Within hours of being expelled from the school, Albert McDonald had his helicopter ready to bring him back to the country side. Albert McDonald did not believe in excuses, he believed in facts. As Joel explained his version of events, he held nothing back at all. He and his grandfather shared a special connection - they had an understanding of each other which Lynette could never understand because of the biological truth of the situation. And although Albert raised his voice and even smacked him aside the head a few times for his use of bad language, Joel explained how he couldn't contain himself from degrading and upsetting Drika as much as she had him.

"Boy... there are very few things in this world that make sense to me..." He said finally sitting down across from Joel, "And why that girl would do that is beyond me."

"Doesn't justify you spitting in her face!" Lynette snarled as she entered with the ice pack for Joel's swollen cheek.

"No it doesn't." Albert said, "Lynette be a dear and give me and Joel a minute will you?"

"Sure." She smiled, but her heart nervous to what Joel might divulge about their lives thinking that Albert might already aware of. "Joel, I realize that your life is very much…disrupted. And perhaps I am to blame."

"You are?" he said through swollen lips.

"I dragged you out here to the Netherlands, put you in a school, pretending that everything would be alright." Albert sighed as he lowered into the arm chair, "I suppose I was only thinking of myself and teaching my son, your father, a well deserved lesson. Truth be told my boy, I'm almost seventy five and life has thrown its fair share of curveballs at me, maybe a man can only take so many hits to the nuts before a big part of you dies and evolves into something else – often something you don't even want or have control of."

A silence hung between them and for the first time that he could remember, Albert McDonald the self-made millionaire seemed relaxed and comfortable in his own skin.

"Boy in my day the world was simple. Men were men, women were women and wars…." He paused as his eyes drifted, "Wars were fought for purpose not for money or greed. These days it's acceptable to have men beating women, child murderers, teen suicides, drugs, rape, incest…. The world is falling apart and the only hope any one my age has is the lineage we leave behind - the tomorrow generation."

"I'm sorry I've disappointed you grandpa."

"Oh nonsense." Albert said huffing, "If you ask me, the little tramp probably enjoyed it. The youth of nowadays are into some pretty diverse themes. I'm not disappointed in you my boy, I'm disappointed in myself for acting abruptly and bringing you all the way out here. I hope you can forgive me?"

Joel shook his head, "It won't matter where I am..."

Although the cut on his lips had stopped bleeding, the taste of blood still filled his mouth and his body ached.

His grandfather chuckled as he got up from the chair, motioning across the study to a built-in wooden liquor cabinet.

"I once thought the same thing." Albert said pouring a brandy, "There was a girl I met once... she was everything I could ever imagine. The time we shared would've made each horrible day of this over populated, over polluted world worth surviving."

He handed Joel the glass, "Here, just a sip for you."

Joel managed a weak smile and carefully sipped from the glass.

"We are not cowards by nature. The blood inside of us is pure and strong. I know because I am strong, I made myself strong and I never quit, I refuse to let things get the better of me again."

His passion mimicked raged as he spoke, pacing up and down along the wall of books.

"Your father is my only son, which means you are the last of my heritage, to carry on the family name." Albert said looking at him, "I don't condone any actions of a man who raises his hand to a woman, or spits on them for that matter…but I realized during your story that I need to reel in my hooks. You are not my son, your father is your father. I think it's time you and your mother go back home."

"He won't change." Said Joel abruptly, without thought and his heart sunk as Albert turned to face him. He knew not to betray his parents in this regard, but as he sat there with his heart raging inside his chest he wanted to tell the old man everything they've endured.

"Do you really believe that the man who has raised you, provided for you and cared for you is a monster because in a single moment of misjudgement acted out?" he asked, "If he could I would have him beaten to a pulp to learn his lesson but violence doesn't end with violence. There are problems at work here Joel, maybe you are too young to understand it. Maybe you are too caught up in growing up to realize it."

Joel sat back, placing the glass on the table – unsure whether or not to feel relief or frustration.

"The behaviour of others should never affect your peace Joel, the Dalai Lama said that." Albert smiled, "Just like you I am angry at my son, I am furious and in shock. But the man we know, the father you know isn't a monster is he?"

The room felt small, silent with only his increased heartbeat slamming inside his ears.

"Is he?"

Louder and louder his heart slammed inside his chest, his swollen mouth dry and sore. He prayed his mother would walk through the door.

"Is your father a monster?" Albert asked again, lowering his head to meet his grandson's eyes, "Or is he the man who puts food on your table, clothes on your back? Isn't he the same man who would spend hours and hours playing blocks with you in the yard? He is Joel, you need to allow for a second chance don't make my mistakes and rush headlong without thinking into any direction just because it seems to make more sense to you."

A silence hung as the old man took his seat again, sipping on his apple brandy. "My point is Joel, for a long time I was lost in the world too. I know puberty can be rough, I understand how it feels to be the new kid in every school every few years or months. It hasn't been very fair on you. I don't think I realized that until today. Perhaps neither did your mother or father. I think we tend to allow our greed and ambition to get the better of us."

The brandy stung all the way down and Joel coughed, his eyes fixed on every word his grandfather said.

"We need to remedy this and get you back on track."

"I'll be fine."

"No. No you will not Joel." He said adamantly, "You need to get yourself back together Joel. Since you arrived here I've seen the depression, the anger. I know it very well because I too have been in that shallow drowning pool. So, we have to have a game plan."

He got up and head to the door, politely stopping the house servant and providing him with instructions.

He made his way back around Joel, taking the glass of unfinished brandy and adding it to his own, "Grandpa has a plan my boy. Now I suggest you get yourself cleaned up for dinner. There is much we have to discuss."

○

The dining room smelt of fresh bread, eggs and bacon. Joel had sunk off to sleep after bathing the night before and the morning air was chilled beyond the great windows overlooking the pond.

"Feeing any better?" asked his mother rounding behind him as they stepped towards the eight seat redwood table.

"Like I've been pissed on mostly." He said with a weak smile as she put her arms around him as they made their way to the table, "My ribs are bruised from Aldert's size nine but overall I feel better than I did yesterday."

"Some rest and now some healthy breakfast!" the chef smiled as he whisked at the yoghurt in the centre of the table.

"Is someone joining us?" he asked noticing an extra place setting.

Lynette looked to the chef, but before he could reply Albert McDonald's voice rounded from within the corridor behind them.

"Good morning family! How is my young man this morning?" he smiled as he neared the table head, "I bet the brandy worked its trick?"

"Slept like a baby grandpa." Joel managed another smile behind his split lips. "Bertie are you looking for a hiding?" Lynette asked shaking her head. Albert chuckled, he was comfortable again. "Morning!"

The voice from the door sent chills down her spine, she felt unable to turn around but with her eyes fixed on her sons face she already knew who he was looking at.

"How did you get here?" Joel asked in surprise.

"No hi dad, check out my face?" Raymond smiled as his head to the table.

"Hi dad." He greeted softly keeping his head low, ashamed of letting his father see his failure.

"Hello Raymond." Lynette said finally looking at him as he moved the table setting to her side.

"I've missed you so much!" he said kneeling by her, "Have you been well?"

"The man is concerned if you've been well but his son sits with a mangled face!" Albert coughed in judgemental giggle, "My boy you really are rather curious in nature!"

Raymond sighed in annoyance and turned to his father, "The woman is my first love, perhaps if you had yours you would understand where I'm coming from."

"Keep it civil Raymond, you agreed." Albert cautioned.

"That we did." He nod sitting beside his wife, "I won't ask because I'm afraid of the answer Joel..."

"I'm fine."

"Good, be bold. It's the McDonald way." Raymond smiled. It was a mock smile, embedded into his face for use around his father and anyone else he was aiming to deceive.

Lynette looked at his hand that he had placed atop of hers and she pulled away and she moved out her seat. The months away from him had been air to lungs long rusted and disabled, the mere sight of him there felt to upsetting to attempt hiding.

"Sit down Lynette." Albert said, cautioning with the same adamant glare behind his eyes, "I took the jet out to fetch Raymond personally. I am slightly tired and would appreciate if everyone at this table can remain civil, we are after all family."

Raymond's dark eyes pierced hers, she knew his thoughts and could feel them screaming and scratching at her soul.

"Shall we eat?" Albert asked smiling, somewhat relishing in the discomfort at the table because he knew his son would hold any cards to keep a façade in front of him.

As the forks and knives tapped the plates and the buffet style English breakfast diminished, the awkward silences and tension filtered across the table. Small talk was Albert's niche, having a compendium range of topics and themes to idly talk about and the breakfast chat was a double blade. On one hand it gave some distraction to the mounting tension and on the other it obstructed their real words to spatter between them.

Raymond had not looked at Joel once since taking his seat beside his wife but instead focused on taunting his father with rebutting most of the conversations. Lynette had difficulty eating, her stomach churning in anxious anticipation and Joel watched how his grandfather would flip-flop between being the wilful and stern businessman and the comfortable grandfather, realizing that he too could yo-yo between personalities depending on the situation. He knew that Drika had broken something inside of him and to fix it, or at the very least keep it from falling; he would adapt too being whatever was needed at the time and simply rotate back accordingly.

"Great!" Albert said with a broad grin, "Let's head to the patio and have a chat shall we?"

◎

Albert's flat hand tearing across Raymond's face stung and he staggered backwards in alarm. Joel and his mother froze in disbelief. The cool morning air circled the gazebo in the lawn and its chill added to the trembling within their guts.

"I think you misunderstand me Raymond." Albert said composing his suit sleeve, "This is not a two way conversation, this is an ultimatum which I am giving you."

He turned to face Joel and his mother, "I apologize for that, I really do but…"

"You still think I work as one of your manservants don't you?" Raymond snarled, "Just who the hell do you think you are? You're my father not my master!"

"I am exactly what you need me to be Raymond, always have been and always will be." Albert turned to him again, "This is not up for discussion any longer. And if you ever disrespect your wife in such a manner again, I swear to you Raymond…"

"You don't run our lives you senile old man!"

"This is exactly why I am taking these steps Raymond, to step back from your lives and leave you to continue your own path. Lynette, you were trying to say before Raymond rudely interrupted you?"

She paused, still in shock from the slap, looking at her husband fearfully, expecting his eyes to scream at her but instead he turned away. "I don't fully understand what it is you expect us to do?"

"I have no expectations of the outcome." He said with a kindness as he motioned towards her, taking a seat beside her on the patio bench.

"In the last few months Raymond has successfully maintained an income, without any help from his funds at all." He said smiling proudly, "I've carried him for long enough."

"You didn't carry me!" Raymond retaliated, "It's my money!"

"No, in fact it is still my money. And you don't need to be making withdrawals from it until the day I finally lay for the last time. Access to it has merely been a benefit, for all of you." Albert stood up again, "But you my son have proven that you don't need any access to it, that you can sail through and weather the storm without it."

"You cut me off and fired me! What else was I supposed to do?"

"You put your wife in hospital, what else would you have preferred me to do?"

Joel reached for her hand, gently squeezing encouragement. Seeing this, Raymond rolled his eyes and stared out at the pond as his father continued.

"Silver spoons do not enrich any person with the fundamental values of life and family." He urged, "You, me, Lynette…we have all overlooked one very important detail about all of this nonsense. Allowing ambition and greed, even your critical commitment to proving yourself better than me to distract us of what is important. And that is family. You are my family but I understand now that this is not about me, this is about your family Raymond."

Raymond turned to face him, his jaw clenched tight in anger. "Your mother and I have been preaching this to you forever... Silver spoons do not enrich any person…."

"I get it father you can dispense with the drama." Raymond groaned, "What is it you want me, or us to do this time?"

"This about Joel!"

"Joel?" Raymond gasped in surprise. Albert nod, "Ultimately, because in the past few years something has become broken in your home Raymond. One of your coaches lost a wheel and the tracks won't hold it forever. Not if any of us continue to be zealous and ardent. You need to slow down your ambitious train and learn to focus on what is truly important."

A frown crossed his sons face and Albert smiled, feeling that he had finally come to a paramount realization on how to finally put an end to the bedlam that had raised its head within his only living family.

"I want you to look at your son Raymond."

"I saw him!" Raymond snarled, his gaze not faltering.

"No." he sighed putting his hands on his sons head and turning him to face Joel, "See your son."

Please! You stupid old fool!

"He is just a boy, a young man in a big world."

Concealing his frustration, Raymond kept quiet. *Redundant.*

"He is your son, he needs your guidance."

My son? You senile ass, if you only knew…he is nothing of us!

"He needs stability. He needs to find himself the way we all did, with fair chance and without constant relocation."

He needs an orphanage! Raymond scoffed to himself, staring at the cut lip, bruised eye and broken pain in his eyes.

"Do you even know your son?"

My son? MY SON?

"You don't know him do you?"

Why bother? He is nothing of mine! If you only knew…

Trying hard to pretend that the attention was not on him, Joel eventually looked up at his father.

"That boy has been in your life for sixteen and a half years Raymond. You fed him, bathed him, took him to sport matches and through you and your wife taught him values." Albert's voice was soft and back to comfortable, "He is your son and right now, look at him."

Lynette turned and looked at her son, Raymond's eyes meeting his and for what felt like hours there was a silence.

In heart he wanted his father to embrace him, to be the man he knew growing up. He longed for his father before he began the abuse, before all the chaos and screaming. The look in his father's eyes ached him and he felt his tears welling so he had to look away. Lynette looked down, her own regret writhing within her guts and she knew that everything was ultimately her own doing. Had she not opened up the door to her past and invited in the man who owned her heart, Raymond would never have known the deception of her lies.

"That boy is your boy." Albert said looking Raymond in the eye, "You are going to make a home for your wife and your son. You are going to work on your problems and you are going to give it your very best because if you don't Raymond, I swear with every ounce of compassion that I have – you will never see a dime."

Raymond looked down, and for the first time in years he didn't care about the money, or the life. He felt guilt.

"Joel." He said turning to face him, his voice and face solemn. Joel's heart raced as Raymond smiled and motioned towards him.

"You are…." He wavered glancing at his wife, "…my son."

Lynette gasped - her mouth dry and her eyes welling with tears. It was the words she had waited so long to hear him say and she put her hands to her face. A smile broke on Joel's face, tears welling in his eyes as well.

"You can retain my access father." He said looking back at Albert who stood grinning bashfully, "I've got good things coming my way, investing what little I had left into a mining project in South Africa. Lynette and I will…"

He turned to her and smiled the smile that thawed her heart almost seventeen years ago.

"I am willing to move forward, if you are?"

She smiled looking at Joel whose teary eyes melted her, "Yes…"

"It's going to be rough…" Raymond paused nervously, "Almost everything has been invested. But we can if we try."

Lynette's face glowed as she looked up at the man who had vanished at the truth seven years before.

"To eradicate further burden and to simply ensure that Joel gets the best tuition, I'll have Wells and Yost create a fund." Albert said rounding his son to face Joel, "You focus on what I told you and you get yourself on track. There will be no more nonsense." Raymond felt the cold slipping in again, fear that he would not be able to succeed in his investment endeavour at the reopening of the mine and that his father would again deem him incapable and again involve himself in their affairs. He head back into the house again with clenched fists at his side, longing for the day his father would be in the ground no longer capable to judge and scorn him, no longer a factor worth concealing the truth about Joel.

Sitting at the wheel of his Evoque with his pretentious friends, he couldn't believe how quickly everything had changed since that day. How for a moment life felt good. But his father was a monster, and nothing and no one could cure the beast.
"Oh my bad." Collin's voice interrupted his train of thought, the beer fizzing on the carpet at his feet. Joel frowned but before he could speak Collin tapped his shoulder grinning.
"I'm really sorry man, I promise I'll have that cleaned for you."
Yes on my expense no doubt.
"Sure man, no problem." He smiled. *Rather be in than out…*
He shook his head, returning to his thoughts as he tried to make sense of his choices. He had taken up swimming, changed his attitude and his wardrobe, his speech, his hair, and even the manners his mother had raised him on. It was safer to be in than out, be what they expected than be who he was. It was a lesson he chose to stop learning the hard way.

◻◻◻

"I have the money." He remembered saying in response to overhearing most of the guys discussing plans for the weekend, obtaining booze and where they'd get the money to throw a party

somewhere other than at someone's house. Those four words are what got it all started, and it rolled downhill since. By using his allowance to cover costs and be the financial backer for most of the plans, Joel became popular within seconds after enrolling in the Seymore College. Word spread through grade 8 to 12 that he was someone who had the means to make any party, any sporting event or any school project stand out. His name was known on every tongue, and he always had plans, people who wanted to spend time with him. Even though he knew most were pretentious, just going with the flow because he had the looks and the money, he kept up the facade that it was acceptable. When he would decline using his allowance, people changed towards him and he'd buckle. It continued through to grade 11 just before they had left to Secunda, when the talk of the school was not that he would be missed by many as a friend, but more so who would be the party payer and booze buyer after him.

He mostly felt empty, even with the genuine people who surrounded themselves with him because it was a façade. He was a person he didn't want to be doing things he didn't really want to do. But being this was far better than being the guy who enjoyed reading, hiking and doing simple things that didn't require money or anything fancy.

Days were good for Joel but he would always feel strain of keeping up the appearance of the person others wanted him to be. After he had stumbled into the middle of an affair between his mother and a long-time family friend Marco, everything changed. More and more things changed.

His father grew darker, and became consumed by alcohol. His mother grew still and withdrew while he got caught in the middle, his being forced behind high walls where they stayed. But when he would feel the shadows crawling over him he would remind himself that he was born a multi millionaire's heir and that would never give him the standing he needed to be someone ordinary that people could speak to without seeing someone on a pedestal. Seymore College garnered a quick reputation throughout the country and had students from all over on campus, he still hadn't met one person who knew him and his story, one person who with enough guts to talk to him like a twenty four year old and not the grandson of one of the country's most esteemed millionaires. He often found himself lost between who he felt like inside and what he portrayed in his smile for the world to see, forced to hide the truth of everything going on at home from everyone, especially his grandfather, through facades, masks and manipulated truths. Joel felt constantly torn between being two people, keeping secrets, doing everything others wanted him to do and he felt it squeezing his lungs dry. Most days were easier to relish in the glory of being the richest twenty-something in the entire province, the popularity, the girls, the expensive toys and never being told off by anyone.

He was living in untruth with nothing inside waiting for someone to help him back to life.

Chapter Three:
Cat's out the bag

Within the confines of an old private hangar that had long been left abandoned sixteen kilometers outside of Johannesburg, two well suited men stepped towards a tall, slowly balding man with piercing blue eyes – Frank Harper.

After hurriedly stepping down as the district executive mayor four years ago, Harper now held the position of member of mayoral committee over planning and development, although as with most of his actions, not at his own will. He felt his palms dampen as the two men neared him from the entrance to the hanger, leaving the four black-suited body guards at the door to ensure security over their secret meeting.

Mr. Cheng Lee, the Asian man to the left was infamous within the Corporation for being a zero tolerance and highly skilled problem solver. Mr. Lee was, in no other general term, the right hand to the most superior element of the Corporation, the faceless man who pulled all the strings who went by the codename King.

Beside him walked a tall dark haired man, who was always clad in a black suit who never removed his dark shades. He never spoke and was always at Lee's side.

"Harper..." Nod Lee with a cocky grin before turning to give a subtle nod for the heavily armed security members to shut the doors and head outside.

"Thank you for coming."

"With all the media surrounding E shaft after the explosion, it's not like I had much of a choice." Harper replied cocking his head to the side as they stopped facing him.

"Mr. Black will be serving as our eyes and ears until we're sure everything that needs to stay buried remains that way."

Harper turned to the silent man with the dark shades who made the air difficult to breath.

"The investigation is commencing in less than four days and we need to be sure that our little problem down there did in fact get disposed of."

"I don't think you fully grasp the seriousness of the implications that little explosion had. When I stepped down I was told I would remain in cabinet at your disposal until the next presidential elections, I was never told that I would have to arrange cover ups for explosions in the middle of the night."

"I think you are misinterpreting why I've called you here Mr. Harper." Lee said walking around him, his stern English accent making each word blunt and firm.

"You should have been focusing on your role with the reopening at E shaft Mr Harper and forming your alliance with Raymond McDonald. So now, due to your lack of better judgement you inadvertently allowed Mr McDonald to announce a full investigation?"

"He would have done it either way, there are unions involved and investors. It was only to ensure the miners security and safety going forward, it is standard procedure." Harper said adamantly.

"Not when it comes to us!" Lee shouted, his voice bellowing over the empty hangar in echoes, "Not when everything the Corporation has been working towards is in jeopardy! Investigations into the collapse of E shaft and you allow this because it is 'standard procedure'? You are only here to act as the first point of contact to the media Frank, and by failing to do the very simple thing you are meant for in this little operation, you have caused a great headache for King."

Harper's lips parted, but Lee was fuming and seemingly unstoppable.

"The only reason - and I am very, very serious when I say *only reason* that you are still walking and breathing in any air is because of King and what happened with your son." Lee snarled coldly, "But he is not happy about this, and when he is not happy it means I have to get involved and kill people. Do you want that kind of blood on your conscience?"

A cold befell Harper and he could feel the tiny hairs on his neck standing up, "Don't I already have it on my conscience Cheng?"

"You got away with stepping down as Mayor Frank, but the only reason you are here right now is because replacing you at this point in the project would be far more time consuming, not to mention the resources it would take to get someone at the right hand of the Mayor to make sure he keeps his brown little nose out of our business."

"You assured me that collapsing E shaft would bury all the evidence left behind by your carelessness!" Harper scoffed looking to Mr. Black angrily, "You too have messed up Mr. Black let us not forget the events that is causing all of this four years ago when you got sloppy!"

"I bet you wish you could forget don't you?" Mr. Black said stepping up to him angrily, "Your son and your wife?"

Harper charged forward but Black gripped his hands and shoved him back, Lee's voice echoing around them again.

"Enough!"

Harper turned to Lee, as did Black and Lee shook his head in frustration as he continued to pace with his hands behind his back. "The simple reality of the situation is this; we made a crucial mistake a few years ago and now the Corporation faces dire exposure. The cats out of the bag Frank, we need to have it shot before it leaps, so Mr. Black will be on site of the reopening as part of the crew checking the shaft as per our beloved Mayor's request. I have personally arranged for this." He smiled, "Mr Black will also be one of the first to enter the shaft for the restoration of the beams. Anything down there that has any relevance will be disposed of including anyone standing in the way. He will be whomever he needs to be in order to ensure we contain the situation – as you put it Mr Harper this is a result of his inability to control himself and follow basic instructions."

Mr Black looked down, recalling the backlash from his actions four years ago.

"It is your job Mr Harper to keep focused on distracting everyone's attention to anything out of the ordinary and engage in a relationship with the McDonald's and ensure that you remain one step ahead of them or any findings at all time. Your function, your one and only objective at this point is to take care of Mr Black while he does what he was moulded into doing and entertaining the media. King does not care about the investors or their interests in the project. The first priority is to shift the attention from the shaft by tracking down the young man in the field with you that night Mr Black. Once we can divert some attention we'll be able to easily move around the rest of the pieces and undo what was done. Is that understood?"

There was a silence among them until Harper finally sighed, "Further concern is a report from the Star, Arnie Pillay. He's relentlessly making it his goal to cover this story, he's convinced that it was an act to conceal a secret within the shaft!" Harper growled, "Your explosion could have been a bit more subtle if you ask me."

Laughing Lee turned to face him, "We used the general mining explosives. What's done is done and the truth is going to remain buried down there. Let us not forget that you Mayor Harper had the chair when this reopening tender began and if you just remained focused you would have been able to put a stop to it."

"I don't have that kind of power Cheng." Harper hissed, "As mighty as the King is, why he not did something about this himself is beyond me. Or you personally?"

"Mr Arnold Pillay from the Star was already dealt with while you lay dreaming in your bed last night." Lee said, his voice riddled with disgust at Harpers failure to respect their head, "As you should know by now this isn't the first time Mr Black had to fix something that should not be broken in the first place. And please Frank, show some respect I would really hate to have to peel the skin from your eyes and feed them to you."

Mr Black grinned and Harper looked away, knowing that there was nothing the Corporation wouldn't do to prove its point – a lesson he had learnt the hard way through losing his own family.

"Everything is about to become very exciting." Lee said with a bright and excited grin, "The Corporation is finally nearing its objective and in a few months when the elections arise, everything we have been working towards will be realized. Have you forgotten the reason behind all our efforts Frank? Have you lost your way in believing?"

"No." Said Harper keeping his eyes fixed on Lee, "After everything I've sacrificed I want this more than anyone!"

"Then why…" said Lee moving towards him, placing his hands on either side of Franks face, "Why have you strayed and lost your ability to control your objectives Frank?"

His childish condescension was insulting and Frank pushed his hands away, "Get your hands off of me."

Lee laughed and round to Mr Black's side, putting his arm up on his shoulder. "You had better get back on your horse Frank because to be frank - Frank, you are making King very nervous and when King is nervous I get nervous. You don't want me to be nervous."

"For you." Said Mr Black, his voice cold and frustrated as he handed Harper the small box from his side pocket.

"Keep your eye on the prize Frank. We have one little obstacle to get through, let us all not forget the greater cause of this project." Harper looked down to the box frowning and Lee turned back towards the guards at the doors, "You boys play nice."

The guards opened the doors and Lee stepped out into the night. Harper shook his head and turned to Black who without expression turned and head towards the doors.

Frank Harper paused, his nerves finally able to settle. He had not been the same since the night all those years ago at the shaft. It was never meant to affect his family.

He head towards the doors, pausing to open the tiny box – inside it beneath a small leaf of silk cloth the two eyeballs from Arnie Pillay.

The night's cool autumn wind captured in its essence the ghostly sagacity of the grave yard and the spookiness it furnished beneath the night sky where dark bands of grey clouds rest lazily over head.

"I don't know why we come here at night Hendry." Mary Watts sighed beneath her chilled breath as she braved keeping abreast with her son as they walked along the cemetery isles. At 82, Mary Watts was a true lady to the term, filled still with the zest for life. Her short thin body held in it a fight, a determination to with hold her complaints of aches in her old age, and despite every concern for her she lived as the age of a twenty year old at heart, with neatly dressed grey hair that hung in a long soft bob style and the sporadic drizzle of make up to her eye lids, lashes and lips.

"I hate to say I told you so, but I did tell you." Smirked her son Hendry as he crossed over the lawn, "You shouldn't be out when it's this cold."

"And leave you alone out here in this spooky place." Huffed Mary sarcastically, "I don't think so sonny."

Stopping beside him as he stared at the grave before him, she knew it had become time to let silence fill the air and let her son be.

Each year on that very day, Hendry Watts would stand before his wife's grave and read to her the very first love letter he had ever written to her as her husband 28 years ago. The anniversary of her passing had never become easier to deal with and he would never let it. Each year for 3 years he would stand by her grave beneath the heavens at the very time she had left the world and remind her of his love and promises to her. As he removed the note from his coat pocket, he felt his heart aching and longing for one more moment with her, the anger of her passing always lying beneath his tears in a silent rage to the drunk driver who had taken her from him, from the world.

At 55, Hendry Watts was a tall, broad set man with dark brown, greying hair and a moustache – the army Admiral he had retired 20 years prior but had never truly let go of. Having spent his life teaching it was no surprise that he would be appointed as the Dean at the Seymore College. Yet as he read to his wife the words from the note, his rage at the driver who had chosen to start the engine of the car even at such a drunken state could not cease and seemed to grow more and more vengeful.

Mary put her hand around her son, her heart too breaking at the loss of a wonderful woman, and yet in the moment so touching and heartfelt, her nerves at the chill of such a ghostly place kept her eyes vigilant to every darkened nook.

"Always, and forever I will cherish you for the true beauty you are. I love you." Watts finished as he closed the note while fighting back his tears with a broken voice. He knelt down beside the grave and put a gentle kiss to his hand and softly placed it against the now faded picture of his wife that sat in the centre of the tomb stone.

"I miss you." He said softly closing his eyes.

"She knows my dear." Mary smiled, gentle squeezing his hand. He stood up again and took a deep breath looking up at sky, trying to see the stars that lay beyond the streaks of clouds.

"I regret so much." He said softly. Mary smiled and snuggled up beside him as he put his arm around her frail body, "We can never go back to do what we wish we had done Hendry, but we can live every day after trying to mend away the regrets."

"Do you have any regrets mom?" asked Hendry looking down at her soft, aged face.

"Of course I do Hendry, but for me it's too late to try and change a lot of them to positives." She said with a laugh shaking her head, "All I can do now is live to forgive myself."

"Forgive yourself?" he said turning to face her, "About the boat?" She nod looking up to the sky with her delicate blue eyes, "I sometimes imagine my life as though we had married and sailed the world in our little boat. And when I look out back and see that boat standing there, for all these years I want to just kick myself for buying it and never making true to my promise."

Watts nod and looked down and she continued, "You know Hendry, I truly did love your father very, very much. And I know you have never understood why I wanted to fulfil my promise to another man. But Bertie, he was my first love, and like you and Ella, the first love is the hardest to let go of."

He knew that he had been privileged to be brought up in a home as good as his mother and father had provided and he know how much in love they were with one another, and understanding her love for a man she had fallen in love with 60 years ago, 10 years before meeting his father, was something he had to make peace with since the first time she told him the story and he respected that as he knew about love and the pain of wanting it back so badly.

Just then the dead silence of the cemetery shattered when the roaring start up of a car's engine sounded a few feet away from where they stood beneath the trees that lined the tar road circling the yard. Then behind the car another set of headlights flickered on as the first pulled away.

"That's just spooky. I didn't realize we weren't alone." Mary chuckled. Watts turned to his mother and put his arm around her, "Let's get out of here." He said holding her as they head back along the darkened grave yard.

Jessie Noordman, once the daughter of one of the surrounding mines general managers with a bright future was now a young adult who had fallen to the pits of debts, alcohol and various forms of abuse. Pulling her underwear up on the back seat as he revved the car, Jessie's lungs craved a cigarette, or more so a joint of marijuana or even a line of cocaine. She had gentle pale, delicate skin and red brown hair that draped in shoulder length slight curls against her face - often in an attempt to hide the torment in her blue eyes that she too felt were a window to her dark and twisted soul.

At the steering wheel sat her lifelong friend Michael Harper, a tall, chiselled 22 year old with a short, smartly gelled locks of black silk-soft hair and brown tanned skin. Unlike his father, Michael Harper was a young man so determined to free himself of guilt that he forbad himself to feel any human emotions. He stared out the windshield at the spooky cemetery feeling over ridden with a sense of loss, constantly feeling torn and confused to the point where each word he spoke, each glance his striking green eyes gave seemed to radiate from the heart of a numbed human being.

Michael Harper was a handsome, well built and at first glance a very together young adult, especially as the son of the former Mayor he was perceived by everyone as balanced but inside still a lost and lonely boy with troubles and depth that despite his handsome and rugged boyish good looks would leave most uneasy in his presence, afraid of how to break silence near him. In the shadows he was the typecast bad boy.

As he waited for Jessie to compose herself in the backseat, he lit a joint, flicked the car into first gear and started out of the cemetery. Jessie and Michael first met on the street they shared as children. She and her parents had been long time Secunda residents while the Harper family had only moved in. His father at the time was a prominent candidate for district mayor and due to this Michael and his brother were often left in the care of nannies. His older brother had easily found friends his age, and she often saw Michael alone cruising on this BMX down the street.

The day he fell was the day they officially met, and for many years after they were inseparable. When her father's body was found out in the fields after his suicide, the life she knew was completely turned upside down and they gradually fell out of touch as friends. The debts Jessie's father had left them in forced her and her mother to sell almost everything they had. The shock and anger and confusion her mother felt became too heavy for a sane mind to cope with and she turned to the bottle while Jessie did all she could to finish the remainder of high school with the hopes of still be able to attend university and make a difference in her own life after the fall from grace. It was during this time that they were forced to move into the local trailer park area just a few kilometres outside Evander en route to Secunda. The park changed everything, as it was there that she met with 43 year old miner, Andre Naude. It was with him that she first experienced the use of drugs and alcohol, two elements that eventually led to Andre becoming her sexual partner, for payment so that she could keep herself and her mother alive. It had never been a lot, but it paid their portion of rent for the plot where the caravan stood, and groceries and text books. Her mother had since the suicide remained incapable of continuing to live, falling into the bottle and becoming a trailer park booty call.

It was the death of Michael's older brother Lyle that brought them together, but the circumstances would never be as innocent as it was before.

Jessie pulled on her shoes and began scooting over into the front passenger seat

She and Michael had no longer remained friends once she and her mother wound up living at the park. Michael hated her for becoming the scum she did after meeting Andre Naude, even more so when he discovered that his brother Lyle was in a manner of terms, working with Andre Naude himself. As she took the joint from him, she could still feel the grip of his strong hands against her thighs, her vagina still tender.

They had just finished having sex while another couple watched and touched them, a thousand rand in only thirty minutes. It was the life they been forced into, a life they shared by with miles of dark despise between them.

As the black Ford Cortina drove out the cemetery gates, she could almost not recognise the young boy she was once playing with. Now he was a bully, not someone to be taken lightly because more than a few knew he had followed in his brothers footsteps into dangerous circles, what she saw now was a reincarnation of Lyle, Michael's older brother.

Michael himself had died somewhere inside of the guy sitting beside her, and he was now just cold hearted and numb - wicked. Jessie, even past the thick make up on her eyes and the long red brown hair that hung mostly over her face was dainty and clearly accustomed to eating lesser than most, who had a vision for her future and a goal, but numb to the world she was still in.

"Why so quiet?"

He sighed and turned to her, his dark eyes filled with constant suffering, "I just am."

"Was it me?" She said exhaling the smoke. He frowned with annoyance shaking his head as his fists clenched the steering wheel, "No Jessie, it wasn't you."

She looked down cautiously, afraid to upset him.

They sat in silence as he drove out of Secunda, the night sky cluttered with smoke pouring up from the SASOL towers, hiding the stars.

She could feel a cold tension between them, and because she knew where his heart stood there was always fear that he would follow his brother's path to suicide.

"Sorry but I have to ask, is it Nkosi?" she said almost holding her breath in fear of his reaction. He turned to her frowning, "What?"

"I'm sorry you just seem so...distracted."

"Was I too rough?" he asked, for a brief second almost sounding again like the sweet boy she knew.

"No." she answered almost cautiously, "Why do you ask?"

There was a silence, his eyes fixed on the road as she watched him waiting for him to speak.

"It's been a long day."

"Like I said I'm just worried about you."

"Don't be."

"As long as you are ok?" She said softly, taking the last drag of the joint before tossing it out the window. Michael shrugged shaking his head; he never could understand why she was always so generous and kind towards someone so filthy and black. He wanted to die inside every minute following the moment he swallowed the last of his humanity.

"They were more hands on this time." She said softly, feeling them still rubbing at her breasts and clitoris while he thrust into her.

"Shut up ok Jess!" He snarled, "You know the drill. No talking, no bonding, no sharing. It's business as usual."

Jessie shook her head, the nausea now filling her gut as she began to feel the dirt crawling through her veins, her skin and her soul. She relied on the money from their arrangement to buy food, pay for her school fees and to save for her future after high school and now had to face living with an addiction to forget about the sin she committed each time with those men and without it, she would feel the dirt alive on her.

"I need a shot." She asserted, avoiding seeing his face, "Do you have any?"

"No."

"Michael please, I just want to take this out of my head." She said softly.

"What do you mean?"

"Were you paying any attention at all back there? The way she held your dick while you made love to me, it was..."

"God damn it!" shouted Michael interrupting her angrily, "What the hell are you talking about? We don't make love Jessie, we fuck and we get paid. End of story! Jesus Christ can you just shut up already!"

"I feel sore."

He sighed shaking his head angrily, his hands clenching the steering wheel.

"Can you pull over? I think I'm going to be sick."

"No, stop over reacting."

"Seriously Mike, stop the car!" she said almost gasping in a panic, already opening the door. "Jesus, are you crazy!" he shouted as he manoeuvred the Cortina off the road and skid to a stop on the dirt. She toppled out of the car towards the grass and began to throw up – something she automatically did every time they had finished a job Nkosi sent them on.

Michael shook his head with his eyes pressed tightly shut to force away the guilt and remorse he would not face. Whenever he tried to stay clear of the drugs, his past would haunt through his thoughts. The night after his brother's funeral, he needed a friend more than ever before and his mother's wailing was unbearable so he left on his mountain bike.

When he got to the trailer park to see the one friend he knew he could rely on, he saw Andre Naude beating on Jessie, forcing himself on her. Everything he overheard sometimes still echoed in his mind as though still fresh a couple of hours. She had been Andre's piece of ass and his brother knew about it.

What transpired that night would change them forever. His brother was gone, he was nothing and the only way to break even would be to become his own man, to be what his brother was so close to becoming before his suicide.

As he watched her puking in the side mirror he felt the bite of guilt and closed his eyes, recalling the day they were called aside by police inspector Brian Nkosi who had evidence of what they had done. He used it against them ever since, making them both his drug pushers and teenage whores. It was never to be anything more than hand jobs or blow jobs, nothing as extreme as Andre Naude had put her through more than three times before they killed him. But now inspector Brian Nkosi had a higher thirst for money and had them running around doing everything he wanted or face jail time.

As she stumbled back into the car, he turned to her.

"We need to stop this." His voice was stern and as adamant as it always was before he would fall back into the realization that they had no way out.

Shivering and trembling she turned to look at him, her cheap mascara running down her face in smudges, "Stop this?"

"I can't live with this guilt anymore." He said, a piece of the boy born Michael James Harper now breaking through, "This world we're in...It's crazy."

"You say this all the time." She said trying hard to avoid any contempt, "You know Nkosi will have us thrown away. I can't do that Mike I'm sorry. We have one year left Mike that was the agreement! One year and we're done, he won't have a hold on us anymore!"

"He'll always have a hold over us Jessie, no matter where we go! How can we trust he will hand it over like he said he would? Neither of us can be sure that he won't lock us up anyway?"

"I won't risk it Mike! I won't! Look at what he did to you the last time! I can't go to jail Mike! My mother will never survive without me being there to take care of her. So what other choice do we have? Kill him like we did Andre, because a fat load of help that did!"

"Shut up about that!" he snarled, shoving her violently, her body slamming into the door. She gasped and he dropped his head into his hands shutting his eyes hoping he could wake up and be in the world he knew before Lyle took his life.

"Fine!" She said breaking the silence as tears fell across her cheeks, "You go and you tell the inspector whatever you want, but unlike you - I don't have the ex-mayor as a father to bail me out. I have nothing but the hopes that this sick shit will get me to university and far from this place, from all this!"

A silence hung between them and inside the car it felt deafening, only the humming of the Cortina's engine groaned outside the car. As they both sat there they each understood the other's plight, but neither knew how to escape Nkosi's clutches without facing trial for murder. For three years they thought they had gotten away with it, but even that was a false hope. They had no hope.

Michael rolled a marijuana joint and handed it to her before rolling one for himself. In the last ten months since Nkosi accosted them, they had done everything from selling drugs, to travelling into the city to buy drugs.

They had photos taken of their genitals, hands and feet for those with fetishes. They had been intimate in front of other people, preformed sexual acts with other people and most disturbingly the rare time's Nkosi had them contact clients into acts of bondage and discipline, sadism and masochism.

They were both whores who felt their sins were visible on their skin like black ink.

The black Cortina spun on the gravel and shot out onto the road again.

The weekend buzz was chunky around the centre of Secunda's business centre as everyone began to spend their month end pay cheques. A cold hung in the Saturday air, yet the sky was opened from the night's blanket, boasting a crisp clear blue with the odd truffle of white fluff lazily gliding across its vastness.

The Hot Spot Café sat adjacent to the mall's main entrance between a book store and an arts and crafts shop and had since its opening eleven years ago always attracted many a customer, some regular and some new with its tasteful menu and homely environment. Inside, the décor was cozy and yet vibrant with plush oak tables, leather covered seats and a long bar. The café catered for sports fans, the elderly, families and children with a play pen. The smell of freshly brewed coffee hung in the dinners air as families and couples began to enter for the breakfast run and the sizzling of eggs, bacon and steaks enriched the noses of all those trying desperately to avoid spending more money other than on their groceries at hand.

Elizabeth Van Rooyen - Liz to those close to her - had been working at the Hot Spot Café since she managed to convince the owner that being the boss of his daughter would not necessarily result in household feuds and guerilla warfare, which after three years had never even touched ground. The money she earned as a waitress on weekends, holidays and certain week nights went directly into completing her B.com degree. Her long tussles of shiny hazel brown hair, creamy smooth skin and intense brown eyes that held in them a great innocence and tenderness applied the finishing touches on the sincere, soft spoken personality that earned her the great tips and welcoming tables.

As she head along the bar, collecting used napkins, spoons, straws, bottle caps and other drab, she bounced to Joan Jett's 'I love rock and roll' when her father tapped her on the shoulder, "Peanut?"

"Morning dad!" she smiled brightly, yet with a cute shyness that would always melt his heart. Her father Fredrick or "Pan" as he was known to the locals was a genuine believer in both the power of the smile and breathing and it showed well in his graceful age of 48. When his wife Helena had abandoned them, his first path lead to alcohol which in due course lost him his job as one of the artisans on the mine, and having always wanted to be his own boss, everything he had went into making the Hot Spot a success, and over the eleven years it had not only grown but doubled his expectations. With the mines within the area closing down and people moving on to green pastures, they had hit a slow run in business, and despite his concern he kept smiling with hope that the reopening would bring the heat back to the Hot Spot.

"I know it's early, but Timmy called in sick and we're already getting crowded and…"

"You want me to take out the trash right?" she said finishing his sentence with a sarcastic wink, "No problem pop."

"Pop?" he laughed shaking his head embarrassed, "Are you implying I'm older than just dad now?"

"Well pop, the early fifties is a half century old you know." she shrugged with a playful laugh. "Early fifties!" he gasped jokingly tossing his bar towel at her, "I should ground you for that!" he said as she laughed walking towards the kitchen, "Or worse, fire you!"

"Oh really?" she said turning to face him with a playful bashfulness, "I'm the best you have daddy."

"Brat!" he joked as she head through the doors into the kitchen. "Independent and strong willed, actually – remember dad? Just how you raised me." She teased with a wink. Shaking his head he couldn't help but admire his daughter, who at 20 was still his baby girl – persistent in paying her own tuition at the new Seymore College.

Busting through the rear swing doors of the Hot Spot, Liz tiredly dropped the two black refuge bags to the ground almost toppling on top of them herself as she breathlessly brushed her soft brown hair from her face.

"Thanks a lot Timmy!" she huffed as she lowered to bring the bags up again when suddenly two hands touched the bags as her did and she looked up in alarm.

"Jake?" she gasped, "Jesus you scared me!"

"Liz, we need to talk." Said the handsome rugby hero Jake with a smile, the only young man she had ever dated and who broke her heart.

"No, no we don't. We're done Jake." She said huffing up the bags and pushing past him towards the trash bins. "Look Liz, I drove all this way to see you." He urged walking up behind her as she struggled helplessly to hoist the bags high enough for the bin.

"Well I don't care!" she said as the weight pulled at her arms.

"Can I help you with that?" he frowned ushering for the bags.

"No Jake! I don't need you help." she said throwing them to the ground angrily, "Is there something in the sentence 'I don't want to ever see you again' that you don't understand?"

"Liz calm down, I didn't come here to fight with you!" he said raising his hand to ease her down, "I just want to talk."

"There isn't anything to talk about." she sighed arrogantly.

"Yes there is Lizzie. You're throwing away two years over nothing baby."

"Nothing?" she gasped surprised at his obnoxiousness, "When a girl says no, it generally means no Jake. Yes we had something good, but you rushed it. The same way you did your rugby and look at how that turned out."

"No!" he gasped lowering his voice, "Jesus Lizzie do you want your dad get his rifle?"

"If you'll leave me alone, then yes."

"How long did you want me to wait for you Lizzie?" He sighed, "Tell me and I will wait however long you want me to."

"Jake, look...We are done, I wasn't ready four months ago, and I'm not ready now. And to be honest, I don't think I ever will be ready to sleep with you. I don't trust you. I never will Jake. Never." she insisted angrily, "Just please, move on."

Shaking his head, the young stud stepped back, "I'm going to be in town until tomorrow afternoon, we're visiting my aunt Dinah so just think about it Lizzie. We could be good together, just like we were when we met."

Shaking her head, she stood watching him as he head back around the side of the building. Frustrated by repeating herself over and over again, she turned to kick at the bags, tearing them.

"Great! Thanks a lot Timmy!" she screamed up at the sky when the door opened to her best friend Troy Bean who stopped abruptly.

"Don't ask!" sighed Liz kneeling down to pick up the trash that had slithered out the slit. Troy, equally petite with blond hair, shrugged and hurried to her side to help her, "I won't ask if you're sure you don't want me to, but why such hatred for trash?"

Liz sighed and propped down in annoyance, "Jake was here."

"What?" gasped Troy in surprise, "That son of a bitch!"

"I feel sorry for him."

Troy grabbed her friends hand, "Liz don't you dare. He's an asshole."

"This is exactly why I feel sorry for him. The knee injury... then losing me." Liz sighed standing up as she and Troy hoisted the trash bag.

"You are much better person than I am, clearly!" moaned Troy angrily looking around, "Where is he? I'd love to give him a piece of my mind!"

"I told him to leave." Sighed Liz morbidly, as they tried to carefully raise the trash into the bin without the slit tearing wider. Troy huffed as the bag flopped into the bin, "You're better than him, you deserve so much more. You do know that right?"

Liz smiled shrugging her shoulders.

The estate where Joel was renting a three bedroom duplex apartment stood silent at 09h30 while the world beyond its giant brick walls already streamed with month end commotion. Joel sat at the kitchen nook eating cereal in silence, the wide open spaces of his lavishly furnished pad not enough to console the loneliness inside of him.

On more than one occasion since leaving the roof above his parent's two story mansion in Secunda's green area, Joel found himself missing the sound of his parents bickering because unless he had girls over or a party on, his life was quiet. And it was in those eerie silences that he found himself still thinking he was at home, feeling fear that his father's all to frequent itch to slap his mother had led to a murderous silence, and he'd listen with his ears pierced through the silence within the walls, his heart beat thumping from his own disturbing imagination and fears.

After washing his own plate, he slumped down on the sofa and immediately turned on the plasma television to break the silence that still toyed with his mind. He longed to feel like his own person, independent from his father's bullying shadow, his mother's obtuse thinking and scheming. He regretted turning down his grandfathers' offer for him to go stay in the Cape Town house, to attend the university there. He felt regret since the moment decided to stay near his parents and attend the Seymore Academic College, which in retrospect, Albert had commissioned especially for him and thus the gesture simply adding to the image he felt so exhausted carrying.

Mindlessly browsing the channels on his bed, he wanted eagerly to shake the feeling of being forever be the guy without life over weekends or friends. His heart was outside in the world and yet his cage was his personality and lack of strength and belief in himself. He felt awkward at home, at college, and commonly in his own skin. For a moment he channeled onto an erotic scene from a movie and his thoughts were distracted. The two people on screen kissing with such passion, desire for the other, their bodies writhing as one. And again, he was brought back to the disorder in his mind. He wanted to break out of himself, soar up far away from the troubles of his life where he could start being a young man and not a boy trapped and bound by the tribulations of his household.

Like a jackal on the prowl Kyle stepped out of the back door onto the steps, the soft sound of the door clicking closed was louder than he had hoped for, but the urge to break away from life was too strong to focus his thoughts and actions.

Inside, Claire and Edward were shuffling furniture and hanging frames while little Bennie unpacked his toys in his own room. The late morning breeze was still cool and full of the excitement of adventure he had secretly longed for.

After carefully making his way up the grape vine that grew on a vertical frame beside the house, Kyle carefully found comfort on his back atop the roof, with a blend of tobacco smoking in his fingers. Earlier, while in the front yard taking out the trash on the sidewalk, he found himself frozen and unable to breath – something lurking a few houses down had him gripped in fear, face from another life when the world was red. Even after he realized that it was pure paranoia, he couldn't shake the way it made him feel, reminded him that he was and always would be 'Boy X'. It happened more often than he could control and he knew that he would have to accept that many faces, places, smells and sounds would take him back there.

The sky was much like the ocean, quiet and calm. The perfect blue vastness and the bright white cottons balls that drift at a snail's pace along it and combined with the freshness in the wind he began to feel alive within the world.

As he lay staring up at the ocean of crisp blue he wondered if he had done the right thing by implying hope to his mother, Edward and little Bennie. He felt a sense of guilt already, at the mere thought of not making it the way he intended to. The nerves of everything stirred at the craving to be free of fear and the more he tried to force himself to imagine being part of anything, the more he felt panic slam into his chest. Since the night it all began, he had led an entirely surreal existence, devoid of anything a normal young teenager would experience. He did not know the first thing about speaking like a guy, or how to approach or reply, engage or joke. He had only gained control over his rage with a program at Crown and Lake, and still he battled to utter words to the people closest to him. He felt guilt for making anyone believe that he could do any of this while the agonizing want to use again gnawed at his soul.

He closed his eyes, trying to recall a time when he had friends, but he couldn't see past the haze of the blackness that overtook his life. Sadness befell him again because he felt cheated of a choice, of a life like other boys with rugby and sports, hang outs, camping, masturbating to dirty magazines in the tool shed, PC games, going to the movies or hanging out at the mall and even the simplest. He closed his eyes, heaving a deep breath to subdue the self pity bubbling inside of the blackness of his heart, realizing that he had never even been familiar any other effortless emotions like love, or a crush, friendship or belonging. All he knew was anger and torment. He sat up, taking another pull of the cigarette, his spirit desperately screaming for something more. He exhaled, shutting his eyes to remind himself that nothing about him or what he was deserved the simple pleasures of live that regular girls or boys had available. Being normal was something he would never likely experience, he was led to be a monster, a worthless user and sex toy for those able to accommodate his desire to get totaled in the numbness of narcotics.

Will I amount to anything? I'm twenty three years old and nowhere.

He sighed, taking another drag of his cigarette.

Stop thinking about your future, you don't have one. You don't deserve one.

Just then an aroma circled through the air, and Kyle's eyes immediately began to scroll the area around him. It was marijuana, he knew it like he knew the taste of his saliva and it stirred something inside of him with aching desperation.

He heard the sound of dry leaves crunching by the wall between their yard and the yard next door and he sat up staring through the vine curiously. Through the deadening leaves and dry vines not much could be seen, and as he tilt his head forward he saw looking over the wall up at him a gray blue figure. He closed his eyes and tried to re-focus through the influence on his brain. Looking again he could still not see what the figure was, but he saw it moving towards the side and just as he was about to call out at it, when the sound of their back door opening echoed from below. "Kyle!" called Claire from below, "Kyle! Where are you?" He sighed shaking his head, trying to form a mantra in his thoughts *You don't need it!*

He hurried towards the vine again, swinging down with ease. "I'm here."

She fold her arms across her chest, her face riddled with disappointment and dire upset and he slowed his pace cautiously. There was a smell in the air, a smell he knew very well.

"How could you!" she screamed angrily, "One day? One day and you turn to drugs!"

The sound of the door slamming open caused them both to turn. "Honey, come on. Not so loud, we just moved in." said Edward putting his arms around her, "We don't need a bad name already."

"Where did you get that? How long has this been going on Kyle?" She snarled on the verge of tears, "I give up! I cannot believe you!"

Kyle bit his teeth and filled with rage and anger, and he felt himself nearing the point he had evaded in Crown and Lake. *Breathe; she has the right to be judgmental. After everything. Calm yourself and talk to her rationally. Rationally!*

"Are you going to say something Kyle?" asked Edward stepping towards him, "I think you owe us something…"

"Why would you do this? I don't understand!" Claire urged - her face riddled in anger, "Talk to me god damn it!"

Breathe Kyle, don't let it out. Breathe!

He felt his rage bubbling, and although he tried to make sense of the situation she too knew that it wasn't called for.

"I'm sorry, hello?" called a weakened voice from behind Kyle. Mary Beth Watts waved over the top of the wall, "Hello, terribly sorry to intrude."

"Who the fuck is that?" growled Kyle, trying hard to avoid the rage pulsating inside of him.

Edward shook his head uncomfortably, looking to Claire in shame as he hurried past Kyle to perform a damage assessment.

"I couldn't help over hearing what you were saying." Said Mary politely with a smile, "Decided it best to call you over before the order of things got upset."

Claire looked up at Ed, her heart sinking already with shame and her eyes pierced through her son who stood with tightly clenched fists at his sides.

"The smell you were referring to is mine." She said interrupting his apologetic introduction. Claire shook her head in total despair and disbelief, looking past Kyle's shoulder where the old lady put held up the joint.

"I'm sorry…" she said stepping towards him but Kyle pushed past her and head inside, slamming the back door angrily.

"You see I suffer from cancer and this is supposed to help with the chemo." She spoke to Edward with a sweet smile, "I really do apologize for any inconvenience I might have caused." She smiled sweetly as any granny would, "I might be 82 years old and far over the hill, but I'm not ready for cancer to take me just yet and apparently this stuff not only helps with the chemo but it defiantly puts a smile on your face." She laughed.

"Oh well, ok." Laughed Edward taken aback and sensing their discomfort, Mary continued to address the neighbors.

"I'm not a user as such, but the doctors tell me if I don't light one of these at least three times a day, the after effects will simply finish me off. I'm 82 like I said and it's taken my old body quite awhile to accept the chemotherapy." She explained, "Please, don't judge me on the smell you caught whiff of."

"Oh! Oh no! Not at all, it was me, I was being silly. I thought my son Kyle was smoking it..." said Claire shaking her head realizing that their own demons with drugs had put on very different faces than they intended. Edward put his arm around her, as he led the conversation away from unwanted suspicion and all Claire could think of was what damage she had done to Kyle.

Police inspector Brian Nkosi was a strong, medium height Xhosa man, 45 years old and well revered by his colleagues throughout the police departments around the surrounding towns. The dark side of the law had attracted him far faster and more powerful than the good and when one of his money making schemes had committed suicide and the other was found dead in the trailer park, he had no choice but to twist his soul to get the market back on track, using the two culprits in the Naude's death as his pawns. Inside a police van parked at the very back of one of the town's stores, Michael handed him their weeks collections, via chores administered to the client base Nkosi had found through the adolescent Lyle Harper - who brought city slick into the small town, and the sales Michael made on drug peddling throughout the region.

Having hurriedly counted through the notes, Nkosi turned to Michael, "This is all?" he asked suspiciously.

"It's been a rough week." Nod Michael lighting a cigarette when Nkosi slapped him across the face and shoved him up against the door.

"I don't have rough weeks!" he snarled, "This collection is getting less and less each week! Not acceptable!"

"What do you expect me to do?" gasped Michael as Nkosi's large hand pressed at his throat. He had been in many rough situations, but this man had brut strength and he felt needles and pins rushing over his face.

Don't pass out! Fight it!

"Please…you're…hurting me!"

Nkosi sighed and shook his head, letting go of Michael's throat, "It's that stupid white bitch. She must fuck the men... I can make much more money if she fucks the men. I have been patient but it is not working this way."

"No. She won't do it." Michael gasped, breathlessly reaching for his smoke and lighter on the floor of the van, "She's just a kid. We are both just kids."

"Kids who can kill!" scoffed Nkosi with a vicious punch to Michael's chest viciously, "I can't tolerate this petty cash bullshit! Are you stealing from me? Is that it?"

"What the hell?" gasped Michael in alarmed surprise as Nkosi slapped at his head, "Are you serious? No!"

"Where is my money?" he said sitting back shaking his head, "Where is my money if you are not stealing it? I will lock you up forever you piece of shit!"

"That's it. I don't know what else to say." Said Michael shaking his head worriedly, "Things are just quiet ok? You have us busy every night with at least one client, and the drugs aren't selling so much. I don't know what you want me to say!"

"They were never quiet when your brother was my right hand!" snapped Nkosi taking the money from the envelope and putting it into his wallet.

"I'm not my brother." Said Michael angrily.

The inspector laughed, "You are very far from your brother, you are like a dust and your brother was the beach!"

Michael shook his head looking away with hatred reveling inside of him. Inspector Nkosi sighed with annoyance, "I will hate to tell your father what you did. You will go to jail both of you!"

"Don't threaten me." Michael snapped aggressively.

"Then make the target!" Nkosi snarled - slapping him through the face, "Easy and simple! She must fuck the men!"

"Inspector with all due respect, we have been your…people…for just over a year now and nothing is ever good enough." Said Michael watching his words carefully, "Maybe you should get somebody else?"

"Somebody else?" frowned Nkosi sarcastically showing enthusiasm to his suggestion.

Michael nod, "Yeah, you're a cop you can anything you want."

"Is that so?" asked Nkosi grinning.

"Yes." Nod Michael when in a flash, inspector Nkosi grabbed him by the neck and shoved him back up against the door with his gun drawn.

"Then maybe I can blow your head off right here?" he said forcing the barrel into Michael's mouth, his dark eyes ruthless and devoid of emotion.

"I am not playing games with you Harper! Two thousand a week, I don't care what you are doing but you are going to do it right! There is not enough teenage murderers I can find to take you place."

Michael's heart pound, the cold metal against his teeth and he felt tears rising to his eyes but he fought it as best he could and maintained eye contact with the inspector.

"I want you to make target, do whatever you have to do or I will arrest you and that murdering white bitch. I will have you put into the worse prison where the big bad men will rape you over and over and over!"

Michael nod fearfully.

The inspector shook his head, "You are a murderer, do not forget that! I give you the customers and the drugs. If it is not making the target then we have no more. Think out the box, understand?" Michael nod and Nkosi moved back, re-holstering his gun.

"The evidence I have for you will crush you to nothing! It will break your father's life. You need me as much as I need you, and you make sure you remember that every day and you tell the bitch also!"

Why God, why didn't you just let him pull the trigger?

"Two thousand per week, if my drugs are not enough, find your own. If my customers are not enough, find your own. If you don't have it right next week I am going to have the bitch's throat cut open and will sell her blood for the Sangoma's witch craft! Do you understand me?"

Michael nod nervously, his mouth drier than ever before, the metal from the barrel still on his pallet.

He hopped out of the van and shut the door, heading towards the back where one of the inspectors colleagues lieutenant Venter opened the back of the van and handed him a brown paper bag filled with the coming week's supply of weed, methamphetamine, ecstasy, magic mushrooms and powder cocaine –taken from the evidence room and local busts.

Michael took the bag and turned to leave when Venter's hairy knuckles grabbed hold of the collar to Michael's jacket - spinning him to face him. Taken by surprise, he had no time to react when the punch from Venter's right hook landed in the centre of his gut, crippling him. Venter held him up against the side of the police van, and Michael fought back the vomit that had charged up into his mouth.

"I want the girl at my house tonight after eleven. I have new leather. Understand me?"

Michael nod, his throat burning along with the ache in his stomach – trying hard not to roll his eyes at Venter's disciplinary fetish. He shoved Michael aside, letting him cripple to his knees on the tar.

"Do you know anything about what happened out at that mine shaft?" Venter asked from the passenger door turning back to face him.

Breathless, he shook his head as he tried to swallow the pain from his gut, "No."

"Are you sure?"

"Yes, I'm sure!" snapped Michael under his breath as he rolled to his knees.

"If we find out you and your chommies were tossing around that shaft the other night Harper, we'll be all over you like a fly on shit, got it?"

"Got it, thanks." Heaved Michael as Venter shook his head and got into the van which drove off as the door shut. As the van veered out, Venter tossed an empty can to the side of Michael's Ford Cortina and Michael sighed shaking his head in relief that they had left.

Chapter Four:
Now, Residence

"I don't see why you made me come with on this little joyride."
Sighed Kyle as the sedan pulled into the parking lot at the front of
the mall. Claire sighed and turned to face him, "Just try and see if
you can enjoy this ok? Baby steps..."
Kyle shook his head angrily, "Me getting into the car was a baby
step."
"Are you going to be mad at me all day Kyle? It was an honest
mistake!" she sighed, "I mean how many people have neighbours
from the Titanic smoking pot?"
Kyle sighed and Edward turned to him, "Look, just take a deep
breath and get a feel for the place, the environment and the
people." he tossed the car keys at Kyle's lap, "If you want to,
come wait here but at least try."
"How do you expect to go to college if you can't manage one
store?" Claire added, 1 reeling from guilt at her assumption this
morning.
Kyle shook his head, biting his lip with frustration. _Kill me now._
"You realise we won't be long right? I don't want to be here
doing shopping on pay day anymore than you do Kyle." Edward
said turning to him again with a sympathetic smile.
"Jesus Ed, please just stop trying to bond with me. It's really
distressing." Kyle replied with blunt snarl as he swung the door
open, "Let's just get this over with!"
"Can you at least mind your language around your little brother?"
Claire said shutting her door as he turned to face her, "And for
god-sakes Kyle, top acting like a child!"
Her stern voice and adamant stare left him speechless as they
head towards the mall.
Inside the store, as Claire and Edward head along the isles inside
the seemingly never ending store, Kyle lazily followed behind at
the allowed distance with his hands slumped into his pockets,
dragging his feet and offering a pretentious nod each time his
parents turned to ensure his presence behind them where they
could maintain watchful eyes over him. Bennie, who had
innocently been sitting in the trolley, noticed a bargain bin filled

to the brim with toys and began to plead for an opportunity to go take a peek.

"Kyle, would you like to go with him?"

"I'd love to but I can't I'm busy acting my age." He grunt sarcastically.

"Just take your brother to the toys." She sighed, "Or else come help me pick out feminine hygiene products?"

"Let's go." Kyle said grabbing Bennie's hand.

Edward put his arm around her as she watched them head off down the aisle out of sight.

"Are you going to be able to buy anything without watching him every second?"

"I feel like such an ass!" she huffed, turning the trolley and heading off

Troy and Liz rounded the cashier at the stores kiosk, Troy counting the notes in her hand as Liz neatly tucked hers into her waist purse.

"The Hot Spot is cooking today! I can't believe the amount of notes I've been given, I was out of change by twelve already. I can't decide if I hate month end or enjoy it." Troy frowned, "At this rate I'll be in my convertible in no time!"

"Oh my god…" said Liz in a numbing tone as her mouth lowered open, her hand gripping her friends arm as she paused to stop. Troy frowned and turned to glance in the direction to where her friends' star struck eyes were fixed, "What? Liz?" she frowned failing to see what had attracted such a sudden loving response from her best friend, "Liz? Hello, Jesus what is it? Is Orlando Bloom shopping here or something?"

Liz, stunned and speechless, could barely manage to shake her head as her eyes fixated on the person a few feet away at the bargain bin. Troy sighed with irritation and scanned around the store again, finally spotting a new face near the bargain bin.

"Oh hell no Liz, not that creepy, gothic, brooding, pervert by that little kid at the toy bin?" gasped Troy, tapping Liz on the shoulder, "So help me god I will blow my rape whistle."

Liz laughed shaking her head, "He's cute! Look at him!"

Troy shook her head, taking another look. His strong arms pressed against the sides of the bin as the kid put a gentle smile over his full lips, his hand brushing the long raggy hair from his face, tense blue eyes watching the little boy with such great care.

"Do you think it's his kid?"

Liz shook her head, "God I hope not."

"Maybe he's a pervert?" Troy sighed, "No guy that gorgeous could possibly be normal, this is Secunda!"

"So you agree? He's gorgeous?"

"Not my type, but yes he's attractive. Yes. Yes." Troy said nodding as her eyes remained fixed, "But you're going to stop yourself from making a big mistake. He's clearly morbid and brooding, tense and full of himself. That my darling friend...is issues on two legs. Besides, look at the way he is watching that kid, I think I should blow my whistle anyway."

"Have you eaten lunch yet, I think your stomach acids starting to eat away at your brain?" shrugged Liz playfully shoving her, "First of all, I was just looking which I am allowed to do since I am single again. And secondly he isn't my type either."

Well...

"Now, let's get back before table twelve has another haemorrhage!" Liz said, spinning around towards the exit when with a wham she slammed directly into Kyle and Bennie, sending Bennie toppling to the ground.

"Oh my god!" she gasped in alarm, turning to Troy in dismay. Kyle, surprised and taken back, quickly fell to his haunches to aid his little brother and Liz, dumbfounded and embarrassed, launched down to help at the same time, connecting her forehead to the back of Kyle's head, the thud making her already overwhelmed thought train spiral off balance and she too stumbled back against Troy.

"Oh. My. God!" gasped Liz holding her forehead, looking for help in her best friend who simply turned away laughing in a rhapsody.

Kyle, smiling to his surprised, gave a polite frown as he too rubbed at the back of his head, "Are you alright?"

His smile! Liz you're such an idiot! Not now, compose yourself and speak to the guy!

"Yes, I'm fine. Are you ok?" she asked dabbing at her forehead.

"Yes, I'm sorry I wasn't looking out for you." Kyle answered shyly, hoping he could hide the agony on his face from the throbbing at the back of his head.

"Neither was I." she smiled, her face burning red. Troy shook her head giggling and Bennie just stood looking up at the two of them in confusion.

"I am so sorry, are you alright little guy?' asked Liz looking down to Bennie who nod with a bright smile.

"I didn't mean to slam into you…" said Kyle looking past her as Troy stepped behind Liz with a composed and stern stare.

"No, this was all me. I did the slamming." Said Liz looking to Troy nervously, hoping the sight of her best friend would ease her racing heart.

"She's like that." Agreed Troy with nod.

Kyle smiled awkwardly, not sure of what to say next as he felt their eyes burning up and down his body and he turned to Bennie, taking his hand.

"Is he your son or do you just follow kids around the store?" Troy asked with a crudeness that made Liz spin around in surprise.

"He's my brother." Smiled Kyle, the awkwardness enveloping him and pressing down on him as though a physical force.

"This is my friend Troy." Liz said trying to break the tension.
Holy crap Liz, seriously! Say something else!

Kyle managed an awkward smile, holding out his hand, which Troy shook kindly.

"I feel like such an idiot." Liz said finally breaking past the redness on her face, "I really am sorry for ruining your entire morning."

"You didn't." Kyle nod, hurriedly looking down at Bennie hoping to elude showing just how gob smacked he was by her splendour and breathtaking adorability. He hadn't ever felt so warm inside, so taken aback by someone.
What is this?

"Her name is Elizabeth Parker." Said Troy leaning over Liz's shoulder, "You both seem to have missed that formality…"

Kyle smiled, realizing that he was so devastated by the way she made him feel he had almost completely forgotten the basic steps of talking.

"Yes, I'm Liz." She said holding out her hand.

Kyle managed a smile and reached out for her hand, "Kyle. And this is Bennie."

The minute his hand touched hers he felt a wave over his body, goose bumps all over him and for a second it was as though everything in the world had melted away, leaving only him and her standing hand in hand. And for the first time ever he had reached out without hesitation.

Liz smiled and waved down at Bennie who had by then already been consumed back into his new figurine. She looked back up, not expecting to meet his deep blue eyes. Something inside of her began to tick and in his chest he felt a pounding warmth, a nervousness he had never known before.

Say something Liz, this is awkward. Stop staring at his eyes. Stop staring at her you piece of shit, you're going to scare her! Liz, say something. Troy? Ghandi? Someone! Say something! What is this feeling? Why am I shaking like this? Kyle, get a grip and walk away.

"So..." said Troy trying to shatter the awkwardness radiating off of them, "Are you new in the area Kyle?"

He pulled her hand from hers looking up with a boyish frown feeling bewildered.

"Well are you?" asked Troy confused as to why he seemed to gobsmacked by conversation. "Yes, we are." He nod shyly.

Bennie looked up at Kyle, "She's pretty."

Kyle's mouth dropped open, unable to utter a word as he felt a humiliation more powerful than he had ever before. Liz and Troy laughed, thanking Bennie and telling him adorable he was and Kyle felt his stomach cease its tightness and breath ran back to his lungs.

"Well this was fun." Said Troy finally breaking the moment, "But we have to get back to the Hot Spot."

"What's that?" Bennie asked from below.

Troy smiled, "The best smoothies in town, you should come sometime and I'll make you a special one just because I could chew on your cheeks!"

"Inappropriate..." Liz said nudging her away from the boys face.

Troy giggled shyly stepping back, "But you should come and check it out, we really do serve the best of pretty much everything. And we have serious play gym!"

"Yes so please..." Liz said looking at Kyle, "You should come check me out."

"The place!" Troy quipped, "Check out the place, the restaurant. Not necessarily her! I mean that would just be unsuitable right?"

Kyle felt confused, they were the first girls he had spoken to in four years and their bumbling couldn't register.

"It's actually my father's restaurant..." Liz smiled proudly, "We're open from 8 to 8 daily and I work on weekends, so if you guys swing by casually, for no particular reason at all..."

"Except to eat!" Troy smiled, "Obviously…"

Liz nod nervously, "Then you should come try me out."

"Again?" Troy gasped, "The restaurant she means. Not her."

Bennie and Kyle looked at each other frowning.

"Well then, this was fun." Said Troy, "We gotta go!"

Liz nod looking down shyly as Troy put her arm around her, "Is there anymore damage you'd like to do Liz?"

Liz laughed stupidly and head after her friend.

"Not a word Troy, not one word!" she said raising her hand over face that felt as if the sun had risen directly in front of her, "Oh my god!"

"What?" laughed Troy, "That went well! You didn't kick him in the crotch! Oh god his eyes are just…"

"I told you!" gasped Liz as they erupted into a collective giggle.

Kyle nod and Bennie waved as they head out the doors to the buzzing square outside.

"Girls are weird." Bennie said shrugging them off and heading towards the bargain bin again. Kyle nod, still reeling from the handshake.

By 4pm, music and people filled the outside of Joel's apartment. Trying hard to recompose himself from the dullness in his thoughts that wouldn't fade, Joel slid up out of the pool from between a group of girls drinking shots off of the floating tray in the rock pool. Everyone with a cell number in his phone had been notified that free booze was available at his house, and everyone showed up.

He dabbed his face with his hands, and head towards the bar he hired.

"A Tom Collins please." He smiled at the bar girl clad only in her bathing suit.

"Hey man, this was a brilliant idea!" Rendani said rushing up to him, wet from the pool, "I think we needed this after the other night right?"

"Yeah for sure man." Joel smiled.

"Can I have two big bulls please?" Rendani asked the waitress before looking to Joel, "You need a place with a bigger pool man, the Delta Caps feel like fish right now."

Joel turned to the side where his fellow fraternity brothers huddled in a corner by the rock pool, crammed like sardines fighting for water over the other guests.

"How are you holding up?" Rendani said lowering his voice, "With the whole mine catastrophe."

Joel shrugged back his shoulders, "Trying not to think about it."

"Hey handsome..." Came a high pitched voice from the side and he turned to the tall blonde with the star tattoo on her left breast.

"Charlene, you made it." He smiled as she hugged up against him, her hand running up his stomach muscles and around his chest. "I wouldn't miss it for the world?" she smiled reaching past him for the Tom Collins from the waitress, "You single yet?"

"Not to my knowledge. Not yet." He smiled biting his lip, watching her slide her tongue around the straw in his drink.

"Pity..." She said handing back to him, "I'll be wet and waiting. In the pool I mean."

She head off and Rendani turned to Joel laughing.

"You know B would have your eggs for that right?"

Joel sighed shaking his head, "Well she needs to stop thinking I'm her property."

"Hey Mac D." came Collin towards him, Michael Harper at his side.

"You know Mike Harper right?"

Joel nod nervously, the stories about Michael far to nerve wrecking to sweep aside.

Michael's eyes scanned him up and down, "Cool party."

"Thank you." Joel smirked, looking to Collin in frustrated concern.

"All a bit too...extravagant for my taste with the bar and all. It's like a desperate attempt to overstate your lineage Joel." Remarked Mike lighting a smoke as he leaned against the bar. Grinning with frustration but knowing his place with the town's notorious thug, Joel turned to him, "Then why'd you come?"

Michael tilt up his head exhaling up into his hosts' face, "You asking me to leave Richie?"

Joel gave a smug laugh and Michael turned to the bar lady with a wink, "Beer please. You got beer right?"

"Why wouldn't there be beer?" Joel frowned, his face riddled with disdain as he turned to Collin with a sneer.

Having entered the party unable to tolerate any thought other than repeating Nkosi's threats in his mind, Michael felt even more discouraged by the reality of his life struggling to make money in sin to pay for sin while one person could so vaingloriously have it all.

Collin looked to Joel shrugging as he tipped his head back to finish his drink, Michael's eyes racing over the students hoping to spot a user in the crowd.

"So are you at Seymore?" Joel asked with forged interest.

"No." said Michael absorbing his beer as he stepped away, not once making eye contact as he head back into the house.

"What the hell is his problem?" Joel turned to Collin, "Why'd you bring him here?"

"I didn't man, he was inside when I got here." He laughed, patting Joel's shoulder, "Besides he brings the good stuff!"

Joel huffed downing his drink, "This is unbelievable..."

"Don't stress about it." Collin laughed, "Get drunk and stop being so uptight my man!"

"What? I'm supposed to apologize for being rich now?"

Collin shook his head, "Seriously man, I never said that. No one cares man. Just relax, this is your party!"

Holy shit I'm going to slam a beer into his face!

"Everyone cares Collin, that's just it! If I had no money, half you people wouldn't give me the time of day."

"You people?" frowned Collin with insult, "Are you saying we're all beneath you? Or because I'm black?"

"Don't go there…"

"Because it sounds like you think you're doing us a favour."

"Aren't I always? One way or the other?"

Collin shook his head in denial, "Whatever man, you have a chip on your shoulder tonight and it's understandable because of who you are. But truth be told man it's tiring."

"I don't know what to do anymore." Joel sighed, turning to order another drink only to find that Collin had gone off into the house.

As he smiled and greeted unknown students, watching how many people had come to his flat only because of him supplying everything for them, just as every time before. And he shook his head angrily.

It's the money that makes you worth taking notice of. Without it I'm nothing but with it I'm still making people upset? Yet look at them, they're here smiling. Sponges!

"You have Calvados brandy right?" he asked turning to the bar girl. "Yes sir." She smiled nodding.

Sir? Is that what people think of me?

"The bottle, just give me the bottle…."

As he continued greeting his guests with pseudo welcome, he chugged back at the bottle of clean French imported brandy, the sting almost choking him but he casually moved to the side, out onto the patio to catch his breath.

Just drink, drink and get totally hammered! Maybe they'll like your spoilt ass then! Look at them, your house but they don't even realize you look like shit.

Watching the party goers, he gripped the bottle again, swigging back another gulp when he noticed his girlfriend Bronwyn Engelbrecht, a curly blonde with green eyes, heading towards him with two other girls in tow. They hooked up for what he thought was casual college sex at a party, but since then she laid claim to him and his money. He sighed managing a disturbingly weak smile as she waved, figuring he'd keep up the pretence because it meant one constant girl in his bed instead of many empty one night stands.

"I have been looking for you all over baby." She smiled pressing up against him for a kiss on his cheek as he arose to meet her. Joel, his voice taken by the strong brandy, shrugged as casually as his choking self could muster.

"These are my new BFF's Tanya and Lindsay."

"Hi." He smiled awkwardly, "What happened to Jackie?"

Bronwyn rolled her eyes handing him back his credit card, "I don't want to talk about that, it's just way to tiring."

"Did you get yourself something nice?" he asked sliding his card into his swimming trunk pocket. She looked up, "I have the most amazing shoes yes!"

No thank you even? She's really getting comfortable.

"I'll stay over tonight and wear them for you, just them."
He smiled nervously.
Too comfortable.
"I thought I told you, I don't like people sleeping over." He said trying his best to charm his tone. She nod, "I know, I'll leave when we're done."
He nod with relieve and swashed back at the brandy.
Who is the biggest slut here?
"You're the guy from Pretoria right?" asked the cherry blond Lindsay stepping to him with a flirty stride, "I've heard good things about you. It's nice to finally meet you."
Jealously giggling, Bronwyn slugged her arm, "He's from Joburg actually."
"No I'm not." He snarled, "I'm from Cape Town."
"Same diff isn't it?" the other girl, a short haired brunette asked with a frown. Looking at them in alarmed confusion Joel frowned, but instead chose another swig of brandy.
"So B tells us your father is some tycoon type investor?"
"Oh yes, Joel drives the new Evoque, have you been inside one yet?" Bronwyn blushed squeezing his behind, "It's so hot and sexy... I told you I've hit the jackpot with this one. He's even travelled the world!"
"So how long have you known each other?" he asked frowning.
"All my life baby..." she said pouting, "I speak about them all the time."
"Jackie's the only name I remember." Joel laughed and threw back another gulp waiting for it to drown the gloom in his chest.
Bronwyn boasted, "He's part of the Delta Capital swim team."
"We need to talk, in private." Joel stuttered foolishly as the brandy began to make everything feel warm and woozy.
Bronwyn pushed herself up against him, "I've been waiting for you to say that."
Joel shook his head and took her hand, leading her to the side. "Look Bronwyn..."
"Call me B. It's an in thing now." She said looking past him to admire her hair in the glass doors. "Alright..." Joel sighed, "I don't think you and I are on the same page here. You don't even know anything about me yet you sleep with me almost every night."
"So?" She said putting her finger over his lips, "You need to

understand something Joel, the minute I set my sights on something, I get what I want. I don't care if you love me! God no! This is college I'm not looking for love."

"I don't think you're following me here….uhm, B."

"If you just relax and have some fun and stop trying to blind side me, I will do things to your dick that will make your mother tingle." She said grinning as she bit her lip, "In time you'll come to realize that we might just work. So what if I don't know you're from Durban?"

"Cape Town!" He insisted with a snarl.

"Whatever, I know you don't have the time to study, swim and play all the games linked to sex. So let's just call it what it is Joel, we're having fun. There's no need for all the mumbo jumbo."

He laughed shaking his head in disbelief as he threw back another gulp of the brandy.

"Why do you look so sad anyway? Isn't this supposed to be your party?"

"Do you care?"

"No." she flicked her hair, "But it's got to change, you're breaking the vibe."

She leaned in, planting her lips on his mouth, her tongue sprung forward to fill it.

Tugging him through the lounge and up stairs, she knew she had to do her part to side line him from the fact she had just spent over three thousand rand on clothing for her and her two new friends. Bronwyn shoved him into the bedroom and slammed him up against the wall. Her tongue again invading every space of his mouth as her hands began lowering his swimming trunks. Within seconds, she was on her knees swallowing him deep into her mouth and he gasped tossing the bottle of brandy across the room onto the bed.

"I don't know about this..." he said looking down at her breathlessly, "I just feel like..."

She stood up facing him, "Would you prefer to put it in from behind?"

His eyes widened - unsure if he had ever noticed how robust she was when they were alone. He shook his head and she smiled, "Then don't talk, let's do this and get back to the party ok? I have a new bikini to show off."

He nod anxiously and she dropped back onto her knees in front of him. He gasped, clenching the wall behind him with his arms out as she bobbed up and down below him, gripping his behind in her left hand and shoving him into her mouth.

"Bronwyn!" he gasped dropping his head in pure ecstasy when she abruptly stopped.

His eyes shot open, "What the hell?"

"We need to talk." She said standing up, taking his hand and leading him to the bed behind her in a waddle with his shorts at his ankles.

Flopping onto the bed with a disgruntled sigh, Joel scoffed, "What exactly do you wanna say that couldn't wait five minutes?" She straddled his legs and gripped his penis in her hand.

"Joel I've been thinking about what you said." She started, while stroking at him up and down, "We aren't compatible, not really."

"Yeah?" he moaned closing his eyes as she continued tugging at him up and down in a slow and circular rhythm.

Stop talking!

"I like spending time with you, but I get the feeling that you don't feel the same way."

"That's…not true…" he said with his eyes rolling back in his head as she increased her pace and rhythm. She shook her head, "It's sweet that you want to spare my feelings J, but I wasn't born yesterday."

Shocker even for me, ssshhh!

"I'm going to do my best to be with you more often, spend actual physical time with you and not just your credit card. I think it will help us grow and bond."

"I'm going to…"

Her hand stopped as she moved her hair off her shoulder, and he opened his left eye.

"I don't think…"

"Ok can you multi task right now?"

"J, I don't think we've spent more than a total of twenty two hours together." She said continuing her stroke up and down, "That means it's only been one day and mostly just having sex."

"Yeah!" he moaned, his body writhing as he neared climax and she continued.

"I'm going to make it my goal to give you all my attention."

"Not…needed…" he moaned - his stomach muscles clenching as he grew closer and closer. "Don't be silly, our relationship needs this if we're going to be living together."

"What?" he gasped sitting up right with wide eyes.

She shrugged, "Well duh. We have to move to the next level eventually."

"But we've only been doing…this for like four months!" He exclaimed, forgetting momentarily that she hadn't eased her rhythm at all.

"Five actually, but that's my point exactly…" she shrugged smiling, going back down with her mouth. "AH!" he gasped, "We need to talk."

Her head bobbed around and he finally sunk back down onto his back, his eyes rolling in his head as his hands clamped the sides of his head as he let go.

"I get it." she said sitting up again, "You don't like me sleeping over, and that's ok. But its part of the problem J. See, I get it. You are unhappy and I want to make you happy so that I can be happy. We're going to have to work on this together. You give, I give, you take, and I take."

"That doesn't mean we have to move in together!"

"I guess." She shrugged with a sigh, "What if I just stay over a few nights a week."

"No!" he gasped standing up and pulling up his swim trunks.

"Ok what if it's just once a week?"

"No. Never! I don't like having people in my private space." He sighed, "Look Bronwyn I appreciate what you are trying to do here but I have to draw the line somewhere…and that is my apartment alright?"

"Oh my god!" she gasped huffing up to face him, "What the hell did I just do if that wasn't invading your private space J?"

"Look there is a time and place to have this kind of discussion…" He sighed walking to the door, "Right now isn't one of them ok? I'm not ready for what you have in mind."

"Then what are we doing J?" she said with a desperate sigh, "I think I really like you."

"And I like you." He said with a sigh of desperation of his own, "I like marshmallows too but I don't sleep with them in my bed…"
Bronwyn shook her head angrily, "This is because I forgot where you came from isn't it? That is what this is about right? I just thought I made it up to you baby!"
"No that isn't it Bronwyn, but its part of it all." He huffed shaking his head, "Look you can't sleep over, not ever because I don't want you to. What we have now is great, let's just keep it that way. We're in college now, there is a whole lifetime ahead of both of us and someday you will find someone who actually wants to be with you."
Her mouth dropped and her eyes widened angrily.
"I meant…have you sleep over."
"I'm trying to reach a compromise here Joel." She bitched, "You make it sound like I barely know you."
"What's my favourite colour?" he smirked reaching for his drink on the bed.
"Like that's relevant…" she huffed, "You aren't seeing the bigger picture here Joel. We are the hottest couple in town, so we have to keep up appearances. Sure you are squeaky clean in all of this, but what must people think of me? I never stay over so I'm just in it for the money?"
"Then tell them the truth!" he said gulping the rest of his drink, "We're in it for the benefits. Me the sex and you the clothes and shoes…"
She stomped towards him, her right hand walloping him through the face.
"You are a son of a bitch!" she snarled, her hand slapping him again. A silence hung and she turned to the mirror to fix her hair before heading out.

He hurried down the stairs after her, grateful that the music and alcohol had most party goers too distracted to notice.
"You are a cheap son of a bitch!" she said angrily, her voice causing the DJ he had hired to stop the music. He looked around at the people nervously and she shook her head. "We could have

been great J." she said slapping him again, this time with her left hand, before storming towards the front door demanding her entourage follow her.

He sighed as the two girls stormed past him, the brunette briefly pausing to whisper in his ear to call her.

Silent awkwardness hung until the front door slammed behind them and he turned to everyone staring at him, his heart beat racing inside his chest.

"I guess I'm single again!" he said raising his hands, and a cheer erupted over the guests as the DJ continued to play. He sighed dropping his head as he turned for the bar. *You are a shameful man whore.*

"Hey, intense action! That shit should be on YouTube!" said fellow swimmer Tiaan grabbing Joel's shoulder and handing him another Tom Collins with a laugh. Joel sighed shaking his head, "That was inappropriate...."

"You are Joel Mac D my brother!" Tiaan said slugging his arm, "You don't have to make excuses for shit."

Yeah, all about the money again.

"Right?" prompted the bald headed Tiaan and Joel managed a weak smile to make him comfortable enough to return to the rest of the Delta Caps.

"Miss much?" asked Collin rounding him, "Where'd you go, I thought you left?"

"No just selling my soul." He quipped, tossing back another gulp before running for the pool and diving in with a splash. The rest of the swim team leapt in after him quickly making everyone rush for the rock pool as Tequila shooters made their rounds inside the crowded water. By the time he managed to crawl his way out onto the grass breathlessly, the tequila had struck him from the side like a speeding car and the light from the sun was mistaken for heaven.

Did I die in the pool?

Just then a head moved over his face, a tall blond with shoulder length hair.

"I know we've never officially met..." Troy said tilting her head to the side, "But here's a piece of advice, I feel I owe you the decency, next time you throw an impromptu party, don't invite kids from the academic club and allow them near the bar."

"Yeah, I'm sorry but there's two guys puking in your stove." Liz said leaning over him with a courteous and warm smile, "Thanks for the party though."

"Laters douche." Said Troy walking way and letting the sun slam back into his eyes.

And as he rolled onto his stomach on the grass, he looked up to Michael who knelt in front of him, "Does Richie Rich want to smoke some weed?"

Joel shrugged frowning boyishly as he stumbled to his feet into Rendani's arms.

"I'm very drunk right now. I might just puke."

"Already?" Rendani asked surprised.

"I know!" Joel stammered with a grin, "I am so rich. It just isn't funny right?"

Michael shook his head grinning and head off to the side of the apartment unit.

"Did you know that I am not a virgin? I lost it in eleventh grade to some chick." Joel sighed shaking his head, "I am many times, *many* times not a virgin."

Rendani frowned nodding worriedly and Joel laughed, the alcohol swooning every fibre of him as he stumbled to the bar lady again.

"Give me the bottle for Cola valhallos" he slurred.

She smiled shyly, "Calvados, yes sir coming right up."

"Don't call me sir or I'll fire you!" he said turning back to face Rendani, "I can say anything I want to. It helps having this face, and like you said, I'm richer than all you people together!"

Rendani looked around uncomfortably, waving Collin over from the pool. When he looked back, Joel had made his way into a slurred conversation with a crowd of students under the thatched roof over the patio.

"I think he needs a bed, he's embarrassing." Rendani said anxiously as Collin rushed up beside him. "But dude, this is his house though?"

Joel erupted in a boyish giggle, stumbling back, "Have a drink, you people all look so parched!"

Collin laughed shaking his head, "I've never seen him like this, have you?"

Rendani shook his head as Joel wailed out loud, "Let's do whatever I wanna do. Because I am rich!"

The students roared in a cheer again and Joel stumbled to face them.

"Wow, who killed your dog man?"

Collin grabbed Joel's arm, "Ok that's enough man!"

"I know! Ssshh!" said Joel putting his finger over his lips, "Can you hear that?"

"Hear what?"

"Exactly!" laughed Joel turning and screaming to the DJ inside the house, "Hey DJ, play something…kick ass!"

"Hey!" Joel said swinging around to Collin and Rendani again, "I know a cool drinking game! It's called 'rich man, poor man'!"

Collin shook his head in a giggle as Joel erupted in a spastic laugh.

"Are you always like this?" asked the bar lady holding out the bottle of Calvados brandy.

"Dunno…" Joel said swigging a big sip into his gullet, "I've never gotten this far before. Cool huh?"

Collin took the bottle and before he put it down again, Joel swooped it back up and began dancing backwards, grabbing the first girl nearest to him and planting his lips on her. "You just kissed the richest dude in town baby." He grinned conceitedly.

She blushed looking down and Collin put his arm around his shoulder, "Ok seriously, I think you need to go lie down."

Joel laughed shaking his head as he stumbled back, "You know what? I always do everything I don't want to nessisararally want to do. And I've decided I'm going to smoke some weed."

Rendani shook his head and walked away and Collin leaned in, "Can you not say that so loud? You'll be kicked off the team if Steve heard you saying that!"

Joel burped and giggled, "Now that's just nasty!"

"Dude, really you have to get control here."

"Why?" snarled Joel angrily, "No one here cares, look at these people. They don't know me, they just came for free shit. How many people are looking at me right now?"

Collin glanced around, "Fine no one is looking."

"I am." Said the bar girl leaning forward with a grin and Joel turned to her raising his eyebrows, "Come with me?"

"Sure." She smiled, hoping over the counter as Joel turned to Collin with a smug grin, "I never said there would be two parties here! That's awesome!"

Collin looked back to Rendani who had just written it off and continued to party with the guys by the pool, frustrated by Joel's blatant personality swap.

"I think you're embarrassing your friend." She smiled, taking his hand in hers.

Joel turned to her with narrow eyes, "Imagine how I feel!"

Five guys, the intimidating dark haired Michael included and three girls stood around the side of the house where the music sounded vague and the shadows of the surrounding trees began lowering as the sun began its plunge below the horizon. They were all taking turns dragging at two marijuana joints and laughing while the girls tongued at the other guys. As Joel and his new companion round the corner, everyone turned to them briefly, before ignoring them and filtering the high.

Joel nod at the malevolent Michael, drinking faster and faster on the clean brandy he fought the urge to run from something he had never before experienced or at most ever witnessed.

"So whose the new guy?" asked one of the girls whose joint consumption had led to severely red eyes.

"This is Joel." He said with a mocking grin, "I'm kinda the host of the party."

"Cool." She said before returning to suck tongue with the guy who had long silver dyed, Rastafarian dread locks and pig tailed chin beard.

"No, not cool." Said Joel stepping forward, pointing at her with the bottle in his hand still, "Get the hell out of my house you…you…bar maiden!"

The guy beside her giggled and Joel point up at him too, "You to Gandalf the what."

Michael laughed looking down and Collin heaved a nervous sigh stepping beside Joel and the two nervously started to head out when Joel laughed in a drunken stupor.

"I'm kidding!" he giggled, "I'm rich, our sense of humour is totally fucked up."

The others began to laugh and within seconds, everyone returned to getting baked. And Joel round past the bar girl and Collin, realizing he had to clear his mind before someone damaged his face.

"So you're the guy who came from Pretoria whose dad's managing the mine's reopening right?" asked Michael taking a deep pull at the joint.

"Johannesburg actually." Correct Collin with a nervous smile as Joel turned to face them, his head spinning.

"You want a drag?" Michael asked holding the joint out to him with wicked smirk.

"I'm good thanks." said Joel shaking his head in the hopes it would regain its former self, "I quit a long time ago."

"Quit?" Michael said laughing, "That's original."

"Yeah, just not that into it anymore like I was back in…wherever I came from…." He said casually, taking another swig of the brandy.

"Sure Richie Rich." Michael grinned as he pulled at the joint again.

"Ok stop calling me that ok…you look like a clean version of John Travolta's kid if he had a kid in grease."

Oh crap! I am so dead. There's two of him and only one of me!
Collin nudged Joel's ribs, his eyes glaring anxiously at Michael as the night began to set in around them.

"Travolta?" Michael asked without exhaling.

"I don't get it either." Said the bar girl taking a deep pull at the joint passed to her. Joel looked to Collin who shrugged.

"I don't know? I didn't have anything to say." Sighed Joel as nausea filled his gut.

"You're pretty funny Richie Rich." Michael said spitting to the grass, "But I don't trust you for shit."

Joel shrugged, swung his head back, gulped at the brandy and then sighed, "So let's go beat up homeless people for fun or drown some kittens?"

"Wow you guys know how to ruin your own vibe..." Laughed Collin nervously, blurting out his words almost exasperatedly. Michael frowned and cocked his head to the side, glaring at him inquisitively and then shook his head and head past him, tapping Joel in the chest before grabbing the bar girl by the hand and leading her away with him.

116

Joel shook his head laughing as the other smokers left the side of the house leaving him and Collin alone in the shadows beside the apartment.

"Are you done?" frowned Collin. Joel nod and slumped his head down onto Collin's shoulder. "I think I'm in the process of dying."

"You'll be fine." Said Collin tapping his naked back gently, the suns redness almost glowing in the shadows.

"No, I can hear my kidneys going on strike. They hate me." Collin laughed and reeling from a spinning drunkenness throughout his being, Joel began laughing too, and as he tried to lift his head from Collin's shoulder he felt his friends hand against the back of his neck. He opened his eyes to meet Collin's and suddenly two lips pressed against his neck and a hand slid up his abs.

"Collin! What are you doing?" he exclaimed stepping backwards in alarm almost falling to the ground over his legs.

"I'm sorry I…"

"No." said Joel raising his hands, "What the hell are you doing?"

"I think I'm gay." He said nervously, "I'm sorry I just, I've been feeling a certain way about you and…"

Joel shook his head, "Hell no, hell no man!"

"I'm sorry man it was just a thing in the moment." Collin said blushing even through the shadows, "But I'm relieved dude, this can be our secret now!"

"I'm done with secrets man, and this isn't one I want on my shoulders ok! I'm not gay!"

Collin's mouth dropped open and Joel shook his head in disappointment.

"This is not cool man, not cool at all I thought you were my friend."

"I said I was sorry."

"Not good enough." Said Joel turning away, "Just get out of my house ok. Just get."

Collin froze, his face distraught and he shook his head in panic as Joel head away, a silence hung in the shadows beside the house, and he felt his body trembling in alarmed disarray.

Standing in the centre of the back lawn, Joel glanced at the remaining guests and then began shouting at them all to leave. He was done, pitted out from the sun, the booze, Bronwyn and now the one person who he felt was remotely close to being a genuine friend who always had his back. The crowds of students began heading out the front door and he chased even the DJ and waiter personnel away too. As he reached the front door ushering the last of the people out, two uniformed officers strolled up.

"Are you the owner?"

"Oh fuck me sideways!" Joel snapped, "The party's over ok, you can go."

The one officer shook his head, "Sir we received sixty seven complaints from your neighbours in the complex."

Joel laughed shaking his head and stepped out glancing at the adjacent buildings in anger, but it wasn't until he saw his Evoque that a true blow hit into his chest.

Bronwyn had scribbled all over the front windshield 'Cape Town Asshole' and the side windows were completely coloured in with three different shades of lipstick.

"Sir?" the second officer said drawing Joel's drunken attention back to them.

"If I give you both a grand will you just go away so I can go lie down and die?"

The Monday morning air was cool, a brisk wind flowing over Secunda and continuing to slither through the fields between Secunda and its small neighbouring town Evander. The fumes from the giant SASOL towers were faint as the thick white smoke rose up to the highest points of the sky.

As Kyle head down the passage for his first day on campus, he felt the tension in his body shiver.

"Grab a plate Kyle." Claire smiled turning to him from the kitchen nook where Bennie and Edward were already tucking into their cereal. Shaking his head trying to be as pleasant as he could, Kyle managed, "I'm fine."

"Are you going to meet the police today about the bomber?" asked Bennie with wide curious eyes from across the table. "Well yes, today we get to do a security walk through of the shaft, if our equipment is ready."

"Are you going to go down there?" Bennie asked, "Into the ground?"

"Well like daddy said, if they have our equipment set up a few men will be sent down, and I have to escort them to make sure they do it right."

"Do they know why someone would throw bombs down there in the first place?" Came Kyle stepping into the kitchen from the side much to Edwards' surprise

"Well, first of all it wasn't a bomb. They actually don't know what it was that sparked off like that and secondly, for all we know it isn't sabotage at all."

"Sabotage?" frowned Kyle looking first to his mother then to Edward with a concern in his eyes, "That's a bit hectic isn't it?"

"Do I sense care in your voice?" teased Claire rounding him with a sandwich wrapped in a Ziploc bag, "You must be coming down with something."

Kyle sighed shaking his head and Claire nod, ushering him to follow her out into the passage.

"Are you ok?" asked Claire turning to face him, the back of her hand gently running his long fringe away from his eyes.

"I'm fine."

"I know today is a big step." She said placing her hands on his shoulders. He froze looking down at her hands, the feeling on his chest alien and she immediately removed them.

"You did so well on your national benchmark tests, just keep in mind what doors this can open in your future."

I don't want a future, I'm already dead.

"I'm so proud of you for agreeing to try out college. It'll be good for you to join the world again." She smiled, "I just want you to know that you can talk to me, we have to face all of this together otherwise it's not going to work. Please Kyle, I want you to know that I am here for you, we all are. And I don't want you to feel pressured into going to college just yet."

"Well I have a NSC level 8." He smiled, briefly feeling self pride, "I got in with my history where others couldn't, and I can't throw it away."

"I just want you to be ready." She said persistently, "Your history doesn't have to affect your future."

"I get it and I'm fine. Really, I'm a big boy." He said managing a weak smile, hoping his face hid the true emotions within him.

As she looked into his sad, deep eyes she felt a lump reach her throat, she knew he was lying, putting up a wall around him. He hadn't been part of the world in years. She knew he was afraid, she knew he was feeling something more than what he let on. She sighed closing her eyes, "The moment you feel overwhelmed…"

"Please!" he said with an impatient snarl, "Just…can we just go please? You are making it worse, making me want to change my mind."

She managed a weak smile to suppress the tears rushing to her eyes, "Alright. Let's go do this."

Clad in grey pants and a white golf shirt, Joel walked down the front porch of his parents' white two story home towards his car that stood cleaned and parked in the driveway. He briefly glanced at the post addressed to him from behind his dark glasses, his head still swirling and his throat sore from the morning of puking. It wasn't until he reached the side of his car when his attention was caught by a white faded gray 4x4 with the slogan "Crisp Cool Pools" that stood parked across the street. His heart beat almost stopped, and coldness crawled over his skin.

No way! What the hell is he doing here?

He slung his bag over his shoulder, taking a deep breath as he readied to head across the lawn when behind him his father spoke from the porch.

"Are you still here? I'm running late so hurry up and move that car out." Raymond growled as he past him towards the driveway. Joel turned back to the van that had started moving off along the street.

"Excuse me, would you like a written invitation to move your car?" Raymond snarled the sarcasm rich in his tone, "I have to leave! I am late Joel! One of the greatest things about you not living here is that I'm on time for work, so get lost!"

Joel shook his head angrily and head towards his Evoque.

"Why are you here anyway?"

"Grabbing my mail before I get to campus."

"You look like shit!" Raymond mumbled as the garage doors

began to ascend. He paused at the door to his car, watching as the van turned the corner and he shook his head, his body screaming to go back inside and beg his mother to stop the affair.

The engine of Raymond's silver Mercedes AMG growled to life and Joel shook his head in defeat, hurriedly getting into his car. The AMG revved like a beast, the reverse lights already on as it began to slowly back up.

"Don't be an asshole!" Joel shouted as he began to fasten his seat belt. Again, Raymond revved at the engine, and the reverse pace sped up. Joel hurriedly turned the ignition and geared into reverse, the nose of his car just centimeters from his father's bumper.

"You're an asshole dad!" he snarled as he shot backwards into the street and veered to the side as the Mercedes sped out beside him. Raymond glanced at Joel arrogantly and then sped off.

Shaking his head with his hands fiercely gripped to the steering wheel, Joel felt rage building inside of him. The white van, Marco's van in front of their house all the way from Cape Town and his father's disgraceful attitude towards him and his mother, Collin's approach from Saturday night, the way everything kept spinning out of control and nothing made sense.

He shifted into first and drove off, surrendering to the fact he would never have control of anything in his life and that he would have to keep facing demons at every turn.

As his car rounded the corner, the white 'Crisp Cool Pools' van steered up in front of the house again, and the front door opened. Lynette stepped out with a smile breaking across her face, her stomach tremulous with butterflies.

The main entrance to the Seymore Academic College grounds led to the front of the central office buildings, the parking lot split by a giant water fountain – in the centre of it the bronze statues of the three key investors.

The campus lawns was crowded with students walking in, cars and busses, a colorful array of faces and back packs that head around the grounds. As the car pulled into the lot, Kyle felt the strangulation of the black hands at his throat as the voices inside of him urged him to break and crumble. He shut his eyes and inhaled deeply, trying to find a calmness within himself as Edward and Claire got out of the car.

"It's a very nice school." Said Claire admiring the buildings stretched across the campus grounds, "I'm very proud of you Kyle, for getting in."

He shrugged and managed a weak smile as he opened the door.

"Are you alright Kyle?" asked Edward rounding past him.

He nod, "Could do with another cigarette."

As he round the car, a red Evoque pulled up beside him and Joel got out, his agitation clear as he flung his bag over his shoulder and slammed the door.

While Claire and Edward walked ahead of him towards the admissions office he felt his body begin to tremble at its core, the marrow inside his bones quivering as the craving to escape reached its pitch. Joel, in his frustrated rush, accidentally knocked into Kyle who was standing stone still staring up at the school. Joel looked up at him, the jolt sending a striking ache through his head and in the second of their eyes meeting he wanted to be his usual polite self, but with Collin's pounce and Marco's van appearing all the way out in Secunda, he could not muster anymore courtesy, he felt that if he cared for one more second he would explode.

"Sorry…" Said Kyle, staring at his eyes – something familiar about them and it made him feel uneasy.

"Look where you are going you fucking worm!" Joel snarled, pushing past him. Kyle shrugged shaking his head as he continued towards the administration's office, trying hard to avoid everyone's eyes on him. He felt it shuddering beneath his skin – the urge to run.

Inside the office, Edward and Claire sat facing the college dean, Hendry Watts, while Kyle sat in reception. Watt's reminded them both that they were allowing Kyle's enrolment as a probationary period of three months. While he did praise Kyle for his outstanding grades on the college aptitude exams, he stressed the college's position on having anything potentially dangerous risking the college's new reputation.

As he spoke with stern reference to the arrangement he as Dean had made with them concerning Kyle's attendance at the school he reminded them of it being based solely on his exceptional level of knowledge and he tried to hide his personal sentiment of dire understanding, feeling that they as a family were faced with a troubled past trying desperately to change the future and deserved a fair chance at that. Hendry Watts had been calm, patient and courteous towards them during each telephonic discussion, but now he held a more stern and indifferent approach as he sat facing them.

"His file is unlike anything I have seen in all my years as an educator. Yet his scores on the national benchmark tests are staggering, of the highest ever obtained for attendance in this college since its opening, and within the top fifteen highest scores in the country."

"He's trying really hard to find himself again." Claire explained nervously, "He's very smart Dean Watts."

"I explained to Mr. Watts the recommendation doctor Naidu gave for Kyle." Edwards said holding her hand, referring to the meeting he had with Watts a few weeks prior to the move, when Watts seemed more complacent.

"I believe every person in life deserves a second chance, but I do have a board to report to at the end of the day. I just want the both of you to understand my situation in this, and understand why there is a need for the secondary terms and conditions contract you were asked to sign."

"We understand sir." Claire said softly, "Kyle will be seeing Doctor Morris and she agreed to supply your office with a monthly personality and behavioral report."

Watts nod with a grin, "I appreciate that we will have to be reassured of his state of mind as he continues his education here. Any information we receive from Doctor Morris will be kept in Kyle's student file. I suspect if he excels here any future employer might, with his history, request as much detail on him as possible to set their minds at ease. Boy X will never surface from this institution."

Claire looked down worriedly, wondering if her son would ever be the success she had always dreamt for him after such a sordid past.

Watts smiled, admiring her desire, her unfailing courage to face what she had faced and still fight for her sons' future.

"Mr. and Mrs. Evans, there are many young adults on campus, all unique in their own way and I can only imagine the jitters you both feel for him being around crowds of carefree, experimental young students. But you have my word I will personally keep an eye on your son while he is on campus. He will be in good hands."

Claire and Edward smiled courteously and dean Hendry Watts arose from his seat at his dark oak desk, "Let's meet the young man then."

The door opened and Edward nod at Kyle, marshaling him in. Kyle heaved a deep breath and crossed the reception.

Be nice, don't mess this up. Don't do anything Kyle-like He said as a mantra to himself as he stepped past the receptionist's desk with an awkward smile. The darkness he held in his soul built in him an insecurity that made he feel wholly out of place, in his mannerisms, his speech and actions. As he neared the dean's door he tried to dig deep inside to bring forth a typical twenty one year old college student who never met the darkness.

Play it cool Kyle, be a normal kid. Think about how kids are on TV and do that! Be normal! His mantra changed as he stepped into Watt's office.

"Nice to meet you Kyle, I'm Dean Watts." Watts said holding out his hand.

"Sup!" Kyle blurt nodding his head up in the same manner he had seen on a music video. He looked down at the Dean's hand and with a determined smile, avoiding the handshake, said, "This is a cool office."

Dean Watts looked to Claire and Edward with a curious frown and Edward shrugged uncomfortably, not wanting to discuss the touching issue with Kyle present.

"I hope you will find Seymore College accommodating, and as I've reassured your parents, my door is always open."

"Sweet!" Kyle said bopping his head with an uncomfortable smile, stepping back awkwardly, glancing at his mother for approval and she smiled charmingly.

"I must say, your final score was really impressive."

"Thanks, I had a lot of time to read." Kyle said matter-of-factly. Watts nod with a smirk, aware that Kyle was merely portraying what he thought he needed to.

"I've asked a fellow undergrad to meet you outside and show you around since you have some of the same subjects. You're only a few weeks shy of the initial orientation program so it'll be useful

to you to have someone around for the first few days on campus."
Watts smiled handing him a paper, "This is a complete map of the
entire college grounds. Unlike Rhodes or UCT or even North
West University that has three separate campus grounds, Seymore
College is one enclosed site with East, West, North and Central
campus spanning in excess of sixty five thousand meters
squared."

Kyle nod, listening as the dean gave him a brief run through of
everything he had already read in pamphlets.

"We have on site health clinics, three restaurants, conference
venues and sporting facilities throughout each campus wing."
Watts smiled proudly, "Make sure you take a trip to the Design
and Architecture hall, I'm sure it will interest you. It's off
Recreation Avenue on the North side of the grounds."

Kyle nod with a weak grin, "Cool."

"Security on campus is very tight, no weapons of any kind are
tolerated and if found on your person you will be immediately
suspended. Campus rules are from page nine to thirteen in your
code book." Watts explained, "Men's and women's dormitories
are on the cul-de-sac around central park just behind this building
and you can collect your pass card from Mrs. Durgean on your
way out."

"Pass card?" frowned Claire.

"Sometimes we have walk-ins who purposefully disrupt lectures
or destroy college property with graffiti and so on. We've
implemented the pass card system so at anytime our security can
request to see the cards, day visitors are given a pass card too."
Kyle nod rolling his eyes, trying not to allow his nervousness to
gnaw at him.

"My door is always open Kyle if there is anything you need."
Watts smiled, holding his hand out. Kyle nervously looked to his
mother, as though still a little boy afraid of strangers, and sensing
the unease to touch, Edward stepped in and thanked the Dean.

Kyle and Joel they head out across the campus and Kyle felt a
slight tingle of excitement inside of him, but neither of them had

uttered a word since Kyle was issued his pass card in the admissions office. The neatly kept campus grounds, the flat green lawn, the giant shade trees, it all felt like a freedom from the walls he had confined himself to for so long. The atmosphere vibrated off the young and carefree students and it sunk into him. Until he felt eyes on him, and he began to sink back down into his self esteem nightmare. He truly was a specimen of beauty and thus girls would notice him and guys would study him as a threat. And as he crossed the lawn, he felt his chest tighten in fear that they could all see the scum crawling on his skin. Realizing that the new student was traipsing behind him, Joel turned shaking his head, "Hello? Can we get a move on?"

It was surreal for Kyle to be standing there, without his parents nearby and without walls secluding him from the world. The sky open above him, people moving all about and his face open to the world. He was part of the world again, the giant world he had so long feared and hid from. Joel tilt his head in confusion, wondering why the long haired guy stood staring up at the sky with his arms out at his sides.

"Look dude…" he said finally tugging him on the shoulder, "I don't know what you are on right now, but I have better things to do with my time ok?"

Looking down at Joel's hand on his forearm, Kyle clenched his teeth focusing on the rage.

"If you knew how hung over I am you would understand, so can you please for the love of god wake the hell up and move with me here?"

Insulted by his attitude and for ruining his first hopeful moment, Kyle shrugged arrogantly, "Move along then dick head, I don't need a chaperone."

Joel laughed in surprise no one had ever spoken to him like that since the days of Wickus or Aldert. Kyle sighed and walked on past him, admiring the architecture used in the construction of the college buildings and Joel stepped after him.

"Do you know who I am?"

"I don't care." Said Kyle walking on, "You're rude, that's enough for me."

Joel gasped shaking his head, watching as Kyle walked along in the wrong direction.

If it wasn't for me there wouldn't be a college you asshole.

"You're going the wrong way."

Kyle turned to him but before he could reply a hand grabbed at Kyle's shoulder, turning him around. Standing facing him stood Katlego Seme – president of the Full Circle society, her face bright and broad with smiles.

To either side of her stood two freshmen Gerrie and Mark, their smiles just as broad as hers but their eyes screaming out their own insecurities as they looked Kyle up and down.

Katlego gave no subtleties in the way she spoke so proudly about Full Circle and without hesitation began to parade the purpose of the society, explaining with great passion the societies purpose to promote camaraderie, scholarship and campus socializing among all students. As she spoke as though without needing air between her long sentences, Kyle nervously scrutinized the eyes of those on him wondering how he would survive a world outside of his bedrooms four walls.

Joel heaved in frustration, trying twice to interrupt her but without triumph. Although with more members than any other society in the college, Katlego's tendencies had often gotten her despised throughout the student population because of her often brut determination to involve people in Full Circle, but more so because she would bully and belittle those who turned away from her offer.

"You have twenty four hours after registration in admissions to decide." She smiled with enthusiasm. Kyle turned to Joel and then shrugged, "Thank you."

"Is that a yes?"

"No, I'll think about it." He said turning away when Matthew reached forward past Katlego and grabbed his forearm.

"Full Circle is more than the average fraternity type club, such as the Delta Capitals for example" he said narrowing his eyes at Joel before looking back to Kyle, "We guarantee you constant support for any issues you might be facing and you'll always be surrounded by someone eager to be your best friend."

"I'll keep that in mind." Kyle snarled with as much civility as he could manage moving his arm free of the boys touch. Joel's eyes widened at Kyle's tone.

"You seem very tense." Katlego frowned as though in disgust, "Full Circle provides weekly social events that include spa massages or since you're a male we offer…"

"I will think about it." Said Kyle taking the booklets she had given him and shoving it into his bag.

"Seriously though…" Katlego said stepped forward and persisted, "Feel good about who you are and soon you'll realize why being part of…"

"Look can you just stop?" Kyle snarled loudly.

Breathe Kyle, just breathe!

A bright grin crossed Joel's face as he watched from the side, watching with baited breath, completely bewitched by the electricity flying off of the boy he had just moments ago rammed into without apology.

"Look, I just started here like an hour ago. I have flyers and brochures coming out of my ass." Kyle ranted, "And yes good for you all that you can stand there with happy little faces trying to encourage me to join your circle jerk. But I haven't even made up my mind if any of this is worth it. So back off and stop touching me!"

Standing with mouths gaping Katlego was briefly taken aback by his flagrant disregard for courtesy and wanted to spit flames, yet when his held darkness unlike anything she had seen and she managed a polite and courteous smile.

"We just want you to know the benefits of joining Full Circle." Said Matthew again reaching for Kyle's arm, to which Kyle responded by wringing his wrist up into the air. Katlego and Gerrie gasped stammering backwards as Kyle brought Matthew's hand up around his head and down against his shoulder blade.

"I said don't touch me…" he said shoving the boy away from him.

"Let's go." Joel urged backing away. Kyle looked up into her eyes shaking his head before following Joel's brisk walk.

"Wow man you are one intense human being! That was fucking awesome!" Joel laughed.

"Who are you?" asked Kyle looking to Joel with daring eyes, cold and untainted by emotion as he turned his attention back to her, "Because you're all beginning to irritate me."

Joel frowned, still amazed at how it felt to be spoken to like an ordinary student and Kyle turned to carry on walking briskly.

"I'm Joel McDonald." He said reaching out for a handshake, which Kyle blatantly disregarded.

"I'd offer you to join the Delta Cap's but I don't want to have my fingers broken."

"I really, really couldn't care less." He shrugged bluntly. He was losing control over the rage building, the tension inside growing and he tried the various mantras as he walked.

"Wow! Hey!" Said Joel raising his hands as he hurried in stride alongside him, "I'm one of the good guys. What's your name?"

Sighing with more flagrant annoyance now, he stopped and turned to him, "What do you want?"

Confused as he turned to face him, Joel shrugged, "What do you mean?"

Breathe Kyle…Breathe. Just breathe. Nobody knows about boy X.

"This is my first day and it's already very difficult to handle. If I stand here any longer, I'm probably going to be late. I don't know where I'm going or what I'm actually doing here in the first place. You were supposed to show me around and all you have done is whine about your hangover like a bitch. You are rude, arrogant and clearly think you have some relevance to me and this school. So tell me Joel McDonald, what is it that you want from me because two minutes ago you barely gave a shit now you want to know my name?"

It took a moment for Joel to apprehend the situation, no other male had spoken to him like that before, especially when they realized who he was and in a matter of 24 hours he had Mike Harper and this stranger taking him on.

"Have a nice day prick!" scoffed Kyle as he turned away.

"Well…" Joel gasped as he watched the stranger walking off.

Amidst the hustle and bustle of the countries capital city Tshwane that was previously known throughout the world as the capital city Pretoria, as the ebb and flow of thousands of motor vehicles, buses, taxis and cycles cluttered the roads and tides of pedestrians filled the centre of the city's sidewalks and stores. Forty eight year old Riaan Kempen hurried from his silver Lexus sedan towards the long black stretch limo that slowed to a halt in the drive of the underground parking.

As he moved across the drive zone of the parking lot in his dark grey Armani suit, he calmly brushed his hand through his side path of faded auburn hair and stepped up to the black limo. Seeing his reflection in the tinted windows of the limousine, Riaan inhaled a deep breath to ready himself for the storm that lay inside the car and opened the door.

Swiftly sliding along the smooth black leather seat, Riaan huffed with a grin greeting the ever malevolently seducing sleuth Mr. Lee who sat sipping on a scotch with ice in a silver grey suit with one leg neatly crossing the other in a relaxing pose.

"Did you do it?" asked Lee with an unceremonious frown as he raised his glass to his lips. With the breathing air inside the limo suddenly vacuumed by the somewhat portentous vibe that seemed to rhythm off of Lee like a vibration he could almost feel against his skin, Riaan offered a nod and answered with a strong certainty, "Yes."

"Good work Mr. Kempen." Lee said offering a raised glass to his eased grin, "Scotch?"

"No thank you."

"You sure?" offered Lee again, this time slyly nodding to an already poured glass on the oak cabinet rest beside him.

"I trust my payment has been deposited as per our arrangement?" braved Riaan now also crossing his legs and clasping his hands, "Along with the extra four hundred thousand for the water cooler."

Mr. Lee puffed a chuckle into the glass as the bronze liquid slid down his tongue and shook his head as he turned his attention to the window that jaded the world beyond it, the tall city buildings and cluttered sidewalks as Riaan cleared his throat uneasily.

"Mr. Lee I don't mean to sound coy but I am slightly pressed for time, is all the money in the account?"

"When is the bomb on the cooler scheduled for?" Asked Lee, his attention still focused on what lay on the other side of the tinted window, the scotch glass near his chin roughly hiding a good portion of his face in a mysterious fashion which caused the now perturbed Mr. Riaan Kempen to uncross his legs and sit forward more pressingly. "Look I already informed you of the time, its four nineteen, just before knock off time. Now have you kept up your end of the deal or not Mr. Lee?"

"Deal?" said Lee with more of stating than questioning in his voice as he lowered the glass and turned his attention back to Riaan. "I sense something here Mr. Lee and to be honest its making me feel very uncomfortable here where I'm sitting."

Lee's head tilt to the side and he smirked, "Uneasy?"

"Well you keep avoiding my question. Has the transfer been made or not?"

Mr. Lee sighed and dug beneath his suit coat with a grunting sigh of impatience, removing a small silver sachet from his pocket and held it up, "This is what I mixed into that glass of Scotch over there."

Riaan looked to the glass which Lee had offered to him and his heart rate began pounding inside his chest. "It would have made this a lot more comfortable and less…manual." Continued Lee, "You would have been dead a long time ago but no, you're too much of a stubborn man Mr. Kempen."

"What the hell is this?" asked Riaan sitting upright in alarm, tapping anxiously on the divider between himself and the limo driver, "Stop the car!"

Lee sighed and placed his glass on the cabinet before swiftly supplying a round-housed style kick across the narrow limousine, sending Riaan spinning in his seat, at which Lee pounced and plucked at his neck, the crack of his spine silencing the panic in the air.

Huffing in annoyance, Mr. Lee plumped back down to his seat fixing his tie and cuffs before raising the glass again as the limo curved along the drive of the underground parking. Like a ghost, the limousine crawled away leaving Mr. Kempen laying slumped face down behind his Lexus.

By mid day Kyle placidly took his seat in the fourth row from the back as the lecture room filled one student and the next, groups of friends and enemies easily became noticeable and as Kyle scanned their behavior he realized how evident it was that this school, one of three in the surrounding area made up of the towns Evander, Secunda, Bethal, Leandra and Kinross, was too divided by social status, money value and class.

"Hey look who takes business and finance law." Joel said smiling with arrogance only money could buy, "This seat taken?"

"What do you want from me?" sighed Kyle as Joel huffed into the desk beside him.

"You really have no idea who I am - do you?"

"I don't care who you are. Leave me alone."

Joel laughed shaking his head, "So what's your major?"

Kyle turned to him with a sigh.

Is this wank seriously trying to bond with me? What is wrong with the people here?

"I don't know."

"Are you just taking random subjects until you figure it out?" Joel laughed, "Risky, wish I had the option. Everything's been figured out for me in advance."

Kyle again turned to him with a heaving sigh, "I didn't ask."

Joel smiled awkwardly, unsure of how to side step the brunt ice of Kyle's demeanor.

"You haven't really gone through life so morbidly dickish have you?" Joel laughed again, "Why all this harbored resentment guy? I'm just trying to be decent here."

"Look." Kyle turned to him, his eyes darkened, "I'm trying to avoid ripping off your arm and slapping you with it so please change seats."

"What the hell man?" Joel huffed with a stunned snort, "Why?"

Kyle raised his eyebrows, sighed, politely managed a weary smile and got up towards an open seat further towards the back and slumped down, glaring into Joel's eyes with annoyance. Joel slummed back in his seat, defeated by his attempts to find himself outside of his normal circle and be in the company of someone else, figuring the new face was easier to approach because it would welcome company. He shook his head.

"Sorry." Kyle said finally controlling the darkness, "I'm very overwhelmed here, it's not easy for me…"

Joel shrugged his shoulders and with an arrogant grin replied, "I didn't ask."

The first thirty minutes of the lecture lulled by, and even with everyone's eyes on the tall, broad shouldered and crescent balding Mr. Collins – Kyle felt uneasy within his own skin. Out of place in a room full of normal, decent, un-blackened youths with promises of a future he couldn't find himself in.

Mr. Collins cleared his throat as he turned from the board, "So can anyone tell me the scope of company law and list the corporate objectives?"

Looking down at the students who began to rifle through her memory to answer, Kyle noticed the girl from the store sitting a row in front, looking up at the student answering. When her glance met his, he immediately found himself experiencing a tense and sensational excitement and nervousness, and the minute she smiled he smiled back feeling warmth transverse over his heart as though he had been given the automatically programmed emotion to respond.

She waved shyly and he again automatically found himself responding.

"Ok very good answer, next question." Collins voice broke his distraction, "Who can list the factors which influence corporate objectives? Anyone?"

"How about you? Up there with the hair." Collins said pointing up at Kyle.

Kyle felt his body squirm and coil as everyone turned to face him. Joel frowned at the clear unease breaking out beside him.

"Come on, list the factors influencing corporate objectives – this is an easy one." He said again, looking to Joel, "Want to give your friend a hand there McDonald?"

Joel shrugged, "I have no idea."

"Does anyone know?" Collins asked looking around the class of students desperately trying to avoid being tasked to answer.

Kyle cleared his throat and responded nervously, listing the thirteen points, the entire time his voice trembling along with his hands.

"Very impressive well done for your first day on campus."

Holy shit you did it! You spoke in a room full of people!

Mr. Collins nod narrowing his eyes curiously, "And you are?"

Feeling as though a magnifying glass was covering him, Kyle realized that the girl from the store was watching, and he lowered his head and spoke with as much fortitude and courtesy he could assemble.

"Kyle."

"Just Kyle?" Collins asked from below.

He nod awkwardly, his head low behind his hair.

Why the hell would you put all this attention on yourself! Do you want them to realize who you are! Idiot!

"Well there you have it, anyone interested in passing this semester should consider partnering with Just Kyle." Collins boasted as he head to the board grinning. Kyle slumped down into his seat.

Yes welcome the masses why don't you.

The air out in the quiet secluded fields, far from anyone who could hear his cries for help – the security guard on duty at the shaft on the night of the explosion lay cuffed to the tow bar of the black Mercedes. Since his abduction from his house earlier in the day, he had endured hours of near suffocation in the trunk. In what felt like hours out in the middle of nowhere he had endured severe beating from a silent predator who never spoke or demanded, threatened or explained. When the hands who had been terrorising him finally removed the black sack from his head, his eyes stung at the brightness of the scorching sun above and it took a few moments before he could clearly see the dark figure in front of him.

"Do you know why you are here?" Mr Black asked cocking his head at an angle.

The guard shook his head, his body and will near destroyed. He had been screaming in both Afrikaans and English and his throat was hoarse. Finally he knew that his attacker was English.

"Please let me go. I don't know you."

"Of course you don't know me." Mr Black teased, "That is what's made our time together so fun."

"Please, I have some money saved. I can pay you." He begged, sobbing in a dry and broken voice, "Please!"

"You can pay me?" Mr Black laughed, "That's hilarious since you have no idea why you are here cuffed to the back of my car, or who sent me."

"Then tell me!" he cried.

Mr Black sighed and head to the driver's door, the guard screaming and pleading behind his tears as the slits on his body began to writhe in fear of being dragged again.

From inside the car, another black suited man in shades hand him a pack of cigarettes and flip lighter.

While he inhaled the smoke and round to the back of the car again, the guard continued to plead and beg to be let go, demanding answers or any justification to his torment.

"You have a daughter, Caroline don't you?"

"Please! Oh God...please don't hurt my daughter!" he cried, "For god sakes what do you want from me?"

Mr Black lowered to kneel in front of him, "She's twenty six years old, seven months pregnant and ironically works with your ex wife Charlene for Oakhurst Insurance Brokers in Pretoria."

"Please, please...don't hurt my little girl..."

"And the ex wife?" a smile cross Mr Black's stern face, "Can I have her gang raped before cutting out her eyes?"

The guard screamed out as much as his lungs and throat would allow and the car jolt forward, dragging him a few feet again.

"No sense of humour..." Mr Black said standing back upright again and slowly walking towards the car.

"What the hell do you want?"

Mr Black smirked, "You were on duty at E Shaft when the whole thing came down weren't you?"

The guard's heart lulled and his body went cold through the blood and sweat covering his body.

"Is this why I am here?" he asked, his Afrikaans accent thick behind the torment in his voice, "Mr McDonald wanted this?"

"No..." Mr Black sighed looking up at the sun in the middle of the sky beating down on his black suit with a vengeance, "At least not that I am aware of. Probably, I mean Ike you were ultimately the cause of all this aren't you? If you just did your job then none of this would've happened, right?"

"Fuck you!"

Mr Black laughed, the sweat streaming down his face and the car shot forward again, this time dragging him only a short distance.

"Please!" he begged, sobbing uncontrollably.

"Dear Ike..." Mr Black said walking to him, "The truth is...you were asleep on the job weren't you?"

"No!"

"Yes you were. I would know. I'm the one who laced your flask with sedatives."

The guard looked up at him through the blood pouring from the cut above his eye, "Why?"

"Need to know." He said with a cold sternness in his voice as he again knelt to face his victim, "Point is, I also know that you and your partner woke up just in time to find someone else on the grounds. A young man dressed in black."

The guard looked down shaking his head, his thoughts spiralling wildly. "You never mentioned this to anyone did you Ike?"

"No..."

"Scared you would lose your job?"

"Go to hell you son of bitch!" he snarled, "What the hell do you want from me?"

The car revved and the guard screamed in alarm as Mr Black stood up grinning, the heat tearing through his black suit and drenching him in sweat.

"I wasn't close enough to get a good look at the man in black clothes but you were Ike. And that leads us to this point, all the way out here in the middle of this god forsaken field in the middle of the day with you cuffed to the back of my car and your wife and daughter blindly going about their daily duties while a bomb ticks away at their water cooler right at sweet Caroline's desk."

"No!" he wailed out again, crying desperately, "Please don't do this! My daughter has nothing to do with this!"

"You're right! She doesn't and she can be saved, so can Charlene and all the other innocent people at work today! All you have to do is give me a detailed description of the person you saw that night Ike. That's it then you are free to go."

Ike the security guard cried out loud, "I don't know! It was dark!"

Mr Black flung down, his hand gripping Ike's jaw and tugging it down while the other hand pushed back at his forehead.

"You were a foot away from him Ike! You have to have some idea what he looked like, Caroline and her work colleagues are depending on you!"

As the students moved out, Kyle paused with the mini map he had been given to locate his lecture rooms around campus, his lungs aching for a cigarette.

Joel head out along side one of the girls from class and Kyle stepped towards them as the tall red head handed Joel her number scribbled on a piece of paper.

Joel turned to face Kyle, and paused.

Kyle sighed longing for his isolation, "Where do I go to smoke around here?"

Heading to the north side of campus, beyond the dormitory and cafeteria, they reached the sport grounds where most smokers not living on campus would congregate.

"Have you got a light?" asked Kyle holding up a cigarette.

"I don't smoke." Joel replied, "I'm a swimmer."

"Then why did you follow me all the way out here?" Kyle frowned, kneeling down to rummage through his bag.

"Are you just naturally a morbidly cold person Kyle?" Joel teased, "Or have I offended you in some way?"

Kyle sighed with relief as he found a box of matches, hurriedly lighting his cigarette obliviously to Joel's existence.

"Hello…." Joel said waving his hand in front of Kyle.

Kyle inhaled deeply, a grin crossing his face - first appreciating the nicotine satisfying only a portion of his needs. When he exhaled he again realized that Joel was standing beside him, frowning with apprehension.

"Is there some reason you keep standing there?"

"Are purposefully trying to be an asshole?"

"Not really, no." Kyle shrugged his shoulders, relishing in the nicotine. Joel laughed, "Wow you are really wound up tight. I'm just being friendly that's all…"

"Why would you want to be my friend?" Kyle asked cautiously. Joel laughed shaking his head, placing both his hands on Kyle's shoulders playfully.

"I'm showing you around, just like you wanted. Besides Kyle you're the most intriguing person I've met in a very, very long time…"

"Look eyebrow monkey…" said Kyle angrily moving out of Joel's reach, "Firstly, don't ever touch me again. Secondly I don't really do the crowd thing, I'm not a 'friends' type person. You seem like a decent-ish type person, but the bottom line is this – you do not want to associate yourself with me at all so just run along and go find someone else to fill their time with your desperate need to have a friend."

Joel shook his head grinning as he answered, "First of all, don't mock the brows ok? Secondly, I'm Joel McDonald, a Delta…"

"Yes I know who you are." Kyle nod exhaling up into the air, "If you expect me to place you on some kind of mantle, you are barking up the wrong tree. If you want me suck you off, that is never going to happen and if you think for one minute that I'm going to give a flying fuck about intriguing you, you better back off because I'm very quickly losing control…"

Joel huffed grinning with amusement by his flagrant arrogance and flung his bag over his shoulder again. As the sleeve of his shirt stuck to the strap of his bag, the black string wound around Joel's wrist flung out and grabbed Kyle's abrupt attention. It wasn't' any string, it was his once. A strip of leather with tiny markings etched into it. Everything felt cold, his breathing stopped and his mind scouring through its dark passages to the day years before when he last held it on his wrist.

"You must have a strangely empty and dark little life Kyle." Joel snarled before heading off without a further word.

Kyle turned and watched him heading off, his entire body paralyzed in alarmed surprise and disorientation.

"Do you know who I am?" he asked, rushing up behind him and grabbing his arm. Joel turned in surprise, "Oh…look, the asshole wants to know if I'm a good guy." He said plucking his arm free.

"Do you know who I am?" Kyle pressed again, his face wild.

Joel stepped back cautiously, "Are you ok?"

"Answer me!" he screamed, those nearby turning in alarm.

"Jesus! No!"

"Do you know me?" Kyle pressed again, this time grabbing Joel's shirt and pushing him backwards, "Do you know who I am?"

"No! Who the hell are you man!"

The look in his eyes was unfazed and scared, and realizing that he was drawing attention to them Kyle let go and stepped back.

"What is your problem?" Joel grumbled stepping forward, "Are you crazy? You cannot just be grabbing people dude!"

Kyle gasped shaking his head, "You don't remember…"

"Remember what?" Joel urged, "Who are you? What are you talking about? Have you lost your mind?"

Kyle looked up at him, his panic and confusion was real and he stepped back with his hands up, "I'm really sorry! I…Sorry!"
He turned away and hurried towards the central campus.
"Wait!" Joel said springing into a jog beside him, "You can't just freak out like that and walk away man…seriously what the hell just happened back there?"
Kyle stopped and shut his eyes, his entire body empty and numb from panic and confusion, everything inside his mind screaming and clawing through the darkness inside of him, his past attempting to break out in a black smoke that would pour from his mouth as it engulfed the world he was trying so desperately to fool.
"Kyle?" Joel pushed again, "What…are you ok?"
He doesn't know who you are! Fix it! Quick!
Turning to face the blond swimmer, Kyle managed a weary smile and replied, "I can't answer you about that. I can't, please just let it go and…I freaked out and I'm sorry."
"What? What are you talking about? What happened? Why were you asking if I know you? Do you have split personalities or something?"
"Please!" Kyle said sternly, "I can't explain it to you so don't ask me again if you want to be friends ok?"
Joel shook his head frowning and a silence hung as they stared at each other in bewildered unease.
"You some kind of a freak Kyle?"
Kyle looked down nervously, "Sometimes the darkness holds me to tightly…"
He spoke without pause or obscurity unlike with anyone before, his walls frailer to the person in front of him, blind to the fact that they had saved each other years before.
"Well I know about the darkness…" Joel said huffing a laugh, "But if you say you won't slice me up or hold me ransom then I guess I won't ask you again. Just...just don't mess with me ok?"
Kyle smiled nodding, "You think you're worth that much effort?"
Joel laughed shrugging his shoulders playfully.
"If you're so Delta, swimming, millionaire cool, why are you being nice to me?" Kyle probed carefully but with a genuine innocence and uncertainty that caused Joel to stop and face him.
"That's just it I think you made me see something..." Joel laughed shaking his head as they walked across the lawn where other

students sat in circles between classes, "You won't understand this but when I saw you putting Katlego Seme in her place, something just clicked…I mean…next to me she's one of the most influential students in the country. Her mere attendance at this school is the reason most of these students transferred and applied to be here and you…you just…you were _real_ about it." Kyle frowned tilting his head and Joel sighed rolling his eyes, "I realize I sound lame, like a real loser but…I'm not capable of doing what you did ever! I've tried, trust me...but being real just isn't something I'm capable of. I'm not allowed to be so instead I wallow in this dark little place where I am Joel McDonald the only way I know how to be without failing or falling apart or... I guess I'm done with the pretence of being that guy."

Kyle frowned as he watched Joel expel all his pent up thoughts into words, realizing that this boy who seemed to boast a rich and lavish life was too tormented by darkness inside. And as Joel spoke Kyle remembered the discovery he had made during his rehabilitation at Crown and Lake – behind the face the world see's, everyone has another face inside amused at them, pushing at them and provoking them.

"I'm probably one of the most worthless, pretentions assholes on campus because I don't know who the hell I am!" Joel snarled angrily raising his voice in desperate aggravation, realising only in that sentence that he had just released so much of his inside thoughts to a person he had only just met, not something he had done since losing his confidant Marco so long ago.

"Jesus Kyle look at me going off, like a girl or something."

"Yeah it got mushy pretty quick…" Kyle joked.

"Totally…what the hell is going on? This is the weirdest day I've had in ages! You're little freak out just flipped shit upside down!" They both laughed, trying to pretend that it didn't feel freeing to let the jaded truths off their chests.

"Baby!" Bronwyn called out in a shriek as she hurried towards him from the side, her high heels clopping on the paving. Kyle frowned, his body telling him to use the timing to vanish but when Joel heaved and his shoulders sunk, he paused – seeing his defeated self in someone else.

"Oooh who is the stud?" she asked winking at Kyle before planting her lips to Joel's mouth in a vicious kiss, her tongue again raping his mouth.

"Wow hang on..." Said Joel pushing her away, "What the hell are you doing?"

"I just wanted to say sorry about yesterday, I started my period this morning so that's why I was so emotional."

Joel looked to Kyle and smiled at the way his face cringed.

"I wanted to let you know that we can talk, as soon as I get back with the girls from our mani-pedi."

"I don't think there is anything left to say." He said shaking his head, "You graffiti my car Bronwyn..."

She frowned with insult, "I was in pain, don't you see? I'm sorry about that, it's a girl thing. Just give me a chance baby, please."

Kyle sighed taking a step back awkwardly.

"Give me your card, I'll get us some champagne and strawberries for tonight, we can try talking it out?"

"Sure ok, I guess."

Kyle shook his head as Joel reached into his jeans angrily, handing her some cash from his wallet.

"I'll also get myself something nice – just for you!"

"Thank you!" she said leaning in again only to have Joel step back with a solemn sigh. Kyle realized that he was a puppet to the money strings and he sighed shaking his head.

She huffed looking turning to him, "And you are who again?"

As Kyle awkwardly prepared to answer the campus speakers beeped and Dean Watt's voice echoed around campus.

"Good morning students, please take note that we have been requested to assist the Department of Mineral Resources with their investigation surrounding the current events in Brendan at the E Shaft. Inspectors will be questioning students throughout the week for any information. We are doing our best to accommodate both faculty and students with their time registers on classes and lectures, please report to the information desks located on campus for further briefing by members of the department. Each student is required to provide full cooperation."

"Sounds like work!" Bronwyn sighed snapping the cash away, "See you later stud!"

The girls head off and Joel heaved a sigh, "I have to head to class, I'll see you around."

Kyle nod and watched as Joel morbidly crossed the stoned pathway. He looked back up at the sky, somewhere inside he was beginning to feel alive and it frightened him.

Liz felt her body heat rise as she motioned towards Kyle, her mouth drying and her heart beat racing the closer she got to him standing beneath the giant willow in the centre of the eastern garden.

"Hello Kyle." She smiled through her nervousness, "How's the head?"

Gripped back from the thoughts of trying to figure out why his black wrist string would turn up so many years later, Kyle turned to her. A smile immediately crossed his lips and he awkwardly looked away from her eyes meeting his.

"I'm surviving. How are you?"

"Good, I was surprised to see you earlier." She said smiling as her palms grew sweatier the more she tried to regain her breath to speak to someone as gorgeous as he, "You sounded pretty unsure before."

He shrugged looking down, his heart now racing against his chest as the heat began to flame inside of him again, feeling frightened by the way she made him feel.

"I don't know why…" he said pausing, "I'm sorry."

"Don't say that!" She said laughing, her eyes fixed on the smoothness of his skin, the perfect colour of his full lips and the way his eyes glistened such an immensity of depth, "I wouldn't have told a perfect stranger who just viciously attacked me either."

"So is there something you wanted?" he asked frowning, his heart beat slamming against his chest with nervousness, his legs ready to run from the way she made him feel. She shrugged, taken aback, "No, I just thought I would come over to say hi."

"Hi." He said smiling nervously, wanting to hide his face into the ground so she could not see the monster he was. She made him feel a fear he hadn't ever felt, and her bright eyes and beautiful smile only made him tremble in fear that he would destroy her, hurt her or blacken her with the filth he was.

"How do you find Seymore College so far?" she asked, realizing that she should walk away after his response but felt it impossible to leave his electricity.

"It's a lot to take in."

She laughed nervously, loving each minute that his mouth skewed to a boyish smile.

Say something else Liz, you can't just stand here!

"So…" she started nervously, "You're not from around here right?"

He turned to her to answer but the way she looked beneath the tree with only certain rays of sun light beaming over her hit him in the chest like a punch and his thoughts scattered in colourful lines through his mind as he stared at her face, her beautiful pure eyes and her anxious smile.

Oh God…Maybe he doesn't want to talk to you, you are such an idiot just walk away!

"Your accent I mean." She shrugged foolishly.

Stop staring like a worthless idiot! Speak to her, your making this awkward!

"North coast." He said finally looking away, his nerves now ripping at him, shaking throughout his body like a violent storm of emotion he had never before experienced.

What am I feeling? What the hell is this?

"I see… I like your accent." She said smiling, looking away now as a crushing weight moved over her chest.

He probably has a girlfriend! It's clear in his short responses – he isn't interested!

"So have you lived in the area long?" he asked, managing to compose himself.

Oh my god he asked me a question!

"Yes I have, all my life." She said biting her lip as she blushed, "It's changed a lot over the years, it's much more a city now than it was in high school."

He nod looking at the students heading around the campus.

"Storm seems to be coming in." she sighed looking to the clouds accumulating above.

Kyle looked up, "I like storms."

"We've been having such nasty weather, I don't like the cold." She explained nervously, trying hard to not keep staring at him.

Then go away, far away from me because I'm cold. Dead inside.

And a small lady bug glide down onto his shoulder and she smiled.

"You have a bug…"

"Excuse me?"

"A bug on you. Would you mind?"

He hadn't responded when her hand reached up towards him and he flinched in alarm, causing her to giggle. "It's ok, it's just a lady bug relax."

The sound of her giggle sent a zeal bolting through him and suddenly he found himself feeling a calm throughout his core. As her hand moved towards him, he felt his breathing slack as a strong euphoria much like a shot of heroine cloaked him. Her eyes were fixed on his as her hand carefully moved towards the lady bug scooting up his shoulder towards where his T-shirt touched the base of his neck.

What is she doing to me? I can't... I'm cold! What is she doing!

"Sorry I can't quite get it." She said stepping closer, her body just inches from his as she carefully tried to get the tiny insect safely into her hand and his body compressed and clenched, his breathing rapid inside his chest.

What is this? Help me! I can't move!

Stepping back, she smiled with such an innocent ferment in her eyes, reminding him of his little brother and the zest for live coursing through his eyes.

"I have to go!" Kyle said abruptly turning for his back pack on the ground beneath the tree, "Bye."

She shook her head confused watching as he dashed away, hurrying around the corner. Looking at the yellow and black little bug, she smiled and held open her hand for it to lift into the air. She turned back to where he had vanished and her smile dropped as she too head off trying to make sense of how she felt.

As the haze of clouds slowly drifted across the crisp blue sky above, the heat began to set in and the hours of day began drawing to an end. Kyle, having spent his time after classes waiting for Claire to arrive, utilized the two hours to study the Seymore College layout to avoid feeling lost again.

As he crossed the parking lot from his Cortina, Michael hurried towards him, lighting a cigarette.

"Need a ride?"

Kyle turned to him frowning, "Jesus another fraternity?"

"Hardly!" Laughed Michael holding out his hand, "Mike Harper."

"I'm not interested in joining any clubs or brotherhoods, fellowships or cults." Said Kyle moving around him.

"Look let's not beat around the bush. I can see it in your eyes, you're into certain things that I might be able to help with."

"I doubt it." Kyle sighed with frustration, turning in a halt to face him, "I'm not interested in anything you're offering."

"Careful bro, you wouldn't want me as an enemy I can assure you." Michael said staring coldly into his eyes, "I know who you are Kyle."

Kyle felt his chest tighten with his fists and suddenly his heart raced against his chest as the unnerving dark haired boy stared into his eyes with such a knowledge about him.

"You're a real life tough guy." Michael smirked, a glimmer rising in his dark eyes, "I have my ears on campus and I've heard a couple of things about you and its only day one. So let's not beat around the bush here. I'm the go to guy for anything people want from sex to drugs to illegally distributed DVD's. And you my friend are just the guy I need for something."

"That's fascinating." Kyle mocked with a grin, "Not interested."

As Kyle turned to head on, Michael grabbed him by the forearm to stop him. Staring in a boldly into Michael's eyes, Kyle answered, "Don't touch me."

Michael had only felt threatened by Nkosi and Venter, never by anyone younger than him, and for the first time he felt a cold dread inside his gut as Kyle's cold eyes tore through him with savage peril.

"I know who you are Boy X. So let's just get the formalities out of the way."

Kyle stepped backwards, his mind in spiral.

"Your secret is safe with me." Michael said lowering his voice, "But I might need your help with something."

"Stay away from me." Gasped Kyle, turning to walk when Michael reached to grab him at his shoulder. And in burst, Kyle swung around and gripped Michael's arm, twisted it and rammed him backwards against the wall with a hard slam. His eyes filled with rage for a monster trying to lure him back into temptation.

"Who sent you?"

Seeing the turmoil from across the square where Bronwyn handed him back his credit card from inside her convertible Mini Cooper, Joel hurriedly took his card from her and dashed across the square towards them.

"Dude relax!" gasped Mike in alarm, "I just need your help! I won't tell anyone anything!"

"Stay away from me!" Kyle growled through clenched teeth.

"You have it wrong! Please just let my arm go!"

Kyle stepped back leaving Michael to breathe and compose himself. Inside he was raging humiliation as Kyle was the first to ever stand up to him and remind him that he was in fact not as brave as he pretended to be. As he stared into Kyle's wild eyes, he felt a guilt crawling over his chest for trying to reach target by manipulating someone eager to change their past – something he himself could never remedy.

"What do you want from me?" Kyle urged again as Joel rushed up to his side. "What's going on here?"

Michael turned to him grinning through his shame, "Nothing."

Joel turned to Kyle who watched Michael with stern apprehension when Michael huffed, "A misunderstanding."

Kyle's wild eyes scanned his face and Michael shrugged, "Actually, a misjudgment that's all. Forget I said anything."

"What the hell was that?" asked Joel as Michael head back towards his car, "Have you got some kung fu black belt or something? Do you have any idea who that was?"

"Not yet. Go home." Kyle said hurriedly heading after Michael. Joel sighed shaking his head in confusion and walked off towards the pool where he had practice with the other Delta Caps. The beast inside had been awakened and Kyle felt everything inside of him begin to mangle and distort.

"Just how is it you know so much about me?" said Kyle walking beside him as they crossed the lawn towards the parking lot.

Michael turned to him grinning with the cigarette hanging out the side of his mouth, "I underestimated you, forget it."

"Listen!" said Kyle grabbing him by the front of his jacket in a choke, "Answer my question fuck-breath."

"Ok chill bro." Said Michael raising his hands in surrender, "I have certain contacts, relax I won't be posting it Facebook any time soon bro."

"Don't call me bro." snarled Kyle shoving him backwards angrily, "Who are you? What do you want from me?"

Michael laughed nervously, "Relax ok? Take it easy, you are causing a scene."

Kyle turned to the few students around watching them, Liz and Troy at the side of their car and beside them a black Mercedes with a tall man in a black suit and shades.

"What do you want from me?"

"I only know the basics alright." Michael said cocking his head to the side with arrogance, "Look I get it. I was out of line but I need the business so I had to try! I guess I figured that someone as…damaged as you would be able to pick things up for me."

Kyle said nothing, instead wondering why Michael held such an anxiety in his voice as though he too were about to crack and fall apart. Instead Michael shrugged his shoulders, "Good luck staying clear of the shadows my friend. I mean that."

The shadows? Like the darkness?

Michael head towards the Cortina.

"How did you know who I am?"

"Look Kyle Evans…" Mike sighed exasperated that what he thought would save him now could not, "Your secret is safe with me…and for what it's worth man…I'm sorry."

There was a gentility in his voice and Kyle felt his guard lowering as Mike flung open the car door.

"Forget we met." Michael said adamantly as his engine roared to life. He eyed out the man in the dark suit who turned and head towards the main building and then spun the tires as the shiny Cortina flung out of the bay and sped towards the Toyota Fortuner that had just cleared the gates.

With the usual droning of the city drowning out the commotion caused by the security guard's struggling, Mr Black and his assistant successfully plucked him from the trunk of the black Mercedes in the back alley between two buildings and threw him to the ground. After once again removing the black sack from his head, Mr Black stepped back to admire the wounds caused by the dragging before pulling out a filled syringe.

The guard cried out, trying desperately to crawl away through the burning pain in his body from the flesh that had tore off in the dragging. Mr Black knelt down and effortlessly shoved the needle into Ike's thigh causing him to wail out in agony.

"That was adrenaline. In a few moments you'll have enough to get yourself to Caroline's office and evacuate them all before the bomb goes off. Head east from here, you will know your way I trust."

The guard felt the core of his exhausted body begin to thrive again and Mr Black turned and got into the car, its wheels spinning as it shot away out of sight.

Within minutes the battered guard had crossed two streets, his body alive with the adrenaline as the fear and rage and desperation coursed through him to reach his daughters office.

Those on the street who he passed hurried out of his way in disgust and alarm as he scurried desperately through the agonising pain. By the time he reached the front steps, the security guard on duty hopped off his seat in panic and rushed towards him. "Help! Call the police!" he screamed as the guard rushed to aid the bloody man who begun to collapse from pain and exhaustion on near the doors.

Desperate and realizing that the guard was too concerned for his wellbeing, Ike reached for the guards Tazer and jabbed it against his neck. "There's a bomb inside, get out of here! Call the police!" he called out, waving at those on the sidewalk near the front doors causing them to disperse in panicked screams as he slammed through the doors into the foyer.

"There's a bomb! Get out!" he cried, his body near total collapse as he stumbled towards the elevator as the people around him cleared and gasped in confused alarm.

By the time the elevator doors slid open, the mine security guard had filled the floor with a puddle of blood and urine, his body unable to function as the adrenaline helped him to move.

Screams and gasps erupted from the insurance staff as he wobbled out into the passage, his pregnant daughter just behind the thick glass wall. He smiled, his bloodied hand pressed against the glass as she gasped and stood up from her desk.

He cried out, "I'm sorry!"

In seconds, the sight of his daughter vanished behind flames as the cooler beside her desk erupted and just before his world went dark the guard shut his eyes for a final prayer.

As Troy pulled up to the parking in front of the duplex in her Volkswagen Polo, she couldn't help but giggle at her best friend's frantic exasperation over Kyle.

"Liz you have it bad." Troy giggled, "In fact I don't think I've ever seen you like this, not even in nursery school when that kid with the big nose slobbered on you!"

"He didn't have a big nose, he had a small head." Liz said as they got out of the car, "And it was a gentle kiss, it was sweet."

"Are you kidding? EW! I think that was the first time I ever saw my food in reverse! I'm surprised it didn't turn you into Lesbian!" Troy teased, leading Liz up to the front door of the duplex she shared with two other Seymore students.

Liz laughed and then heaved exhaustedly, "I don't know, I mean who am I kidding anyway? Someone like Kyle Evans would never in a million years date a girl like me."

"Well you did say he was trouble, maybe it's not meant to be?"

"I never said he was trouble, I said he was troubled!" Liz corrected as they head into the apartment.

"Besides Troy, I can't be sure, not yet, not by the brief conversations we've had this far." Liz said slumping down onto the couch, "He's very tense! He sure takes brooding to a whole new level!"

Troy shook her head, putting on the kettle as Liz lamented her hearts disorder.

"I just get the feeling he likes me." She continued, "Or maybe I'm reading too much into the way looks at me. Hell I don't even know if the dude has a girl friend back in Durban or something."

"Won't surprise me, he's like sex on legs." Troy said blushing from crude thoughts.

Liz tried to smile but the complexity she felt outweighed it.

The afternoon heat began to subdue as the sun lowered beyond the horizon in an orange and yellow flare.

Lying on the roof, with a cigarette in his hands watching the clouds above form and deform into shapes only the creator could define, Kyle thought about the past and how his present had become too difficult to handle without something to ease the bedlam inside of him.

What does Mike Harper know?

He recalled the countless faces of the others, but he couldn't place Michael Harper. He recalled the red world of 'V' and almost all of the horrors with it. It made him cold throughout.

Yet he was safe now, on the roof of a modest home with a lush yard, and feeling things he thought he had forever shut off. But just as his paranoia suggested – someone would discover the truth about who he was. When he opened his eyes and exhaled a puff of smoke up into the air, a cold breeze meandered over the roof tiles, and cowered over him. The cold carried in it a memory that brought back the night he tried for the second time to rid the world of his existence.

Standing on top of the roof of their home in Salt Rock staring at the horizon, riddled with hatred and loneliness, the knife in his hand gripped tightly that even his knuckles were white. Inside the apartment his mother crying in Edward's arms, cached in hopelessness, desperate to understand why her son had gone missing, why even rehab could not bring him back to her.

"Hey!" Came a voice suddenly, pulling him out of his memories. He sat up looking into Bennie's eyes. Bennie smiled, half on the roof and half on the vine.

"Bennie!" he said hurriedly putting the cigarette aside as he got up, "What are you doing up here? It's dangerous!"

Bennie laughed and shrugged his skinny little shoulders, "Did I give you a fright?"

"Where's mom?" asked Kyle hurriedly pulling him up.

"She's unpacking by the car. I knew I was going to find you, hey Kyle?" he giggled as he rushed up to the top, his collar gripped tightly in Kyle's fist.

"Bennie it really is not safe up here. Don't ever climb up here unless I'm with you ok?"

"Ok." Nod Bennie innocently.

"Promise me?"

"Promise Kyle." Insisted Bennie looking over his shoulder to the yard below, admiring the height he had gained.

"Ok come on little guy, let's get down from here."

"But I wanted to look at the funny shapes of the clouds with you!" Kyle turned to his little brothers innocent, bright eyes. He could not fight the warmth sailing over him and he smiled.

"Sure, ok. But first stand a bit closer, away from the edge and close your eyes ok?"

"Okay." Nod Bennie with an enthusiasm as he hurriedly covered his eyes with his little hands. Kyle grabbed him and swooped him up into the air above him.

Bennie gasped and giggled ecstatically, "I'm a plane! I'm a plane Kyle!"

He wanted to feel freeness the way his brother could in that moment. To live without fear of the past catching up to him, without anyone ever discovering the truth about him or Boy X. But someone had, in only a few days someone had made the connection and was walking about with the knowledge. It would end everything he had begun to feel, and the freedom he was almost discovering would never see light.

Kyle put him down again and the two of them sat with their legs hanging off the edge of the roof, looking up at the sky where massive nimbostratus clouds grouped and spiralled in slow motion to the wind.

"Kyle?" asked Bennie nervously, now looking down to his hands again.

Kyle sensed heaviness in his little brother's aura, "What's up?"

Bennie sighed, still keeping his eyes focused on his hands, "Mom really wants you to be a happy boy. Like me."

"I know." Nod Kyle with a heavy chest.

I wish I could be, I wish I knew how to let myself be happy little guy. For you at least.

"Will you want to tell me about what makes you sad then?" asked Bennie looking up at his big brother with hopeful eyes, "Maybe I can make you feel better?"

Kyle's heart filled with unyielding weight and he managed a smile to break the sense of crying building up in him. He pulled little Bennie under his arm against his chest, hugging him tightly. "That's really nice of you Bennie. You're a great little guy, you know that?" Said Kyle swallowing his tears behind his voice, "But I can't....It's my own pain and my own problems that I need to deal with and come to terms with myself. Do you understand that?"

"No."

Kyle smiled, "It means that I am trying, very, very hard. But sometimes I get stuck, and when that happens I have to go back and keep trying again until I don't get stuck again."

"And when will that happen?"

"I don't know, but you and mom can't wait for me. You have to be happy inside your own hearts too, for yourselves."

"Do you need me to help you when you get stuck?"

No one can help me.

"No buddy. No you can't." he said hugging him tighter.

He nod, enjoying the warmth of his brothers body against his cold ears and cheeks, "But it sounds hard to do it by yourself, don't you think if you have a friend then your friend can help you not get stuck?"

"It is hard." Nod Kyle, wishing heavily that he was free already of the darkness within him, "And I'm sorry that you have to have such a mixed up brother."

Do I have a sign on my back saying 'Friend needed apply here'?

"You don't have to be mixed up." Said Bennie pulling away, looking up with bright eyes again, "We are brothers. We can share anything cant we?"

Kyle nod and looked down as the tears grew heavier to withhold and Bennie continued, "I don't like you sad all the time."

A weight cracked in Bennie's five year old voice and he looked down sadly, "I don't see other boys being as sad as I am for you."

Kyle took his brothers face and forced him to look at him, "Don't be sad. Not for me. Things will be better and you are too young to be sad about anything Bennie! I love you so much! So much and I don't want to make you sad. I'm trying my best to change! I promise I am trying!"

Kyle pulled him against his chest again, his arm over him and hugging him tightly as he kissed his little brothers head, "We're brothers, and no matter what I will always be here for you and I promise you that I will really, really work hard to not be sad anymore ok?"

The words had barely escaped his lips when red glare images of the missing years tore through his mind. V being pumped into his veins, his body being raped as he lay lifeless and weak, the fights and the violence of his life came roaring through his head and he felt his body dive to coldness and he sat up, away from Bennie trying to suppress the craving from clawing it's way back into his blood. It was the recollection of the dead boy in his arms, his body blood soaked and the taste of the blood splatter in his mouth as he screamed into the darkness.

I'm such a worthless human being, why am I meant to make everyone suffer?

"Kyle?" asked Bennie worriedly, "Are you alright?"

I shouldn't be alive, why am I such a coward? I can't even kill myself! Worthless! Ugly! Pathetic! Sinful!

"Kyle?"

"Yeah, yeah I'm fine." Kyle nod, "Just know that I love you ok. And even though I can't talk to you about this, you can talk to me anytime about anything and I will always, always be there ok?"

Bennie nod and looked down, a short silence filling the chilling air between them before Bennie looked up at his big brothers face again, "Am I always your brother even if you have a different dad than me?"

"Nothing will ever change that!" Kyle said managing a smile again.

"Then you know I'll be around when you also wanna talk to me right?"

Is this why I'm alive? Is this my punishment? To live a life of watching the best of people suffer because of me? Or can I change who I was? I can't, it's all over me like a stain! His thoughts were haunting.

"You are way ahead of your age little dude, way ahead!" Kyle said playfully brushing his hand through his brothers' long blond hair.

"Hey, oh my God! Kyle! It's not safe up there!" called Claire from below, her arms full of grocery bags, "What the hell do you think you are doing Kyle?"

"It's ok mom! I'm with Kyle!" shouted Bennie proudly waving his skinny little arm in the air, "We are watching the clouds!" Claire looked to Kyle, her eyes scornful, "Kyle…You should know better!"

"We're fine…we're safe."

"Get down there right now!" she snapped angrily, "I think we both know what happened the last time you went up onto the damn roof Kyle Evans, now get down with your brother immediately!"

Bennie's face dropped and he looked up at Kyle, "Sorry Kyle."

As Claire slammed the packets of groceries onto the counter top, she realised that she had crossed a line saying what she did, but she couldn't escape the reality of her life, of the situation her son was facing. Seeing him sitting up there with little Bennie made her feel powerless from fear as though her own son was a stranger. She began to unpack when she felt overwhelmed with sadness, tears immediately rushing from her eyes. Resting against the counter, Claire shut her eyes tightly, heaving in and out deep breaths to gain composure.

His eyes now had grown ever deeper with sadness and pain, she saw it every day, developing over the last four years into a type of normal existence for him. She could not understand why he wanted to harbour whatever agony and pain he held, nor could she understand what it was that kept her son locked into such a darkened lost soul. She exhaled looking up, her eyes dry and she continued to unpack the groceries, recalling all the times she and every doctor at Crown & Lake had tried to uncover the full history behind his missing years – only to have him keep everyone at bay, and keep himself tormented behind a wall no one could break. It frustrated her and she found herself slamming the tin cans into the cupboard.

Seeing him on the roof just took her back to a place best forgotten, but she almost knew for certain it would never leave – she would always be left wondering if she would ever know her son again; her little boy that once had such a beautifully bright smile and such a passion for life.

Her train of thought was disrupted as the kitchen door flung open as Bennie rushed up to her, squeezing her legs in a hug as he greeted. She looked up to Kyle who stood by the door as though an orphan waiting to be welcomed inside. Bennie hurried to his bedroom and Claire stepped forward.

"Kyle..."

"No." He said shaking his head, "I get it, you have no right to trust me with him."

She knew it would bite her, she broke his confidence, she implied he was worthless and untrustworthy.

"I wasn't thinking." He said looking down, "It won't happen again."

"That isn't what I meant." She said stepping towards him, wanting with all her heart to drape her arms around her son and hold him as tight as she could.

But she refrained, knowing that touching only sent him into a tension she couldn't understand. She saw in front of her not her 21 year old son, but a little boy in desperate need of attention, of a mother's hug. She tried hard not to let her tears show.

"Kyle I shouldn't have said that. I was just overwhelmed seeing him up there." She said smiling, "I do trust you, as much as I can."

He shook his head, "You shouldn't."

She wanted to hug him, but did not want to send him further away - back into whatever dark torture raged inside of him.

"How was your first day on campus?" she said looking up again, but the doorway was empty.

Having spent almost the entire afternoon and early evening stifling the fire that spread through four of the eleven floors of the Oakhurst Building in the CBD of Pretoria, the local fire brigade began finishing off their canvassing of the scorched area where eighteen men and women lost their lives and a further seventeen were seriously injured in the bombing that ripped through four floors owned by an Australian company Oakhurst Insurance Corp. As the smog and smoke rose in the autumn wind, Mr. Lee watched from behind the tinted windows of a black Ford Everest parked a distance away from the calamity area, speaking into the cell phone by his ear.

"The Oakhurst investigation will buy time for me to get to the identity of other player sir. I've requested our media connections to specifically focus on placing the blame on the security guard for the bombing at Oakhurst which in turn identifies him as a chief suspect for the collapse at the mine. The trail will earn Riaan Kempen quiet the spot on their watch list too, naturally bringing down with it any vote of confidence in the National Democratic Movement. I'll be meeting with Mr. Gavin-Smyth soon so everything is in order." Lee said in a deathly calmness, signalling the driver to head off.

The night carried with it a chill in the air, a soft gentle breeze that circled the trees lining the streets and rounded the homes and stores in the small town of Evander that lay dead centre between Brendan Village and Secunda City. The black Ford Cortina with sparkling silver 18 inch rims and a turbo stood in the dimness of the moonlight under the dense willow trees that rounded the dam known as Unicorn, a place for trailer homes and occasional fishing. The breeze howled across the empty park, the swings slowly moving to the ghosts from the day and inside the Cortina, Michael lay in the dropped seat with both his hands up behind his head with his eyes closed, moaning softly to himself. Beside him on the passenger seat with her head bobbing up and down at his lap sat forty one year old Brenda Visser, wife to one of Evander's largest privately owned 7/11 type grocery store.

"This ok for you baby?" she asked lifting her head up, moving her long dark auburn hair from the side of her face as she continued to massage at his penis.

"It's good." He sighed, relishing in the sensation as he tried to shut out the fact that what was happening was indeed very wrong.

"Michael, I've been thinking." She said nervously, still circling up and down his shaft with her hands.

"What?" he said clenching his body tightly as she manoeuvred her hands over his manhood.

"Well I'm tired of paying the same two fifty each time we meet up for this." She said, "I want you to start thinking about dropping my costs since I am a regular. You know I need to see you at least twice a week."

His head now spinning from the orgasm waiting to erupt from him, Michael sighed, "Do we have to talk about this right now?"

"You close my young baby?" she asked smirking at him as she intensified her grip.

"Yeah…" he breathed closing his eyes as the feeling through his body now amplified. She grinned and hurriedly put a condom onto him before crawling up onto his lap, sliding down onto him as he squired beneath her, gasping and clasping her thighs.

"Yeah." She grinned as the thickness of his youth filled her.

"I'm gonna cum..." He said, his voice high pitched as he fought for air.

Brenda pound down in his lap grabbing his hands in hers and forcing them onto her breasts, "Squeeze them baby."

He gripped them hard as she had taught him through their visits, allowing her to slam down onto him, deeper and hard.

He began moaning out loud and fighting the seat until she had emptied him.

"Oh my god..." she exclaimed, breathless and bewildered as she put her mouth onto his lips.

"Alright!" He said grabbing her thighs, "Enough! Please!"

"Give me what I've paid for." She said looking up with a grin as she continued to grind on his young penis.

Michael clenched at the sides of the seat, frustrated at the woman who would never know when enough was enough and forced himself to remember the charge he offered to perform as the client wished. Her eyes lit up at the sight of his young tight body clenching and tightening and she kept on grinding herself down, his member deep in her, running her hand through the semen streaked over his young abs – a sight her husband could never provide.

He groaned out loudly, more out of agonising joy than pain as she continued to stroke and lick at him, running her hand up and down his tight six packed stomach and chest until she finally stopped at the sight of tears in his eyes.

He gasped fervently, the muscles around his entire body falling to a mush. "Stay hard for me my baby." She urged, sliding up and down over his throbbing erection.

He shut his eyes and clenched down his teeth, his muscles again contorting to the over bearing sensation, and the sight of the slight water build up coming from his eyes excited her fetish even more. As she gripped at his strong chest, gripping her nails all the way down his tight young stomach, she felt herself heating up to the point where she could finally get what her husband couldn't give her and Mike could not muster the energy to contain the sensitivity on him any longer and he screamed.

"Shit!"

She bit down on her lip as she began to ride his waist. His hand grabbed at her thighs and she gripped at his arms, digging her nails into his skin as her hips twirled and grind harder and harder. "Don't make me stop." She demanded with a sadistic grin, grabbing his face in her hands, "Say it..."

He clenched shut his eyes.

Gripping his flesh in her hands beneath her long red nails, she urged again, "Say it!"

He tried to shut out his soul and softly uttered the words she was paying him to say.

"Fuck me mommy."

She gasped and pound harder and harder, her nails clenching into his abs. He put his arms up behind the head rest, his body tight as she pounced on and on. "Say it again!"

Saying it again, he looked out of the window to the moon light that broke through the thick blanket of clouds above.

He shut his eyes as the pleasure below his waist became more and more intense, trying with all his strength not to shove her off of him as she was paying exactly for this and his second release as always, and he gripped his fingers tighter to the seat, his hands going white as his lungs collapsed to the immense pleasure, his head spiralling and winding out of control to the severe pleasure thriving now through his shaking body.

Brenda Visser relished every moment of his youthful tight body, and his gasps but it was when he reached his second climax without any pause in between that she found her ultimate desire. Stamina she craved for at home. He shut his eyes as the numbness engulfed his body, the tingle and orgasm rush that built only seconds from eruption, and tears began to trickle down his face.

"Ok you can do it!" she urged, slamming down on him over and over again. And he reached the moment where his guilt and self hatred felt justified, overridden by the alarming sensation savagely scourging through his entire body.

"God I love that!" she said moving in for a wide French kiss, rubbing her hands over his stomach, her tongue wrapping around his as his body trembled and rocked in his seat beneath her - the wetness from inside her running down his throbbing hard, agonisingly sensitive shaft.

She sat back into the passenger seat smiling widely as she removed the wet condom off of him. As always, she'd slap him hard through the face for that final thrill.

"Thank you." She said tossing it down to his stomach, "Now catch your breath and take me back before Pieter locks up the store your dirty little boy..."

For most of the drive back, he sat silent as she redid her face and hair, the torture of having sold his soul disgusted him but he had to remain strong and not cave in, allowing his shame and remorse to engulf him whole.

As the Cortina steered into the vacant parking lot outside the school in Evander, Michael turned to Brenda Visser finally breaking the silence that had hung ever since they had driven out of the gates at Unicorn Dam.

"Thanks I needed that." He said shifting into his seat. Brenda, still wiping her hands with scented wipes turned to him smiling slyly, "And the price?"

Michael sighed, "It's the going rate."

"Then charge me less for that, but keep the price for sex and anal the same." She said with a bluntness she would never portray in any other place. Nodding Michael managed a pretentious smile to her stirring trouble making question, "I'm sure we can work something out."

"Good." Brenda smiled putting her hand on the door handle, "I want to see you again over the weekend. Sunday night at my house, I have a new dildo I'd love to watch you try out."

"Excuse me?" asked Michael laughing from behind the unlit cigarette in his mouth.

Brenda laughed, "You heard me. Don't worry; I'll pay whatever extra you ask. Oh and Lucinda will be joining us again, so make sure you bring that other toy with, with the three prongs."

He felt his mouth dry instantly as she got out of the car, rushing towards the metallic blue Toyota Corolla that stood alone in the empty lot. Michael looked down shaking his head as he lit his cigarette, waiting for her to drive off before leaving the parking. He head across town to where he had left Jessie at her appointment with one of her more easier clients Mr. Lloyd, who only paid for manual stimulation and never spoke a word, insisting the session only last for the duration of what was needed and nothing more need be exchanged other than cash.

Standing beneath a bus stop one block away from the Lloyd residence, Jessie stood quivering in her knee high skirt and low cut shirt, eager to leap into the car as it slowed down.

"You alright?" asked Michael driving off as she shut the door. Cold and craving for a cigarette of her own she hurriedly grabbed his box and lit a smoke, already in the mindset of cutting out of her memories of the vileness to her struggle to take care of her mother and get out. "You ok?" repeat Michael softly touching her chin so as to make her face him. "I'm fine, just cold. What took you so long?"

Michael sighed as the filth crept over his skin, "I'm sorry." He said, his voice dry and shaken.

"Are you alright?" she asked with her ever present sincerity as she huddled lower in the seat to evade the wind seeping in at either window.

"You know Brenda…" he sighed trying to keep his legs and body from shivering. Jessie managed a weak smile as the car head out of Evander towards the dam ten kilometres away. "Lloyd wants a boy next time." She said nervously.

"To hell with that."

"He'd pay six hundred."

Michael clenched his teeth. If only his suspicions about Boy X were remotely correct, he would have made a new junkie customer. He was certain that someone with such a violent and extraordinary past would be a user – or be damaged in some way or other that could help them reach target. The truth made him feel utter guilt and disgust for how desperate he had to be to save Jessie from having to do the one act with strangers she couldn't do.

Silence remained within the car until the wheels hit the gravel road leading down towards the caravan and trailer home. Turning off the engine, Michael turned to her with irritability in his being, "Jessie, I want to say something to you."

"Yeah well I want to talk to you too." She said disregarding the solemn look in his eyes, "I was thinking we need to consider cutting our portion of the week's takings."

"What?" Frown Michael now clicking back to his usual cool.

Jessie nervously sighed and flicked the ash from the window.

"At this rate we'll have to carry on doing this for another year! I can't do this anymore, I'm breaking apart."

He turned to her with a stern frown, "Then take on another job!"

"Christ Michael!" she said raising her voice, "I can barely manage the two jobs I already have! Unlike you I don't have…"

"Oh don't, just don't!" snapped Michael.

"I'm working my ass off to finish my studies Mike, and Nkosi keeps messing us around!" she said as tears of rage built in her eyes, "I'm barely making payment on my study material, not to mention supporting our rent, food! But I'm willing to cut where I can to get us on target."

"Just stop it ok!" snapped Michael loudly, "God damn it Jessie I will help you out with some money!"

"I don't want your money!" she screamed, hitting at his arms, "I want to be free! I want to be a pretty girl again!"

She screamed as she finally broke into tears, dropping her head down into her lap.

Michael sighed shaking his head, his body now filling with a heavy sorrow, "Jesus Jessie, it's too crazy to go against him. He has our lives, our future right in his hands and there isn't anything we can do about it until we've reached target to break even with him and his goon gang. I can help you with some cash in the mean time."

Jessie raised her head, her soft brown red hair soft against her face as she wiped away her tears. "Michael…" she said her voice breaking to the break in her heart, "I can't live anymore and I don't want to die either."

A coldness hit him and he grabbed her hand, "No, don't talk like that."

"It is Michael." She said looking into his eyes, "I can't do this anymore."

"You're talking crazy…" said Michael opening the glove compartment and pulling out a small black sued sachet, "You just need a high again."

"No." said Jessie sternly from behind her tears.

"Don't do this Jessie." He insisted strongly, "You are Jessica Noordman, a strong and brave and wonderful person who is doing this to keep herself out of jail. And it could be worse."

"Can it really Michael?" she snarled, "Look at what we are doing? We have no soul."

"I don't know what you want from me Jessie. God if I could just figure out a way to save you I would but I can't do this by myself, I don't know how to get us out of this." He said shaking his head as he fought the urge to release tears inside that have built for years. She looked up at him, for the first time in a long time hearing the sincere and wonderful boy she had once dreamed of marrying and parenting with.

"Look Jessie none of this is easy. Not for you and not for me but you know what will happen to us both if we don't finish what my idiot brother and Andre Naude started. Nkosi will have us thrown into prison and we will never be free." Michael continued, "I've tried to get you uninvolved in the sex stuff, but Nkosi knows everything we do and everything we don't do. Every day I pray that you can be forgiven for this and you know what? I think you will be because there's a lot you aren't giving up."

"Pray for *us* Michael, pray for both of us."

He grit his teeth and Jessie slumped in her seat with a heavy sigh. "Michael…we should kill him."

Coldness seemed to engulf the car and Michael sat back.

"Like we planned the last time but this time really go through with it. We kill that mother fucker and we free ourselves of his bullshit."

Speechless, Michael turned his attention to the window and the somewhat ominous looking dark water of the dam that flayed waves in the gentle wind.

"There is no concrete evidence to prove we did anything so with him out of the picture…" she continued when he shouted.

"Stop it! Are you listening to yourself? Is this what you have become? A cold blooded killer?"

"Opposed to being a 20 year old whore?" she screamed, "Screw you Michael! I don't have a rich father like you do! I don't have anything! All I have is this God forsaken life my father left us when he died and now this hell!"

"You know very well my father couldn't care about me so don't play that card! If you want to blame someone, blame your own dad!"

"I already do, everyday Michael!" she said as tears fell down her cheeks, "I don't want this anymore! Won't you please just help me?"

She wept for a moment and everything was quiet, he didn't know how to deal with her increasing breakdowns. They had grown harder in the months since it all began and each time he saw more of her dying.

"I just want to go back to my life before….I want to be a pretty girl with make-up and nice clothes." She said softly, "I want to be a real girl, I want to be loved and laugh again."

He reached out for her hand, seeing her broken devastated him.

"What do you want me to do Jessie??" he asked softly refusing to cry and let everything behind his massive inner wall to come rushing out because he feared it would suffocate him and he'd end up shattered like his brother.

"You want me to kill Nkosi and then what? Either way how will you pay for your text books or your college or take care of your banged up mother? How will you survive? You won't accept my help so if you don't do this, what's the plan?"

"I don't know..." she said wiping her tears and turning to face him, "This is the life I am supposed to have I guess. Until I can finally get the courage to end it all."

"Don't speak that way…Let me help you." He said with urgency in his voice, "I can handle the clients and Nkosi, just stop doing this to yourself."

"I don't have a choice do I Mike? The damage is already done, there is no way I can ever take back what I've become these last few months, never! I can kill Nkosi and Venter. I know I can because I'm glad we killed Andre, I don't regret it for one second!"

"It wasn't all him." Michael said softly, acknowledging that his brother was also a major part to blame in the events leading to them taking a man's life.

"Oh wake up you stupid asshole!" she snarled angrily, "Look at what this life did to your brother, he's dead! The same will happen to us, whether we off ourselves or leave it up to Nkosi and Venter! God I wish you would stop idolizing your dead brother because that's all he is Mike – fucking dead!"

Like a viper, the flat of his hand slapped across her cheek, and the second it stung on his palm he felt his body tremble in regret.

"I'm sorry!" He said reaching of her but she moved to the side in her seat. A silence hung in the car between them.

"You don't know who he was before, to me." He spoke softly, "You were in this life long before Nkosi or my brother."

"Not like this...." she said opening the door before turning to him, "I was young, I thought Andre loved me and wanted to take care of me. I never thought of myself as a whore until you came back." He turned to her alarmed and she face contort in disgust, "What we do might be fun for you because you're a guy. But know this Mike, every time I'm expected to give a hand job to some lonely loser or dead beat husband, it makes me feel like gutter filth. You can't stop me from that forever Mike, Nkosi is going to force it soon if we don't bring in what he wants and I'd rather die a convicted killer than die a whore!"

Her words stung deep behind the clouds inside his soul and she slammed the door.

"Do you think I don't feel sick about this?" he asked stepping out the car, "I feel it every day too, just because I'm a guy doesn't mean I'm dead inside Jess. It doesn't mean this is fun for me. You never, ever have sex with any of the clients. I do! Because I'm trying to spare whatever is left of your screwed up soul you grateful bitch! So yeah I get it… to hell with Mike he's a loser like his brother. At least I'm trying! I'm trying to get us out of this!"

She shook her head trying hard not to see the boy she once knew, "And it's made you blind Mike. We're stuck in this now and we'll always be stuck in this. And even if Nkosi lets us walk away from this, do you have any idea *who* you will be after? Because I don't Mike, I will never get back everything I've lost."

"What do you want me to do Jessie? I don't understand what you want from me?" he urged loudly with desperation, "I have been beaten and kicked, I've been attacked inside my own house! I've had guns shoved in my throat and I'm inches from being raped by a man. I'm scared of everything, every day Jessie!"

She felt a shiver through her body as she looked into his dark eyes, and for the first time in years, she saw something different in them. It was a deep pain as he continued to rant from the core of his soul.

"God! If could kill him I would, but that isn't going to stop anything! He's not alone in this there are other cops in this thing too. So where do we turn exactly? Where? We are totally screwed so either we kill ourselves or we make it through the year until our debts are clear!"

Jessie shook her head shrugging her shoulders in defeat, "I just don't want to live."

The night fell silent between them, and he walked towards her digging in his pocket.

"Take this." He said handing her a small sachet of heroin powder, "I don't want you talking like that." He said putting it in her hand and holding her hands shut in his, "I can't lose you."

She could feel the urgency within him from the fear of losing her and she could see in his eyes through to his heart the boy she once played with, young and carefree. Her best friend looking back at her as though she was the only thing in the world that mattered and she looked down with a heavy heart. So many times she would see pieces of the boy she once knew, but she knew he was to far gone to ever be that boy again or the man she thought he would be.

She turned away and head to the trailer, shutting the door without turning back to him and Michael slumped back into the Cortina, dropping his head on the steering wheel.

Chapter Five:
Euphoria Town

Carrying still the crisp chill from the previous night, the morning sky was filled with hazy white clouds that carefully shifted and hooked into each other lazily constructing what would by the break of dusk become a thicket of storm clouds.

The crew had begun readying themselves for their decent into the mine shaft. The first decent would merely be standard protocol for the safety of the investigative team who would need clear and safe access to the structuring walls, beams of the underground tunnels and stopes in order to uncover the truth behind the blast.

Detectives Jordan and Underwood from the South African Special Task Force head across the area surrounding the shaft and mine workshop buildings where the activity was hefty as numerous amounts of construction, security, canvassers, site men and crew men persisted with their duties, pushing overtime through the dark hours of the night before to hurry the clearance and create entrance for investigation.

The tall red headed and broad shouldered Simon Underwood had only recently been transferred from the police department in Johannesburg Central to the special task force where he was partnered with the Latino officer, Eva Jordan. Having had arrived in South Africa shortly after her 3rd birthday in 1971 with her grandparents, detective Eva Jordan was well familiar with the mining industry as she had spent her youth moving across South Africa between the various mining communities her grandfather had served with. Being a Latino with natural an exotic charisma, hazel eyes and caramel skin, Eva portrayed both charm and strength in her position within the task force, having her long black hair always remain in a ponytail and accustoming herself to wearing very closed pants suits - as means to brace herself and assert herself as a serious female police detective. Her partner, Brian Underwood, was a tall African man with short dreads tied like wheat fields along his head and wide brown eyes. They had been rookie partners in the Johannesburg police force since graduation and naturally Simon followed Eva to the SASTF once a position opened. As they head past the massive head gears waiting to be mantled, she could feel the eyes of the crewmen undressing her.

"Detective Jordan!" smiled Raymond heading away from the crewmen towards them as they neared, his hand out greeting them both. "Mr. McDonald." Nod Underwood, his eyes somewhat judgmental and almost accusatory.

Raymond smiled, talking loudly over the noise, "You probably here to discuss the ETA on the surveillance walk?"

Raymond turned back to where the elevator cage was being erected over the shaft area then looked back at them, "Right now everything is on schedule and we should be able to lower in a couple of days. Did you find any prints on the fuse chord?"

"Not entirely no." answered Eva with a softer approach than her partner, "As I explained before Mr. McDonald…"

"Please…" he interrupted with a smile, "Call me Raymond." Turning first to her more obnoxious and judgmental partner who already had a sour taste for Raymond's flirtatiousness to her, Eva smiled with a gentle conviction and initiated a continuation of her sentence when Edward stepped up to the side of them greeting.

"Ah, detectives, I'd like you to meet my mine captain Edward Evans." Introduced Raymond, "The gentleman who couldn't be present at our previous meeting due to his move from Durban."

"Pleased to meet you, I'm detective Eva Jordan." She said shaking his hand with a stern warmth opposed to her partner simply nodding, "Underwood."

"Has your office been made aware of the events surrounding Ike Magnus and the Oakhurst explosion Mr. Evans?" Eva asked with an ease facing him who didn't X-ray her clothes.

"Who?" Raymond frowned. "Ike Magnus." Underwood said stepping forward holding up the security guard's picture, "Surely you can remember him?"

"Right, yes sorry I've got many things on my mind…" Raymond smiled awkwardly. "What are you asking detective?" Edward asked worriedly, "Did something happen to Ike?"

"For the moment it's difficult to say, we've spent most of the evening in Pretoria at the site of the fire."

"The insurance building in the city?" Edward frowned, "I briefly caught it on the news this morning."

"Yes that would be the same." Underwood nod sternly, "We have reason to believe that Ike Magnus, the same security guard on duty at your mine Mr. McDonald is responsible for planting a bomb in the Oakhurst building."

"What?" Raymond gasped, "Why would he do that?"

Eva turned to her partner, her eyes pleading with him to be more cautious of any information shared with Raymond McDonald.

"That is what we are trying to figure out." She smiled looking at Edward, "Did you know Mr. Magnus at all Mr. Evans?"

"I never had the opportunity to meet with him no, I've just moved here from Salt Rock actually. Most of my involvement has been via Skype or day visits." Edward answered calmly, "I never had the chance to meet him or any of the security team yet, with the exception of the security chief and his assistant."

"I'm not sure I understand you detective…" Raymond interrupted, "Why would Ike Magnus want to blow up a building?"

"Why would he want to blow up the mine?"

Edward turned to Raymond, "If he is capable of blowing up a building in the city, then maybe he is the one who did this?"

"But what motive?" asked Eva nonchalantly watching their faces carefully as they stood trying to contemplate a possible intention before both shrugging up their shoulders in defeat.

"The chord the assailant dropped the night of the attempted sabotage does have prints but nothing on our system to match." Explained Underwood, "Mr. Magnus served a few months sentence for a drunk and disorderly charge back in the late seventies, so his prints are on file…"

"Which means he never had any contact with the fuse chord." Eva finished, "But due to the texture of the chord it makes reading the prints very difficult. And as I've said before Mr. McDonald it's clear they used ANFO, we're waiting to confirm if the same charge was used at the Oakhurst building. In the mean time I'd really appreciate your consistent updates on the ETA for the walk through Mr. Evans."

Edward nod with a weak smile, "We are getting a lot of pressure from the unions and investors, so we're hoping to be ready to send a team in by Thursday at the latest. There are a lot of smells down there detective, not very pleasant."

"Smells?" Underwood grunt from the side.

"It's a dark hole that's been flooded for eight years detective."

"Don't get us wrong, the re-commission was granted, we still have much to do before we can just let anyone go walking around down there."

"We understand." Eva smiled.

"We'll do our best to keep you up to date on the progress here detectives. The compression systems are functional, we're cleared to begin re-=commission now that we ordered new gears and cages." Said Raymond checking his wrist watch, "If you'll excuse me, I have a meeting with the mayor in a few hours, he's growing even more concerned each day and I'm as desperate as you are to get in there."

Eva and Underwood turned to each other and Raymond smiled, shaking their hands as he greeted.

"Thank you for the information detectives."

The two task force partner's nod and he head off crossing the noisy bustling mine grounds.

Watching him head off, detective Mendes turned to Edward, "Why on earth would the mayor be putting pressure on this operation Mr. Evans? I was under the impression this was being handled by Frank Harper's department?"

Edward shrugged his shoulders, eyeing his boss as he waited for a crane to pass in the distance, "Perhaps he just wants to prevent loss of life in the tunnels that haven't been used in over nine years? There's a lot riding on this re-opening detectives and at this point we are getting heat from all sides. This isn't just about E Shaft anymore, the mining board itself is having difficulty with this because they authorized the re-commission."

"No one saw this coming."

"In the fourteen months we've spent on this project detective, I'm having a very difficult time figuring out why anyone would sabotage the shaft when there were no previous threats or attempts to blatantly shut down the operation here. I want answers as much as you do, my job is depending on it."

"Have you been threatened?" she frowned worriedly.

Edward heaved a sigh and put his hands on his hips, "I was down there with them on the surveys eight weeks ago. I am the one who signed off the all clear on tremors and faults in the ground. It's technical but basically if we go down there and there are further delays intended…I can't help but think they blame has to be put on me."

"You are over thinking this Mr. Evans, surely."

"I have over forty unread emails from spouses raising concern for the men on site. The news certainly isn't helping with all their angles of speculation." He sighed, "I guess I just want to know what the hell is going on."

Underwood huffed a laugh shaking his head, "Then we are on the same side here Mr. Evans."

Eva took Edward by the arm and ushered him aside, out of earshot of her partner.

"Surely it's clear that this is more than just a random act of vandalism, we are both adults here Mr. Evans and for some reason I feel I can trust you, so let's not avoid the clear and simple truth that whoever has the biggest gain with the intent to do damage to E Shaft is a suspect. Right now, just like the reporters, we are just about scrambling to find anything conclusive. If we don't come up with something soon we risk another explosion, more deaths."

Edward frowned worriedly, "I don't understand why the Oakhurst fire is linked to E Shaft?"

Eva shrugged her shoulders, turning to her partner who stood watching her in annoyance, "Everything we have on the fire in Pretoria at the moment leans to Ike Magnus. Oakhurst we can try to explain because his ex wife worked there with his estranged daughter – it could have been a simple psychotic breakdown – but E Shaft just doesn't sit right. There's no clear motive for him to want to damage the mine in anyway, this was his bread and butter."

"Everyone stands to gain from the mine reopening detective, and we've been through the same list trying to figure out who gains from it not opening."

"And came up empty?" she confirmed with a weary smile, the sleeplessness now beginning to provoke her.

"If Ike Magnus set the charges here Mr. Evans, we'll find out. Right now I really need your assurance that you will keep in touch with me on anything relevant to my investigation. I'm sorry for my blatant honesty about this and maybe I'm close to utter exhaustion but I need all the help I can get. Once we are able to get closer to the shaft we'll hopefully find something for us to work on."

Edward nod and encouraged her confidence with giving her his business card and cell phone number.

"Thank you Mr. Evans. We'll be heading to the city again, if anything conclusive about Ike Magnus shows up I'll be sure to let you know, I'm sure Mr. McDonald would appreciate it too."

Her statement barely hit the dusty breeze around them when news vans begun pulling up to the site.

"Took them longer than I expected." She smiled offering him a handshake, "Please, I trust your confidentiality Mr. Evans."

He nod and greeted with a smile as she head back to her partner, the crew of reporters setting up to uncover the story about Ike Magnus. Edward grabbed his two way radio from the clip on his belt, "Get me security – we have reporters on site. I don't need them talking to anyone today, move them off site and call the police for assistance."

He shook his head in frustration and turned to the laborers nearby who stopped to watch the fiasco unfold at the vans.

"Get back to work! You're not paid to be on television, back to work!"

Without shoes or shirt, only a tattered blue jean and a bloodied lip, twelve year old Kyle tried to walk but could not muster the energy in his numbing, disorientated body, the energy that seeped from his muscles causing him to stumble and tumble jaggedly along the dimly lit alley way that smelt of stale urine and sewerage. He didn't know where he was, everything was chaos in his mind but the thought of going, not stopping until he found anyone who could help him and direct him to safety.

Looking at the world through the red euphoric vision he could see lights at the end of the alley. He tried to run but the pain in his bruised insides from the tournament proved too much for his mortal human body to withhold and he toppled forward to the ground, cutting his knee. The world was spinning in red as he tried to maintain balance getting up again, stumbling and finally toppling into the trash cans.

Lifting his head he could see lights a few feet away, the giant yellow 'M' of the fast food drive through and he mustered the power to push forward, shivering from the cold and the pain that cursed him from the battle earlier that night.

Again, he toppled to his hands and knees but he kept fighting to keep the 'M' in sight, he knew there was life there and exhausted, he dropped his head for what felt like only a second.

"Hey." A voice drew him back and he looked up at the young boy kneeling to his side.

"Are you ok?"

Kyle fought to find his voice through the exhaustion and the boy held out his cold drink. Kyle wearily perched his lips and the boy carefully helped the straw to his mouth.

"Thank you." Kyle said slowly shifting himself upright.

"You're a runaway aren't you?" the boy asked nervously. He couldn't reply, there was no answer to that question that made sense in the chaos of his damaged and V controlled existence.

"I guess I don't blame you." The boy said with a weak and hesitant smile, "I am too but…you just changed my mind."

Kyle looked at him, the small backpack on his shoulders.

"I…" he started when he noticed that the sky above the alley was now darker than when he entered it and he realized hours had passed and he jolt against the trash cans.

"I'm sure someone wants you home?"

"I don't remember." Said Kyle softly, wanting to cry but unable to know why.

"Here, take this." the young boy said holding up his hand, in it a folded pack of notes that he carefully placed it into Kyle's palm.

"I hope you can remember…" the boy said with a kind smile.

Just then the pounding of foots steps rushing from the back of the alley way sounded and the boy gasped anxiously.

"I better go!" he said getting up when Kyle reached up and grabbed his arm.

"Please…"

The boy managed a smile and placed his hand over the boy's cold wrist when a voice yelled from in the shadows, "Hey! You!"

With the footsteps growing closer, the frightened boy tugged away from him, the thin black strap from his cold wrist in his hand.

"Run!" urged Kyle, tears now finally building in his eyes. The boy nod and ran towards the light at the end of the alley, turning only once before rushing across the street towards the glowing 'M' and vanishing inside.

As he shimmied himself up against the trash cans, the tight grip of cold hands clutched at his bare shoulders, ripping him back towards the dark shadows. In a frenzy to free himself he tried to evade the clutches of the cold hands on his body before the dark shadows swallowed them from anyone's possible sight and the sharp sting of a needle jabbed into the vein of his arm and he screamed.

Kyle leapt up in his bed. Their new home in Secunda still quiet as he sat drenched in sweat and feeling dehydrated beneath his breathlessness as he clutched the duvet cover, panting and searching the bed room for the monsters of his past that he could never out run. There were too many questions plaguing his mind, and he already felt he was losing control.

Who was Michael Harper? What did he know? Was Joel McDonald the boy he saved that ultimately saved him? Why was everything falling apart now after four years? He should have stayed hidden.

The sound of voices and footsteps was loud within the narrow walls of the college corridor as Kyle bent to drink from the water basin, hoping the water would cool the heat arising from the core of his bitter and tormented nightmare.

Just then from behind came a hand gripping his shoulder and spinning him around. A tall, shaven head Afrikaans boy with dull green eyes and freckle spots across the skin under his eyes rammed him against the wall, pressing his elbow up against Kyle's chest. Immediately adrenaline spiked as Kyle clasped at his opponent Jaco Minaar. Two others rounded behind with grins, curly red headed Jeffery Bank and skin head Tinus De Kock crowd behind him.

"Let go of me." Said Kyle angrily, his eyes mad.

"You think you can just walk in here and take over?" asked Jaco, "Eye out my cousin's girl?"

"I said, let go of me." Kyle repeated more forcefully now, his eyes growing darker as the tension from Jaco's close proximity began to cause a claustrophobic reaction throughout his body.

"You leave Liz alone or we'll have to kick your ass good and solid." Said Jeffery pointing over Jaco's shoulder, "Got it?"

Their Afrikaans accents were heavy in their English speech.

"What? Who?"

"Don't play stupid!" snarled Jaco again, "My cousin Jake saw you talking to her in the shops over the weekend boytjie! And we saw you chatting her up yesterday. So stay away from her ok! She's taken!"

With all his might, now disregarding whatsoever could happen to him by disobeying the schools policies, Kyle forcefully shoved Jaco away from him. It was tournament energy all over again.

"I said…." He said raising his fist when Michael's arm slung in around his.

"Hey calm it down…" said Michael pulling Kyle away, "What's the problem here boys?"

Jaco stepped up to them both, his entourage dazzled as the rest of the students carefully moving back and watching with anticipation. One person in particular was staring in awe, heart beating at the sight of Kyle Evans standing his ground like a lion on attack, the long haired Elizabeth Parker.

"This isn't your business Michael." Kyle warned, fighting his arm loose of Michael's grip.

"Why are you on campus again anyway?" asked Jaco who's face had fallen to a pale shade of white as he stood there trembling with adrenaline.

Kyle angrily shoved Mike away from him and turned to Jaco with wild and vengefully dark eyes, "I don't know who you think you are, but if you ever touch me again I'm going to knock you the hell out – got that?"

Breathe! Breathe!

"Do it!" he said shoving Kyle again.

Screw this! Kyle responded with a swift, yet mighty punch sending Jaco propped down to the ground, the other students gasping and gawking around the corridor as Kyle propped down and begun to punch. It was the old world again, this time not red. A tournament he had to win, the beast within was lose.

Michael grabbed for Kyle's arm and forced him backwards.

"Just stop!" Michael warned holding his hand out at the three Afrikaans boys, "Whatever it is - it's over. Back away."

"What's going on?" Joel asked rushing up beside Kyle.

Jaco wiped the blood from his mouth with a grin as he carefully got back up to face them, "Op 'n ander dag broer."

"What the hell does that mean?" Kyle raged forward, caught back by Joel and Michael netting him in their arms as he lunged forward savagely.

Jaco looked to Michael as Joel tugged Kyle aside, and up against the wall urging him to calm down.

"Mikey, jy't nou kak gemaak waar jy nie moes nie boet."

"Walk away Jaco." Michael said in a cold voice, "Or put your money where you have a snatch for a mouth!"

Jaco laughed shaking his head angrily before turning and heading off in the other direction with entourage following like sheep.

"Get off of me!" said Kyle shoving Joel off of him angrily, storming off across the lawn angrily. *Breathe! Breathe!*

"What the hell was that about?" Joel asked turning to Michael who had already placed a cigarette in his mouth. "No idea." He sighed putting flame to the tip, "Jesus do you have a knack of just showing up all the time?"

Joel managed a cocky grin as Michael hurried past him after Kyle.

"You don't seem to stay out of trouble long do you?" mocked Michael playfully as he slowed in front of Kyle who stood smoking beneath one of the wide willow trees.

"I don't need your help." Said Kyle rudely, also riddled now with adrenaline.

"You need to keep it cool Kyle!"

"Who the hell are you? How do you know me?" said Kyle turning to face him angrily, "I'm only going to ask you one more time Michael so you better answer me. How do you know about Boy X?"

"Sshh!" said Michael pushing him towards the back of the bathrooms, "Are you insane?"

"Don't touch me!" Kyle snarled, slinging Michael's hand from his shoulder, "Answer the goddamned question!"

"My father was the Mayor so I have a few connections!" Mike said whispering, "I am the only one who knows so you back off of me Kyle I'm not your enemy."

Kyle stepped back, his chest struggling to breathe.

"I swear to you, I won't tell anyone ok? I just thought that you might be all screwed up and on drugs ok? I thought I could make target by getting you as a client. That's it!"

"Stay away from me Michael."

"I'm only trying to help you stay out of the spot-light, you are doing all the damage yourself!" Mike snarled, "You are screwed up, just not in the way that benefits me."

Joel reached them frowning worriedly, "So what was that about?" Michael laughed, "You shouldn't mess with Jaco and his cousin dude. They're real life masochistic weirdo's man. Not so much Jake, he was cool, but Jaco is a different kind of dangerous."

"And coming from Mike Harper that's saying a lot." Joel added with a smug grin. Michael turned to him with narrow eyes and Joel shrugged, "Just trying to make a point here."

Kyle angrily exhaled smoke from his cigarette, his body pounding as he tried to control his clinical rage.

"I don't care, I have no idea who they are or why the hell he just attacked me." He said fuming, "But I didn't need either of you acting like trawlers back there!"

"Clearly not!" Mike gasped, "You move with some serious skill!"

"Where did you learn to move like that anyway?" added Joel.

"Are we done here?" Kyle asked.

Michael sighed shaking his head with a grin, "Look Kyle if you want to go around getting your ass kicked then so be it, I thought I was doing you a favor back there."

Joel wittily added, "Same here and I don't even know the story."

"Are we done here?" asked Kyle turning to face him, his eyes an icy blue, wild and dark. Michael sighed shrugging his shoulders, "Are we cool Kyle?"

"Like I said, just stay away from me!"

Michael nodded cautiously, scanning them both before heading across the yard. "What the hell is going on Kyle?" asked Joel worriedly.

"Everyone just needs to leave me the hell alone!" Kyle scoffed as he shoved past Joel and head across the campus.

Standing beside the concrete benches beneath the overlapping branches of the giant willow trees, Kyle observed his fellow college students, trying to calm his breath and the rampant beat of his heart. Suddenly a tall Indian girl with glasses sat down beside him with a wide grin from ear to ear.

"My name is Ferzana." She smiled, plucking a note pad and pencil from her blazer's front pocket, "I'm a columnist for the campus paper the Seymore Statement, its printed bi weekly so I doubt you've seen it. I would like a minute of your time to interview you."

He frowned moving up on the bench, "No thanks."

"Why not? You're new on campus and my ears know that everyone's talking about you."

"Stay away from me..."

"Hey Kyle." Came Liz Parker crossing toward him, Troy smiling at her side.

"I see you've met Ferzana."

Ferzana smiled up at Troy, "She and I go way back. I'm decent they can testify to that."

He looked between the two girls frowning worriedly, unable to find any words to say that would make sense of anything to him in that moment.

"You want to do a story on Kyle?" Liz frowned curiously. "What gives?" added Troy.

"He's hot news." She shrugged turning to face him again, "Very quickly earning yourself a reputation on campus and I'd like to cover something different from the investigation by the mineral department investigators. He's hot."

Liz smiled and Kyle rolled his eyes. "Give me three minutes Kyle, come on. People are talking about you, give them something?"

Kyle looked up at Liz anxiously and she smiled.

"I can't say I'm not curious too." She shrugged, "It won't hurt will it?"

"I'm a very private person, no thank you." He said managing a courteous smile.

Why can't people back off!

"You know I bet Jeffery Dahmer said the same thing." Troy said looking to Liz with a witty grin, "Bundy too. And probably that Boksburg butcher a few years back."

Ferzana aimed her camera at him and he pounced upwards, covering her lense and pushing it down.

"Seriously! No!" said Kyle trying assemble a smile, "I really don't want my picture taken! Find someone else!"

Ferzana shrugged her shoulders in defeat as she head off again, "I'll get you Evans, you'll see."

"And believe me Kyle, she will get you. She's got Pulitzer written all over her." Troy smiled before noticing how her friend began to lose color from holding her breath waiting to speak to the electric stranger.

"Anyway…I better be going that way now. For no reason, I just like that way. So I'll be going to it now, just randomly…."

Liz's cheeks went red as her friend head off towards the fence. Kyle heaved a deep breath, relieved that his space had gotten less jammed.

"So you waiting for someone?" she asked carefully sitting down on the bench beside him, just close enough for their knees to touch.

He swallowed nervously as he moved up, "No, I just hang around the parking lot for fun and watch everyone drive home."

She laughed shaking her head, "Right, stupid question."

"Apparently, there is no stupid question." He replied, a smile gleaming over his face, "Or so they say."

"Yes but *they* are the same *those* who invented finance." Said Liz playfully, "So *they* are not to be trusted."

He smiled looking down, unsure why his teeth were showing behind his smile for the first time in very long time.

"I just wanted to say how sorry I am for what happened earlier, with Jaco and his stupid friends." She explained nervously, "See I left Jake awhile ago and well, he's the kind who doesn't let go of things very easily."

Kyle turned to her frowning in surprise.

"But we are over, we have been over for awhile, Jake just doesn't seem to get it."

"That cup cake attacked me because of you?" he asked scowling in confusion. "Well, yes." She said nervously, "But please I already called Jake and explained everything to him so you don't need to worry."

He felt again the charge of electric sensation engulfing him as it had the first time he saw her smile. The way her eyes touched his face, her smile, her hair and the way she smelt. Her very presence making him feel inundated in emotions he had never felt before, not in the darkness inside of his tortured soul. And he remembered the way she smiled with blushing cheeks when she introduced herself, Liz. He felt a warmth inside his heart that he had not known, a warmth and passion so exhilarating that it frightened him at the same time it made him want to kiss her lips and pull her against him in a way he had never done to a female.

"Worry?" he said raising his eyebrows boldly, "Look here Liz…" He gently ushered her to the other side of the willow tree as students moved to the bench, the flat of his hand against the middle of her back, the feeling of her silky skin against his palm making him feel as though she was the reason for the air passing in his lungs and he didn't want to let go.

Lowering his voice as he turned to face her, Kyle's face glittered with a smile.

"Firstly, your life should in no way have any effect on the people around you, whether it's you're friends or just some guy you hit heads with in a shopping market. So don't ever apologize for something outside of your control. Secondly…"

Liz watched his eyes and the silkiness of his skin as he spoke through soft red lips that almost screamed for her kiss, yet her fear for the strength inside of him that crept out in his persona and voice subdued her thoughts to focus on what he was saying.

"If you dumped the dude, don't bother trying to explain anything to him. If he or any of his girlfriends try and jump me again, I'll handle it. You don't need to worry about me. I personally think you deserve better than any relative of that fuck-tart." He said, almost unable to swallow past the bulge sitting in his throat. Liz frowned, her body trying to recover from the weakness he sent through her bones, and she watched his riddled face try to muster a smile as thought someone had just whipped at his back. His eyes were dark again, withdrawn back into mystery and depth she could not wait to uncover.

"Thank you." She managed a smile.

"My pleasure Liz."

"No really, I think I really needed to hear that from a stranger."
Was I out of line? Great! He frowned awkwardly.

"I mean…" she said, her soft skin going red again, "From someone other than Troy."

"Well…you're welcome." He said looking up at the world around him to avoid staring at her subtle endearing charm and drawing eyes.

"And again, I am sorry about that cup cake." She smiled looking out to where his gaze touched, "Maybe sometime you could swing by the Hot Spot and I'll make you a killer smoothie to make it up to you."

"The, what spot?"

"The Hot Spot Café." She giggled, "I work there remember? It's a restaurant in the Secunda plaza, right next door from where we met."

Her giggle was something of a remarkable sound, and he felt a charming warmth inside himself as he relished to its innocence, its truth.

"So if you're ever around there again, feel free to drop by. It'll be my treat." She nod, "And I won't even give you a concussion this time."

"Thank you." He nod looking to her, feeling the overwhelming need to kiss her lips.

Don't do it you sicko!

He looked down, his legs urging him to run but he knew he couldn't make her feel bad about herself because of his own demons.

"So do you miss the coast?" She asked with a nervous tremble in her throat, determined to find a way to ask the only question that really mattered.

"I miss the ocean." He said softly.

"I bet you left behind a whole lot of friends." She smiled, "Girl friends…"

He shrugged shaking his head, "No, nothing like that."

If you only knew how lonely it is for me, you would run. I'm dangerous why am I leading her on?

"What about you?" he asked turning to face her, his eyes so deep and strong that he felt unsure of where to look.

Her hair gently flayed in the breeze, her dark eyes filled with a glimmer of life and hope and excitement. He felt himself aching inside to kiss her lips or touch her hair. He looked at her hands that she toyed with nervously and he wanted to hold them and make her feel safe near him. She finally braved the depth of his eyes and looked up at him, and like a bolt of lightning striking at his chest he felt something sizzle across his core. He stepped closer, he felt as though he had lost all control of his body, the fire inside of him making him feel things he never knew, or imagined feeling and before he realized it – he raised his hand to her face, gently lifting her by the chin to see into the eyes that made him feel normal.

"You're…" he said bravely through the screaming of his conscience as his breath escaped him from the overwhelming emotions crossing through him.

"Yes?" she said looking into his eyes, her knees weakening at his touch. Her body trembling with electricity to press against him and feel him against her lips.

Don't do this to her! What you are, what it will do to her!

He stepped back again, his eyes blinking in alarm as he felt his body return to its cold and hard self. She frowned as the current fell through her, dissolving into the ground.

You're worthless! WORTHLESS!

"I'll see you around Liz." He said managing a smile through the fear drenching him. She nod, her voice lost still to the overpowering disappointment that she never felt him. He head across the lawn towards the parking lot, his skin crawling at the disgusting thought of allowing himself to be anything but black and worthless.

The soft navy grey color of the clouds lay like cotton packed tightly against one another below the white '98 Dassault Falcon 900EX Jet plane that crossed the sky's above them.

Within the cabin of the custom 12 seated jet, Mr. Lee sat facing the somewhat tall yet moderately heavy set commercial business man, Mr. Donald Gavin-Smyth in a maroon shirt that complimented his dark jacket and trousers.

Seated on the soft beige cushioned leather seats nearest to them was either man's form of security and defense.

"Eighteen people dead." Continued Lee now hoping to finally crack the dark curly haired man's tough protection over the cash in the briefcase cuffed to his side kicks arm, "Not half bad even if

I do say so myself."

"Still not what we had agreed on Mr. Lee." Came the heavy set man's reply as he sipped at his sparkling champagne. Lee sighed with a sarcastic grin nodding, "And this flight is still another fifteen minutes long until we land Mr. Smyth and I am confident that you are as eager as I am to conclude this deal."

Huffing a grunt like grin he replied in a rather determined tone, "Its Gavin-Smyth. And I cannot agree to the total amount since the target wasn't met. Riaan Kempen was supposed to die from the poison because it would have been easier to swing confidence if he was found as a suicide. Business is business."

"So it is. However should any of the opposing delegates discover your involvement in the bombing of the Oakhurst building, I can almost guarantee that you will regret forfeiting on you're companies part of the deal." answered Lee with a collected coolness, unfazed by Mr. Gavin-Smyth's attempt to back him down on collecting the sum agreed on.

Laughing now, Gavin-Smyth turned to his body guard and then back to Lee, his smug laughter eating at Lee's already thin patience.

"You dare threaten me with that?" he grinned cocking his head arrogantly.

"Let me ask you something…" started Lee, leaning forward now causing Smyth's guard to nervously sit up ready to react, "The Corporation does not exist Mr. Smyth, nor does Mr. Lee. Nothing you have is concrete because that's how it plays out when you sign a deal with the devil. So do not under estimate the extremities the Corporation will adhere to in order to successfully evade conviction."

"I never have." He grinned with his nose in the air, "You assured me they would all be destroyed in the fire. Yet Miss Moodley escaped unharmed."

"Unforeseen." Lee said tweaking his necktie with a raw frustration, "It wasn't easy getting all three of them in the same parking structure without Kempen figuring out what we were doing. Besides, Kempen's body is lying beside the car where Greef and Moller are. It will look like a professional hit."

"And Moodley? Now she's gone off the radar?"

Lee sat forward with a disgruntled huff, "We will continue looking for her, as I've said. But the fact remains that Greef and

Moller are out of the equation, she'll be too withdrawn to make a move now."

"Do you realize that Moodley can bring us all down? You seem to take this so lightly Mr. Lee?"

"Kosta Moodley is only a threat if we don't find her."

"Or so you hope. How can I be sure? You gave me your assurance Mr. Lee."

"You seem to think you have the dice in your hand." Lee laughed sitting back.

A strong silence befell Gavin-Smyth's lips and it continued to hang until Lee finally sat back in his seat, playfully tapping his finger tips together as though to demand a response.

"You're threats are nothing to me Mr. Lee and since its almost time to land, I suggest you reconsider taking the portion I'm willing to pay for the services."

Lee smiled brightly, "Perhaps I can Mr. Gavin-Smyth, but since I have the exact coordinates of where little Sara-Jane and Keith are at this very moment and I can almost willing bet my life on it that you are not going to sit back with a briefcase containing one hundred and eighty five million rand in you hand and allow me to authorize my men to take them out."

"You son of a bitch!" he snarled tossing his champagne into Lee's face before grabbing him by the neck. Gavin-Smyth's assistant leapt up, weapon drawn when Lee's associate drew his weapon to his head and with a silenced shot sent the bullet into his head sending him down to the cabin floor like a falling tree.

The thud of his body on the cabin floor beside him caused Gavin-Smyth to stop cold. He released his grip around Lee's neck and slowly slumped back into his seat, hurriedly removing his neck tie as the silence within the cabin echoed in a loud ringing within his ears.

The stillness broke when the middle aged cabin girl entered with a tray to clear their drinks screamed, a scream silenced within seconds by three bullets directly into her chest. As her body slid down the side of the plane to its end on the ground, Gavin-Smyth realized for the first time just how deep he had become involved in the conspiracy.

"Mr. Gavin-Smyth we have five minutes before this bird perches. What do you say we have ourselves a serious little chit-chat?"

The waiting room outside of Doctor Andy Morris's office was silent, humid from the air conditioners and yet Kyle found himself cold. He could vaguely hear Claire speaking to the doctor, their voices muffled beyond the dark wooden door and he sighed wishing he had been normal all the years that had gone since his eighth birthday. He huffed back into the sofa, he didn't want those thoughts, not now.

"I will be in the car downstairs."

"You know you could always buy me a car."

"Sure, here just grab some cash off my back. Oh wait..."

"I'm serious. I know dropping me at college and picking me up everyday cuts into your time."

"Kyle... If things were...different, with you. If things were normal maybe, it's just such a big..."

"I know, I was kidding."

"I'll be done stairs ok?"

"Sure."

The door opened again and he cleared his thoughts of the stinging word 'normal' his mother had used, knowing he would have to keep it straight to get his first session with the new psychologist over smoothly without complications she might read into.

Just keep it cool. Talk like a regular guy, not like the worthless asshole you are.

"Hi Kyle." She smiled as he thoughtlessly sprung up to face her.

"Yo! Hey... Sup?"

You should have died before.

Her eagerness to finally meet the infamous Crown and Lake patient that only the world knew as Boy X had been bubbling inside her stomach all day and as she stood there seeing him for the first time, she felt herself becoming almost 'star struck'. He bobbed awkwardly and she immediately captured control to not show the most high profile patient she had ever treated just how overwhelmed she was feeling at the sight of him. She had to have confidence, the notes all over his massive files made clear indication how high the walls within him were.

She frowned awkwardly, her face warm and she had something he hadn't seen in neither physiologists nor therapists previously: a genuinely sincere smile without the Boy X factor scribed into their eyes. Claire greet and head off, leaving them as they entered her office. Doctor Andy Morris found herself utterly bewildered by his appearance. To the world, Boy X was a blurred black and white image of a boy whose face was hidden behind swelling and blood, bruises and cuts. The identity of Boy X was known only by very select doctors and policemen, for the sake of keeping him and the family out of the media spotlight in order to help him overcome the dark matter torturing him - so she had seen classified photos taken of him during his stay at Crown and Lake throughout his treatments and physical therapy sessions from his file and she was pleasantly surprised that it did him very poor justice.

"So let's like, get this thing moving."

"I know what you are doing Kyle and it's very unnecessary. Just get comfortable."

She was very pretty, more than he had expected from a doctor of the mind. She was tall, slender with layered brunette hair and light hazel eyes.

"Please sit." Andy said using her hand to usher him to a seat as she round behind her desk, "I'm sure by now Dr. Naidu gave you enough information on me already, so any questions?"

He shook his head, "No, they gave me all the information I need so we can skip the introduction phase please, I'm sure we both are pressed for time."

"You have something better to be doing?"

He huffed frowning.

"How's things at college? Three days in, you must have a lot to share."

"Not really."

"Make any new friends?" she smiled, silently observing each detail about the young man in front of her, surprised the more she looked at him at how beautiful he had been created.

"Yes Andy, I think I have, I'm not sure." He cocked his head to the side sarcastically.

There was a brief silence and then Andy got up and went to the water cooler beneath her window sill that over looked the side of the courtyard.

"You obviously have all the details about me, my file from Crown and Lake, and the notes from Doctor Naidoo so you should know

I'm not the extrovert type." He said shrugging his shoulders with a coy sigh. "So let's cut the formalities and why don't you just dive right in, you must be burning with curiosity."

She laughed as she swallowed her water, then head back to her seat behind the desk. A stillness hung as she sipped her water again, her eyes not leaving his face and he felt extremely uncomfortable and angered that she clearly hadn't read his file or she would have known that her gaze was making him highly irritable and uneasy.

"Why don't you tell me about Seymore College? How's the classes? Who are the people you aren't sure whether or not are friends. What do you think of the dean and the faculty?"

Kyle sighed and slumped his shoulders, "The College is fine, the classes are typical, I met a few people but since I'm so scarred and full of shit, I don't know what is classified as a friend. Hendry seems fine, reminds me of a general and the faculty are just superb. In fact I'm so infatuated I'm writing a book about how amazing and wonderful Seymore College is and how it's affected my entire life. You should keep an eye out for it, or actually no, I'll send you a signed copy."

Raising her eyebrows with a grin, she reached into her drawer for the jar of éclairs, offering him one which he declined. After unwrapping the small sweet, she placed the bottle back in her drawer and leaned forward on the desk.

"Hendry? I think he deserves the right to be referred to as dean Watts, don't you?"

"I couldn't care less."

"He's actually a good friend of mine."

"How do you know him?" he smirked, attempting to lead.

"I treated him."

"What's his deal?"

"Confidential."

"Then why'd you bring it up?"

"I didn't." she smirked.

He shook his head grinning as he admired the plaques of merit on her wall.

Andy smiled and stood up, rounding the desk again and taking her seat, "Leave if you want to, there is no chain on that door Kyle. I only want to talk to you, as a <u>friend</u> nothing more."

"Are you shrinking me right now?" he frowned dropping his

hands at his sides, his head reeling from bemusement, "I've been through this shit before Andy."

Oh yeah I've done this a lot, and I know your going to be a lot of fun. Hope you have the energy to keep up with me because you'll never get in.

She laughed and shook her head, steadily sipping at her water before answering, allowing the wait to linger in him.

"I gave up being a shrink a long time ago mister." She said finally lowering her glass, "Now I just want to be a friend without prejudice, without judgment and without any other cause other than to give a shoulder and offer unbiased advise. I know you have no respect for me or actually anyone. And if you want to leave then there's the door."

Kyle dropped his head, sniggering sarcastically, "I'll give it to you Andy, you're approach is unique."

"I doubt it, and judging by the list of specialists in the field you've seen, I think you know your only ruffling my feathers for your own amusement."

Holy shit, that's unique.

"No one has ever told me I could leave before."

"Kyle I realize you have so much on your shoulders, hiding things away inside. You're afraid your past, which is justified. But I'm not here to break down Boy X, I'm here to know who Kyle Evans is. If you want to give this a shot, then I'm here. But this isn't Salt Rock, this isn't Crown and Lake. I'm Andy Morris so either you are going to give me a chance as much as I will for you, or you don't and we call a spade a spade."

"You're blunt."

"And you are playing games with me." She huffed, "I get it Kyle, but truth be told in fact I cannot imagine what you've been through. I cannot imagine the toll it must take to have that kind of darkness inside. So my job is to help you, to try and save you from it."

"No one can save me from it."

"You can, with a little help."

He looked down.

"So are you going leave because I do have other patients that actually want to be saved from the darkness inside of them?"

Darkness?

"I don't need saving. I'm here because if I don't see you, you don't provide Hendry with feedback about what a socially acceptable young man I am. Because if I don't come here, my parents will lose their mind and if I don't come here, everyone is going to stick me in some asylum for my own well being. My family will fall apart and my mother will lose it, so her marriage to Edward will fail and because of all the trauma, she'll end up neglecting Bennie. Eventually she'll lose custody of him because the strain of failing and losing me again will drive her to drink very heavily. And since I probably would have killed myself somehow, in a few years mom will be sitting her across from you as your patient." He grinned sarcastically, "And you're going to pull all the same old tactics out on her, as her <u>friend</u> right?"

She laughed and gave him a brief applause, her eyes filled with amused admiration and he smiled bashfully.

"Well done, did you have that rehearsed?"

He shyly shook his head as she took another sip of her water.

"So what do you want from me doctor?"

"Just conversation I guess, we'll take it as it comes. I'm not a pusher Kyle." She said sternly, "And you can continue calling me Andy."

He sighed with irritation, "Ok so where do we begin the protocol? Do I talk about my mother or my father first? Or my step father maybe? Or are you going to prefer if we start on the more subtle influences in my life?"

She sighed with a frustrated grin, "Ok, you've made your point Kyle, you've been through this shit before…"

"Yes I have, so where do you want to start? Jump straight into the missing years?"

"I don't know Kyle, take the lead since you've done the course before." She said leaning back in her seat, "Tell me what your problem is, maybe we can wrap it all up today."

"What is my problem?" he frowned, "No one's business I guess. I can take care of myself, I think I've proven that. This is just another formality for both of us isn't it?"

"Not for me." She sighed, "And how are you caring for yourself exactly? By hiding in your room and confining your social circle to therapists and doctors? Or by locking away the truth about yourself, which by the way; is simply you destroying whatever tiny chance of a life you can have IF you would just leave behind the fact that Kyle Evans made headlines as the notorious Boy X? You are just killing your own soul every day Kyle, that is the fact here."

Her forthrightness to the topic came as a surprise, usually others had more tact especially about the subjects that added to his self loathing.

"Why is it you want to do everything alone? Surely someone with your brain can see that you are going to lose?"

"I'm doing well so far." He huffed, "I'm at college, and I met a few people. I interact."

"Do they know you?"

"Know me?"

"Do they know what you enjoy listening to? Your favorite color? Do they know that Kyle Evans lives or do they just know you exist?"

He looked down and answered softly, "They don't know me."

"Why not?"

"Because it's better and easier that way, no one gets hurt."

Wow, how the hell?

"Enlighten me on that please." She said shaking her head almost mockingly.

"Everything I've done, been through…that truth will kill them."

"Not everyone has to know everything Kyle. You just need to learn that letting people in can be easier than shutting them out completely."

"I shut people out because I am covered in it! In this god damned nightmare crawling in my skin and I don't want to hurt anyone anymore!" he said almost shouting.

Holy shit Kyle!

"Why do you think you are going to hurt them?"

"Because there's blackness that I cannot undo." He said, tears welling in his eyes, "I don't want to do this."

"I said you could go. You chose to stay. Why is that?"

"Are you being serious?"

"Yes. You can still walk out of here. Continue ruining whatever chances you have of living again, in the world away from this stigma of Boy X. Return to your complete isolation and stay that way forever. You are twenty one you are not a minor Kyle. You're legally entitled to make your own choices, yet here you are even after I told you that you could leave. That makes no sense because if you're capable of taking care of yourself and handling this darkness alone - you'd tell everyone to back the hell away so you can do whatever you wanted to do right?"

Ok she's different!

"No…well yes…but no." he said cautiously, "I do not want that. I don't understand emotions or how normal is supposed to be. But I made a promise to Claire that I would try, and I promised the same thing to Bennie. I clearly can't rid them of me I have to try for their sakes."

"Bennie? Is that your brother?"

"Yes, he's five."

"Step baby brother right? Not blood brother."

"Makes no difference, he's my brother and I love him."

She smiled with great conceit nodding before taking a sip of water.

"Why are you smiling like that?" he frowned curiously.

"I just…" she shrugged now shaking her head, "I find it strange that you speak with such a gentleness about your step brother who is only half blood, but you fail to call the woman who gave life to you and continues to love you unconditionally by the name 'mother'."

A smile crossed his lips, "I did that on purpose. You're paying attention Andy, very good."

"I know." She said winking at him with a grin, "I'm not like anyone you've seen before Kyle so you can stop the games."

"But let me stop you from wasting your time there." He sat forward, "I love my mother and I don't want to hurt her anymore. In fact I've tried everything I can to avoid hurting anyone but it's difficult to be…"

"Normal?" she asked.

"Yes."

"So you admit you want to live Kyle, outside of the past?"

"I'm scared all the time. They can come back for me."

Jesus Kyle, put some brakes on it will you!

Andy paused cautiously, "Do you think you are the biggest problem?"

"I'm not the one who has a problem with me. Everyone else does, because they keep insisting that I 'live'."

Andy laughed and shook her head, "Fair enough. But if you want to really turn your life around and live on the side where you can wake up to the warmth that the world, that people offer, you need to make all the choices with everything you got. And you can't always do it alone Kyle. Regardless of how bull shit you think things are. Because I know you want to live, you are not ok with being numb like this and lost and confused. Because unlike you, the people in your life care about you and they want you to live, really live."

Kyle kept quiet and simply offered her a nod, avoiding her eyes.

"If I may ask, you said you have tried everything to stop hurting people, does that explain your Haphephobia?"

He shrugged, "I don't like being touched for a number of reasons but yes that helps me keep a distance from people getting to close to get hurt."

"So it's coping mechanism then?" she frowned, "Something you have control over?"

He shook his head, wishing that he could control it.

"I see." She said reaching back for the jar of éclair sweets in her drawer, again offering him one to decline.

"So tell me about these maybe friends of yours."

He wanted to mention to her that there was someone with the knowledge of his past walking around, but he knew it would cause a panic to his mother as this would be something Andy was required to divulge apart from doctor – patience confidence. He wanted to mention to her that there was a boy he had met in the missing years now prancing around school trying to be his friend. And then he wanted to mention Liz Parker. But he didn't understand what it was he wanted to say about how she made him feel. He heaved a deep breath trying to hide the anxiety.

"What is there to say?" he asked confused.

"Well…who are they?" she asked chewing her sweet. Kyle shrugged his shoulders awkwardly, "They're all twenty something college kids. I don't know them."

I'm scared to get close lady…duh. Especially with Liz.

He felt the warmth again, her eyes, her lips, her hair, the way she smiled so innocently, so purely.

"Kyle?" she said trying to bring him back from his deep stare.

"Yo." He said looking up with a stupid smile.

There you go again you worthless swine. Were you made in China?

"Where were you just now?" she smiled, "You had a sparkle thing going on in your eyes."

He looked down and put his hand over his mouth anxiously, the flush over his face was warm and completely foreign. Sensing his awkwardness, she chose not to press further.

"Do you miss your old environment? Salt Rock?" she frowned looking down to his file. A grin crossed his lips as he stared at her, reading her curiously, trying to place what about her made him feel unthreatened. Her characteristics and trait, the questions she asked and how she brought him forward were so different from the specialists he'd seen before.

"So you don't want to talk about my failed suicide attempt?" he asked abruptly.

"Is that something you want to talk about?" she asked elevating her head with a curious frown. "I'm surprised you haven't used the normal first consultation techniques." He smiled with arrogance.

"We don't have to talk about it unless you want to?"

"No we can skip that." He said looking down.

"Why?"

"Because it reminds me that I…" he paused, realizing she had gotten him to bring it up anyway. "What?" she said matter-of-factly expecting a response, "What does it remind you Kyle?"

Say it! Say it out loud and wear it until you love it you valueless pig!

"That I failed, that I am worthless." He said holding his breath, succumbing to the darkness inside of him. As the words left his mouth he felt an anxiety building, he had given her something already. He hurriedly shook the memory of his 8th birthday, the door to his bedroom opening and the eyes behind the light and everything that followed

Smiling, she got up from her desk and rounded towards him, resting her hands on the arms rests at his side as she lowered to his face level. Her presence over him making him feel the claustrophobia he'd get whenever he was touched, when his own dark and disgustingly filthy black space got invaded.

"We all have scars Kyle…" she said moving her finger down his forearm and over the wrist band covering his knife wounds, "You just wear yours on the inside too."

He felt his chest tighten at her touch, his body beginning to panic at her close proximity, her hand resting on his.

"Andy…" he said, his words tight as they left his mouth without air. She moved back as he immediately got up out of the chair and moved to the side of her office, his body riddled in angst.

"I wasn't thinking, Kyle." she frowned worriedly, "I didn't mean to upset you. I apologize."

He nod, inhaling a deep and vigorous breath, "I don't like to be touched. Just…just don't ever touch me again."

She hadn't realized that she had crossed into his space when all she wanted to do was stress how desperately she wanted him to trust her. "Will not happen again."

"Don't come into my space again Andy." He warned, his eyes cold again, "I wouldn't want to hurt you."

"Hurt me?" she frowned alarmed.

Yes! I'll knock your fucking teeth out if you touch me again!

"We're done here." he said moving for his bag beside the chair.

She nod with a smile, "I understand."

"It's in my file for fuck sakes! Do you have any idea what they did to us? No, you're just another dickhead and you know what? Curiosity killed the cat Andy. If you want into the darkness I can't promise that it won't kill you!" he snarled.

Andy stood speechless watching as he ripped open her office door and slammed it as he left, a portion of the wooden frame cracking from the force.

On the outside of her office, Kyle slumped against the wall taking a deep breath, regretting that his memories caused his outburst more so than her intention, and he shook his head feeling guilty for how he had spoken. For a second he moved his hand to the door handle, wanting to go and apologize and explain just like he had always wanted to drill into everyone's minds – it was all him, not them. But he turned instead and head out off the office park building towards the car.

The drizzle had slowed until its eventual end and the fresh coolness that followed the fall of rain was sweet and fastidious.

The swim hall echoed with sounds of the teams practicing in dark maroon Speedos and swim caps. As a fellow Delta Cap undergrad hoist him from the pool, Joel immediately felt like falling back into the water and sinking away.

"Alright scum bags, freestyle two hundred meter front crawl." The coach roared rounding past the freshmen towards the senior Caps.

The undergrad Delta Cap's moved to the far side of the pool as the seniors took to the water, Joel noticed that Collin was still fully clothed and sitting on the bench.

"Are we good?" he asked below his voice.

Collin shook his head and eyed the water, "If you're good?"

"The way I reacted… It was un-cool."

"Are you sure about that Joel?"

There was a pause, Collins face solemn.

"The guys are going to speak to coach about getting me off the team."

"What?"

"So it wasn't you?"

Joel shook his head, "What are you talking about?"

"Someone saw me kissing a guy."

"Oh my god!"

"Obviously they don't know it's you, so you can relax."

"That's not the point…"

"Don't barf in the pool Mac D. Better move away if those shorts don't have a chain keeping them up!" Another team mate teased as the coach ordered them into position on the dive boards.

Nearing the bench as Joel stood up the coach grunt, "Come on you maggot, why aren't you suited up?"

"Sprained ankle sir."

"Get it healed ASAP." He nod turning to the others, "Give it your best you shit stains. Dave you bloated son of a bitch don't go dying on me."

"Wouldn't want anyone catching anything…" Collin slummed back in the chair as Joel stepped to the dive board still in shock. Standing in position, his fraternity brothers lined beside him, he couldn't understand why they wouldn't want Collin on the team and how he had somehow missed their double standards all this time. The shot went off from the cap pistol. They flew off the starting blocks into the water and Joel stood still, turning back to Collin with a heavy heart.

"Excuse me Joel?" the coach said, his voice calm and concerned unlike before, "Is there something wrong?"

Joel shook his head and leapt forward into the water.

For Joel, being in the water was the only time he felt like himself and not the young man faced with the burdens of his father's disgrace, his mother's fabrications and being made to feel welcomed because of his ability to possess the water and the money lying behind his family name. The caress of the water he was gliding through and the rush to push himself to his full capacity to beat the water, break it, slice through it and make it his own made him feel whole. It was the only time he was in charge of his life, making his own decisions within seconds of thought. But the snickering and stares of his team at one of their own haunted him as the sliced the water. Collin was in the same shadows that he had been in for so long, being someone he wasn't. Suddenly everything made sense and as Joel's head broke up through the water in the middle of the pool he felt it rising inside – the voice he had forgotten.

"Is something wrong McDonald? Must I get you out?" the coach called as Joel swam for the side, his team continuing without him. Joel raised himself up out the water, his thoughts streaming as everything grew clearer.

As he head out of the swim hall, the coach hurried up alongside as he wrapped his towel around his waist, his bag still open as he made his way towards his car in the lot.

"Talk to me here McDonald what's wrong?"

The coach's voice and tone had always changed each time throughout the time spent at the water. He would handle Joel differently. When he was blinded it made no difference but now Joel could barely stand the sound of his caring concern.

"I quit."

"What? What's the matter?"

"I'm done coach, thank you." Joel said turning to him briefly as the rain drummed down on them. "You can't….the team…"

"Fuck your god damned team!" Joel snarled before turning towards the car again.

Feeling dwarf, the coach watched as the Evoque sped back out of the parking, arrogantly ignoring any other student in the process of leaving, and raced out the gate.

That felt so good!

Joel head across town, his hands trembling in such adrenalized fear that he could barely hold the steering wheel, nor clutch or accelerate with his legs wobbling under him. He laughed shaking his head, "Holy…shit…"

The stretch of road between the fast growing town of Secunda and the trailer home park only a few kilometers outside Evander was quiet, with the overhead storm and the ever so often flash of lighting that tore open the immenseness, an omen seemed to whisper in the wind.

Inside the car, Michael sat in silence while Jessica simply sat staring at the lights of the SASOL plantation glimmering in the darkness on the horizon - wishing with every fiber of her human body and soul that she could transform her existence to that of a dove so as she too could fly away from all the world, especially the world she found herself forced into not long after her father took his own life.

"I feel sick." Michael said heaving a sigh as the tobacco flared up at his lips.

"Was it painful?" Said Jessie softly, her thoughts still swallowed by her dreams of the life beyond the horizon. Michael chose to remain silent.

He, in the bowels of his soul, secretly desired Nkosi to be omitted from life and to break free of his clutches, yet feared too greatly the concern Jessie invoked in her proposal in killing him themselves. His heart broke at the thought of his dearest childhood friend Jessie who had been swallowed into the tunnels of deceitful soul breaking, and yet as he pitied her and the suffering of her fading spirit he too felt the sickening vileness eating at his gut every day like a constant feeling of euphoria, an acid slowly ingesting him.

Having lost his brother to the same pits of self-spiritual mutilation four years ago and to face a life of solitude and loneliness with a father who blamed him for his brothers' suicide. A father who hated him every day, assuming that this life was the path Michael himself chose in order to fill his brothers' shoes.

There was a stillness again as they neared the park that surrounded a large natural dam out in the fields nearest the mines. "Do we have business on Friday?" asked Jessie breaking the stillness in a soft morbid voice.

Michael shook his head but remained quiet to the screaming inside his core as the car slowed onto the gravel leading through the trailer park, carefully steering towards the trailer she and her mother were staying. She kept looking at him, waiting to see a glimmer of the Michael she once knew. But he was quiet and she knew it was because of their last discussion. She knew she wasn't the only one selling herself to the will of Nkosi and Venter's scheme and especially now as he sat there after what he had just done for eight hundred rand, she knew he too was as broken as she. His eyes were dark, fixed ahead on the road and his jaw muscle constantly in clench.

"Can you believe I was once living in a street just next to you?" She said trying to lure his mind to a lighter place, "Huh big man Michael."

"Shut up Jess." He sighed shaking his head, "Get out before you say something you'll regret."

"Relax, I'm only saying. We've come a long way since then."

Michael leaned over and opened her door, "I know you blame me for all of this."

"No I don't." she said shaking her head, "I blame your brother. If it wasn't for him maybe we never would have killed Andre."

"You would have been Andre's whore either way."

She looked down angrily, unable to look at the man he had become.

"I'm sorry I just…" he sighed staring ahead, speechless and devoid of energy to try and feel anything but sick.

"You have no idea what it's like." She turned to face him, "I hate him you know, my dad. If he didn't die and leave us with all his debts none of this would have happened we would have still…None of this would have happened."

She looked down, her eyes filling with tears and a silence hung between them, only the engine of the Cortina droning beneath the black hood. Michael sighed and put his hand on her leg with a gentle squeeze in the hopes it would comfort her, "Go home

Jessie, get some sleep ok?"

She turned and motioned out of the car, slamming the door shut, heaving a deep breathe of the cold night air before walking up to the faded white trailer marked 1307. She knew that what he once felt for her was lost in the haze of black turmoil they had fallen into the night they both caused Naude's death. Yet as she walked back out of the trailer, watching him drive, she wondered if she would ever sever the last fragment of love she once felt for him.

The interior of the one bedroom, narrow little trailer smelled of stale beer, throw up and long stale smoke. The violent disorder and lack of clean space on anything within the trailer again hit her in the stomach and she sighed, looking down the left side to where the bathroom and bedroom stood with both doors shut, then looked ahead at the small cramped sitting room kitchenette, her dyed blond mother no where to be seen.

Jess stumbled to the bedroom compartment and opened the door to find sitting up on the bed, a plump overweight man with hairy shoulders and chest whom she had seen in the park before, fishing and drinking, his long greasy hair hanging somewhat over his eyes as he looked up from the ashtray.

"Where's my mom?" she asked clearing her throat uncomfortably looking down, her tongue feeling large and uncontrollable. The man sighed and pulled off the covers where her mother lay past out. "Right, okay." She said hurriedly heading out of the room and sliding the unhinged door shut as she dragged her feet through the musty kitchenette, her spirit blank as she flopped down onto the faded green and brown couch. She removed a small sachet of fine powdered cocaine that she had taken from Michael's car before he returned. Neatly lined, she knelt on her knees eager to dissolve out of the reality of her existence and she snorted it. She closed her eyes to allow her body to be taken by it. Soon the buzzing rattle of the small bar fridge fell away and a deafening silence consumed her and a memory began to be submerged into her thoughts as she crawled onto the sofa, desperate to evade her life.

The sunlight breaking through the pink floral curtains hanging by the window of her childhood bedroom and she seated on the ground at her small plastic table where guests Lilith the fluffy white teddy bear and Casey the rag doll with long strings of blue hair sat enjoying the tea party. The sound of the car driving up the drive way filling the room with a humming drone as she hurriedly excused herself, dashing through the warm house past her mother in the kitchen baking scones and out the front door, running around the side of their comfortable home to the car as her father got out, "Daddy!"

Just then a loud crash ripped her from her cocaine induced graceful dream and she lifted her head lazily to find her mother laying on her hands and knees beside the counter at the kitchen in only her bra and panty. Behind her stood the grease man shouting, but she could not hear the words through the deafening drone the cocaine filled her with and the induced sound of the underwater like murmuring from the bar fridge.

Jessie smiled and for a moment her eyes rolled back into her head, seeing all of them happy and together, a family. Her life as her father's princess and her mother's pride.

Another muffled clatter burst through the droning and she raised her weary head again, this time to find her mother against the wall with his greasy hand to her throat. Their mouths moving but only a muffled noise to her pulsating mind and with her eyes too heavy to keep open even through her fight to overcome the cocaine scouring through her system - she dropped her head back again.

She could recall the day her father died, the day she stood sourly beside her Opel as she and her mother both stood waving to him as he drove off, the last time they would ever see him alive.

Regret filled her and she clenched shut her eyes, recalling how she had fought with her father before he left, typical teen angst and hormones, only to never have a chance to make it up to him.

Another loud noise crashed and she opened her eyes, her heart pounding inside her chest and her eyes wide. Her mother pressed up against the counter with her underwear torn hanging by her knees, trying to cry out from behind his hand as he rammed into her from behind. Jessie closed her eyes and suddenly everything went dark, and silence like she had not experienced before. Then a scream filled the trailer and she tried to see past the dense blackness, but could not. Her heart racing against her chest, her pulse at her wrists almost breaking through her skin in a strong euphoria as images of her memory - she had hoped to bury deep into a forgotten portion of her life - began to play flashing through her mind. Her father's car heading off as she waved, and then the images of his body hanging from the tree beside the road, the men carrying stuff out of their home in boxes, the first time she saw her mother submitting to alcohol. She saw in her mind flashbacks of the night Andre Naude forced himself on her and Michael barging through the door. She saw snippets of memory, she and Michael watching from around the corner as Michael's brother Lyle Harper traded drugs with clients and before her mind swallowed the blackness of exhaustion she remembered screaming at the sight of Andre Naude lying on his back – the picket fence torn through his stomach. And then her heart beat calmed and her thoughts went black.

The morning air still held within its clasp, the brisk chilling whispers of the night's secrets and a low fog covered the plateaus of the low land areas of Mpumalanga.

The shaft that had been flooded upon its close eight years prior had, after almost two weeks, finally lost its horrid stench.

The compression systems were now fully operational, the water mains were cleared. Since the explosion, further surveys were done to ensure that the ground stability was suitable to proceed with the reopening. The tension was heavy at surface level as the double-decker cage lowered the crew of fourteen down into the shaft. Each member of the team, known as a 'Proto-Team', had all previously descended down the gullet of E Shaft in the months before. Before the re-commission was authorised, each of them had previously accompanied the Inspector of mines and quarries and his associates into the shaft and its many stopes and ore pass tunnels.

They were tasked with the goal of survey each and every section of the support beams holding the colossal shaft in place, from surface level all the way down to the shaft bottom. And during their decent also surveying as much of the stopes, dumpy levels and ore-passes as possible for any additional signs of damage from the explosion.

Normally these shift bosses, mine captains and other well trained artisans would endure this decent into the blackness of the mine to scout and survey for safety within the tunnels from any sign of methane or ground tremors. Cracks in the walls, the water pipes and ventilation systems…but now they were tasked with something far different…body hunting with the giant spot lights attached to the cage. All further work around the shaft had been put on hold since the explosion, the situation was direly delicate and all of them on the control room knew this as they stood waiting in tight suspense, watching the CB radio control desk with baited breathe.

"Team One here, we're heading down to the third level now." A voice crackled over the radio finally relieving the air, "I have no reason to regard the deterioration of the stockade this far down as a hazardous, some restoring to the chute on level two's eastern stopes one through to five."

Raymond turned to the inspector of mines and quarries, nodding with a confidence and the radio crackled again this time with the engineer on team nine.

"Hoppers are totally rusted on tunnel 2B and some of the fencing seems weakened."

The broad shouldered man turned to Raymond, his face grim and his dark eyes very displeased.

Noting that it was only the usual defects found thus far, Raymond smiled and nod.

"We are having a problem reading team two, can any of you guys reach them?" asked Edward taking over the control mic, slightly apprehensive since the last time they had communication from team two was after the cage lowered to the fifth level taking them deeper ahead of the other two teams.

"That's a negative." Answered the first.

"De Graaf and his boys were lowered to level 5 that was the last I heard."

Detective Jordan sighed and Edward turned to her, "Don't worry detective, breaks in signal are not that uncommon at that depth. Back in the old days the tech didn't really allow for communication from surface level to shaft bottom, so this is better than how it used to be."

She smiled awkwardly and whispered, "I'm just impatient." Underwood, who had no prior knowledge of the operations of a mine watched the cage operator in awe of his ability to move the cage with such discipline and accuracy.

In the silence of his apartment, Joel lay on his back as the wind tampered against his window. He had tried getting out of bed for college, but couldn't face the Delta Caps or his coach, Kyle or anyone else. He felt a weight crawling over him, uncertain how to apologise because Joel McDonald never had too. Everyone had always wanted a part of him and he had grown so accustomed to living a life that being just Joel felt alien. His heart was tearing to dial Collin's number into the cell phone in his hands, to apologise and tell him how he knew the struggles of being someone else behind a smile, beyond the water, the money and the neatly gelled hair.

Finally, he dialled.

The ringing made his heart race.

"Joel..." Collins voice was solemn and empty, "Why are you calling me?"

"Hey man, I didn't go in today." He said smiling while he felt an eagerness to tell Collin that he wasn't alone in living a double life and that together they could burn their masks.

Collin was silent.

"You there?"

"Why... are you calling Joel?" Collin sniffed, his voice soft and empty. Joel sat up, "Are you ok?"

"It doesn't matter."

"Dude where are you? You don't sound ok? What happened?"

It was silent again.

"Collin?" he said again, desperately trying to hear more through the phone and in a few seconds he knew that the faint undertones coming through the connection was tears and sniffling.

"I wanted to talk to you..." Joel said awkwardly, "You there?"

A strangeness befell Joel as the phone muffled a sound from the other end of the line and he pricked his ears as desperately as he could.

"Collin?" he said as tears broke from his eyes, "Collin!"

He screamed into the phone, realizing that it was a stool hitting the carpeted floor, the odd squeaking the rope around his friend's neck.

By the time Joel reached Collin's dorm, the entire hallway had filled with students, paramedics and uniformed police officers. A few of the Delta Caps stood huddled nearby, Collins roommate standing pale in shock as Dean Watts and an officer tried to comfort and console him.

As the sky above tore open with a light rain, Joel stepped out onto the steps facing the lawn, students all around carrying on with their classes hurried to the front of the fraternity block after the news spread. The air and drizzle was cold and sinking deep into him as he walked to the car; unable to speak or think past the reality of his delay in making the call to someone he could have saved. He turned back to the face the dorm, wanting to cry but unable to face that someone he had spent so much time being angry with for being oblivious to his agony was in a dark pain himself. *I'm sorry Collin. If I just told you who I was, how I felt maybe you would have trusted me sooner.*

Kyle carefully stepped up to Joel, having heard the news he knew that somehow he would need to say something to the person who saved his life and offered friendship oblivious to the darkness inside of him, a chance he had never gotten in years.

Joel turned to face him as he stepped up beside him in the drizzle.

"I'm so sorry about your friend." Kyle said awkwardly. The agony in Joel's eyes bore in them the same he saw in the mirror every morning getting ready to face another day. Joel nod and Kyle carefully placed his hand on his shoulder. As the paramedics cleared the way to bring out the stretcher, students begun to cry and gasp in the shock of the first suicide on campus. Dean Watts stepped aside after ushering students out the way and held open the door for them to cart the young man's body to the ambulance, at his side stood Andy Morris with her umbrella open above them. Trying hard not to sob, Joel realized that Collin had been seeing the doctor because of the demons inside of him and that he had been so overcome by his own darkness to realize that so many others were consumed in their own.

He finally broke into tears, trying bravely to hide it and subdue it and knowing that weight and what damage it did to him; Kyle moved in and sincerely placed his arm around the shattered swimmer. Joel bravely cried into his chest, freeing himself of the burdens of his own life of lies as he gave into the fracturing on his soul.

Still standing beside Edward at the console inside the newly built control building, task force detectives Jordan and Underwood listened anxiously along with everyone else in the room to the broadcast as the drizzle tapped at the ceiling above them.

"Unsteady ceiling here boys." Came the leader of the second team, "We're definitely going to need some restricting or support beams down here. This is tremor related, probably from the explosion."

"Location?"

"South of level 2C at the junction meeting the ore pass X East 3, its really flimsy and..."

The voice of the leader cut off when a crackle over the radio brought De Graaf through.

"Are you reading me?" his voice broke through, "De Graaf here, are you reading me?"

"We are reading you team one." The operator said calmly.

"We have a situation down here!"

Raymond, Edward and the other foremen huddled nearer to the control desk.

"Go ahead De Graaf, what is your situation?"

"Jose found something on the support beam. Level nine."

Underwood turned to his partner in awe that they had taken so long to move through the various tunnels, unaware of the vast network beneath them.

"Explain please De Graaf..." The operator spoke again, his voice still calm and controlled.

"Oh my god..."

"What is it De Graaf?" urged Edward into the microphone.

"De Graaf hold your team back, I am on my way to assist."
Moorecroft urged.

Raymond grabbed the mic, "Negative Moorecroft, we need every level secured. Remain with your team at shaft bottom."

There was no response, the radio crackled.

"So much for new technology…" Underwood sighed anxiously beneath his breath.

Raymond hand the mic to Edward worriedly, lowering his voice, "Doesn't sound like a problem with the timber supports that's for sure."

"What is their location?" asked Eva turning to the map. As the survey officer pointed to it, the radio crackled again.

"Sir we have something here. We need confirmation of how to proceed with this. Are you copying me?" De Graaf's voice cracked through again, "Did you receive my previous communication? Die kak werk…"

"We did not, that is a negative De Graaf." Advised the controller, "There is interference. All teams please take note of this, copy?"

"Copy that. We heard De Graaf's message…" A voice came through when it was interrupted by De Graaf again.

"We have….."

"Repeat please?" Edward urged worriedly as a cold euphoria riddled over them all.

Raymond lunged forward, ready to request that Pieter just convey the message De Graaf was unable to transmit when his voice broke through on the com.

"I repeat! We have a human hand! We have a badly decomposed hand down here."

Eva turned to Underwood in alarm.

"Been here awhile…years…" his voice said in the dry fuzz.

Chapter Six:
Four years ago:

21 year old Lyle Victor Harper was all about image. This was clear in his pitch black hair that was always sculpted neatly, his facial hair styling and his well-built physic. His clothes were always branded and of the highest quality, his shoes worth hundreds. He had always been proud and daring, living on the wilder side of the family name. His true pride and joy was the Ford Cortina MK3 GXL four door that he had purchased on his own from years of savings. The car had been a dream of his since he first received a collectable Die Cast model as a gift. He had it sprayed, reupholstered and almost everything in the engine had been redone, modified and souped-up. The pitch black body always shone and its silver mag wheels glimmered without fail. It was a metal version of him and would always be well cared for at any cost.

As its turbo fuel injected engine roared, the muscle car slowly crawled into the parking bay where the complex signage read: 'Units 18 – 34 Visitors Parking'.

Clad in tight fitting navy jeans, a tight red shirt and his infamous black leather jacket, he corrected his collar and turned to lean back into the open window.

"I won't be long and leave my CD changer!" he said looking to his younger brother Michael, "Got it?"

"Sure!" Michael said huffing, his 16 year old hormones focused on the girls at the swimming pool across the lot.

He heaved a deep breath before heading up the narrow stairs. After knocking rapidly on the door and waiting in anxious anticipation, it opened to a tall blond with perm hair in early thirties wearing only a night gown.

"You must be Lyle." She smiled opening the door as her friend Heidi slumped up beside her in only her underwear.

"You ready for us gorgeous?" smiled Heidi flipping her blazing red hair. He nod awkwardly, they had been drinking.

The girls giggled drunkenly and yanked him inside, the door shutting with a slam. Wasting no time, the fiery red head gripped at his jacket and slammed her lips up against his as they stumbled backwards, heaving his jacket off and shoving him down onto the sofa.

"You've done this before?" he asked trembling as the two girls began to swop tongues. Giggling and wiping the spit from her lips, Heidi shook her head, "No but you can trust me tiger, for four hundred bucks, you can be sure we wont let any time go to waste!"

Inside the car, Michael sat staring at the glove compartment at the small compactor his brother had just used to get a hit of cocaine before his visit. It frustrated him because he knew his brother was on a dark road and wouldn't listen to reason.

As the dashboard clock struck 14h15, two hours later, Lyle hopped up to the door and got in with a bright smile, "Hey bro! Miss me?"

"Have fun?" asked Michael shifting up in his seat from his sleeping position as his brother revved the engine to life.

"Dude, I can so do this!" he said shifting into reverse.

"You're at least using condoms right?"

"What kind of stupid question is that for the younger brother to ask the older brother?" laughed Lyle, feeling extremely proud of himself and he scrimmaged his hand through his brother's hair.

"Are you?" Michael asked again.

"Hell yeah little bro! Of course!"

He nod feeling relieved that his brother hadn't utterly stumbled into insanity. Lyle lit a smoke, "Oh man! That was awesome man! Hell I did things in there…Shit I actually did it! We did things in there that would make you stay up all night with tissue paper!"

Michael laughed shaking his head, "Yeah and at least this time you got paid for it."

"Shit!" gasped Lyle slamming on the brakes. Knowing that Andre Naude wouldn't easily take any failure of payment, he swung the Cortina around and sped back to the complex.

◉◉◉

By the afternoon, Michael and his brother had made two other visits and a drug pickup just outside of Alberton north of Johannesburg. As the Cortina veered up the curving driveway to double story home and circled the water fountain in the centre of the wide paved road, Michael had to finally ask the question burning him since he had went to spy through the window at the second visit.

"Why won't you let me be part of it?"

Laughing, Lyle shook his head brushing his nose, "The reason I'm doing this shit is to break free of this pretentious life they have us living." He nod up at the house, "They push to hard for me to be what they want, and I'm tired of doing it. I have a good thing going now bro. Constant sex, constant cash, drugs... You are doing well for yourself bro, and that's who you are! Not this! Unless you grow up to be a total drop out then we'll talk again."

"I could do it, I have some moves…"

Lyle smirked, "I know you saw us and that's ok, but seriously little bro you have to keep this to yourself. I get you want in on the action but you're just not ready for it yet. You can do better for yourself, for now just have my back ok?"

Inside the house, Michael head up the curving stair case when his mother called from below nearer to the kitchen, "Don't you greet anymore?"

"Hi mom!" He smiled turning back down, "I didn't know you were home?"

52 year old Mrs. Alice Harper smiled behind her tired hazel brown eyes and stepped to the banister, more fragile and aged than she would have been if her life hadn't been shattered two years before having suffered a stroke.

"Your father and Maxwell are still out there campaigning, I need the break." She smiled. Her soft brown eyes watching him as he neared, "Was that Lyle who dropped you off?"

Embracing her supplied him with enough time to acknowledge that should he answer truthfully she would only probe further into his brothers recent whereabouts and undoubtedly only supply her with more reason to refuse him any leniency and keep him close to her as the only son left under her roof.

"No that was Steven's mom." He said stepping back, "She had to do some shopping anyway so I caught a ride with her."

She shook her head with concern, "Oh Michael, why don't you make use of the driver? It'll make me feel so much better knowing that you're always alright. Unlike your brother, I worry about him all the time and it's like he just doesn't care." She said leading him towards the kitchen.

"He cares mom." Sighed Michael, "He's just busy that's all."

"Busy with what?" she said opening the cupboard, "I hate how he and your father just don't communicate anymore, its ridiculous really."

"Dad doesn't have time for any of us, what makes Lyle so special?" he said slumping up against the marble top counter as she began unpacking bread and condiments.

"Rubbish!" she snapped, "Your father loves you Michael, both of you. Sure he is busy running this campaign and all, but it's almost over and we can be a family again but your father doesn't favour Lyle over you."

Michael shook his head, "I'm old enough now to know how things work. Besides, everyone in the area knows that there is only one thing more important to dad than being district mayor and that's Lyle. I've made peace with it!"

Mrs. Harper shook her head and handed him a cheese sandwich, "Well your still my boy and you are all I have left now."

"You say it like Lyle's dead mom." Said Michael chewing on his bread.

"No but..." She said, a glaze falling over her eyes as she stared off into the distance as though her mind simply stepped out the path of tears that streamed down her face. She had been battling the first stages of dementia for three years and it was a sadness like no other watching her mind switch on and off at will.

He hurriedly put down the plate and half eaten sandwich and put his arm around her, "Hey, its ok. Let's get you to bed for a nice lay down huh?"

He ushered her out into the passage when the house maid Deloris stepped out of the dining room with her feather duster in hand.

"Everything alright young sir?" she asked rushing up to them.

Michael nod with a gentle smile, "She's fine, she just needs a lie down and take some of her pills."

Deloris nod and proceed to help him with his fragile mother when the front door opened and his father's associate Maxwell Keagen entered.

Michael nod for Deloris to continue without him and head towards the front door where he could see the black BMW outside, his father heading up the stairs with a young Korean looking man and his associate beside him.

"You're fathers busy." Said Keagen with a stern yet childish kindness in his voice as Michael, whom he treated like a toddler, approached down the hallway.

Ignoring him, Michael stopped at Keagen's side waiting for his father to enter.

"Really, now is not the time, go to your room!"

"You're not my father..." frown Michael with insult as his father entered the house in his powerful stride commanding attention and reverence, "Hi dad."

Mr. Harper stopped and looked to Keagen uncomforted by his son's attendance.

"You must be Lyle..." said the Asian Mr. Lee with a smile, "I understand you are quite the sportsman?"

"Oh no..." Harper chuckled uncomfortably, "Lyle is my oldest son. This is just Michael."

The man nod with a pretentiously kind smile, "Apologies young man. Nice to meet you Michael."

Michael shrugged, taken aback by his fathers blatant disregard for him and Harper turned to Keagen with annoyance, "Shall we?"

"Yes of course this way Mr. Lee." Keagen said leading them across the oval entrance hall, "We'll be having our meeting in the study. Can I get you some refreshments?"

Harper turned to Michael sighing, "Don't ever embarrass me like that again."

Still speechless, Michael watched them head towards the back of the house wishing to find a way to accustom himself to the coldness of his fathers shoulder in the strife to be recognised as his son albeit nothing as infamous as Lyle.

◻◻◻

The stillness of the night ruptured with the roaring of the black Cortina's engine and skidding of its tyres on the driveway and 17 year old Michael leapt up in his bed in alarm. He listened through the silence as the sound of a slamming car door echoed from the yard and he dart for the window where he saw Lyle dropping to his knees beside the car just ahead of the front steps, the guard at the gate rushing up the way in alarmed confusion.

By the time Michael had rushed down the stairs, the security guard and Deloris the house maid had come to the scene and were

210

already helping Lyle into the house.

"What happened!" asked Michael as his bruised and battered brother tumbled past him towards the lounge area. Lyle slumped into the couch, his lips cut open and both his eyes swollen almost shut.

"Should I call the police?" asked the guard looking to Deloris worriedly. "Where is my father?" asked Lyle breathlessly.

"Here I am." Came Harpers stern voice from the stairs, "Move that noisy tin can to the back where it belongs please Rodney." The guard nod and asked, "Should I have the police come around the house sir?"

"Just move the car. I don't need this kind of publicity right now." Lyle sighed and Deloris hurried to the kitchen for some ice and towels.

"Are you alright? What happened to you bro? Who did this?" asked Michael stepping closer, his body shaking in alarm.

Lyle heaved, "A couple of clients got out of hand. How bad do I look?"

"Who was it?"

Lyle looked down in shame, his brother admired him to much to know the darker side of what he had been doing all these years.

"Michael get out of here!" snapped his father entering the lounge, "I'm certain you still have school tomorrow morning."

"Leave him alone." Said Lyle carefully pressing against his bruised ribs. "Michael, go to bed – now!" said Harper sternly.

"I'm not a child!" Michael snarled when Harper's hand tore across his face.

"Get out of my sight." He said coldly, "You're the biggest regret of my life."

"Bro…" Lyle said sighing wishing that he had more vision through his swollen black eyes, "Just go to your room its ok. Let me hear the old man out."

Michael shoved past his father for the stair case, stomping his feet as he head up and Lyle lay his head back in agony.

"Why do you have to be so abusive to him?" Lyle snarled when they were alone.

"What happened to you?" asked Harper as though without any pity or concern in him. Lyle shook his head, "Just got into a fight that's all."

"I told you before Lyle the next time you want to act like a hooligan you can take your belongings and get out of my house because I will not tolerate this kind of blasphemy against our family name."

Just then Deloris returned with warm towels and ice, "I think we should have you taken to the emergency room…"

"There will be nothing of the sort!" said Harper looking up at her angrily, "Go back to your room Deloris, there is no need to pamper him."

"Oh can you just stop being such an asshole already!" snarled Lyle taking the towels and ice from her, "Jesus I get the point!"

"To your room Deloris!"

"Good night sir." She smiled nervously before turning to Lyle with a concerned and sincere smile, "If you need anything just holler."

"You can leave us now Deloris thank you!" said Harper strictly. Deloris hurried to the back of the house and Harper sighed sitting back in the chair shaking his head.

"You think are you so cool, poisoning your brother against us, turning him into a rebel. At what gain exactly?"

"Mike's not a rebel!" Lyle scoffed, "You wouldn't know anyway."

"I've allowed your little rebellion phase to go on long enough, look at you! You are a mess, is this what you want out of life?"

"Does it even matter?" Lyle scoffed angrily, carefully dabbing the cloth over his broken lip, "You only want me to do what you want me to do! Everything's always about you! Your campaign, your status, your image! No wonder mom chose to have a stroke!"

His father's slap sent him wobbling off the chair, his face and head screaming from the sting.

"If you chose to carry on this way then I'll have no choice but…"

"Suck my dick." He said spitting blood down at his father's slippers from his knees on the floor.

A silence hung as Lyle carefully placed the ice pack over the warm dish rag and Harper stood up, "I want you out of the house as soon as your eyes are open enough to drive. I wash my hands of you."

◖◯◗

"I just want him back!" cried the thin and frail Mrs. Noordman laying in a ball in her daughters lap across the only sofa they had managed to salvage from the repossession of their home. 16 year old Jessica sighed with apprehensive frustration and said, "Mommy you cant keep doing this to yourself, it's not good."

"Look at what we have become!" she cried, sobbing into her daughters lap, "Trash!"

"No mom it doesn't have to be that way!" urged Jessica, "Just because we've hit rock bottom it doesn't mean we can't fight our way back to the top!"

"Oh what do you know?" snarled her mother sitting up and heading to the small bar fridge in the kitchenette, "You're only a child for god sakes, and it's easy for you to say!"

Watching with an annoyed sigh as her mother took the bottle of Jack Daniels her father had been saving, Jessica demanded, "Will you just stop drinking for once!"

"How dare you!" she snarled turning to her angrily, "I'm a grown god damned woman!" she screamed as tears filled her eyes.

Jessica sighed and looked down as her mother continued to pour herself a glass on the rocks.

"I've been out everyday since we've moved into this dump looking for work Jessica, I deserve a drink! Who are you to tell me what to do?"

"I am your daughter mom." Jessica said looking up at her with tears in her eyes. Mrs. Noordman shook her head and gulped down a quarter of the glass.

"You still have me." Continued Jessica softly, "Think of me before you become a drunk."

"A drunk!" laughed her mother, "What do you think we're going to do next Jessica? Huh?" she said raising her voice, "We have no more money, we're running out of food and yet you still see a silver lining! What world do you live in child!"

"I'm sixteen years old mom, I'm only starting to live now, none of this is fair but we have to believe in hope."

"Well then you make a god damned plan for a pay check darling because no one wants to hire me! I've tried everything but we are nothing more than gossip on everyone's lips. Hell I don't even have standard eight! So wake up and know your place young lady because this, this is your life now and nothing you or I do will ever get back what we've lost!"

"We'll see about that!" said Jessica storming towards the small bedroom to the side of the trailer. "Oh really?" laughed her mother, pouring another glass of whiskey.

"Yes really!" said Jessica crying with a bravery in her tone, "I'll finish high school and get out of here, become something! Just like daddy wanted."

"You can forget about it darling!" snapped her mother turning to her angrily, "No trailer park rubbish has ever become anything!"

"Dad wouldn't let us slide backwards!" said Jessica under her breath as she stormed into the room. "What did you say!" shout her mother rushing after her with her glass in the one hand, "What did you say you stupid little cow!"

"I said daddy would never let us slide backwards! He'd never quit on us the way you have!" she shouted when her mothers whiskey splashed into her face.

"You're good for nothing father left us in this shit with unpaid bills and debts!" said Mrs. Noordman behind a broken voice and tears, "If it wasn't for him we would still have our house, our stuff, and a chance at some kind of life! If it wasn't for him you would still be able to have schooling Jessica god damn it!"

Jessica's body fell cold, "What do you mean?"

"Everything has been ceased by debt consolidators in the estate. We lost it all Jess."

Tears filled her eyes again and she asked, "What about getting a social grant to pay for my schooling? You said we could do that?"

Mrs. Noordman reached up to her and pulled her close against her in a tight embrace, "We can't afford to use that money for schooling. Jessie baby listen to me. We are alone now, not even the state can help us because of the tax money he never sorted. It's that amount that's paying for our rent here, your fees haven't been paid since the funeral so it's only a matter of time before they send you packing. I'm so sorry but we need a roof over our heads, or god knows what will happen to us. Your father left us in so much debt. God damn it don't you understand Jessie!" she cried, "Everything we have is gone and the little bit we have is just enough to keep us off the streets!"

Jessie shook her head, "I've got a job! I can get a second job to get through college. Mom! Please! Don't give up on me or us! We can't give up on hope."

⊙⊙⊙

The engine of the small black Honda VFR roared as the motorcycle veered down the gravel road in Unicorn Trailer Park. It had changed over the years since he last saw it, more run down, the grass un-kept and more trailers set up on the grounds. Michael sighed with a heavy anger as he leaned his helmet on the handle bar of his motor cycle. He looked up over the grounds of Unicorn Dam, across the murky water to the other side, eager just to find the one person he could always count on. He had to be with someone who cared enough to give him advice. He had returned from the University of Cape Town at the news of his mothers passing, and the longer he stayed home he more he began to find out about the life he had left behind. With everything spiralling inside his mind, all he wanted to be sure of was Jessie. As he moved towards the Noordman trailer, he noticed the black Cortina shining in the glow of the afternoon sunlight parked near one of the trailers on the opposite side of the dam and his heart beat bounced. *Andre Naude.*

Michael head towards the Noordman trailer 1307 marked in black paint. He knocked on the door, eager to see his long time friend.

"You're the other Harper boy aren't you?" Her mother asked looking him up and down through drunken eyes. He nod, "Michael, how are you Mrs. Noordman?"

"You aren't any more welcome here than that *sleg* brother of yours." She said readying to slam the door.

"Wait, what do you mean?"

"If you want to kuier with Jess you do it somewhere else!" she scoffed, "You Harpers are not welcome here!"

"I don't understand, has my brother been visiting Jessie?"

She grunt shaking her head, "Get away from my property!"

"Where is your daughter ma'am?" he urged worriedly, "I just want to see her."

Mrs. Noordman looked across the park nodding to where the Cortina was parked, "By the boyfriend."

Michael gasped in alarm, but when he turned the door shut in his face and Mrs. Noordman yelled through the door that he never come back. He turned to the Naude trailer in alarmed confusion. *Jessie is dating Andre? Andre Naude? Lyle's Andre Naude? No that can't be! Or is she dating Lyle? That's worse! What did she mean? Does Jessie know about the HIV?*

Carefully prowling towards the trailer, he pressed up beneath the window where he could hear only a soft murmuring of voices. And he carefully raised his head, peering in through the dull netting that hung behind the glass - his heart beat felt almost blocked.

Did he tell Jessie he has HIV? Why wouldn't she tell me they were dating? That makes no sense!

Shock kicked in through his system as he saw his brother sitting with a rubber band strapped around his upper arm, the heroine needle still injected into his veins, the bed covered in money and hand guns and various packs of drugs. The malevolent forty eight year old Andre Naude lay on his back with his best friend in front of the bed on her knee's performing fellatio to him. Michael stumbled backwards, tripping over the Webber braai and hitting the ground with a thud, the coal from inside the braai'er messing out beside him as he tried to scurry back onto his feet. The trailers door flung open and the broad shouldered Andre stepped out tying is belt.

"Wie's jy?" Andre snarled in alarm, "What do you want?"

Riddled in deceit and shock he shook his head and stumbled backwards in a frenzy to escape the reality he had suddenly found himself flung into.

"Where do you think you're going!" demanded Naude grabbing him by the arm and spinning him around, "What did you see in there?"

"Michael?" gasped Jessica from the door in alarm.

"You know this boy?" asked Andre turning to her in distress when Lyle stumbled up behind her, dazed and drugged.

"Let go of me!" said Michael flinging his arm free of Andre Naude's grip and looking hatefully at Jessica who stood with her hand over her mouth in awed alarm.

"Michael..." said Lyle staggering towards him, "What are you doing here?"

"Get away from me!"

Andre shook his head, "Lyle*tjie*, wie's die ou?"

"My brother..." said Lyle shaking his head, "Michael wait!"

"Fuck you!" he snarled turning away when Andre grabbed his arm again.

"Leave him alone Andre!" cried Jessica now shivering.

"Let him go Andre!" snarled Lyle aggressively, "He's my kid brother."

"Not anymore you son of a bitch!" he snarled, turning away when Lyle rushed after him, grabbing him by the shoulders.

"Calm down bro, ok. Take it easy...I can explain this."

Michael shoved at his chest and then punched him in the nose, sending him toppling over Andre's feet and to the ground beside the braai.

Back in front of the Noordman trailer, Michael grabbed his helmet, deciding that he would go back to Cape Town and never return. Everything that he once held dear had vanished and there was no further reason to ever come back.

"Michael." Jessie said stepping behind him just as he was about to put the helmet on; Lyle at the far side of the waters edge with Andre belittling him for taking the punch and not retaliating. Looking into her eyes, he felt his heart wrenching inside his chest as she explained everything he had missed since he left so suddenly four years ago. Everything she tried to do to continue her studies through the post proved effortless, juggling two jobs and home studies couldn't pay for everything she and her mother needed to survive. At a point in the years since they had last seen each other, she was maintaining three jobs to support them, her mother had truly fallen far from grace and during the weakest of her moments, and Jessie turned to Lyle for something to keep her going. Ecstasy added speed to her nervous system and acted as the mood enhancer she'd emotionally lost. It made her feel all the usual effects, happy and relaxed amidst the war of her life. The added energy would help her stay on her feet while still attempting to redo her course and hold onto the work she had.

"He made you pay for drugs when you didn't even have enough money to survive?"

"He helped me keep my jobs Michael." She said angered by the disgust in his tone, "It was worth it to get through everything I needed to."

As she tried to make the one person who mattered see sense of her situation, Michael felt nothing but vile disgust at his brother and at himself for leaving his best friend. She continued to explain how bad her mother's alcoholism had gotten, as means to cope with the numerous men she'd bring to the trailer for some cash in the hopes they would stay long enough to keep supporting them. She explained that cocaine soon became a replacement for the Ecstasy and that during the countries recession she lost her second job and struggled for months to find a job worthy of her time and energy. Both were already running on low due to the extra shifts from her first job and thus struggling to pay for Ecstasy and cocaine lead to her meeting with Andre Naude who agreed to help support her habit in return for favours of a sexual nature.

"You're his whore?"

"No!" she snarled insulted, "It's not like that."

"Then what is it like Jess?" he fumed, "God why didn't you call me? I could have helped you!"

"I don't want your help Michael, I never have!" she snarled, "It's never been anyone's responsibility but my own to keep afloat, to get out of here."

He shook his head angrily, "So you'd rather be his whore than my friend?"

She slapped him across the left side of his face and stepped up to him angrily, "You don't get to judge me! You don't have the right you selfish asshole! The minute we moved out here everything changed, you changed so don't you dare throw it in my face that you are better than me?"

"What?" he gasped stepping back, "Jessie it's not like that, I hated every second knowing that you guys were suffering."

"But you never came Michael! You never once came here, I'd greet you in town you'd ignore me!" She said as tears fell from her face, "You were never around for me when I needed you. That's all I ever wanted Michael, just to know that you were there for me. The way you used to be."

"I was Jessie." He said as lump pitched in his throat, "I never came because I couldn't stand to see you like this. I knew you never wanted my help, you made it clear you'd do it on your own and I couldn't deal with it. How can I greet you if you won't even let me help you?"

She looked down shaking her head, "It doesn't matter now anyway... We're different people."

"I'm not." He said taking her hands in his, "I'm still standing right here, trying to help you..."

She looked down, the hurt in his eyes to much for her to bare.

"Let me help you Jessie. Please!" he urged, "Please let me take care of you. Better than Lyle or Andre ever could."

"No!"

"You can't stay here!"

"And I can't leave my mother!"

"We can figure something out! For both of you!"

"It's too complicated! There are things you don't know about, I cannot just leave I have debt to pay!"

"To who?" Michael gasped, "Andre? Lyle? To hell with them both! I'll take care of it, just please...don't make me beg you again Jessie because I won't come back if you send me off. Please!"

"It isn't your obligation to do anything..." She said stepping back, letting go of his hands, "I'm not the girl who once lived down the road. I'm a different person now and I'm stronger."

"Are you? Or is that the drugs talking?" He said stepping forward as her face flared in anger again, "Jessie, you're the strongest person I've ever met. But that doesn't mean you have to do it alone Jessie. It doesn't mean you have to resort to this...."

"Andre looks after me." She said crossing her arms and looking back to the trailer again as the cold trickled to her bones, "If it wasn't for his money we'd starve."

"And the drugs?"

"Shut up! You don't understand!"

"Jess!" he grabbed her hands again, "I can't walk away knowing that you are here. I won't be able to ever return here if I walk away now."

She frowned shaking her head, "What are you trying to say?"

"I'm saying that I can look after you, and your mother. We can figure this out together, just like when we were kids!"

"Jessica!" Andre's call broke the moment and she stepped back awkward.

"We're not kids though Michael. I did what I had to do to survive and I know you frown on the drugs and on Andre. But I'm ok, whatever he and Lyle have going on that is their business."

"Are you fucking my brother?"

Her mouth dropped open and he quickly added, "I have to know that much at least. You owe it to me."

"I don't owe you shit!" she scoffed angrily, "Go home, to wherever it is you live. This is my life, I've accepted it years ago, so you might as well too."

"Jessie please! Don't do this." He said pleadingly, "Let me…"

"No Michael." She said, "I'm many things, but I'm not a whore."

He frowned confused and she looked down, "I might not love Andre, and I'm not proud of the drugs either. But I have never turned my back on my mother, even in her worst moments. But you did Michael, you turned your back on me the minute we weren't neighbours. The truth is…you are no better than the father you hate."

"That's not true."

A smile crossed her face and she shook her head, "I did your brother Michael."

He looked down, her words like a punch to his gut and she turned off, heading to Andre and they walked off down the hill. He turned towards the sun set, his life slowly slipping away from him like the sun leaving the sky. Every word she had said put a chill inside of him and he knew there was truth in what she said about his father. He had become so swallowed in making his parents acknowledge him, and he refused to give them any reason to write him off as they did Lyle. He had wanted his father's love so badly each day that his mothers' dementia ate away at her that he became the very person Lyle tried to outrun, losing in the wake of it every fibre of what he dreamed of being.

"Bro… Can we talk?" Lyle said stepping up behind him.

◯◯◯

"Please just talk to me bro."
"I don't care Lyle, just get away from me!"
"No! Not until you understand what's going on!"
"I don't care asshole! I hate you!"
"No you don't, you're just angry!"

"I'm sick of the lies man! I'm sick of the bullshit you've been spoon feeding me my whole life! You never wanted this life, you fell into it because of Andre and now you've gotten Jess mixed up in it too!"

"It's not like that bro."

"Don't ever call me that again! I'm done living in your shadow Lyle. It's time dad knows what you are up to, it's time he knows what his beloved son has been doing all these years!"

"He knows Mike. He's always known."

"Is that what this is about? Pissing him off?"

"At first yes it was. Remember that first time I did a gig? I was scared shitless, by that time I was already so deep in debt with drugs..."

"I don't want to hear this."

"Well you have to because you should know, you deserve to know! I got caught up in some bad shit bro, real bad shit. I'm working with Andre to clear my debt with some cops."

"I don't care!"

"I am not letting you leave here thinking that I'm some kind of a monster bro! I did what I had to do to stay alive!"

"So what Lyle? You had some debts, paid them off by becoming a gigolo and now you and Andre are running some kind of business from his trailer. How amazing! While you're at it why don't you just make Jessie pregnant and neglect the baby while you're at it!!"

"What?"

"You knew I loved her since I was a kid!"

"I've never touched Jessie...I swear!"

"Even if you did, I wouldn't be surprised at what you are capable off. God all the years of thinking you were my hero and yet, here you are at the bottom like scum. I don't care what you did or didn't do Lyle. She's done with me, and I'm done with you. You've messed up so much already Lyle, how can I ever love a brother like you? Dad was right...you are disappointment even to me."

"Oh please! You aren't this guy! Look at you with your fancy shoes and bitch jersey! This isn't you Mike! This is you desperate for daddy's attention! You're living a life you don't want! You're doing it all for a man who will never give a shit about you!"

"Screw you asshole!"

"No Mike because the joke's on you! He will never acknowledge you! You aren't even his son! You're not my brother college boy."
"What?"
"That's right Mike. You were adopted. I had a little sister, Linda, who died when she was two. Frank Harper agreed to adopt you to give mommy dearest something to do again. He never accepted you, you were a replacement like one of his staff."
"How can you do this? How can you go so low?"
"I'm sorry but it's the truth. You've spent your whole life trying to get Frank Harper to love you, to see you through my shadow. But it's always been for nothing, and now that mommy dearest is gone and there's no need to play doll anymore, he won't even admit you exist. So run home college boy, I dare you. In this world I'm all you got because I'm the only one who ever truly loved you like a blood brother!"
"I know about your HIV Lyle. And you know what brother? I hope you die alone."

Their last conversation echoed in his ears as he raced across the highway full throttle, eager to leave behind everything and never look back. He knew that Lyle wanted to tear at him but refrained even at the harshest moments and he fought back the guilt of what he had said. He didn't care, he never wanted to.

In the months that followed, despite him trying to study or focus, party or keep up the charade in Cape Town, Jessie's words still ate at the twine of his soul and the more he tried to deny it the more it rang true in the people he had surrounded himself with at the university. He was everything his father wanted Lyle to be and he had been so desperate for the affection that he didn't realize the counterfeit in the short and small moments he saw his father. It was always something to whisk away to, a meeting to attend or a phone call. Frank Harper couldn't look at the adopted play thing and pretend it was anything close to the son who denied him.

In the course of three weeks, Michael struggled to make the phone call to his father but when it finally happened, it was the hardest call he ever had to make.

"It's true, you are the bastard son of some woman who wanted nothing more than get rid of you. We took you in and we all tried. What a relief that you know, I'm surprised you called. What do you want to do about it exactly?"

By midnight that night he found himself standing in the glowing neon lights outside of the club 'Influence', one of the best known rave clubs in the Cape area where anything and everything was possible to obtain. Going inside would mean shedding the skin of what he become since Lyle was banished from the family. He knew that once he stepped in he would be walking out as everything against what his father had so badly wanted for Lyle, against everything he had worked to be – he would be surrogate prince no more and instead mould himself into anything to hurt his father. As he head home in the early hours of the morning in a circle of new friends, he knew through the rush that he was nonetheless retracing the same path that Lyle had.

◻◻◻

The screen of his cell phone lit up on the table beside his bed in the dorm room, the ring tone blaring beside his head but he couldn't force his eyes open. He reached for the phone but it was only inches from contact, his arm fell beside the bed exhausted from the week's non-stop partying following the night at club Influence. The cell rang and rang, but he felt depleted of life, he couldn't answer it. And finally the ringing stopped. He turned his head, waiting to fall back into a deep sleep when the door to his room burst open at the hand of his two room mates Viran and Alan.

"Yo! Are you dead Harper?" Viran asked leaning against the door post. He wanted to talk, but even his voice was exhausted and instead he just groaned. The partying never stopped, he barely recalled the faces staring at him.

"Your phone has been ringing non stop!" Alan said nudging him in the back, "You're behind on your share of the rent and there's a note on the counter from headmistress Delubom, you're getting expelled."

Michael growled again, his voice dry, "Go away."

"It's been ringing all day non stop." Viran sighed, "Please try get up so we can talk dude, and you're behind on your share of…."

"Everything…" Alan huffed.

"Back off! Leave me alone!"

The two boys head off sighing and huffing angrily and the phone rang again. Michael grabbed the phone, "What?"

"Michael! Where have you been?" Max Keagen's voice said anxiously, "We've been trying to reach you!"

"What do you want Max? I have nothing to say so tell my father to go to hell." Michael said cutting the call.

It rang again.

"Jesus Max what the hell do you want?"

"Michael please don't hang up." Max urged, "I have some bad news Michael, you're brother's dead."

"What?" Michael said shooting up.

"They found him on Saturday morning, I'm so sorry Michael." Michael's heart raged inside his chest, his head spinning as his body fell cold and numb, "What? I don't understand…"

"Come home Michael, this isn't something to discuss over the phone."

"Where's my father?" Michael asked, regretting the word as it left his parched lips.

"He's broken Michael. I've never seen him like this. You need to come home, I think he would appreciate that."

"Saturday? What day is it?"

"I know what you are thinking Michael but…"

"It's Tuesday." Said Michael as tears welled in his dark eyes, "You waited all this time to tell me?"

"This is a time for the family to be together, and you are all he has now. Please come home."

Michael clenched the phone, "How…how did it happen?"

"Michael this isn't something to discuss over the phone, please come…"

"How did it happen Max?" Michael snarled interrupting him, "Please…just tell me…"

There was a silence and Michael stewed in remorse, suffocating on the last words he said to his brother. Finally Keagen sighed, "Suicide. He…he was found in a shed at the old Leslie mine. He hung himself Michael."

Keagen's voice, for the first time in all the years that he had known him, held in it a sincere sadness and regret as he spoke. "He was full of drugs…he left a note." Keagen paused, "Please, come home."

For eight days after the funeral the world still felt cold and empty. Nothing made sense, the suicide note plagued him. He wanted more from it but no matter how many times he stared at the page there was nothing more but empty words. He couldn't believe that his brother had done it, the words didn't seem to be from him and he kept wishing there was a page somewhere that could prove it was his hand writing on the back of the post office mailing sheet.

I am done now. I have lived and I am ready to meet God. Dad, Mikey don't be sad. I want this. It's my time. I did this because I want to be happy and free of this world. Forgive me for being so selfish. I love you. Lyle.

Diving head first into the life his brother once lived, Michael began wearing Lyle's favourite leather jacket and using his car. Being home just drove him further and further to craving anything to numb him from the guilt and remorse. He took residence at the bachelor townhouse where Lyle lived, leaving only briefly through the bathroom window after a few men in black suits and shades came turning the place upside down looking for something they couldn't find. There was food in the fridge and cupboards and enough drugs and alcohol to keep him out of site long enough to figure out what would happen next. Everything was Lyle Harper, except it was silent and would never be refilled with him again. He retired into solitude and would sit for days without eating or sleeping properly. He made use of all the drugs he could find in the unit and surrendered to a different numbness.

It was only when Jessie knocked on the door begging for his help that he realized how much time had truly passed since he first walked into the townhouse.

They head off in the Cortina, the pedal to the floor as it shot across the tar with the sun beginning to set on the horizon. Everything she had explained riddled him with anger and pushed his thirst for revenge. As she spoke about his brother's involvement in the business two policemen controlled, the more it became clear to him that only one person was responsible for his brother's death and the only verdict was death.

As the Cortina's black wheels skid to a stop on the far edge of the water near Andre's trailer, the rage within him was staggering and driving him forward.

There was never truly any real chance of taking Naude down but even with bruises and cuts on his face, Michael kept pushing himself back up from the trailer floor. Seeing Jessie strewn on the ground crying in pain, he knew he had to do everything he could to save her because he had already ignored everything his brother was trying to tell him the last time he saw him alive.

"Ag nee…You don't have what it takes boy'tjie." Andre laughed wiping the spit from his moustache, "I didn't kill your brother."

"Who did?"

Andre laughed shaking his head, "Wasn't me…"

Michael hobbled to his feet and motioned forward but his knees collapsed from exhaustion and pain and he toppled down by the door. Andre had punched him repeatedly in the ribs and it was crushing any chance of survival.

"I'm going to let you get out of here boy'tjie, and don't come back for this bitch. She's my pussy now."

Leaning over him, Andre shoved open the door and kicked him three times before he finally hit the gravel outside the trailer. As he lay there, everything was on the verge of breaking within his soul. The sky above dark now as stars glimmered as though to offer hope down the road of blackness he had found himself on, beaten and worn. The pain of his brother's death, his mother's death, his father's hatred, his friend's innocence stolen, and his life so severely off course balanced on what he would do next.

Gripping Jessie's hair tightly in his fist, Andre dragged her to her feet to face him, slamming her into the wall.

"There is no quitting." He snarled, his mouth foaming with thick spit that sat on his moustache, "I need you to bring in the dough bokkie, there is no quitting now."

"Please, let me go!" she cried, her ribs aching from the kicks he delivered in front of Michael. He shook his head grinning, "You are my piece of ass girlie, now stop it before I teach you a lesson."

The door opened behind him and turned to Michael who spat blood to the steps. "I'm not done yet."

Andre grit his teeth and turned to him.

"Nou is ek gatvol vir jou kak…" He heaved, stepping down two of the three steps. Michael raised the plank he tore of the white picket fence and rammed it towards Naude, but with his hairy big hands Andre caught it just inches before it hit his fat belly. Michael pushed with all his might, crying from the pain in his body but Andre held it firmly, laughing at his face with only 3 feet between them. Every fiber of his muscles began to burn and Michael was just about to drop back and let Andre have the plank to further destroy him when Jessie pounded a kick into Andre's back from behind causing him to lunge forward. Between Michael's force and Jessie's kick, the plank tore through Andre's belly and Michael gasped.

Gargling blood, Naude turned on the step to face Jessie, his hand reaching out for her and his eyes wide with betrayal and terror. Michael rammed him forward, and it was only when his body slammed down onto the steps into the trailer that the sharp end broke through his back, allowing a flow of blood to gush from him.

In the hours of the night that passed, he and Jessie hurriedly washed and watered away any signs of the fight, leaving Andre's corpse on the stairs. There was no plan, there was no speaking – they just hurried to cover their tracks and any evidence of the fighting that night. When they were certain, the sun began to rise and finally Jessie spoke.

"I haven't seen him since he hit me, I know he was drinking and doing drugs in the middle of the night. He probably fell through it and crawled back into the trailer."

Michael shook his head with solemn concern, unable to feel any remorse for the fat abuser, "We're screwed."

Sanctuary only lasted for three days before the police were notified of the smell inside the trailer. Nkosi and Venter were the first to arrive and the first to pull Jessie into their van.

She held herself throughout the drive out into the fields, and even more braved them hitting and slapping at her to get the answers they wanted. Their concern only for who to use as their mule and nothing more. When Venter threatened to rape her, and began tearing off her panties she reached the limit and the truth bubbled out. Within hours, she and Michael were in the back of the van together being taken out into the nothingness where Nkosi and

Venter could ensure that no one would ever hear of their plans to ensure survival of their business.

—╫—Chapter six cont—╫—

Pandora's Box

The fields surrounding the dark mouth in the earth stood silent. A breeze moved in the shadows and it was cold.
Mr. Lee stood looking out at the blackness and he could almost feel the darkness looking back at him. He turned around again, shaking his head he grinned.
"There is no point in arguing this any further. There is not enough money to shut you up."
"Please! Please don't kill me!"
"Then you should not have ran." Lee said coldly, "And why come to this desolate place anyway? Just too convenient…"
Removing this customised Nighthawk Bob Marvel, Lee took aim and almost instantly fired the shot. The blast echoed into the empty field and the body of the tall African man flung backwards. The force of the shot into his chest, sent the body stumbling – his legs propping against the concrete maw surrounding the mouth of the giant abandoned mine shaft.
Mr Lee and the two men in black suits rushed to grab hold of him before he went over into the blackness, but the body tumbled down just out of their reach. Slamming into the support beams they could hear it descending into the rotting darkness.
Turning to face the two men standing near the black sedan parked to the side, Lee felt his breath escape him.
"Well, we'll have to get it back up here." Said Lee heading back to the dark sedan. "That won't be possible sir." Mr Black said matter-of-factly. Lee nod with a heavy sigh and opened the car door, sliding in.
"The body will be forgotten down there, in fact it's almost too perfect. In a few years the heat and moisture would have decayed it beyond recognition." Lee said with a grin.

General Gondwe looked to the gaping shaft nervously, "That wasn't the plan Lee. You said you had control over the runaway." "I did, clearly. Look this wasn't part of the plan at all, but here we are and I'm good at making split second decisions, it's why King trusts me. General Gondwe, as alarming as it might seem right now, this does work in our favour."

"Tonight we finalised the end stage of the Face program Mr. Lee and any other loose ends need to be tied up now, we don't need anything standing in our way. Not a single thing." Said Gondwe sternly, "You have this misfortune on your shoulders Mr. Lee, any ripple effect is on you!"

Lee nod nervously and Gondwe looked to the door handle. Rounding the car again as the suited men tried in vain to see any glimmer of the fallen man, Lee turned and offered a wave as the sedan rolled off along the grassy gravel.

"Sir!" came a breathless call from the side as one of his men came rushing back through the dark field, "A vehicle just sped off from behind the brush about 400 meters south."

Mr Lee's eyes turned and in the distance the red rear lights faded in the darkness. "Sir, I gave chase, but he got away. I can't be sure sir, but what caught my attention was a flashing red light much like one on a camcorder. I got a clear visual on the make sir, black Ford Cortina."

"Find that car!" Barked Lee angrily, heading towards the shafts concrete maw and looking down into the blackness.

"Decomposition over a year or two, no one will ever know." Came Agent Black beside him, his arms folded over his waist and his black shades covering his eyes. "Deal with that." Said Lee cocking his head to the black SUV that skid away after the black Cortina, "I'll deal with Mayor Harper, I want someone on this shaft every day for the next two months just in case. Make sure they find that car Mr. Black."

He nod and they head to the remaining SUV, "From this point onwards, anyone who stands in our way dies. I don't care how much they know or how much they think they know."

Before getting in, Lee looked out across the blackness surrounding them and he shook his head, returning his stare into the black abyss of the old E Shaft where one of the biggest conspiracies in South African history now lay miles below.

Chapter Seven:
Fixation

The storm had come and the sun shone following it. In the three weeks following the macabre discovery of the human hand on the fifth level of the mineshaft, the small communities of Brendan, Evander and Secunda had been riddled with a suspenseful excitement as the buzz surrounding the mine grew into a production fiasco.

Within 48 hours of the discovery of the decayed and rotting thumb, index and middle finger portion of the black man's hand, all production on the sections of the mine had been enforced to a strict halt by the national counsel. Police had cordoned off the area as the search and rescue teams began their decent into the shaft in the hopes of finding the remainder if any of the hands owner. Intense discussions were held across the board of investors pertaining to the delays expected on the reopening as well as the costs involved. After having searched out the mine's former security executives, it became apparent that on the mines original shut down an 'all clear' was given, the tunnels and stopes were entirely evacuated and the shaft was flooded.

Police forensics found that the hand had been laying in the murky, putrid waters of the shaft for a period of four to five years - ruling out negligence on the mines part. Further inquiry into missing persons commenced, but to assert the identity on the decayed hand was proving difficult for specialists due to the water damage to the skin and tissue.

As specialized search teams continued to descend deeper into the shaft to examine and search each and every nook and cranny of the underground tunnels and man made caverns of mine, another item of concern was discovered. A size nine, left, male Armani shoe was found lodged between debris on the sixth level on the south western side of the shaft, the explosion had caused the securing net to tremble and release the debris. All the material previously used to fill the shaft at its shut down was being searched with microscopic detail, but the amount of debris meant much delay to the police investigation. The courts were still to rule on who had jurisdiction over the matter as the police special unit and department of mining went head to head. The politics had grown out of proportion, there will too many unanswered questions and numerous investigations into the shutdown procedures from eight years before to get through.

Mr. Lee and the rest of the Corporation he represented were fuming at saga unfolding, their secret on the verge of being exposed as the hounds of teams continued to search to through the cleared debris and mine tunnels, with them too fighting on either side of the court battle to, regardless of the outcome, secure a position in the investigation.

The tension, upset and angst grew thick as more and more pressure befell the reopening of E Shaft as media channels around South Africa hounded the story for scoops.

Joel and his mother had barely spoken since confronting her about the 'Crisp Cool Pools' van at their house. Since Collins memorial, everything about his personality had flipped and no longer was he bound by money or name to be someone he didn't want to be. The Delta Caps had all but fallen apart within their circle because it was difficult for any of them to truly come to terms with Collin taking his life and blaming it on everything he endured having to live in secret.

Although they were trying to pull together and form back to what they were, everything around campus and the mood that hung on all the students walking past the giant memorial erected against the fountain made it difficult for anyone to move past the suicide on campus. He found it easier to be Joel by having Kyle at his side because it was Kyle's demeanor that encouraged him to stop carrying the family crest as a branch for other's to perch on. With Kyle, he no longer felt timid and bendable to the people around him, although inside he felt timorous but remained fixed on his goal to no longer be who others wanted him to be. He valued Kyle for never once speaking to him like anything but the guy next door, and the more he withdrew from the flaunting of his trust fund the easier it became to forget about the problems at home. He had broken a link of his torment chain and each day more links would follow. He was adamant to be open to everyone around him by being real and never leaving anything for another afternoon because he had lost it being to proud to dial Collin. Kyle's torture was evident in everything and although Kyle tried desperately to hide it and deny it, Joel knew that he was merely well trained in the dodging of any form of personal poking. Being free of the Delta Caps and any other person only sponging from him gave him a sense of freedom in his mind, not having the constant turmoil to keep quiet and pay. But to have that freedom, meant being set aside and starting all new friendships and trying to find out where he would fit in.

The breakup with Bronwyn boosted him into popularity throughout the campus, mostly because of his charm during Bronwyn's melt down. Each ounce of pent up aggression he harbored began pouring out in private swim practices, but he kept an unintentional distance from everyone who knew him because he felt it was time to be alone and to figure out who he was going to be after college. The strange and mysterious Kyle Evans had grown close to him because it meant being able to hide behind him until he was able to figure it out and not suffering pure isolation in the process.

Liz had found herself trying to follow Kyle around as often as possible, always trying to cross his path for another chance to see him and exchange a few words. She had found herself obsessed with him, every move he made, the way he smiled, his hands, his walk, the way he frowned whenever he realized that girls were staring at him or trying to chat him up. She cherished the way he twitched nervously, breathlessly when girls or guys were talking to him and it even angered her to see how many girls wanted to engage him. They'd been spending more brief moments together in passing on campus, often pausing for chit chat or sharing a bench in the shade. It was clear that he was a very private person and that he had some demons in his past, but more than fixing him it was her goal to simply know who he was behind the pretense.

She found herself constantly watching him and thinking about him, in esteem and admiration, lust driven over every single aspect about him. Her mind was all Kyle Evans, she had never felt so turbulently fixated on anyone and more than air, she relished each moment he would talk to her even when his mysterious electricity was both frustrating and tiresome. And each time she brought up a get together after school he would withdraw again. It was his depth that stirred her lust, his body that stirred her desires and it was his smile that made her know that he was the one. And the thought puzzled her because she barely knew the boy she wanted. And more so, it was evident that to him that such a place was forbidden, and she desperately wanted to know why he felt that way. And the more it felt illicit, the more she felt certain that it was what she needed, what she had been waiting for.

For Kyle the days were long and difficult. Portraying what he thought was close to normal took a very taxing emotional and mental toll – having to somehow be one step ahead of the typical befriending questions, gestures and activities. Although he knew that he had control over his Haphephobia and could easily part take in high-fives or fist bumps even, he chose to maneuver around them. The constant paranoia followed him from dawn to dusk and beyond, with the ever tormenting thought that he could be recognized at any given time and as a result be found by those he knew were looking for him, waiting for their chance to sink their claws back into his skin.

He found himself constantly making subtle moves to get people's hands off him without being rude or aggressive, constantly having to be patient and polite, constantly have to force himself to be a way he had long forgotten how to be – part of more than just the darkness of his soul. Andy had gained his respect, but she too became harder to lead on as the first weeks of their sessions progressed. He found himself living in two places at the same time. One, the dark and bare world he deserved, isolated from feeling anything but utter guilt and self loathing and the other was the reality of his new life in the public eye, where he could no longer just release his rage and tear people down.

With Liz, he found himself suffering from emotions he had no understanding off, and it was frightening and freeing at the same time. But as with everyone, the more he tried in vain to distance himself from his sudden reality, the more he failed. With Liz failing was welcomed, and he couldn't make sense of it, which frustrated him and pushed him to want to end the chaos in his mind. Every second he spent with Liz, made him feel further from the darkness. In their talks he had found himself more and more able to smile and laugh and share ideas with her, more than he had ever done before with any person. And through this, he grew closer to Joel and began to feel, very slowly, at ease with his ever growing popularity on campus.

Home, college and everything in between were beginning to grow exhausting and although it was rare Claire or Edward could pick it up, he himself felt that if he didn't make a choice regarding playing it out it would eventually lead to him suffering a form of fit.

Michael, after having failed to meet Nkosi's weekly target, had remained locked up in his brothers flat. He hadn't heard or seen his father or anyone else since the findings at the Leslie Mine E Shaft. Jessie nursed him, even though he hated her seeing him weak and vulnerable. Each time she came with soup or ice packs, he'd feel a part of him engulfed in shame. The swelling and bruising felt to him like a blessing of sorts. It was time borrowed to avoid exploiting his body to their usual clients or approaching dealers and users for whatever substance Venter expected. Through this, his mind remained preoccupied with worry for Jessie who kept up the drug sales. Nkosi had beaten him with his police baton, smashed the windows of his car and tore off both side mirrors and the petrol cap door. And as he recovered, the more stressful he became of them doing something to Jessie in his absence. The more panicked he became to get back into the swing of things again, and as per Nkosi's violent instruction – increase revenue no matter what it took.

Jessie found herself surprisingly adept to liaising with Mike's clients during drug trades, even in how she handled Nkosi's disconcerting behavior each time he'd meet with her to give her supply. She hadn't until that week realized how busy the cell phone Nkosi had supplied was - it rang and received texts almost each hour on the hour. It had never occurred to her that she was doing much less than Michael towards keeping Nkosi happy, but she refrained from thanking him because the hand jobs and other sexual acts she engaged in with him still upset her aggressively, even though she insisted to do her part for their crime. And because of the cell phone she learnt more about him than she had ever known, especially about how he had constantly been protecting her from Nkosi's instructions to sleep with anyone who asked. As well of all the other deals that could have helped them reach target but that were ignored for her sole benefit. Each time she'd reach his flat and see him shattered and bruised, she wanted to tell him how grateful she was, but she knew it would only push him further away. He had grown closed over the years, but in everything he kept her safe.

He wanted to run but knew he could not outrun what was inside. He started off so fixated on being like his brother, but so easily found it sickening who that person was.

The more time they spent together in his flat, alone as though the outside world had never existed, the more they began to see their old self's evolving from the dark lives they had been cast into. He noticed her smiling more often, and she realized that not everything about him had been completely lost. They spent time playing cards, talking about their childhood memories and just being twenty something adults without the vile of reality peering at the windows. Each frightened for his wounds to heal.

The nibbling bite of the winter air had already begun to sting, the suns dim glow touched the earth but gave it only a glow and no real warmth. The bare trees and deadened grass simply gave eeriness to the small towns in the area, as though forgotten and abandoned of the living. With the police and department of mineralogy sitting down with students, Collin's suicide began to be an after-thought as the tension grew surrounding the findings at E Shaft. Alone at the pool, Joel swam and swam the length of the pool hoping to escape the guilt inside. But the water did not clear him as it once did, instead it added weight to his thoughts. As he burst up for air beneath the diving boards, he noticed the legs hanging beside his head and he moved in alarm.

"Sup." Rendani said frowning awkwardly.

Sitting on the bench in the quiet swimming hall, the two of them spoke in low voices, careful for the echo in the emptiness.

"It is our faults the shaft collapsed, I think we need to go back and say something." Joel sighed worriedly, "I just didn't know how to when they sat me down…"

"First of all, it isn't entirely our fault." He raised his hands, "You lit a fuse that night, nothing more. Whatever brought that place down was more than just fuse chord dude."

"But we have to say something about us being out there, our stupid fuse chord could be throwing them off. Jesus Rendani, a man died down there!"

"Yes, four years ago." Rendani said, "So that isn't on us. Besides who is going to take the fall for this? It's supposed to have been a tradition in the Caps – five of us went before you did."

"And your fuses were dug up or pumped out with the rest of the shit down there! I went when the damn thing was pretty much cleared!"

Joel sighed in frustration that his nerves were constantly tense since the fuss around E shaft began.

"Well you came to me Rennie…so what is it you want to do exactly?"

"I just wanted to know what you said to them, Brian sent me to ask you. We all just need to know you didn't say anything. I mean, face facts here Joel it was just a fuse! It couldn't have done anything and the police know that. I just need to know you have the Delta Cap's in your best interest here."

"Like you all did with Collin?"

Rendani sigh with a heavy heart, "We've learnt that it's…"

The coach's whistle echoed in the swim hall as the Delta Cap undergrads hurried through the doors towards them.

Joel for a moment watched them, missing the team but sighed and turned to Rendani, "Well you can all relax, I never said anything but I'm not going to promise you anything either."

Mr. Lee hurried down the steps of the small Jet plane across the tarmac to the golden SUV where two more men in black suits stood waiting. As he stepped into the car the driver leaned back holding out a cell phone, "It's the director general sir."

Lee sighed and grabbed the phone, "General." He smiled answering.

"Is everything arranged?" came Director General Gondwe's short reply.

"Yes sir, everything for plan B is set to go, I've just landed back in South Africa and am currently en route to the mine as we speak."

"What about Harper?"

"He's handling things."

"Agent Black removed from the assignment?"

"No general. He's inside now, I do regret he wasn't there to find the hand, but we're past that point of control now. As long as he is inside McDonald's circle, we have a way to direct the situation to suit us."

"For everyone's sakes! No loose ends Mr. Lee." Gondwe said dropping the call.

Lee sighed with frustration, slumping back into the car seat regretting having fired the shot four years ago that started it all. Yet he knew that there was no way to control which way the body fell, he just wished the members of the Corporation would acknowledge it.

"So here we are again." Andy said smiling up at Kyle as he entered, "Enjoying the cold?"

Kyle nod with a sarcastic smirk and took his usual seat.

"So, how you feeling today?" she asked.

He shrugged, "Fine I guess."

"Is the campus still so heavy for you?"

"For everyone I think. It's been a strange few weeks since that boy hung himself." Kyle said softly, "Everyone is so sad all the time even those that didn't know the guy."

"It's in our nature to feel and experience loss at the thought of death."

"Only if you haven't been around it enough."

She looked down at his file, recalling the grizzly notes inside.

"So, what are your thoughts about the E Shaft?"

"Are you really interested in what I think about that?"

"Well, I'm not going to attempt discussing anything else since you'll just refuse and we'll spend our time arguing again."

He smiled, "It's been rough this last while Andy, and it's not that I refuse, we do speak about a lot of things."

"Yes, vague discussions at best." She wrenched back with a sigh, "Discussions that you keep using to lead us from where we should be heading to."

"And where is that Andy?"

"I want to know who you are, and after all this time, I still don't."

He shook his head frowning, "I don't think that's true."

"I don't know you."

"No one should."

"That is what I'm talking about!" she sighed irately. "Is that really who you are Kyle, cold, closed, withdrawn?"

"It's who I choose to be." He replied looking up with an uncompromisingly certain tone, "It's the way I survive."

"And what happens next?" she asked leaning forward on her elbows, "Where do you go from here? Can you imagine anyone wanting you to work for them? And I'm not only referring to your history Kyle, I'm referring to the way you engage with people."

He looked down as a weight befell his shoulders, realizing that he had never given his life a future, he had always assumed he would never make it. She felt the tautness radiate off of him and she sat back in her chair.

"You have no clue do you?" She frowned sympathetically, "I don't believe you even want a future Kyle."

He laughed shaking his head, "Why would any person not want a future, that's insane."

"Is it really?" she said with a frustrated stern glare, "Because you have taken almost every single subject Seymore has to offer without any particular major. You don't know where to go from here yet Kyle, and you know what? That's fine. Most of those college kids have no idea where they want to be when they graduate. But eventually Kyle, you won't have any more time to play with. Eventually you'll be in the real world, and trust me it happens in the blink of an eye and one day you'll realize you spent a good part of your life missing life itself."

He sighed shaking his head, "Did you know who you wanted to be when you were in college?"

"I knew I wanted to help people."

"Are you happy with where you are in your life Andy?"

She grinned shaking her head in disbelief, "Stop trying to lead, it's getting old."

He too grinned and looked down nervously, the pressure in her tone uncomforting.

"Moving on, you seem to have made a few friends at least, mighty popular I believe." She said moving off the subject that caused a vague sign of tears forming in his eyes, "That's a good start, something I didn't expect so suddenly."

"I don't have friends." Said Kyle matter-of-factly, "I don't know why people insist on talking to me."

"I refuse to beat around the bush, it is what it is Kyle. You can't move on until you accept it and own it. You are no longer Boy X, you are Kyle Evans. Step out of the dark room and into the light."

"There are a lot of rooms to get through."

"So pick a room, which one do you want to walk out of first."

"All of them."

"Pick one."

He looked away, "It's not that simple…"

"Then let's talk about the fighting." She said taking a deep breath, "Two years ago you briefly touched on it with Doctor Naidu."

"There's not much to say." His voice shuddered, "It was cold. We had to do whatever it took to stay alive, to avoid punishment."

He sighed, his eyes welling with tears.

"You feel guilt don't you?" She asked softly, "For being here while so many others are still lost."

"How can I not?" He said looking up at her, his dark blue eyes piercing and filled with fear, "I shouldn't be so lucky to be here, free again and with a life."

"But you are Kyle. There is no denying it." She smiled, "Your story all those years ago has already saved so many others."

"Not enough!"

"It's a start."

"It's too late for so many of them." Tears filled his eyes, "Andy its cold there. It's like…death."

She looked down, "Take me there Kyle."

He shook his head and the red life flared through his memories.

"I don't remember how long I was there." Kyle said softly, "Beaten near death, some never made the training at all. Bodies were taken and I don't know where they were put. Some of us stayed together, helping each other. Others were just there to die. They knew they wouldn't make it so they never tried."

She nod, watching his face as her heart weighed on her for the horrors of his past.

"Boys and girls weren't separated, it didn't matter to them. We were just pawns." He said as the red life echoed behind his eyes, "The younger ones were weaker and we couldn't…"

She looked away as tears fell down his face.

"We weren't allowed to have any sympathy for them, we weren't allowed to show anything. They wanted killers."

He heaved a deep breath and turned to her, "There was a girl they called Boa. I had already been there a while, I don't know how long. They were training the younger kids by having them go up against the older ones. Boa couldn't go against the kid anymore and she tried to stop, to refuse but…."

Silence hung, she knew he was back there.

"After they slit her throat we were all made to watch them continue the training with the kid boy. It only lasted a few minutes." Kyle looked away and a silence filled the room again.

"We had to train and we had to be the best. If it wasn't against each other it was against one of them. Didn't matter because if you weren't what they wanted you would be beaten to pulp or die anyway. Every day the same, it never stopped. Not once."

"Do you remember how long you were there?"

He shook his head, "Time changes when every second is a fight to live, where you don't know anything but pure fear every waking moment."

The room was silent and he dropped back his head, staring up at the ceiling.

"When they knew you were good enough to kill without remorse or fight without being afraid of pain then we were moved again, back to whomever wanted us or owned us."

She nod, her notes hurriedly scrawled along the pages of her book as her eyes watched him.

"You say owned. How many owners did you have?"

He dropped his gaze back to her and shrugged, his eyes almost grey as he stared at her.

"I don't remember much of the beginning, flashes mostly. It never

really mattered, nothing made any difference. I was dead from the moment they had me anyway. Or at least I thought I was."
His voice quivered.

"When they take you…you become nothing. Saying that you are property isn't even close to what you really become when they have you. You are expendable and will be whatever they want you to be. If they want fighters, you do it or you die. If they want you for sex, you do it or you die. Whatever they want, you be. 'V' would make sure that there was nothing else that mattered. If you run, you die. If you refuse, you die. If you make a choice, you die. You become something that exists outside of the natural realm, something numb and grey – empty."

She listened and watched him intently, her body cold to the words coming from his mouth, his dark blue eyes were chilling and wild.
"There are so many of them, you wouldn't believe how easily they walk among us." He said softly wiping his cheeks, "They move in the daylight disguised as normal, as humans. We are blind to their existence because the world is trained to recognize the devil as a red beast with horns and a pitchfork. But in reality he lives in the shadows of broad day light, watching and waiting, scanning and looking for the right moment to take what he wants and drag it with him to a place where you live only because God enjoys the show."

"Do you really believe that God enjoys watching people suffer?"
He shook his head, "There is no other way to explain how I am alive today."

Andy smiled, "Because you are survivor Kyle. You are the strongest person the world has ever heard of."

"But I'm not the only Boy X." he said composing himself and pushing back the pain, "There are hundreds of girls and boys out there."

"And you survived to tell the world about it Kyle." She said putting the book down and shifting the recorder to the side as she leaned forwards on her desk, "You are here today because your story saved lives, you survived to save others."

He looked down, his hands clenched tightly together.
"It's ok to save yourself now Kyle." She smiled, "You have to let yourself be saved."

"It isn't fair." He said looking up at her again, "I don't think it's fair to save myself."

She heaved a sigh and smiled again, "You will Kyle, if you let go of the past."

"Let go of it?" he frowned with a snarl on his face, "There is no letting go of it Andy! It's a nightmare I live every day, every time I see my reflection or walk into a dark room. Every time I notice someone looking at me. I live in fear every day that I am going to taken. I can't forget it, I can't let go of it. I can't escape where I've been or what I've seen."

Tears crawled back into his eyes.

"I'm tired all the time. Because truth is Andy…I'm scared…all of the time."

Dr. Morris heaved a sigh, the torture and torment behind his eyes was crystal clear and for the first time she could see the boy called Kyle Evans.

"I just want to be left alone. I'm comfortable numb." He said cumbersomely shaking his head in surprise that he had exposed his raw self so openly to her after years of trying to hide the turmoil within him.

"Everyone wants to save me somehow and bring me out of the darkness…But the truth is Andy, I like it here because it's all I know. It's the only way to be ready for the day I get taken again."

A silence hung and she looked to the recorder on her desk. There was a vast depth to Boy X, to the deep mysteries of his missing years and she looked up at him feeling a world of sympathy for his sordid soul.

"For every day that you allow your world to get a little bigger, a little more light will come in." she said smiling, "You might never forget it, but as time passes you might just find that it doesn't control you."

He looked up at her and managed a weak smile, "Sounds like a tomorrow I don't believe in."

"Let's not pretend any of this is going to be easy. But I promise you Kyle that I believe in your tomorrow. So you can add me to the people in your life that bring you such rotten misery by trying to love you." She teased.

A smile crossed his face, "You really are different Dr Morris."

"I just want you to feel safe Kyle. It's what everyone wants." She smiled, "None of us can ever take away what happened, or your memories or even the terror you feel every day. But we can protect you from it by doing our best to help you find a way to live past your history and have a future."

He looked down shaking his head, silently screaming.

"Let's talk about why are you afraid of being touched?" she said reopening his file. "I'm not afraid." He said defensively, "I just don't like how I feel when people are close to me."

"How you feel?" she frowned, "And how do you feel?"

"Scared, for them." He sighed, "It's in my file because I've answered this before."

"Yes you have" she smiled, "But I don't buy it."

He smirked watching as she found the transcript from one of Dr Naidu's recordings.

"I am scared that I make everyone black by what is inside of me. You motherfuckers won't understand that because you are all blind fuckers who think I am safe to touch. I will fucking kill you all."

He huffed a short giggle shaking his head, "That was a very long time ago, early stages of progress."

She shrugged her shoulders, "Then explain it to me now, why the issue with touch?"

Kyle sighed and crossed his legs up on the chair, "The minute someone gets close to me, I risk hurting them."

"Because of what? The rage?"

"The rage." He nod, "And because I don't think I'm healthy for anyone. It's too easy to hurt them if I get taken again."

"What makes you so sure you are still being looked for? Why are you so certain that you will be taken?"

"No one ever got away, not alive."

A silence hung and she sighed, taking a moment to think before speaking again.

"Kyle can I be frank for a moment?" she paused awaiting his approval. "I think it would help if you start taking on new things in your life, it's a great distraction from what's in your head. You've walked in here a different person the last few sessions and it's because you are surrounding yourself with people at college. Dean Watts reported that the way other students treat you, it's with a reverence and intrigue. Most kids seem utterly fascinated by you, especially…Liz Parker."

"Your stalking methods are both creepy and intrusive Andy, and you really should seek out professional help."

She laughed.

"I want to show you something Andy."

He heaved a deep breath standing up.

Other than the medical doctors who saved his life, the last time any person saw him without a shirt on was in the ring back in the world where everything was jaded by red and since then he had constantly kept himself isolated. He removed his jacket and placed it on the chair, carefully trying to find the strength to reveal his body to her. She sat back as he stood up and began to raise his shirt from the bottom up. As the fabric slid up over his stomach and chest, she felt herself lull at the sight of his perfectly toned abdominal muscles, his pectorals, biceps and triceps all perfectly proportioned and healthy. Carefully he turned his back to her and she realized that he was showing her more than just his body. The scars on his body were not clear at first sight because of the way he was toned and carved, but once the cast of his meticulous body got absorbed, she could see the faint impressions of his turbulent life. He stood with his eyes shut allowing her enough time to see the scar markings that scattered his skin.

A silence hung and she fought away the breaking heart inside, wondering how she could ever bring him back to live again.

"I see so much potential in you Evans…And we've only recently met." she said staring into his eyes, "Your mother, Edward, Bennie, Liz and everyone else can see it because you aren't all bad, you aren't the sin you think you are. Nor are you the poison you fear will spread by a simple hug. I just wish you could see it in yourself."

He shrugged flicking his head to the side for his long hair to fall back in pattern after his shirt flung it amuck. "I think our times up doc. Thanks for the chat."

"The timer hasn't rung yet Kyle." She said standing up with him.

He heaved a deep breath as he drew conclusion to his internal debate over whether or not to show her something more or not.

"See time can be viewed as nothing more than gesture through the three dimensions and I'm not sure if you know this or not, but this is why it is often called the 4th Dimension."

Andy frowned with intrigue, folding her arms as he continued with his somewhat conceited explanation.

"It's reflected in the fact that we measure years by the Earth's orbit around the sun and we measure days by the Earth's revolutions, and our measure of hour's, minutes and seconds are nothing more than simple fragments of these greater measurements. All these things involve motion."

Stunned by his informative knowledge on time and its keeping devices, Andy continued staring at him in surprised interest and Kyle smirked looking down to his wrist watch.

"And on my first day here while I waited for you to greet my mother, I figured out that your clock over there is working on one minute's delay, which means it's about to ring right about….now."

They both paused, looking up waiting for the sound of the timer on the corner of her desk. Realizing he was off, he frowned with a grin, the first grin she had seen that made him look like the young college freshman he was and the timer rung out.

She laughed clapping her hands in applause while also shaking her head in disbelief, "Innate accuracy! That was so awesome Kyle! How did you do that?"

He managed a weak smile as he reached the door turning back to her, "No, sometimes, I just know things."

Andy nod, still dumbfounded by his impressive intellect and he opened the door, turning to her with a wink, "See you later Andy."

"More than scars and old wounds, eventually someone will want to know who I am and if they find out, if I let them get close I risk seeing pain in people who don't deserve it. Sometimes it's better to know less Andy. I hope you understand that?"

She nod and gave a smile, "It's my job to help you Kyle, to feel alive in your skin. I can only understand from a personal point of view, can you understand that?"

Again he flicked his hair and walked out with a smile.

She turned back to her desk in utter admiration in him for having such a valued mind even despite the time spent out and between schools with a past as sordid as his.

The interior of the ex-Mayor's office held a glaze of white cigar smoke that hung like drapes in the air above the four men sitting there.

"The only way for us to break ground here is a full on sabotage at the shaft." Said the ever placidly comfortable Mr. Cheng Lee, turning to the tall broad shouldered man at his right, "And we have the perfect way to do just that without any questions being asked."

"And how do you suggest I keep the barking dogs at bay if you and your henchmen send that shaft crumbling down?" asked the grey haired, Frank Harper as he sat forward in his lush brown leather chair, his strong blue eyes untainted and cold.

Maxwell Keagen changed his attention between them both, remaining silent after his previous run in with Mr. Lee.

"Do you people realize what this is going to do to the town? How the mayor is going to handle it? The press coverage?"

"It's the least of our concerns Harper." Lee said shaking his head with a grin, "Your position in all of this is undeniably understandable but you must bear in mind that the Corporation knows the sacrifices you have made to assist in getting operation Face as far as it has come. We haven't overlooked that in the planning of this operation going forward Frank. You will have your seat in the next elections and eventually you're title in the new government."

"My concern lies with the town after all of this." Harper said with a solemn frown, "People are relying on this for job security, economic development."

"And rebuilding the shaft will just increase labor." He shrugged, "It's a winning situation Harper. Once this is done you no longer have to have any stress and strain about keeping our dirty little secret your main priority. It will be done with for good the moment the charges go off."

He shook his head grinning with admiration for the way Lee always seemed so certain, without a microscopic doubt. "If the investors don't care to rebuild and the entire plan to re-mine E Shaft falls through, a lot of people are going to have it very difficult. This entire thing is getting out of control!"

Lee laughed shaking his head, "Why do you care about everyone else in this shit-hole district? Once the elections are over and our man is on the high chair you will move to far greener pastures.

What happens to this little area is irrelevant in the greater scheme of things wouldn't you agree?"

"The greater scheme is falling apart by the seams Lee." Said Harper sighing, "Not everybody lies within Gondwe's little pocket! A part of me has always known that this was going to be uncovered, ever since we put my son in the ground!"

Lee sighed with impatience as he too stood up to round the desk to where Harper stood facing out the window. "Operation Face has been in the works for over eleven years and I can assure you, not that you don't already know this yourself, the Corporation has thought this through rather intensely. Yes I will not lie the recent events at E Shaft has made us all very uncomfortable, but you forget that we are everywhere Frank, we are inside everything we need to be to always have control. Whatever little hiccups that surfaced over the years have been dealt with. Gavin-Smyth's funds have been received, and just like the fire at the Oakhurst building and the Hout Bay mobs, this hiccup at E Shaft will be entirely accidental and unforeseen."

"The Hout Bay mobs?" Frank asked in surprise.

"It was a distraction technique, basic." Lee grinned, "Stay focused Frank, you seem to forget the vast scale of this operation Mr. Harper and what is at stake here."

"You think I don't know what's at risk?" asked Harper turning to him with a mocking grin, "I think I, more than anyone else, understands the sacrifices made to get this far."

"With or without your assistance, we are going to proceed to go ahead with burying our little problem, shifting the blame and resolving this insanity." Lee interrupted arrogantly, heading back to his chair and reaching down for his briefcase.

"Blow that mine down for all I care, my main concern is what will happen when investigations get underway and how many more innocent people have to die for this thing to be over."

Lee grinned shaking his head as he stepped to face Harper, utterly disregarding Keagan's presence.

"Mr. Harper you worry me. I thought by now after so many years of loyalty you of all people would endure, but it seems you are starting to grow soft." He said holding his hand out in front of him. Harper looked down and walked around him towards the door of his office. Lee smirked and head after him.

"Everyone in this country will benefit from what we are doing

Harper, in the long run. A few innocent lives lost on the way is well worth the sacrifice. It's how it always has been throughout history. South Africa needs a change, needs a new president to take this country to places most people only speak of in pipe dreams. That my friend is definite." Said Lee turning to face him. Harper chuckled shaking his head, now holding his hand out, "Only a few things in this life are definite Mr. Lee, death, taxes and that you can never trust a politician."

Lee laughed nodding, "Back in the day when we first approached you about E Shaft your greed was equal to our own."

"Yes but that was before I had to bury my son."

"That was unfortunate." Said Lee softly, looking down.

"No!" scoffed Harper angrily, "Faking Eugene Noordman's suicide was unfortunate. The post office workers, that was unfortunate but for the greater good. Lyle was never, ever unfortunate and when all of this is over I will have my minute with Mr. Black as promised."

Lee nod, his smile pensive, "Yes it was unfortunate that all this happened in your district wasn't it? All the more reason for you to take a deep breath and bring back the man we approached four years ago."

"A lot has changed since then." Keagen said in the mayors' defense.

"Four years ago!" Lee snapped, finally acknowledging him angrily, "And we have come a long way since! This country is standing at the dawn of a new era gentlemen. We stand so close to the goal. This is the last stretch? Twenty four months and everything is going to be realized. There will be millions lost if the reopening is forfeited. And if it isn't, by that time there will be no evidence relevant."

Harper looked to Keagen nervously, and Lee opened the door. "I'll keep in touch closer to the time." He said walking out.

"It's utterly chaotic out there, like something out of movie or something." Edward said as he scooped a spoonful of green beans into his plate, the family sitting around the dining room table. The house smelt of divine cooked vegetable and roasted meat and potatoes. Bennie was seated beside Claire and Kyle across Edward.

"Do you think it was murder?" asked Claire lowering her voice to keep Bennie from hearing. Edward nodded and dug his fork and knife into his steak, "It's certainly foul play, who would voluntarily throw themselves down there?"

"Anything's possible I guess. What do the police say?"

"Well they only spoke briefly but I don't know, it's such a nightmare. Thank god for the rain or we'd still be out there." Edward said scoffing a fork full into his mouth.

"Can't you work in the rain?" asked Bennie with a cute curiosity, "Or will it flood the hole?"

Edward smiled shaking his head, "We can work in the rain my boy, it's just the generators powering the supply of electricity down into the shaft that provides ventilation and light down there - broke and we have to hold off until we get a new one."

Kyle continued to enjoy the vegetables in silence while Bennie swapped his attention between the two adults curiously.

"Why are things happening so slowly though? I mean it's been two weeks and there doesn't seem to be any rush in finding the rest of the, well, you know…" Claire added digging into her potatoes, again avoiding saying upsetting things near little Bennie.

"Well according to the police the prints were too badly deteriorated to identify, well, you know and since we are operating on levels that haven't been used in almost a decade it isn't very safe down there just yet. I mean we have cranes holding the cages and equipment left all over the place, its utter chaos I tell you. Just yesterday a stope wall collapsed almost trapping a couple of guys." Ed said taking another forkful into his mouth.

"Oh so I'm guessing we won't be going away on the weekend of the 4th then?" asked Claire while chewing politely. Kyle looked up frowning in surprise and Bennie gasped, "Are we going back to the sea!"

"No kiddo" laughed Edward chewing his meat, "Mommy and I wanted some time alone."

"But…" Bennie said pausing with confusion, "What about us?"

"Well since uncle Jimmy's back for awhile, we thought…"

"Dad's coming?" frown Kyle in surprised alarm.

"Yeah he sent through a text message a few days ago."

"Why?" asked Kyle trying to mediate his emotions, his body already trembling.

"Well, he's getting married to that…" Claire paused, "…tramp and she wanted him to ask her father the traditional way. And since he's here he wanted to see us, we figured we'd use the time to get away and be alone for a bit."

"So soon?" asked Kyle softly trying to regain control of his spiraling panic, "We just moved here…I can't believe you guys already want to break away?"

Claire smiled reaching out for his hand, but she paused and looked to Bennie.

"Kiddo why don't you take your plate to the lounge and put the TV on, mommy and daddy want to have big people talk ok?"

"Ok mom." Said Bennie with an eager smile as he hurried down the chair, carefully took his plate and hurried to the sitting room.

"Kyle I don't understand what is going on between you two?" she asked with a loving concern, "Is there something I should know because nothings been ok between you guys."

He paused, his brain spiraling to make sense and his body raging in dire upset. He finally shrugged, "No but…"

"It will only be two days." She said, "But we don't have to go anywhere if you feel like you need us to be here. But I just assumed since you haven't seen your father in years you'd want to catch up."

"I think he'd appreciate some time alone with you Kyle." Edward added, "I think he is eager to see you after everything."

Kyle realized his lip had began to shiver and he stood up, "Well we'll see if he can make it or not." He said taking his plate to the kitchen.

"Let's see what happens. We don't even have to go it was just a suggestion. " Edward reached out for Claire's hand, squeezing it gently, "I love you."

"I love you." She leaned across the table, kissing him.

Kyle mumbled under his breath as he ripped off his shirt, clambered up along the metal frame holding up the grape vine and began doing pulls up. His body was riddled with frustration and when he felt the rage building it was best to get his temperature down. As the cold air circled him he felt his thoughts spiraling out of control, his body shivering with fear, dread, panic and nausea. In the red world there was a man behind the glass whose face was recognizable to him in the haze of 'V', and as he stared at it trying to place the familiarity he couldn't. There was a number of naked boys and girls with him in that room, but when the man looked through the glass their eyes met almost instantly.

In Crown and Lake Jimmy denied it and although he was still in the darkest part of recovery, Kyle was adamant. In the time that had passed he often tried to make sense of it, but it was easier to simply lock it out for his own sanity and for his mother because if the face was Jimmy, his father – it would crush her to a place unrecoverable.

It's paranoia, your paranoia.

He kept repeating it to himself as he pulled himself up again and again as though his body only weighed a total of 20 kilograms.

"It doesn't take a blind man to see your upset." The old neighbors' voice came over the wall, causing him to drop down in alarm.

"Jesus Christ!" he exclaimed stumbling back, "Lady! Are you trying to give me a heart attack?"

"Wasn't planning on it, no." smiled Mary Beth, taking a drag of her marijuana joint. "Christ, what do you want anyway?" he said carefully maneuvering back onto the vine to continue his work out.

"What do I want?" she frowned playfully, "Well there's a lot actually. A toilet bowl made of pure gold…To ride in a helicopter with that handsome fellow from 'Lost'. A headboard made of diamonds and…"

"Ok smart lady, I get it." He said heaving up and down as he spoke, "I meant - why are you lurking around in the dark spying on people?"

She laughed and shook her head, "You seemed distraught. You know for a lad who smokes dope you seem so tense all the time."

"Hey!" He snapped dropping down again, walking up to the wall, "Would you mind not blabbing that out to the world? Besides granny you have it wrong, I don't smoke dope. It was a misunderstanding that's all."

"Oh I know everything dear I'm a witch you see." She said looking up at him.

He frowned, "What?"

"It's a joke nut head." She laughed, "It's the weed see…" she said lifting a joint over the wall, "I get these weird spells if I hold my breath a bit longer than I should."

"You're a weird old woman." He said unconsciously speaking his mind. She giggled shaking her head, "That about sums it all up sonny. Care for a drag?"

"No thank you." He said looking down and heading back up to continue the pull ups, "Why are you smoking this anyway? You got cancer or something?"

"Yes I do." She nodded somberly taking another pull at her weed stick. Kyle propped back down to his feet. *Nice going jerk!*

"You're rude. Do you know that kid?" she said exhaling up into the air, "Granted, you don't know me but I am trying to be nice, plus I'm older than the Ark so stop acting like a Jew on his way to circumcision and be nice to me."

He laughed shyly, "I'm sorry ma'am but I'm not really good with people, much less really old people."

"Please, call me Mary Beth." She smiled, "My son Hendry is the dean at Seymore College, I believe you recently started going?"

He looked down, still reeling in from the alarming news at diner, "Yes."

"Small world isn't it?"

Nodding clumsily, Kyle asked, "Is it the bad kind?"

"Aren't they all?"

"I guess so."

"Well kid don't have sleepless nights, I'm doing good. Chemo's over so that's like having your cherry popped by John Lennon." She said taking another drag.

"Lennon?" he frowned cocking his head back to flip his shaggy hair out his eyes, "No it was Ringo that gave the Beatles edge."

"Ringo Star?" she smiled surprised, "Thought that would be way before your time."

He smiled resuming his work out.

She giggled shaking her head, "You are one of the few people I've met, and I've been around for centuries so I have met a lot of people, that laments Rings Star." coughing up smoke and she shook her head.

"My name is Kyle." He said politely, "Sorry about your cancer."

"I'm sorry about my cancer too. I guess we have something in common now right Kyle?"

"Seems that way doesn't it Mary." He smiled, inspired by her age carrying in it such a charm and bashfulness, something at twenty one he had nothing off.

Another short pause filled their conversation as she dragged at the joint.

"Well, good night then." She said lowering behind the wall.

He wanted to ask her, beg her for a drag of her joint, but he clenched his fists and shut his eyes.

In the darkness of the night, he stepped deeper beneath the vine into the blackness of its shadows. He knelt down almost choked out of fear. As quietly as he could, he began to punch down at the soil, harder and harder with each blow, trying desperately not to scream out in defeat or frustration. He wanted answers to the tormenting questions that plagued him.

Why me? Why did they take me? Why am I alive? Why did this happen! He kept on hitting and hitting at the soil with all his might, silently breaking the seal and allowing rage to filter back in. As the damp soil broke and mashed at his pounding fist, he began to cry.

Across the stretch of vast open veldt between the small community of Brendan Village and the ever expanding Secunda, the McDonald house stood lit only from the tall three headed golden lamp that stood beside the front door and was silent just minutes past twelve pm. Joel had not intended on staying over, but the long overdue conversation with his mother had dragged on well past midnight and she did not want him driving so late.

As he moved down the steps in only his bright red boxers that were comically decorated with Mickey Mouse, Joel scratched his hand through his hair to shake the sleep from which he had just woke, from a dehydrated thirst that derived from the nights overly spicy lamb curry.

The kitchen floor was white tiled and cool beneath his feet as he stepped towards the refrigerator, the white light from within glowed brightly, almost blindingly. With the bottle of orange juice in his hands, he tipped his head back and began to gulp it down. After placing the bottle half drained back into the fridge, he turned to the large window that faced out into their vast back yard. The light from the full moon glimmered upon the swimming pools clear water and the night air was silent. For a brief moment he pondered on the urge to go for a swim, but that wouldn't be appreciated by either his mother or father – if he indeed had yet returned from his usual late night work meetings. Staring out, he enjoyed the gentle coolness of the breeze that slithered through the slightly opened window.

Shrugging off the vague wish to fly away from everything he knew, he turned to exit the kitchen when he slammed into his mother who gasped in fright, scrambling to turn the lights on.

"Joel! God Almighty! You scared the cholesterol right out of me!" she exclaimed in a breathless whisper as the florescent lights above flickered on.

"What the hell, I was just getting juice."

"What are you doing up this late sneaking about?"

"I wasn't sneaking I was thirsty." He explained with annoyance, "Why are you up?"

Lynette sighed shaking her head, "I also just came down for a glass of water. I forgot you stayed over, sorry."

He moved for the light and switched it on.

"But I really do appreciate you coming over tonight." Lynette said shutting the fridge, "I miss you since you don't live here anymore. It was nice to just talk."

"Pity we had to talk about Marco."

"Joel listen to me." She said stepping forward and putting his head in her hands, "I know it's hard for you to understand, or accept. But Marco and I have been in this…thing for a long time…We have a history."

"I get it ok!" he said lividly moving past her, "You love him, there's feelings, blah! I don't care! I just don't want to see you in hospital again! Or me for that fact!"

254

Is this his concern? Is this why he wants it to end? She thought looking down.

"We've covered it, I can't listen to anymore and it's late." Joel sighed shaking his head, "I just…I can't hear this anymore mom. I have my own life to live and all the time I'm living under something else's shadow. If you love the guy, leave dad and marry him. Otherwise just stop before dad finds out!"

"Dad finds out what?" Raymond asked stepping around the corner behind him with his suit jacket slug over his forearm.

"Honey, I didn't hear you come in." she smiled nervously, "I didn't think you would even be home tonight. Joel stayed over." Raymond nod and tossed his car keys to the counter as he placed his briefcase on the floor.

"It's past one in the morning…" Joel said confused, "I can't believe you have to work so late."

"Someone has to do it."

Maybe just tell him about the fuse chord. Now rather than never.

Lynette hugged against his back "I've missed you."

"It's been a long day Lynette, please just heat my food and stop hanging all over me."

She nod and stepped back.

"How's things on campus?"

Joel shrugged, "It's been ok, since Collin's suicide I guess everything's a bit upside down."

Raymond nod as Lynette hand him a glass of water.

"The people from the mine investigation are still on campus." Joel said fishing, "Had a sit down with them a few days ago. Routine questions I guess, but do you have any idea why they think someone from school had anything to do with what happened?"

"No idea." Raymond shrugged, "Everyone's following up leads. One of the security guards on duty said he saw a college aged person on site the night of the explosion. He's dead now."

"Dead?" Joel gasped, "The student?"

"No, the guard." Raymond grunt, "Really Joel it's late I don't want to get into this right now."

"Sorry, we just don't really get time to talk about it." Joel said pulling out a chair. "Why do you care anyway? You've never cared about my work, why the sudden interest?"

"Don't think about work. Joel let your father eat so he can get into bed." She said closing the microwave as he stepped aside and pulled out a chair by the nook.

"Besides you don't want to be late for school and upset your dear grandpa." Raymond grinned. Joel rolled his eyes and got up, "Good night."

"Oh Joel…" Raymond said causing him to pause in the hallway, "That boy's suicide…your friend…"

"Yeah, you met him. His name was Collin."

Raymond nod at him, his face solemn with sympathy but he did not say anything further and Joel knew his intention so simply head back towards the stairs.

"Good night sweet heart." She smiled as Joel disappeared along the railing. Raymond began eating and trying desperately to avoid any snap in his long dormant temper, she asked, "Would it hurt you that much to be nice to him at least? He's grown up to be a really good man, just look at the sacrifices he makes for us to survive our debts."

Raymond dropped his head in tired frustration, "I just don't need to think about that right now, I have enough on my plate. For god sakes Lynette are you trying to cause a fight? Is that what you want? Is that why you are throwing his valiance in my god damned face?"

"No please, no fighting. I hope you like the lamb curry." She smiled cautiously, "It's a recipe I got from Hannelie down at the spa. She and I went shopping after."

Raymond sighed and looked up at her, "Where are you going?" She turned shaking her head, raising her eyebrow, "What do you mean?"

He shrugged confused, "This small talk? I don't follow, is there something you want or are you scared Joel is eaves dropping?"

"I'm just trying to be civil."

"Don't." he said shoving a forkful into his mouth, "It's only making things more complicated. We can dispense with the small talk Lynette, this is what it is."

She smirked shaking her head, "I was only trying to be civil, nothing more. Besides darling, by the looks of your collar the last thing you need is your old ball and chain around."

He looked down to the lipstick on his collar and heaved angrily. As she head up the stairs his plate flung out from the kitchen into the passage wall, splattering everything out onto the floor and she froze, looking up as he stepped out of the kitchen towards her.

Her heart raced and her mouth grew dry. He grabbed her hand and led her to the large rectangular mirror that hung in the entrance hall.

He shoved her in front of him to face it, not knowing that Joel stood at the top of the stairs.

"This is why…" He said shaking his head in disgust, "This is why I have other women hump my brains out Lynette, because you are all used up."

His snarl was vicious, his eyes teetering on rage and she felt frozen with terror. "You are the reason we can't be anything more Lynette. And I don't appreciate your games."

Joel heaved a deep sigh, his heart racing in his chest.

"Maybe if you'd had a tighter pussy I'd be faithful." He snarled, "But no, you never had a tight pussy did you Lynette."

"Stop it Raymond." She said pushing away from his grip, "It's been a long day, neither of us are in the mood so just stop."

He smiled, "You don't get to push me Lynette, you lost the privilege remember?"

He sighed and began heading up stairs. She had always known he was nothing more than a common bastard in a charade behind the glitz of his family fortune and every so often that side of him would peek through.

"One more thing, you can sleep in the guest room." He said going into the darkness past Joel who hid in the bathroom.

Chapter Eight:
A breath of madness

As the cage filled with teams of four ready to do the final sweep of shaft bottom and the last levels stopes and ore passes, detective Jordan and her partner Underwood head up to Edward and Raymond beside the crane that stood holding the thick chain that lowered the cage. The winter air was icy, the fields surrounding them barren with dead grass and leafless trees.

"Morning!" smiled Eva with a warm friendliness not previously present in her attitude, "You going in there with them?"

Edward looked down to his suited gear and smiled almost shyly, "Today yes."

"Bring us back a face." Nod Underwood with an attempted joking grin.

"Yes." Said Raymond awkwardly trying to overcome Underwood's somewhat tainted humor, "Hopefully by the end of today we can put this mess behind us."

"Perhaps it's a mess to you Mr. McDonald." Said Underwood, "But it's a father or son to someone else."

"Well until you have jurisdiction, we're doing what we need to do to feed families detective." Raymond snarled, "Simply talking to you is a courtesy we are not actually allowed to offer according to the court at this point. But rest assured, if we find a face you will be in the loop."

Underwood's eyes narrowed and Raymond walked off.

Edward nod and Eva pat his shoulder, "Good luck."

As they head off, he turned towards the crane, passing agent Black who remained under the facade of Moorecroft.

Observing the other students from the spot of shade beneath the tree stood Kyle slowly dropping caramel glazed cashew nuts into his mouth. The day had reached a high of 20 degrees.

"What you doing?" asked Liz Parker rounding from behind him with a bright smile.

"Observing..." He answered with a slight grin. She turned and looked around at the students. A brief silence draped over them as she stared at his soft, picture perfect face and hair. She felt a strange tension within her stomach each time she stood close to him or saw him, yet accompanying it the gentle relish of butterfly kisses against her heart that warmed her and almost compelled her to him like a drug. Standing at his side looking at his strapping forearms and biceps she knew that something about him had her addicted, afraid, lustful, mystified and compelled her to want more than what her eyes saw.

"Well, the reason I came all the way over here is to ask you if...." She started, hurriedly pausing as she realized that her palms were clammy and the pounding of her heart in her chest seemed to leap to her voice as she spoke. "Ask me what?" he asked turning to look up at her, his eyes causing her heart to race inside her chest. She shyly cleared her throat, realizing that she had begun to tremble as the butterfly kisses grew more intense as his eyes met with hers, "Well I wanted to know if you wanted to come over sometime? I mean, like to the restaurant sometime. You know like for that smoothie or whatever. Remember the smoothie I mentioned awhile ago?"

He frowned and looked down to hide his laughter to her adorable fumbling and she heaved a breath, "Tomorrow actually, would you like to come for that Smoothie?"

Kyle looked back up at her with a smile, his heart suddenly drawn to the charm she had such a radiance of, "Tomorrow, just the two of us?"

Feeling the embarrassment smoldering on her cheeks she looked down, "Yeah if that's suitable for you."

"Just the two of us?" he asked trying to shun his own sudden awkwardness.

"Well us two yes, along with everyone else who might be dining at the Hot Spot yes…why would you prefer we didn't? We can do anything, anywhere. Whatever, I'm easy you decide. You probably have plans anyway, so it's fine…another time?" She was breathless and more awkward than ever before, "But would you like to come on tomorrow night? Because I just asked… and then cancelled for you…so, I'll shut up and let you answer now. Go ahead..."

Pausing first, he felt the rush of his crush on her filling him with warm needles and pins, yet hidden at the far corners of his soul, the fear of being in love frightened him and he nod, "Sure ok. Sounds good."

Again her body filled with flutters and she smiled broadly, "Really? You sure? You seem a bit uneasy about it every time I bring it up?"

"No, no, it's a date." He said looking out to the campus yard again, trying to remind himself of what and who he was, his thoughts screaming *You are filth and your going to ruin her you worthless bastard!*

"It sure is." she said, her dark innocent brown eyes glimmering with excitement. "Thanks, I'd really like to go with you."

"Go with me?" he frowned looking up at her again.

"Tonight, the date…I mean." She blushed, "Sounds great."

"But…you asked me?" he said smiling confused.

"Right, I did…" she said, her smile dropping as she gripped her hands together trying to bring her heart back to the ground, "What I meant was like…like cool then. It's a date then. I mean, not a date – date, but like… you know…we're on. Let's do this thing!"

"I know what you mean." He laughed looking down again to rid his face and soul of the feeling he fought to avoid due to the complications it brought, "Are you always this… bouncy?"

She laughed, trying desperately for her crush on him to subdue, "Bouncy depends who I'm playing ball with…" she answered playfully punching him on the chest before gasping at her nerve to actually physically abuse him.

Stop acting like a high school girl Liz or I swear to god I'm going to slap me!

Liz smiled shyly putting her hands in her pockets, wishing she could undo her puppy like behavior and erase it from his mind, "Well I'll see you later Mr. Evans."

"Later Miss Parker." He replied with a warm smile as she started back across the lawn.

Joel head into the bathroom to wash the ink his black pen had soiled his hands with. As he leaned over the basin Kyle entered towards the urinal.

"Hey."

"Joel."

"So how are you doing?"

"I'm good, you?"

The door flung open as Rendani entered, behind him Jaco and Tinus. Seeing Joel, Rendani nod a greeting, and Tinus boorishly shoved past him. Jaco's eyes were fixed on Kyle in the mirror but Kyle simply looked down and shut the faucet. Tinus stepped up to the urinal and Rendani head into one of the stalls, while Jaco folded his arms across his chest staring at Kyle in the mirror.

"Evans."

Kyle sighed turning to him.

The tension felt like physical weight on his body and Joel shut the tap.

Just then, Tinus turned to face him from the urinal, his member peering out of the zip. "Look out!" he warned as he un-squeezed and send a squirt of urine down near Joel's shoes.

"Pissing on a millionaire bru!"

"Oh come on man!" snarled Joel, when in what happened like a flash of lightning, all the rage Kyle had overcome unleashed. It was the moment to drill.

Swooping his hand up behind Jaco's neck, Kyle shoved him face first into the wall before bringing his knee up into his ribs in two swift motions. Joel barely had time to react when Kyle swung up behind Tinus, swinging a punch that hit him off his balance and backwards into the urinal. Rendani turned in alarm as Joel stepped aside. Jaco swung a punch from behind, his fist landing on the side of Kyle's face as another connected low in his back. The two boys slammed up against the wall, Jaco choking at Kyle as Kyle's fists flung left and right, each time ramming in his stomach until Jaco had stepped off just enough for a kicks space – sending him tumbling backwards into the stall against Rendani.

"Kyle!" warned Joel just as Tinus tackled into him, both of them crashing down on the ground, Tinus punching and punching down at Kyle. Joel hurriedly reached in, trying to force Tinus off of Kyle as Jaco regained his feet.

Tinus grabbed at Joel, flinging him aside angrily swearing at him.

Kyle stepped to him, but Jaco whacked into him from the side, the blow to his face dazing him and he lost balance, going down into the side of the urinal.

Rendani got to his feet in alarm, wanting to run out in fear of being caught up in a brawl but could not move his legs.

Tinus gripped Joel's hair backwards, bringing his fist down into his face letting Joel collapse down onto the ground.

"Jy dink jy's vokken snaaks jou kont!" Jaco said flicking open his pocket sized switch blade as Kyle stumbled up onto his feet, "Kom ons dans boet!"

Tinus charged at Kyle, aiming to pin his hands behind his back, but Kyle swung aside, his elbow slugging Tinus across the jaw twice. Jaco clawed around Kyle, gripping him around the chest, and put the blade to his neck from behind.

Touching was not allowed, but Jaco's grip from behind was strong and all Kyle could do was twist free of it.

"Jaco los hom!" said Tinus breathlessly as Jaco continued to slash the knife out at Kyle who had stepped back against the wall.

"Stop it!" shouted Rendani finally getting feeling back in his body. Joel raised his head, blood trickling from his mouth on the ground.

"You want kak? Let's do it then bru!" snarled Jaco, swinging at Kyle again, when out of sheer chance Kyle managed to swing around and grabbed hold of the back of his collar. Joel wearily rolled to his knees as Tinus looked on, both of them knowing that the blade was only going to end everything they knew. With Jaco's collar gripped firmly in his adrenaline pounding fist, Kyle swung him forward into the paper towel dispenser with a bang, the knife dropping to the ground.

"Do something man?" Rendani said helping Joel to his feet. Disorientated by the blow, Jaco stumbled and Tinus reached down for the blade. Kyle grabbed Jaco again, swinging him around back into the dispenser, his elbow across Jaco's throat as his hand right pound at his side as fast and hard as he could. Tinus stumbled forward, and Joel grabbed at him.

"Stop it…" Joel said trying to get a grip on Tinus's arms as they scuffled and swore at one another. Kyle stood bewildered and confused as Jaco heaved breathlessly away from him to grab the small knife.

"Come on bitch!" he screamed as the blood from his nose pour into his mouth, swiping the knife through the air, "Bring it *soutie* boy!"

Joel and Tinus flung around and Kyle stepped back raising his hands, "Put it down there is no point to this!"

Jaco clenched his teeth, "You think you so cool? Show me soutie! Show me!"

"Jaco man put the knife down!" Joel urged, protectively shoving Rendani behind him.

"Sny hom!" Tinus said shoving Joel back, "Cut the fucker! Deep!"

"What the hell?" exclaimed Joel in alarmed disbelief, entirely taken aback by their impulsive brutality that he never knew secretly existed within them.

Jaco's heart beat pound with a vengeance as blood trickled down over his lips and chin, standing on the edge of a fight he went into with blind incomprehension.

"Cut him!" Tinus continued to press breathlessly. Jaco looked deep into Kyle's blue eyes, trying desperately to find fear or surrender, never imagining that in a flash movement, Kyle would leap forward and grab his arm. Joel and Rendani watched in distressful surprise as Kyle forced Jaco into a twist, bringing his hand towards him, pulling the blade towards his very own neck.

"Do it!" said Kyle staring into his eyes, his voice filled with sincere and dead cold as he fought for Jaco's hand nearer to his neck with the blade in grip, "Do it!"

Jaco's blood-blotched hand trembled as he fought to further the blade away from Kyle's neck, but Kyle's strength surpassed and the edge of the small blade finally pressed against his skin.

"Kyle what the hell are you doing?"

"Don't be stupid Kyle!" Rendani growled, "Jaco! Stop this shit!" The coldness of its steel nipped as he felt its sharpness tingle against his skin and he continued to force Jaco's hand closer.

"Cut him!" Tinus urged, when Joel shoved him and found in himself a courage he never thought he'd possess, swinging a left hook as hard as he could to get Tinus falling against the urinal with a bloody nose.

The small knife was now hard-pressed against his neck and Joel and Rendani still pleading with them to stop.

Jaco felt his heart racing within his throat, palms and chest – a fear he had never known as he bleakly tried pulling his hand away or at least free his grip from Kyle's hand that held his grip tight to the blade's handle.

"Go on…do it big boy." Kyle insisted in an icy calm tone, with a wild animal wrath in his eyes – a cold wish that sent terror through Jaco's veins. Joel shook his head, "What are you doing?"

"What the fuck man!" wheezed Rendani from behind them, "Let him go man! Let him go!"

"Kyle stop it!" urged Joel in distress as Jaco continued to fight the blade away from Kyle's neck. "You want to play with a blade you better be willing to do it right." Kyle said again, his eyes dark and filled with a menacingly unafraid fury.

"Let go of me." Jaco said behind clenched teeth.

"You wanted dance bro, let's do it. Cut me you chicken shit!" For those moments of the blade being pulled to and from Kyle's neck, there seemed to derive a slowness in the hands of time as heartbeats and breathing seemed to slow to a close stop, both echoing and booming. Staring deep into one another's eyes, Kyle sought relief from the life he could not take and Jaco the freedom of this crazy event that he knew would forever change his life regardless of how it ended.

Then Kyle kicked with full wrath of his being up into Jaco's stomach, forcing him backwards up against the stall, knocking his breath from his lungs. Jaco's cough had barely left his mouth when Kyle's hand came hurtling through the air as he screamed, the knife stabbing just beside his head into the metal dispenser. Joel, Tinus and Rendani each felt the air ripped from their lungs as though their hearts had for that instant paused, each looking at Kyle who stood facing Jaco with wild eyes. A silence hung in the air as Jaco's trembling hand fumbled up beside him for the knives handle, plucking it out of its hole in the canister nervously.

Kyle stepped to Jaco staring deep into his eyes.

"If you come near me again, I'll kill you."

Rendani turned to Joel and Tinus scrambled up.

"Liz is off limits. If anyone says otherwise, I'm waiting."

Jaco nod, his eyes wild in fear of the crazy person who tried to cut his own neck. "Come on man…" said Tinus pulling his friend by the arm as they backed for the door and Kyle turned to face them as they scuffled out.

"What the hell is wrong with you?" Rendani barked stepping to face Kyle, "You're crazy man…"

Kyle turned to him, "Who are you?"

"No one, if anyone asks I wasn't even here." He said heading out. The door flung shut and Joel stepped up against it, sighing in relief that the bathroom had gone quiet again. Turning to face Joel, appreciative of his attempt to help, Kyle winked with sarcastic and heroic charm. "That was wild right?"

"You are insane…"

Kyle smiled up into the mirror, a look on his face that Joel hadn't seen before, a young and carefree Kyle.

With a coat of silver grey clouds covering the sky, the afternoon seemed dark and foreboding as the tension again hung thick over the mine near E Shaft, as the second decent into the shafts final sweep went underway.

"We have what seems to be a cufflink here on the eastern stope of level 7C." Came the first voice over the radio and Eva sighed turning to Raymond folding her arms against the bite of the air through her suit.

"Yeah, yes it's a cufflink alright - got a smart little rectangle type ruby smack in the middle of it. It's rusted but it's defiantly a gem stoned cufflink." Confirmed the voice.

"So we have a piece of hand, a shoe and now a rusted cufflink." She said shaking her head, "I'm sorry Mr. McDonald but seems you have a homicide on your hands."

"It could be anyone's."

"Was it an easy find?" Eva asked with a bitchy frown. Raymond shook his head, turning to the mining commission's representatives before asking the operator to confirm.

"Please clarify, was the cufflink on surface or was it dug up?"

"In the wall actually." The voice advised, "Found it by pure accident."

Raymond sighed with frustration and turned to the two detectives, "Homicide? Does that default jurisdiction?"

"I'll call this in." Said Underwood ignoring him as he motioned for the door.

"We'll need to determine the age of the cufflink first, I assume…" Eva explained trying to subdue her disregard for him.

"You will." The blond haired representative of the mining commission added from over Raymond's shoulder, "If you can prove beyond reasonable doubt that the cufflink and the limb are connected, the distance between the two finds will indicate that the link got lodged when the shaft was flooded after the excavation."

"Then I would suggest you have these men pulled out until the forensics arrive to determine just that, wouldn't want anymore miners stepping on our crime scene…"

Raymond turned to her shaking his head, "This is my mine detective! You still require my courtesy if you want to bounce through my stopes!"

Eva smiled and nod, "Don't worry Mr. McDonald, I still think you have the biggest shoes in the room…"

He gasped in surprise as Eva head out after her partner. "Wait, what gives you the idea that this is a murder scene?"

"There are only a few men who wear cufflinks Mr. McDonald and much less one with a ruby stud in his cufflink and the average Joe isn't one of them and don't get me started on the Armani shoe." She said confidently, winking at the representative before shutting the door behind her.

Stepping into the cage for their accent upwards, teams as far down as level 7 begun filling the cage, both eager to escape the heat and claustrophobic hug of the underground and hungry for the purity of air. Carefully kneeling down to fiddle with his safety boot laces Mr. Black, the sly team member, deviously looked up at the others around him as he carefully removed a single dynamite stick from inside the leg of his boot.

"You ok?" asked one of his fellow mates placing his hand down on his shoulder in concern.

"Just tying my laces." He smiled with pretentious assurance, moving his head from the light from his team mates' headlamp that glared into his eyes. "We're almost out of here. I bet the news is going to have a field day with this cufflink." He smiled reassuringly as the cage jolt, slowly ascending towards the light that seemed like a tiny spot in the distance. Standing up in a turn, he carefully removed his small pocket blade and slit a piece of the fuse off, shortening it rather severely – his ears pierced through the loud cranking of the chains and the murmuring of the men and his eyes scouting with peripheral agility to ensure that nothing would jeopardize his mission.

Shouldering towards them and eyeing down through the grid walls of the cage, he carefully placed his lighter to the nipped fuse line when a hand grabbed his forearm.

"What does this mean about our jobs?" asked one of the mine foremen whispering to Raymond as they head out of the building towards the shafts entrance, "Everything will be put on hold, we're going to need to address this very quickly before we have a strike on our hands."

Raymond shrugged angrily, "I don't know Scherman, I don't know. …"

Just then a loud grumble sounded beneath them and the floor at their feet trembled. The crane holding the cage squeaked and moaned, buckling some as a ball of dust bubbled from the shafts mouth. Within seconds, panic spread and frenzy broke out among all the crew around the site as people began rushing towards the shaft.

"Get that cage out of there now!" roared the foreman turning back to the chains that still hoisted from the crane. "I've got the cage, I can feel the weight!" the operator called back. "We need to secure the area now!" called another foreman stopping those scurrying towards the surface platform at the shafts mouth, "This ground could be unstable, everybody back. At least 15 feet please!"

"What was that?" asked Eva rushing beside Raymond as the crew hurried away from the shaft mouth.

"I don't know." He said turning back to the shaft as the roof of the cage broke surface through the smoke. The two ambulances that stood in preparation came roaring nearer with sirens blaring, trying to get as close to the mayhem as they could. The crane began to reverse, crushing over the barricade behind it as it carefully swung the cage away from the threatened area and the crowd offered a cheer of relief to the sight of the men standing and huddling together in shock. "Medical personal only please!" Barked the foremen as the cage lowered to the ground, "Everybody back."

With the assistance of his men and the few uniformed officers on the scene, they created a barricade with their arms as the medics rushed to the cage doors.

As the doors burst open to the twenty nine men covered in dirt, coughing and gasping as they stumbled out into the arms of the paramedics, Raymond too rushed towards Edward who hurried aside coughing for air as he fell to his knees.

"What the hell was that?" asked Raymond hurrying to his side. Shaking his head he choked out the last of the dust filling his lungs Edward could not yet find the clear air his lungs craved and Raymond turned back to the pandemonium where Eva rushed towards them amidst the fog of dust that still hung in the air.

"What the hell was that?" she asked breathlessly, looking down at Edward, "Oh my god, are you alright Mr. Evans?"

"Something… something went off down there!" exclaimed Edward still coughing, "It hit below the cage…"

"Jesus Christ!" raged Raymond putting his hand on his head as he watched the alarming scene before hurrying across the chaos.

"Shook the cage like an animal, I don't know what it was!" said Edward as Eva knelt down beside him, turning to confirm that her partner was calling it in.

"Fatality!" came an alarmed voice, "I need a medic!"

Both Eva and Edward spun back to the cage in bewilderment. Rescue teams and paramedics alike rushed across, into the dust and Eva helped Edward slump to his feet, still choking on the dust riddling his lungs.

"Jesus!" gasped Raymond standing over the body of one of the search members as blood filled the floor of the cage around his upper body. Underwood pushed through as the paramedics looked up from the man's side. "He's dead."

Raymond gasped and head away from the cage, his world spiraling out of control.

"The wound seems to be a puncture to the side of his neck." The paramedic said standing up and pushing past Underwood calling to his colleagues at the ambulance for a stretcher and body bag. Underwood knelt down, now coughing from the dirt tickling his throat and then turned to one of the mine's foremen, "I need this entire area cleared out."

"What's going on?" asked Eva as she and Edward pressed closer, their eyes stinging from the dust. Underwood sighed shaking his head as he momentarily covered his eyes with his arm, "We have a dead guy here, that's what."

"Who is it?" gasped Edward in a cold distress. Ignoring him,

Underwood grabbed his partners arm and pulled her aside to a clearer zone as a paramedic draped Edward with a blanket and led him towards the ambulance regardless of his protests.

"Please, I need this area cleared!" instructed Underwood as they past more crewmen who hurriedly obliged. Raymond turned to the ambulances where the other crew stood being doused in the face with water to clear their eyes and he realized that everything within his expectations of coming here was about to be crumbled.

That night as most families began retiring to bed, Mike and Jessie begun their monthly show for Kallie Waldeck at his un-kept garden flat in Leandra. At 207 kilograms, Kallie had only left his flat on the rare occasion each month end to go shopping with the help of his mother Dorah who lived in the main house. His life was lived in social networks during the day, pornography sites at night. His weight kept him sitting most of the time and because his mother wasn't any lighter, she too didn't always make effort to walk down to the flat at the bottom of the garden. When the first police raid to his flat uncovered his vast collection of illegal pornography download from the net, Kallie thought he would be jailed, but Nkosi saw opportunity in his file and the evidence against him went missing. Since then, Kallie paid a thousand rand a month for Michael and Jessie to perform for him. He urgently wanted a younger cast, but they still brought to life his addiction to see two young bodies become one in a smutty sex session. The glow from the lamp made Jessie's pale skin seem a soft bronze and she heaved a deep breath, waiting just for the acid to take its effect on her mind. Stumbling to the doorway, Kallie grinned boyishly as his stubby fingers shifted the small glasses on his nose.

"Are you almost ready?" he asked snickering. She turned to him and managed a weak smile. Standing in front of him in a thin lace navy blue teddy, she still felt uneasy even after months of doing this in front of him.

"Is Mike ready?"

Kallie nod grinning, stepping aside as Michael entered behind him and Jessie smiled with relief at the sight of him. His outfit for each occasion would vary, and standing there in the doorway with the glow from the lamp stretching across him, his body glowed golden. Wearing only a black waiters pants with a black tie hanging down to his belly button, he head towards her with a tray in his hands.

"Wait, wait." Said Kallie rushing to the side where his camera stood on its tripod, "Ok start again."

Michael looked down at Jessie and then head back outside the room.

As he moved towards her, she stood up nervously - wishing the acid would take over sooner. Looking into her eyes, Michael asked, "You ordered room service ma'am?"

She reached for the tray, its contents a glass jug of body oil, a bowl of strawberries and a bowl of dry icing sugar. With a strawberry in her hands she smiled, "Thank you Jason."

She reached forward putting the strawberry against his lips, then run it down his chin, slowly along the contours of his neck and circled his nipples.

As the scene Kallie had given them progressed, the more he sat snickering behind the camera, his mouth watering as he watched them.

Laying on his back on the bed, she run the tie through her fingers as she straddled his waist, and she tilt her head watching him, forgetting in that moment that Kallie was in the room with his tripod. The way his body glistened in the light awoke a tingle inside of her, his tortured eyes looking up at her in anticipation. She reached for the belt at his waste and unbuckled it, sliding it down his legs as she got off of the bed. Laying naked in front of her felt natural, yet he found himself blushing as she crawled between his legs and very gently placed a single kiss on the tip of his penis. He gasped, his body glowing hot. She reached for the tray again, this time taking the jug of oil. It felt cold as it dribbled out of the spout onto his chest as she strew it in a thin line all the way down to where his hair began.

Her hands caressed the oil into his skin, rubbing it slowly over his chest, circling his nipples and streaking her hands down his sides, before swooping up over his abdomen and massaging it all the way up again. He gasped and shut his eyes, blushing hot as his erection pressed against her. She bit her bottom lip at the pushing against her vagina, and again she found herself forgetting that Kallie was there and that they were acting out for him. And she leaned forward over him, gently kissing his lips. Kallie, too caught up in the sensation from rubbing over his crotch, didn't realize that she had broken script. Michael looked up at her frowning confused and she sat back nervously, looking to Kallie who shrugged impatiently at her to continue.

Laying on her back with only the top of her teddy off, she watched his muscles glisten with the oil as he straddled her, drizzling a thin sheet of icing sugar from his finger tips. The white dust landed on her skin and blushing still from his throbbing erection, he lowered down and began to scroll the tip of his tongue up her body, collecting the small white dust as his tongue laced over her soft skin. She gasped, tilting her head back.

Kallie's stroke over his pants grew feverish. Her mind was racing, from both ecstasy of the acid she took before they got out of the car and also the thrill of his warm wet tongue against her skin. She lowered her hands, gripping his strong biceps and she felt her wetness tingle below her waist.

"Ok nice." Kallie said standing up from behind the camera grinning, "Lets cut to the good stuff."

She sighed looking down, back in the reality of it and no longer lost in the boy she had known all her life. Michael looked down at her blushing as he covered his erection, "Are you alright?"

She managed a weak smile, again captured by his dark eyes and she couldn't place what had changed inside of her. "Alright, action." Kallie ordered, smiling brightly after having moved the tripod.

He slid off her panties with a deep breath and she shut her eyes. Slowly, he lowered down, licking around her navel, then going lower across her smooth pelvis. Kallie zoomed in to capture the wetness of her vagina as Michael's tongue circled her clitoris. She clutched the bedding, gasping a soft moan as he continued to circle and move up and down her wet lips. He looked up at her, his heart racing. His thoughts were always the same each time they acted for Kallie, or performed for anyone.

I hope she really does like this. I hope she can relax and enjoy this, and find forgiveness for me.

She looked up into his eyes and he froze, and she reached for him, pulling him towards her, kissing his lips again with the gentleness

271

from before and he felt himself losing everything in the room. She kissed him passionately, their tongues circling and intertwining, her hands pulling his face against her mouth lustfully. He couldn't understand why she was kissing him the way she was, but everything didn't matter. Not Kallie, not the camera, not the money. Her lips and her body beneath him, safe, was all that existed.

Her hand reached down for his manhood, her thumb rolling over the wetness forming at his tip and she stroked him. Never before had he felt himself ready to come so soon.

It must be her kiss? What is this? What's happening to us?

He grabbed her hand away and pressed it down on the bed beside her head, their lips not parting. Kallie's hand raced over his crotch as he watched them.

She moaned into his mouth as the moisture from his throbbing hard erection oozed down onto her stomach and she opened her eyes to meet his. Something electric was sizzling between them like never before. And she grabbed the back of his head, kissing him again, her tongue ravishing his. His hand streaked down her stomach and he parted her below, slowly easing in two of his fingers. He gasped as her hands grabbed his body, her hot craving body begging for him to take it.

She felt her body heighten its sensation, heat burning through her as she reached the moment where everything erupted. He felt it on his hand and fingers as she released against him, grinding her pelvis against his hand harder, her hands grasping his strong body and she moaned his name out loud, "Michael…"

She wanted him more than she could understand given the situation, the camera and Kallie's grunting from the side. Michael lowered himself down, gently putting himself into her.

"Michael…" she whispered, and he lowered to kiss her.

Their bodies moved as one, slowly, the oil from his skin rubbing against her and her hands wanted to be all over him, she could not understand it. Their naked bodies began to heat up as he gently thrust in and out of her, hitting her spot each time and she felt herself swallowed by every fiber of him. He kissed her neck, circling his waist as he pressed into her, gasping beneath his breath as her hands ran over his abs.

"Michael…" she said raising her mouth to his ear, "Come inside me."

He wanted to stop, ask her what was happening, figure it out and demand an explanation for everything he was feeling inside, feeling radiate from her. But he couldn't and he cried out, his body tightening all over and he fell weak against her, shivering subtly but she could feel it and she kissed his shoulder.

"I wanted the cum shot." Moaned Kallie standing up, his sweatpants at his ankles and the fat rolling off of his thighs and belly. Michael sprung up away from her at the sound of his grunt, covering himself in alarm. He looked to her, then back to Kallie, his eyes wide and terrified of what had just happened. Everything suddenly felt cold and surreal and Jessie shifted up in the bed, covering herself with the sheet looking down, feeling everything he did, except she felt love. Kallie shook his head, "You didn't do anything I told you to do. It was nice, but you have to stick to the story next time got it? What the hell am I paying you for? You fuckers didn't listen! I will refuse to pay! Venter will hear about this!"

By the morning, the clouds had dissipated to the clear blue sky. Cutting across past the hall, Joel head for professor Holtshausen's lecture hall when Troy hurried up alongside him.

"Ok so how is Kyle feeling about tonight?" she asked staying in stride.

"Excuse me?"

"They're meeting at the Hot Spot for a date tonight." She said frowning in confusion, "You are Joel right? The millionaire boy." He nod and she continued, "Well I just assumed you knew about it."

"I wouldn't say we're friends as such." He said shrugging his shoulders, "Not like that, not really. We don't hang out."

She cocked her head to the side, her perfectly straight blond hair flaying in the breeze.

"I see. Well I'm sorry I asked, I just assumed someone like you would be in the loop, Liz is kind of freaking out because, well, she really likes him."

Joel smiled nodding, "I'm sorry I don't know you. I don't even know who Liz is."

"Troy." She said insulted flicking her hair back, "You sit behind me in Business. But don't worry I wouldn't expect someone like you to know the little people."

He looked down shaking his head, "Sorry, I…"

"It's ok." She smiled, "Well just pretend this never happened and uhm…well I'd say see you around but…you wouldn't remember me."

"Hey that isn't fair." He said reaching for her arm as she turned away, "Would you know me if it wasn't for Kyle dating this Liz person?"

"Oh please…everyone knows you." She smiled with a cheeky wit, "Joel McDonald, do you ever let people around here forget it?"

He nod his head with an impressed smirk, she bore in her the same determination as Kyle to utterly disregard his status. "My name precedes me."

"Yes, just like Hitler." She smiled sarcastically, flinging around and heading off.

He laughed, shaking his head taken aback by her sudden flittering overconfident charm and continued towards class when a hand grabbed his forearm.

"Michael?" he frowned stopping in surprise.

"Yeah look, I just wanted to know if you had a minute? There's something I need to talk to you about?"

"We aren't friends…You know that right?"

Michael smiled, "I get that. I just, I need to discuss something with you and I would appreciate your time."

Joel frowned, "What is this about?"

"You can call it a business venture."

"No." Joel said turning and walking away.

"Look I get it, this probably happens to you a lot, but I really think you can help me if you'll just hear me out. Please?" asked Michael walking along side him.

Am I in another dimension suddenly?

"Look I know what kind of shit you're into Harper." Joel said bluntly, "And I doubt there is anything I can help you with. Because if you have the nerve to approach me for money you have a serious set of balls on you."

"Look if I had a choice I wouldn't ask you shit. But…" Michael paused awkwardly, "I need help, please."

Joel frowned, "I'm busy right now, but we can meet up later and I'll hear you out."

Michael smiled, "Thank you."

The afternoon sun grew closed behind a blanket of dark clouds again and a strong icy wind blew across the fields.

"She said that?" Kyle asked turning to Joel as they head along the corridor.

"Yes! I don't know it was weird, it's been a weird day." Joel smiled with bright enthusiasm, "But she said Liz really liked you."

Great this is just what I need! Why did I agree to this? Worthless!

"So why didn't you tell me about this Liz chick?" Joel asked putting his hand on Kyle's shoulder as they walked. Kyle immediately stopped and looked at Joel's hand, "No."

Raising his hands Joel shrugged, "Sorry, so what's the deal?"

"There isn't a deal. I was being an idiot. I think I have made a mistake."

"Well then just cancel."

"Can I even do that?" Kyle asked with innocent eyes looking desperately for help in Joel.

"Sure you can, if you really don't want to go just call her an hour or so before and tell her that your car broke down."

"I don't have a car." Kyle said nervously.

"That's not the point!" he laughed, "Just make something up, and reschedule. That way the next time she brings it up, you can just decline. Or better yet, just avoid her."

Kyle shook his head worriedly, "This is complicated."

"What's complicated? You act like you've never…" Joel paused, "Wait, have you ever been on a date?"

Kyle tilt his head angrily, "I'm not a virgin."

"That actually isn't at all what I mean, but good to know none the less incase it comes to organ donating and they need your hymen." Joel teased. Kyle's face was stern, concerned and clearly unimpressed with the opportunity to use sarcasm.

"So wait, you're twenty one years old but you've never had a girlfriend?"

Kyle sighed impatiently, "I'm going to slap you in the eyebrows Joel - friendly warning."

Joel smiled, "You're such a strange human being Evans. Do you know how to smile? Have you physically mastered the ability to move your facial muscles…?"

"Are you going to help me?" he sighed turning to him, "Please I don't know what to do."

"Yes fine."

"Without any more sarcastic remarks about my previous dating history?"

Joel frowned anxiously, "Sarcasm is my coping mechanism, and I draw the line there. But I will try and avoid getting you upset, heaven forbid you force me to shove a knife into your neck."

Kyle nod pleased, "Then Joel I think we are about to make history here."

As they cut past the cinematography building, Joel raised his hand to his ear as a phone.

"Hi Liz, it's me Kyle Evans, you know the guy who thinks the world starts and ends on my shoulders? Yes that's me." He said acting bashful and cold in an attempt to convey Kyle's usual mannerism, "Listen, about tonight I won't be able to make it. I ran out to save a goldfish that flung out of a car window in an attempt to escape its bag, and as I ran out, a truck came along and bumped over some old guy crossing the street. I've been at the hospital since seven and I've just heard my bone marrow matches a dying three year old and I offered to donate so I won't be making dinner. Yes I'm amazing I know. Great stuff, chat later."

Kyle shook his head and Joel nod proudly, "See what I mean?"

"Do you want to ever swim again?"

Laughing, Joel shook his head, "Look man it's not hard, just tell her something came up."

"This whole thing is such a mistake, what was I thinking?" Kyle grunt angrily pressing against his temples.

"Look you can do a lot of things when it comes to fighting, but you can't do this date or get out of it? I don't get it."

"That's just it, the thing I've tried to tell you about, everyone about. I'm not a people's person, only bad things come from hanging with me. I'm such worthless piece of shit!"

Puckering a brow worriedly as Kyle turned his back, his temples still bearing the brunt of his fingertips, Joel stepped to face him. "First of all dude, you are being way too hard on yourself, just relax. I know it's a very unique term for you, but chill out. Take a breath, relax your shoulders and chill the fuck out. Or if you really can't even do that, just go on the date."

"Kyle!" Called Liz as she and Troy head towards them.

He gasped, turning to Joel in alarm, "Give me a lie, quick!"

"That's Liz?" Joel wheezed with wide eyes, "Elizabeth Parker? What the hell is your problem? Do the date!"

"Typical Friday afternoon right?" Liz smiled as they stepped up to them, "Even the teachers are chill."

Kyle managed an awkward smile and looked back to Joel anxiously.

"Hey." Troy smiled with a nod to Joel, "Just hanging with your non friend I see."

Joel rolled his eyes, "Yeah the Nazi get together doesn't start till after school."

Frowning confused, both Liz and Kyle shrugged off the strangeness radiating between them and Liz turned to face him smiling with a deep breath.

"So you still want to hang with me tonight?"

Kyle turned to Joel, his eyes pleading and desperate for him to intervene with skill and practice, but Joel raised his eyebrows and turned to Troy, starting up a conversation about which subject they were in the middle of.

"Well the thing is…I have a fish." Kyle started, his words spoken without breath available through the awkward tension gripping at his chest.

Liz nod and tilt her head in uneasy anticipation for him to utter the words he was clearly choking on.

"It uhm….there was an old lady in the road and…" he blabbed, "Look Liz…the thing is…I don't have a car."

"Which is why…" Joel said wrapping his arm around Kyle's shoulders, "I offered to drop him off at…wherever it is that you are going to be."

Looking to Troy in a baffled uncertainty, Liz agreed, "Oh ok."

277

Joel nod, realizing that he was still clutching Kyle's shoulders, but this time Kyle was too distracted and lost inside his chaos to notice.

"Are you ok Kyle?" asked Troy folding her arms suspiciously.

Kyle turned to her blinking, "Excuse me?"

"The fish, he was close to the fish." Nod Joel patting Kyle's back, "Anyway, we gotta run so, see you when we see you."

"Okay." Liz smiled, still confused. "Bye Liz." Said Kyle as Joel ushered the zombified Kyle across towards the parking.

Turning to Joel, Kyle shook his head, "Thank you."

Trying desperately to not keel over laughing, Joel simply nod biting his teeth to keep his mouth from opening.

"That was intense!"

Joel smiled shaking his head baffled how Kyle could never have had a girlfriend, and as he watched Kyle walking beside him with a grin on his face, he saw an innocence that he had never seen in any other person in their twenties, an innocence he didn't expect to see in this particular boys being and he smiled. "It's cool Evans, we'll get through this."

"I just want to run away man." He sighed, "I just can't keep doing this."

"Doing what?"

"Lying." He said looking up into Joel's eyes, feeling an alarming sense of trust and comfort in his first friend in years, "I don't know who I am anymore."

"I've been there my friend." Said Joel managing a wearily comforting smile, "You just have to take it easy man. It's just a date."

"No it's not just a date." Kyle grunt angrily, "It's everything about me, my entire history is just…" he cut himself off cold, clenching his fists tightly.

Joel shook his head, "Look I can have a plane by tomorrow, why don't we fly out to the coast for the weekend and just break away from everything? I know I need a break from this place."

Kyle frowned, "A plane? You have a plane?"

"Well no, it's my grandfather's plane but I can use it whenever I want to. It's kind of a family plane?"

Shaking his head with a laugh, Kyle nod, "Joel I don't know you - do I?"

"I don't think so no." Joel laughed with a smug smile, "Let's do it, let's ditch this place and just go wild for a few days. Drink booze on the beach, pick up some hot babes and just forget about Secunda and everyone in it."

Kyle felt the urge to go wild since he got into the car back in Salt Rock, and Joel's words were tempting but he declined politely.

"Alright then listen up, let me explain how this is going to go down." Said Joel taking a seat.

As the members of mayoral committee adjourned from the board room, Keagen hurried up to Harper in stride, lowering his voice as they walked.

"Sir, Graham Knox just called. They're considering shutting down all mining procedures indefinitely. We need to leave for Johannesburg immediately to attend the share holders meeting. The Mayor is already on route."

"Did you hear anything from Gondwe's office?" asked Harper as they hurried down the marble passage way. Keagen shook his head, "Nothing, they're saying nothing. I have our people at the papers searching to confirm the rumors out at E Shaft but Agent Black is on site."

"He confirmed?"

"He's the source."

Harper stopped turning to him, his face riddled with concern, "What about Lee?"

"Can't reach him sir."

"I knew this was going to be the outcome. Damn it!" Harper hissed as they continued to walk down the hallway towards the elevator.

"Sir…" said Keagen nervously, "I've sent my family to Australia."

Harper turned to him alarmed, "Australia?"

The elevator doors opened and they paused as the load emptied.

"With all due respect sir I have my procedures in place should the shit hit the fan." Keagen said as the doors shut them in, "Only

God knows how this is going to over complicate things, especially at the mine with new specialists being brought in. This falls directly under planning and development Sir."

"I know that, thank you Max." he snarled, "I respect you sending your family out of harms ways but when and if Mr. Lee's arrogance proves frivolous, then we jump boat together is that understood? Until then every action we take must appear normal."

"What if we can't sir?" Keagen shrugged worriedly, "They are all sitting pretty and we're left with the fall out. There is a zero guarantee that the blast did what they wanted it to. It's a police matter now sir and we don't have high enough connections to keep a lid on any findings down there. I doubt Black is going to remain on site. And sir, there's something else…"

"Well…"

"Sir, deputy president Twain is said to be visiting the area." Keagen sighed, "Typical political stunt to visit with the families of the miners who died in the blast."

"Jesus Christ." Harper hissed rubbing his brow, "If they shut the mining of E Shaft down, the problem falls directly into our lap, and any audit into your department will reveal that you have been trying to get involved in the shaft. Moorecroft is on our file, the security detail from a month ago, and can you imagine what would happen if they found out what you did for Michael Baden?"

Harper heaved an exhausted sigh.

"It's enough to pose a lot of questions that we can't answer without ratting out Lee, Gondwe or deputy president Twain. Why would he risk coming out here at a time like this? It's ridiculous!"

"It can only be something approved from higher up sir. That means King wants him out here, they're arrogant enough to send Twain here because they have nothing to worry about. We are the link this side, and we both know what they did to Noordman and Lyle."

"I understand." Harper sighed as they stepped out of the elevator towards the large glass doors, "Keep trying for Lee, or Gondwe. I will not go down with this ship! Call the madam speaker, I want a meeting with her as soon as she is available. If I can get her to agree to help convince the committee to push for the reopening to commence for economic purposes, the sooner equipment and men down there will ruin whatever's left to expose us all. We can only expect the worst if our beloved Deputy President Twain rocks up here to speak with grieving widows."

Keagen shook his head, "They're over confident. It makes me nervous sir. Just what else are they aware that we aren't?"

With his black Cortina parked off the side of the road facing the front of the police patrol vehicle, Michael got out with a smoke in hand as he head over towards the patrol car where Nkosi sat eating a burger.

Without greeting, he reached into the inner pocket of his black leather jacket and handed him the week's earnings.

"Feels light." Said Nkosi shaking the white envelope as he chewed, "How much?"

"Three thousand eight hundred." Michael answered nervously.

Nkosi shook his head, chewing with a frustrated sigh.

"We're getting better." Said Michael shrugging his shoulders anxiously, "With me out of commission it was a bit hard to see clients."

Nkosi scoffed, admiring the bruising he put on the side of Michael's face.

"You are short."

"I have until tomorrow don't I?"

"You can make target in twenty four hours?"

Michael nod worriedly, "I might surprise you."

"If you don't, you know what I will do this time?" Nkosi said with a cold glare, "And she has such a pretty face."

Michael nervously looked down as he exhaled a ball of smoke into the icy wind, "I need a favor."

"Well now, since when do I owe you any favors?"

"Don't worry, you'll benefit from it." frowned Michael looking up at him with an arrogant grin.

Nkosi laughed shaking his head doubtfully.

"I want to throw a party." Said Michael puffing again, the icy wind now chilling up his back as he huddled from its blow, "A big party, I can't push E mostly."

"Where?"

"The old storage facilities off the R13."

Nkosi laughed starting the engine, "With everything going on at E shaft you want to party on more mine property?"

"It's not anywhere near E shaft, I just need to know we can go big without being raided." Nkosi shook his head licking his teeth and Michael sighed, "It will be fine. We'll leave it just like we found it. I can assure you."

"Are you sure you want to be throwing a party out there? It's not far from where your brother was found."

Michael sighed, "I know. But it's irrelevant. I can't let ghosts spoil my life. Those stores are big enough to host a big event, which is what I need to reach your target. It's secluded and big enough for the amount of people I'm expecting."

Nkosi laughed shaking his head arrogantly, "Alright Harper, consider the area yours."

Michael nod with a smirk and Nkosi turned to him cocking his head with a curious frown. "Speaking about your brother, the one who killed himself." He said with intentional egotism, "What exactly was in that box he gave you?"

"What are you talking about?"

"After he died, that thing he sent you." Said Nkosi with a curious frown, "My cousin was working at the post office at the time he chickened out."

Michael looked down angrily trying to ignore his deliberate disrespect.

"He told me once that a there was a big fuss at work about men asking questions about the parcel that was delivered to your home, after the funeral."

"What are you talking about?" frowned Michael as curiosity began to nibble at him.

"He told me your brother had a package sent to you if he did not sign in on it every week. He kept it in safety deposit. I wanted to ask you the first time we met, but Naude's blood was still fresh on your hands and I forgot. Now you talk about that place and I'm curious Harper, what in there that caused such a big drama?"

"My brother left me a box?" said Michael frowning worriedly, "I don't know, I don't ever remember getting that."

Nkosi shrugged shaking his head, "Well whatever it was, my cousin said it caused a lot of trouble at work. He was even fired."

Michael sighed, his head reeling through his memories for one he could not find.

"Enjoy your party Harper."

Michael nod, still in great awe and confusion as the patrol car skid off past him, onto the road with the sirens blaring.

With his tires screeching to a stop outside the Harper Mansion, Michael leapt out of the car angrily, pausing briefly to admire the mansion he hadn't returned to since his brother's death four years ago. He clenched his fists and head towards the front door.

"Michael!" Gasped the family steward in surprise as he walked in.

"Hey Ned." He managed a smile, "Where is he?"

"Your fathers busy with a very important meeting sir, perhaps you would like to have some coffee while you wait?"

"I'm not staying long Ned." Michael rushed past him towards the back of the house. As the doors flung open his father and the three men in the room spun around in alarm.

"What's the meaning of this?" asked Harper stepping forward, his face utterly devoid of the surprise to see the son who he had not spoken to in months.

Michael sighed breathlessly, his body filled with anger, "Hi dad, got a second?"

"Get out of here Michael!" Harper said rounding past Mr. Lee and Keagen, "I don't have time for your shenanigans."

"Was there ever a package delivered here from Lyle a week after he died?" he asked abruptly as his father tried to usher him out of the room.

"What package?" frowned his father with annoyance, uncomfortably looking to Mr. Lee who raised his eyebrows in surprised curiosity. Keagen sighed nervously, looking down.

"It was supposed to come to me if he didn't sign it every week." Michael said adamantly taking another step forward, his fists trembling.

"Are you ridiculous? I'm in the middle of a very important meeting here!"

"I want to know. Did Lyle have a box delivered to his house after his funeral?" Michael questioned more calmly now, "Yes or no?" There was a pause and Harper turned back to the others, providing them with both an apologetic and courteous smile before grabbing his son's arm and ushering him to the door.

"Now listen here Michael." Harper said softly, his voice riddled with fury, "I don't know what you're talking about. There was never any type of package delivered to this house after your brother died ok. Now let it go and get out of here."

"Are you sure about that?"

"Who told you such a rubbish fable?

"A cop did, his brother worked at the post office when Lyle died."

"I'm begging you, please just let the idea go, you are mistaken alright?" said Harper in a pleading urge, "Just get out of here Michael, I don't want you here. Ever."

Michael sighed in aggravation, shoving his father's hands from his arms, "Whatever."

He head out and slammed the door shut.

Harper turned to the other raising his hands, "I'm terribly sorry. He just…"

"What was he asking about Frank?" Mr. Lee asked with a determined stare, "What parcel?"

Harper shook his head, "Nothing, I've taken care of it four years ago."

"Is it what I think it is Frank?" Lee said stepping towards him with a cold stare locked in his eyes, "Because if you withheld anything from us, I can assure you everyone you know will die in very terrible way. Every single person you know."

Harper sighed shaking his head, "I told you I handled it Lee, and I did. He knows nothing about what Lyle did."

"You better not mess with me Frank." Lee said staring into his eyes.

"You have my word Mr. Lee, there was never a package. I took care of everything right after you snapped my son's neck."

A tension hung and Harper shook his head, "Keagen and I handled everything that needed to be handled Mr. Lee. We aren't standing here because my mishaps, we're standing here because of yours. Everything you mishandled at E shaft has brought us to this point Lee, let's not lose focus because of what a drug addict might think he knows."

Lee smirked angrily and turned back to the schematic of the underground tunnels.

As Michael drove along the streets avoiding going home after school at least until the night had grown much later, he chewed on a stick of gum with music blaring from the speakers and subs in the back of the Cortina. His body was pumping with adrenaline from an ecstasy he had taken and he felt almost more open and alert.

As he stopped for the red light on Main Street, a white Opel pulled up beside him with two guys the same age as himself. The one had his entire arm hanging out the window, their music pumping too.

Mike sighed and laughed at them before looking back to the front. "You got a problem?" called the passenger. Michael turned to him and said nothing. The light flicked green and the car shot forward, the passenger motioning to him a jerk off.

Mike laughed and floored the Cortina and within seconds it sped up beside them, its mighty engine not near its full capacity. Mike threw up his middle finger before flooring it and leaving them in trail. Suddenly the blue Alcatel cell phone rang from its spot clipped onto his sun visor, the cell phone that only rang when it meant business.

Slowing down again, the white car in the distance of his rear view mirror, Mike answered.

"Lloyd here."

Michael felt his skin crawl. He had taken the job after Jessie mentioned his interest to have a boy being the one to donor a full body massage.

"What can I do for you Mr. Lloyd?"

"I have something I want to try."

"Alright, let me know which night and I'll bring Jessie over."

"Not the girl. But there will be more this time."

Suddenly Mike froze and began to slack off until pulling to a stop at the pavement in front of the stores.

"Oh?" said Mike nervously, his gut trembling inside.

"I have a daughter, a virgin."

"Yes?" he asked as his body fell to an eerie lull, Mr. Lloyd's strong Afrikaans accent creepier now than before as he spoke English.

"She lives with her mother in Roodepoort, but she is visiting this weekend. I want you to come and have the sex with my daughter."

Michael's heart raced, his Afrikaans tone dark and soft.

"Are you there?"

"Yes, yes sorry… Ok, how old is your daughter?"

"She's eighteen her birthday was a week ago." His voice was rasp, ghostly.

"She is going to start college in Roodepoort, but she…" he paused sighing, *"The details isn't important ok? She knows that I want you to do her. Fuck. Sex with…with her. She wants it."*

"Mr. Lloyd I…"

"My daughter…she's a virgin." He said cutting him off as soon as he heard the hesitation in Michael's tone.

"And she knows you're going to pay someone to…do this to her?" he asked as courteously as he could, "I don't understand Mr. Lloyd, why would you want her to lose it to me?"

"It's the only way I can be sure."

"Sure of what?" he asked, his heart racing anxiously. The line remained silent.

"I will pay you two thousand rand, no questions asked. Just come and fuck my daughter and go home again."

Michael felt nauseous as his stomach writhed and churned, but the money would take him to target for the first time and he heaved a very heavy sigh nodding with closed eyes, "Alright. I'll do it. What time?"

Heaving out a morbid sigh, he wiped his hands down over his face, the concern and fear tingling around his body. He hurriedly dug into the glove compartment and dashed a line of cocaine out on the mirror, regretting that he had answered the phone. His nose stung as the white powder flung up and he clenched his teeth torn between the desire for the two grand and the awful reality that he had just agreed to lay with a man's daughter without knowing why Lloyd wanted to be sure of something.

Pulling to a stop behind the Evoque in the parking across from the mall, Mike got out lighting a cigarette and round to the passenger door.

"Feels like some illegal meeting." Michael said, "I could have come to your house Mac D."

"No this is fine." Joel said anxiously, "No smoking in my car."

Michael flicked the smoke out the window, "Excuse me sir…"

"What do you want Harper? And I'm warning you if you reference any drugs or weapons or anything illegal in my car I'll report your ass to police."

Mike smiled.

"What do you want Harper?"

"I'm in big shit." He said sighing, "Really big shit and there's a girl involved too."

"I'm not paying for an abortion!"

"No Jesus!" Michael sighed angrily, "Can you just let me get it out? This isn't easy for me either so…so don't be a jackass about it ok?"

Joel sighed nodding, "Go ahead then."

As Michael carefully began plotting out how Nkosi and Venter got him involved in their syndication of drugs, pornography and escort services, Joel fell cold and numerously wanted to interrupt with objection and various other judgments, but when he noticed the tears in Michaels eyes as he spoke about Jessie Noordman, the beatings he endured and how he had been swallowed into his pit of despair, he knew that Collin was somehow giving him a second chance to try and save someone from their own demons.

Michael sighed shaking his head, "I know it's a lot to take in but, this isn't for me it's for Jessie."

"I don't have that kind of money Michael…" Joel said, "Jesus you need more than money because it's never going to stop. There has to be a way through this."

"I've been on this road Joel, I've thought of everything I could do to get us out of it." Michael explained careful to omit anything to do with Andre Naude. Joel huffed, "So what are you asking me here exactly?"

"I want to get Jessie out by paying Nkosi her debt and try and get her out of Secunda as far away as possible. I know your family has the resources and the money to help."

Joel shook his head, "It's not that easy."

"I know, but now someone else knows how deep I am." Michael looked to him, "Put yourself in my shoes Mac D. I took a big risk talking to you because I don't know you from shit. I am asking for your help because I can't save Jessie alone and if I don't ask you, I have no one else to turn to."

"What about your dad? You have resources of your own."

Mike scoffed a laughed, "Please, he's not even my real father. He's a liar and a sadistic pig. He wouldn't help me with money if my life support depended on it. Trust me! And he's lying about Lyle and whatever he sent me so I couldn't possibly turn to him with this. You are the only person that knows."

Joel frowned and a silence hung in the car.

"Who is Lyle?" he asked finally. Michael sighed shaking his head, "Long story and it's irrelevant to what I'm asking."

"No. No everything is relevant here Michael. You're asking me to get involved in something really dangerous, I mean dirty cops? I think I have the right to know what else is lurking in your story if I'm even going to consider putting myself at risk here."

"So you'll help me?"

"Lyle your brother?"

Trying hard to keep the story contained to only the facts and not his suspicions, Michael told Joel about his brother's death, the suicide note and the package he wanted him to see that never made it past his conniving father and his henchmen. Putting his hands over his face, Joel shook his head.

"Jesus Christ this is getting unbelievable."

"Please, I swear I'm telling you everything and it's true." Mike urged, "My life isn't about silver spoons the way everyone thinks Mac D, yes I'm a screw up and I have some twisted stories but I really just need your help! Please!"

Joel turned to him, "I need time to think about all of this, I can't tell you right now because…I mean Jesus…"

Michael nod and the alarm on his cell phone began to beep.

"I have to go anyway." He said plucking it from his pocket, "I'm going to follow up on a lead about my brother's box. Can I contact you tomorrow?"

Joel turned to him, his curiosity and thoughts spiralling in shock, "Why do you think you can trust me with this?"

"I'm desperate and…" he paused with a weary laugh, "The way you freaked out at your party…I could see you through your bullshit. If I had any other option trust me, I wouldn't have brought this to you."

Just then Joel's cell phone alarm beeped from the cup holder by the gears and he hurriedly shut it off.

"I've got something to do, for Kyle." He explained clipping in his seat belt. Michael nod and reached for the door handle.

"If you want…" Joel said to his own surprise, "I can come with you on this lead of yours?"

Michael scanned him and offered a smile, realizing that it could be pure proof that Joel needed in order to give second thought to what he had been told.

"Sure, why not."

Joel nod with a smile and turned the ignition on. As he head out the mall parking, he filled with nervousness and confusion as to why he had suddenly felt so compelled to help the dark haired menace.

Chapter Nine:
Rendezvous Night

For the remainder to the late afternoon, the storm outside grew stronger as a downpour washed over the town. Sitting in the Evans' silent lounge holding a cup of coffee, Joel and Michael both felt uncomfortable. Kyle felt the eeriness of the storm inside of him as he watched the rain drops racing on the windows.

"I can't stay locked up in this house anymore. You said so yourself."

"Yes but…" Claire paused looking to the two young adults on her couch awkwardly, "I don't think you going out on a Friday night of all nights, is a good idea I mean…what the hell? This is totally new Kyle. We don't know how things are here, drunk drivers, parties that get out of hand…"

Joel looked down nervously, "It's just a movie ma'am"

"Yes I know that." She snarled unintentionally, "I'm surprised."

Edward sat forward, "Michael, Joel would you give us a moment? I'm sure you understand that this is a very sudden thing and well…we don't know you."

"You know my dad actually." Said Michael grinning, "Frank Harper? And his dad is Raymond McDonald your boss."

Edward frowned and Claire stood with her mouth agape looking between all the men in the room in utter surprise. Kyle sighed shaking his head, "Can you guys give me a sec'?"

Michael and Joel nod and hurried to the entrance hall, going outside to wait on the front porch.

"You wanted this damn move to make it all better but how am I supposed to make friends when I'm chained to the house?" snarled Kyle again.

Edward barked as courteously as he could, "Do you know what a surprise this is to your mother and I? Out of the blue we find out you have friends and ironically both of them just happen to be somehow linked to my employment."

"It's all just a bit to strange Kyle!" Claire said, "It's very, very sudden I actually feel like I've had this dream before."

"I'm not asking to have a place of my own…" Kyle urged, "I just wanted to go out with some friends from campus. I really can't believe you guys are acting like this."

"Drugs, alcohol…" Edward scoffed, "We don't know these guys Kyle. How long have you known them?"

"Awhile…Since I started there about."

"And you never mentioned this to us?"

"I didn't know they were my friends."

Claire looked to her husband shaking her head, "I just…I'm shocked. You leave the house one way, come back with two friends. One a millionaire and the other…who is he?"

Edward stood up and put his arm around her shoulders, explaining the connection as Kyle huffed into the sofa angrily.

"Look I'm twenty one years old. Technically I don't need your permission!" he scoffed, "Why are you being like this?"

Claire moved to sit beside him, "Kyle…do you seriously not realize how strange this seems?"

Outside on the porch, Joel raised his concerns in a whisper as to why someone of Kyle's age needed his parents' permission and Michael, having a clear idea of who their friend was, tried hard to show convincing uncertainty. He checked his watch anxiously and then head back inside.

"Excuse me…" he said peering in at the lounge, "If I may just say something…because I don't think Kyle's had this type of experience before?"

Claire and Edward turned to him, their bodies falling cold in alarm and Kyle shook his head with wide apprehensive eyes.

"Kyle's told me a little bit about his past, not much but I know enough to understand why you and Mrs. Evans are reacting this way." He started, Kyle still shaking his head.

Joel carefully stepped in by the front door just enough to eaves drop without being seen.

"The thing is, Kyle deserves to have some fun." Michael continued respectfully, "I get it, Kyle doesn't want me to tell you that he's opened up to me..."

Claire and Edward, both stunned that their son had opened up to another person outside of therapy, turned and looked to Kyle.

"Kyle's a good guy, I'm a good guy. I realize this must be totally strange and unexpected, but the fact of the matter is Kyle needs to know what the world is like. What the mall is like, what the movies is like. He's never been inside a cinema for fuck sake." Edward and Claire's glare turned cold and Michael carefully apologized. Kyle watched Michael's show and found himself holding his breath.

"You have my word, Kyle will be home on time and in good health. I don't do drugs, Joel is the heir to millions so he's squeaky clean – in fact frustratingly so." Michael smiled, "I don't know Kyle all that well but he's a really decent guy just trying to figure out how to get back to normal after everything...and as much as you both seem to have every right to be concerned, I just think he needs to be given some credit here."

"Maybe you should go." Said Kyle sitting forward.

"He is a grown up, technically speaking. And he doesn't need your permission, but here he is with two grown up friends asking for it." Mike insisted turning to Claire and Edward, "And yes you don't know me or Mac D, I mean Joel, but Kyle does and having the balls to bring us here and ask you for permission is saying something. He wants to have some fun, to feel remotely normal and we three know that Kyle needs that."

At the door Joel frowned, his thoughts racing in curiosity as he listened to Michael's scene unfolding behind a brilliant charm.

"Let's face it…most of the time Kyle's nothing but a self absorbed, arrogant and blatantly cold person. He's so lost already that it depresses flowers."

Claire huffed a smile shaking her head, "Thank you Michael, can we just have a minute please? I appreciate you standing up for him but this is very much a family matter."

Michael nod with a smile and head back to the front, opening the door just as Joel hurried back towards the edge of the porch. Kyle dropped his head into his hands wondering if it had always been an age old tradition for boys to struggle so greatly for a chance to meet with a girl. He wanted to tell them the truth but realized that due to Michael's gambit about the cinema that it was too late to admit to a skew truth.

"He's right." Edward agreed turning to face the sofa, "Kyle doesn't have to ask us if I can go out with his friends."

"But I am because I owe you both that. Or would it have been better if I just snuck out the window?" said Kyle realizing there was a gap to take. Claire dropped her head wearily and Edward laughed, "You opening up to someone like that…I'm proud of you Kyle."

Claire heaved a sigh, "I'm also very proud of you Kyle. Surprised as hell but proud."

"As the head of this household…" Edward winked, "I want you back by eleven sharp."

"Eleven!" gasped Claire in alarm.

"We can arrange with Beth next door to take Ben for a couple of hours so you and I can still have a romantic time together like we planned when we thought Jimmy was taking the boys. Kyle in turn can go out until we return at eleven." He suggested.

Kyle smiled, admiring his step father and appreciating that somehow the dilemma had made his parents proud of him.

Claire sighed anxiously, "Eleven Kyle, not a minute later."

"Thank you." He got up to face Edward.

"And don't think for one second we aren't going to touch on this whole…everything when you get back young man." Claire added standing up beside him, "And I don't want to have any excuses. I think you owe us an explanation for all your secrecy."

Kyle nod nervously and managed a weary smile, heading past them to the front door.

"It worked?" Mike asked grinning as Kyle shut the door behind him. Ignoring the elephant in the air, Joel shook his head, "Dude you can at least go put on a new shirt."

"Why?"

"Because she saw that one today…" Joel said, "Go get a new shirt on, and put something else on your feet. Just change everything."

"And maybe do something with your hair?"

"My hair?" Kyle frowned. Michael laughed, "Are you guys for real? What is this like his first date?"

Kyle turned to him with a scolding glare and Michael realized that Boy X had probably never even really kissed a girl.

"Ok listen up." Michael said stepping to him, "You go back in there, make it snappy. Get a new shirt, jean and some decent black shoes. Wash your face and comb your hair."

"Aftershave too." Joel added, "In case she moves in for a hug."

Michael nod, "If you tie up your hair she'll see more of your face."

"Good point." Joel nod, "There's not enough time left for a shower, so do a quick basin bath for all the key areas."

"Chick's dig clean nails so give them a scrub."
Kyle raised his hands, "This is way too much…"
Joel and Michael laughed, "Ten minutes dude, make it count."

Drumming down now a lot less heavily than before, the drizzle was almost invisible to both the eye and the ear. The interior of the Hot Pot was warm, lit with soft lights along the walls and large steel chandeliers that hung above each table. The smell of strong coffee and grilling steaks greet all those who entered and with almost every table fully seated, the atmosphere was both lively and homely.

As Kyle neared the bar counter where waiters and waitresses hurriedly got their tables their beverage orders, he caught a glimpse of Liz in the back with Troy. The soft golden glow of the lights touched her soft skin delicately and for a second he felt peace.

"What can I get you?" came a loud voice from over the counter. Kyle turned to the tall strong man with dark hairy arms and broad friendly smile. Kyle shook his head, "Nothing thank you. I'm waiting for someone."

"You're not Kyle are you?"

"I am actually." He nod awkwardly, "Who are you?"

"The names Frank." Said the man holding out his hand, "Liz hasn't stopped talking about you since…I don't know."

Kyle managed a shy smile and shook his hand, careful not to over squeeze as per Joel's instruction, "You must be her dad?"

"I am." He laughed warmly, "Lucky for you - you didn't order Scotch right?"

Kyle managed an awkward smile and nod as he took a seat.

"So, what are your plans with my daughter son?" frown Frank leaning in over the counter, "Marriage, babies and then…divorce?"

Kyle frowned, gasping nervously, "None of the above sir."

Joel never told me about this!

Frank shrugged rudely, "So you don't think she's good enough to marry?"

"No sir!" said Kyle defensively, "It's not like that at all, and your daughter is a kind and very decent girl! She deserves much better than settling down, or divorcing, someone like me."

Frank frowned with a serious scrutiny building behind his eyes and Kyle felt himself shrinking in the bar stool.

Once more Frank ruptured out with laughter, "I was just teasing anyhow. If Liz speaks so highly of you then well, I'm sure you're a nice boy." He said holding his hand out to Kyle again.

"Thank you sir." Said Kyle, again careful not to over imply his manliness in the strength of his hand shake.

"No Kyle, thank you. For reminding me what a lucky man I am for having a decent and kind daughter." He laughed, "But I'm not sure if your response impressed me very much, you don't have a high opinion of yourself and I wouldn't want my daughter wasting her time on someone who thinks he is worthless."

Kyle shrugged, "I just meant…"

"I know son, I was kidding!" Frank laughed again, "I know you're nervous, relax son. I won't give you any further grief."

Kyle nod smiling shyly.

"I do have a gun license though so keep that in mind college boy." He said with a straight face, "Have a good date."

Kyle smiled, "Thank you sir."

"Please tell me my father wasn't giving you the gun license speech." said Liz as pulled up the chair beside Kyle.

"Just letting the young man know where he stands." He grinned.

Liz rolled her eyes and turned to face Kyle as her father head off.

Kyle smiled, "Hey."

"Hey."

"Very nice guy your dad." He said looking down awkwardly, running Joel's breakdown of do's and don'ts through his head

"Yeah, he's a great person." Said Liz proudly.

"Your mom work here to?"

Liz sighed heavily, "No, she died when I was seven."

Ok left foot in mouth.

"I am sorry I didn't…"

"It's a fair question, don't worry." She said smiling. The way her face glow in the dim lights made his body lull with warm bubbles and he could not help but smile.

"Are you ready to go?"

Kyle frowned worriedly, "You mean we're not eating here?"

She laughed and shook her head, "I didn't plan on it no."

"Oh." He said looking down worriedly.

"I don't mind we can stay here, I kind of assumed you would be uncomfortable with my father being in the same building with his gun license in easy reach?" she smiled.

Kyle laughed and shook his head, "No, why would I mind? I'm not going to try anything I shouldn't. Besides you owe me a smoothie, you promised."

Liz laughed nodding her head, "I did, didn't I?"

The drizzle sounded almost relaxing as it hollowed against the roof of the black Ford Cortina. Parked facing one of the many shebeens in the Embalenhle township, Michael tried to gather together what exactly he would say when he walked in, trying to convince himself that being the only white people inside wasn't going to cause a disruption to the patrons Friday night recreation and beside him Joel sat anxiously regretting offering his support. Inside the air hung thick with smoke, dimming the lights on the ceiling and it smelt of sweat, beer and stale smog. Not yet noticed, Michael and Joel made their way to the bar and smiled as best they could to hide the nervousness on their faces as they asked for Gabriel Kesha.

Making their way through the crowded round tables, nodding and smiling at those staring at them in surprise, they finally reached the side of the shebeen shack.

"Gabriel?" he asked loudly over the Pop-Kwaito music blaring from the speakers.

The short round man turned to him, "Yes?"

"My names Michael Harper. I'm a friend of your cousin Brian Nkosi." He said nodding, "This is my friend Joel. Could we sit for a second?"

"Go for gold my laaitjie." He smiled ushering him to the seat beside him, the others at the table simply continuing their game of cards.

"I know you must be surprised." Michael smiled, "But I have a question about the work you did when you were still working for the Secunda post office."

"Yes that was many years ago umlungu." He laughed referring to him as 'white boy'.

"I know Gabriel, but I really need some information." Said Michael sliding him three fifty rand notes, "Four years ago you delivered a package to my father, he was still the Mayor, Frank Harper."

"Yes! They fired me by the post office, lost my job… it was nothing vir die suits." he said hurriedly putting the money in his pants pocket, "I know, I know what you talking about."

"That's good Gabriel, because I need you to tell me what happened."

Gabriel shook his head, gulping back his milk stout before lowering beside Michael in a whisper.

"I don't know what was in daai box my laaitjie, but your father's suits were very sick about it umlunghu. I remember it was in brown paper by the boys in the back office."

Joel frowned, "So there's no way you can tell us what it was?"

"No only the post office manager and security are allowed to know what gets wrapped and sent. Safety regulation so we don't do the delivery for bombs or illegal stuff."

"Who do I speak to? Do you remember who was working that day?" Mike asked, his heart beat throbbing in his throat. Gabriel took another gulp of his beer stout and looked down deep in thought.

"It was four years ago umfana." He laughed finally, "I remember little about it."

Michael sighed and nod with disappointment, "Alright, I understand it's a long time ago."

Joel hand him a two hundred rand note, "Can you try remember?" Mike turned to him in surprise and Joel shrugged.

Gabriel laughed taking the note directly to his pocket, "I delivered the package to a guy, a tall whitey, hoekom you don't ask him?"

Michael shrugged his shoulders shaking his head, figuring it was probably Maxwell Keagen, and that would lead him nowhere.

"Die suits." Said Gabriel pausing to gulp back his beer stout, "They didn't like that we gave that box away. Everyone on duty that day was fired. Some even went missing, some died in snaaks accidents."

"Are you serious?" Joel gasped before Mike nudged him.

"How do you know it had anything to do with my brother?" Gabriel laughed sitting back in his chair, his chuckle loud over the music, "I know but I keep quiet, your pappa's suits make me scared."

Joel smiled putting another wad of money on the table, "Give us something, please it's his brother."

Gabriel leaned forward, "Your brother he saw something, something that made him kak scared for the suits. We all knew it because they said his name over and over. But you will have to see the mense at the office if you want to know more, I only know what I know."

Michael smiled and stood up, handing him another three fifty rand notes, "Thank you Gabriel."

As they head out back to the car Joel shrugged, "So our next move would be finding out if the post office keeps any kind of record on their staff register."

Mike turned to him, "Ok look Mac D, I get it – you need some kind of proof that what I've told is real, but there is no 'we' ok? I don't want you in my affairs, I just want you to help Jessie get out of this mess."

Joel laughed shaking his head as they got to the Evoque.

"I'm in your affairs either which way. At least this way I can see firsthand where my money will be going. If you can't trust your father, I can't fully trust you until I know what I'm dealing with. And a key factor in this story is your brother. He was mixed up with Nkosi before you were, and now your dad is hiding something about him. Just to protect myself I deserve to know where this rabbit hole leads. Or I step back and you can forget about me helping you or Jessie, my safety is my only concern here – sorry to say."

Mike sighed shaking his head, "Fine whatever."

For the entire time Liz and Kyle sat talking in the rear booth against the window, he struggled to talk about himself without letting the blackness ooze from his mouth and send her screaming for her father's gun. They covered the general topics Joel had briefed him about, but she wanted inside and he felt himself battling to breathe on more than one occasion. But she was so lost in him, she hadn't picked up on his apprehensive tenseness. Questions directed at his childhood were the hardest to answer, without letting tears seep from his dark eyes. But he was able to talk to her about the very few memories he had, before this eighth birthday, before all the darkness closed in.

There was a presence between them at the table all night, a physical force pulling them together and drawing them closer on a connection he had never realized could exist to a person as torn and broken as him.

"What's the one thing about your life you would do differently if you had a time machine and could go back and tell yourself to do it differently?" she asked sipping the smoothie.

Kyle looked down, his chest tightening.

"I would go back and tell myself to hold onto my mother more often that I did." She said smiling bravely, "To kiss her and stare at her so I could remember her face without needing to open my purse for a picture of her."

He smiled, "That's really sweet."

"What about you Evans?"

"Well…" he said nervously, heaving a deep breath as he swallowed, "I have too many things to change, and I wouldn't know where to start."

She frowned curiously, "You're being evasive. Does the mystery thing really work for you Kyle?" She sipped the smoothie again.

"What do you mean?"

"I bet you had girls lining up all your life, hot guy on the beach, popular no doubt." She giggled, "Speaking of which, how many relationships have you had?"

He looked down in frustration, "Do we have to go there?"

"Yes." She smirked teasingly, "Are you shy Evans?"

He shook his head, sending a forkful of baked potato into his mouth. She tilt her head watching him, the muscles in his face bulging as he chewed, his lips oily and she found herself gently biting her bottom lip. He looked up frowning with a skew smile and she went into a putty state leaning forward, amazed at how someone so beautiful could be sitting having dinner with her.

"Are you waiting for my answer?"

"Yes." She smirked.

Why didn't Joel tell me girls were into this kind of thing? Why are they?

He shook his head smiling shyly, "I've been with a lot of people."

"A lot?" she frowned curiously, "Classify, but spare the details."

"I don't know, a lot."

"Were they all serious?" she frowned still. He shrugged, "I don't know what you mean?"

"Well all these girls, were any of them serious relationships or are you a bang and blame kind of guy?"

Did I just say Bang? Oh my god I can imagine him banging...

He froze tilting his head cautiously, "I don't think I understood the initial question."

Laughing behind her hand, she felt her face redden, "Were you talking about sex?"

"What were you talking about?"

"Relationships Kyle!" she giggled, "Oh my god..."

He looked down shaking his head in embarrassment.

Right foot in the mouth. No more feet, no more room.

"Wow. Ok." She said composing herself, "So that was awkward..."

"Yeah." He said looking down still, feeling the filth seeping out of him.

"So how many *relationships* have you had?" she asked smiling, passionate of each second of his shy smile hanging from the corner of his lips and the boyish blush in his tanned face. He looked up into her eyes and the strength of the awesome in her gaze felt like wave of ocean crashing over him with a great intensity.

"I've never had anyone before like that." He said softly, "This is my first date."

She frowned gently, touched and bewildered by the amazing specimen of young man before her with eyes so intense – she couldn't move her eyes off of him.

A lot of women but I'm his first date at twenty one? Is that even humanly possible for someone who looks like this?

Her thoughts spiraled inside her mind, but she couldn't move. Her heart raced rampantly against her chest, her blood heated beneath her skin and her breathing shallow.

A part of him wanted to speak and break the silence between them, but in seconds he realized that the best part of his day was that very moment of being with her, nothing said, no words spoken, just the two of them alone in the booth with the drizzle gently rapping against the window. He looked down, realizing that her hands were over his and he hadn't even noticed or flinched. Everything inside of him begged him to get up and leave, take this worthlessness away from her and absorb it in the confines of his torment, alone. But he couldn't move, he couldn't take his eyes off of her or ignore what he felt coursing through his entire core, tissue, bone, skin and blood. It was entirely natural.

"I'm not who you think I am Liz." He said softly, "I'm not the guy on the beach who had girls all over him, I'm nothing like what you seem to think I was."

Liz smiled, "I know, I can see it in your eyes Kyle. You're in pain and…that's ok. I might not know why you have this thing about you, keeping you from kissing me or just relaxing when you're with me. But I like you Kyle and I'd really like to explore what this could be because I know you feel it to."

"I felt it from the moment you cracked my skull." He smiled, "But I'm not a good person inside. I'm not ok inside. I don't want to hurt you."

"Then don't."

"I don't understand what's happening to me." He said almost gasping as the electricity between them sparked each pocket of blood rushing through him.

"I think you could if you gave yourself the chance." She said softly.

"You don't know me."

"I want to know you." She smiled, their eyes not disconnecting, "If you can do that I would be really lucky, really honored."

He smiled and before he could think he felt his eyes close as his body leaned forward.

She too felt her eyes close, her skin burning to feel his against her as she moved towards him, her lips parting slowly waiting for his to touch hers and ignite everything they could be.

But a horn screeched from the street outside as a bus swerved for a cyclist crossing without looking and they both sat back in fright, his hands quickly at his sides.

"It's almost time for me to go." He smiled nervously, "I have to be back by eleven."

"Curfew for a college guy?" She nod trying to hide her disappointment, "You get more interesting by the second Evans."

He smiled shyly, "I must say though, this was the best smoothie I've ever had the pleasure of tasting Liz."

She smiled looking down and he frowned, "What?"

"Nothing." She smiled blushing again. "Tell me, please."

"That isn't the smoothie I made. This one is." She nod down to the smoothie she was drinking.

Three feet? Really?

> **Sender: Jessie**
> **Time: 22h06**
>
> Ok Harper I haven't seen you & its coz
> I had stuff to deal with in this head of
> mine. ☹
> I got your 10000000 calls & texts. Im
> ready to chat, call me.
>
> J

He looked at the text message on his cell phone with a heavy sigh, looking up at the Lloyd residence in uneasy anticipation. He felt paranoia following him since he left Joel back at the mall parking and he found himself checking the surroundings for the Evoque before he hurriedly texted a reply message.

He hurriedly sprayed deodorant and got out of the car popping a breath mint into his mouth as he head up the driveway towards the front porch. Everything inside of him screamed to turn and run, but he held his hand out and knocked on the door.

Inside, the house was very dimly lit, the furniture all wooden framed with flower embroidery on the cushions. The house smelt of curry and Lloyd ushered him to sit in the lounge. The walls all around were cluttered with keep sakes ranging from different patterned plates, teaspoons from around the country and globe, and other trinkets. He felt his skin crawl, the house was silent and everything but the lounge was in darkness.

Mr. Lloyd entered from the dark kitchen with two glasses in his hand, one a white wine and the other a red. He was a very tall thin man with long black hair in a side path that curled at the tips. He wore spectacles and had a reddish brown moustache.

"I don't know if you drink white or red." He said holding both glasses out, his Afrikaans accent strong in his English as it had been over the phone. Michael reached for the wine, noting that if he had spiked the drink it would be easier to observe in the white. Mr. Lloyd had only ever made use of the mobile number for Jessie to visit and administer hand jobs. Michael had only met him the one time before after Lloyd specifically asked her to send him. Silence hung as Michael cautiously sipped at the wine, its cheap bitter taste mixing badly with the breath mint.

He cleared his throat nervously, "So Mr. Lloyd, what am I doing here exactly?"

"You came to have sex with my daughter." He said looking down, his voice clearly holding back a nausea of anger and disgust as his eyes failed to look up.

"Is she here?"

Mr. Lloyd nod, and then sipped at the red wine.

Michael looked down uncomfortably

Where is she then? In the dark bedroom?

"She's a good girl." Mr. Lloyd spoke, his gaze still fixed on the carpet, "She does well in her studies."

Michael nod, the silence warping the walls around him, bending down over him.

"She's always been her daddy's little princess."

Oh my god he molests her. Michael felt his heart racing.

"But she is a virgin." Mr. Lloyd said finally looking away from the carpet and up at him.

"I don't understand." Michael said trying to sooth his rampant heart, "Why would you want her to lose her virginity to me?"

There was a long silence, Lloyd's eyes now fixed on the surface of the wine in his glass.

"She wants to go study at UCT. But before she goes I want her to lose her virgin when I can be sure she will not be hurt, so she can learn of sex from you, safe here at home."

He felt a rapture of laughter building inside of him and Michael hurriedly sipped at the cheap white wine.

"You can sex her now." He said standing up abruptly, calling down the passage, "Allie."

Michael's heart leapt up into his throat and he nervously arose to meet the figure heading out of the dark passage. She was young, very young in her face. Dark black hair tied in a pony tail, wearing glasses and thin like her father with small breasts.

"Allie, is jy reg my prinses?"

Oh my god is she ready? What kind of a father is this?

The girl nod excitedly, her entire body trembling and Michael shook his head turning to Lloyd, "Excuse me, is she legal?"

"I'm eighteen." She said nodding, "I can show you my ID."

Lloyd heaved a deep breath, "You can begin."

Michael turned to her nervously, and she smiled shyly taking a step towards him. He looked to her father and then back at her, his body at a halt as his heart tore through him.

She moved up against him, looking to her father nervously before wrapping her arms around him. His hands moved up her thin body against her side, hovering but not touching as she carefully leaned in to kiss his lips.

Michael's eyes remained open the entire time, eyeing her and her father anxiously. She smiled stepping back and turning to her father, "Is dit reg pappa?"

No eighteen year old calls her father 'daddy'. This is wrong, I'm out of here!

"I can't do this, I'm sorry." Michael said rounding past her for the front door when Lloyd grabbed his arm.

"Don't go." he demanded irately.

He sat on the couch beside his white wine, and she sat beside him. Mr. Lloyd took his seat as before, nodding at his daughter to continue. She smiled, leaning in and kissing him with more tongue than he cared to accept. Her left hand slithered around his neck, and gripped his shoulder as her right hand rubbed up and down his thigh. She moved her tongue down his neck, kissing him softly and nibbling at his ear. His eyes reverted to Mr. Lloyd who sat watching calmly on the sofa across from them.

She unzipped his jean and reached for his erection, moving it out of its shelter and out where she began to stroke it and Michael felt his entire body squirm uncomfortably.

Within a few seconds she turned to face her father and he gave a discomforted nod, allowing her to proceed to put Michael's penis in her mouth. Michael wanted to shut his eyes to avoid seeing the suffering and anger in her father's eyes but he felt such discomfort and unease, he feared shutting his eyes even for a second to blink.

"Is she doing it ok?"

Michael's eyes filled with tears, Mr. Lloyd's agony clearly evident as he tried to brave through watching his daughter's head bob up and down. "Should we stop?" he asked nervously. Mr. Lloyd shook his head and gulped down the rest of the red wine. *I can't do this, this is not right. But Jessie.* She continued to bob up and down at his waist with his manhood in her mouth and Michael clenched, "You need to stop now." He said gently tapping her shoulder. Mr. Lloyd sprang up just as she raised her head and he forced her mouth back down on him. His eyes were fiercely staring down at her as Michael clenched the seat as he finished into her mouth.

"Moet nie spoeg nie!" her father said in a dark whisper, instructing her to swallow, his hand on her head. Mr. Lloyd finally let go and stood up, grabbing Michael's glass as he turned back towards his seat, huffing down as he drank. His daughter gagged to the side of the couch, spitting into a pot plant and feeling over ridden with guilt and torture, Michael carefully put his arm on her shoulder.

"Are you alright?" he asked patting her. She sat upright anxiously, braving a smile at her father. "Are we done?" asked Michael with wide terrified eyes. Mr. Lloyd downed the entire glass of white wine and got up without a word, heading to the kitchen leaving the air as tense and thick with vile silence until he returned with the bottle of red wine in his hand.

"Finish it." Said Mr. Lloyd with a broken voice, hurriedly tipping the wine into his gullet.

Michael felt his soul breaking inside, trying hard to remind himself that he needed to reach target before meeting with Nkosi in the morning. He had to reach target or Jessie would meet the brunt of the failure.

As he lay her back naked on the couch, trying to be as comfortable as possible against the wooden arm rests he felt her father's heart break as he carefully inserted himself into her.

He hadn't been with a virgin since his days living in the dorm at the University of Cape Town, but with the circumstances he could not feel it as anything but the world's greatest sin. He thrust only a few times, carefully as she winced below him, every now and again looking over at her father who sat with his hands clenched under his chin, his eyes filled with torture and sadness. He thrust again, only a few more times until he could no longer stand the nausea filling up inside of him, bubbling up into his throat. He shook his head, "I can't do this Mr. Lloyd."

He turned to face him, but something met the side of his face and he toppled off of her onto the ground as more and more lashes ravaged down against him. The girl screamed, backing up in terror on the couch as Mr. Lloyd swung and swung his thin wooden cane at Michael screaming and cursing him for the vile act of penetrating his daughter. He had snapped, lost his mind at the sight he thought he wanted to witness and even as his daughter tried to stop and scream sense into him, he would not stop swinging the cane, and eventually he turned his anger towards his naked daughter.

"You are only mine!"

As the Range Rover Evoque head through town, Kyle regaled Joel with everything said and done during the date, and Joel felt pleased that his advice saved a potentially dangerous evening. He felt like a big brother, sitting at the wheel listening to an excited Kyle ranting on about how strange and wonderful he felt, asking questions about the emotions he was feeling and about what to do next. But Joel still found himself curiously studying Kyle Evans with uncertainty. He knew so little about him, yet so much at the same time. Kyle heaved back in his seat with a smile and Joel took the opportunity to dig.

"So what was up with the goodbye?"

"What do you mean?" he frowned worriedly, "Was it awful?"

"No." he laughed, "Just looked very awkward."

"I have a thing about being touched." Kyle said shaking his head, adamant to not let the darkness devastate the great feelings inside of him. Joel frowned confused, "Is that like a clinical thing or…" Kyle sighed turning to face him, "I had a very rough life ok? Can we leave it at that please? I just want to relish the good right now."

Joel nod smiling and the car slowed to a red light. As much as he wanted to enquire about what he heard earlier during Michael's speech, he knew it would only cause a rift on a night not needing one.

"You know we have some time if you want to catch a beer or something."

Kyle shrugged grinning, "I can't drink."

"Oh?" Joel said shaking his head awkwardly, "So how long do you know Michael?"

Kyle turned to him frowning, "Michael? I barely know him, why?"

"Oh, just figured you guys know each other from Durban."

The roads were quiet and they only had a few minutes to be back in time for Kyle's curfew.

"Is that Michael?" asked Kyle looking to the side where further up in the designated bus stop, a dark figure lay on hands and knees puking beside a black car with the drivers doors still open.

"I don't know, I think so." Joel shrugged, "What the hell?"

The light flicked green and Joel swung the Evoque around, slowly heading towards the stop. "That's him alright."

Michael stumbled to his feet hurriedly as the headlights pulled up behind the Cortina, but the sting against his legs caused him to topple down again. As Joel and Kyle hurried over towards him, he tried to subdue his tears but he couldn't, he kept on weeping from a place far from the reach of his control. They gasped in alarm at the red marks across his arms and face and they both knelt down beside him.

"What the hell happened to you?" Joel asked as Michael dropped his head between his legs. "Go away! I don't need you to see me like this."

Kyle sighed worriedly, looking into the car and around them for signs of anyone responsible but the night was empty.

"Please just go away." He said, his voice broken through his sobbing.

Having a background on Michael that Joel wasn't sure Kyle knew, Joel felt unsure how to proceed and wanted them to let the elephant in the air finally reveal itself. Kyle knelt down in front of Michael.

"Michael, talk to me. What happened?" he asked slowly, calmly. He wanted to scream, he wanted to run, and he wanted to lash out at them, at anything. But he could not move, everything hurt, everything was broken inside of him. Joel turned to Kyle worried, mouthing quietly for permission to call the police but Kyle shook his head. They sat with Michael as he cried into his hands, the night silent all around them.

"Go away." He pleaded softly. Kyle shook his head, putting his hand on Michael's arm, "No, we're here and we're going to stay here until you can tell us what happened."

Joel could see there was a trench between them that somehow Michael knew the story behind Kyle and that Kyle was only scratching the surface of everything Michael told him earlier. Michael looked up at him, and in that moment Kyle froze. It was as though he was looking into his very own eyes, torn, shattered and filled with pain as a darkness from inside clawed at the soul. Michael saw it too and without thinking or pausing or debate, he began to spill the ooze from his mouth, releasing the blackness he had always kept on the inside. He told them about every minute of his life that he could recall from his childhood at the brunt of his father's every disapproval to the death of his mother, and his brother's desire to escape the lie. He spoke about Lyle's suicide and how he gave up everything in Cape Town to come be with Jessie. He spoke about Andre Naude and the night they accidentally killed him. He explained how they evaded the truth until Nkosi found evidence proving that Michael had delivered many of the blows on Andre's body and how he had traces of Jessie's hair and skin under his finger nails. And he told them everything he could muster to recall about what they did to meet with Nkosi's target, leading up to the moment where Mr. Lloyd went blind and began whacking him with the cane before raping his daughter. His sobs echoed in the silent street as they sat there listening to him break free of the torment inside his soul, both Kyle and Joel silently understanding all too much about the silent torment and anguish he had been enduring all the years. Joel felt himself engulfed in Michael's tale in a sense of disbelief that the person everyone in town knew to be a rough and tough go to guy, had all the while simply been a lost and lonely boy with no purpose left but to keep going in order to save the one person who meant anything to him.

A silence fell in the air as he continued to cry and sulk into his hands, knowing that when the tears had stopped everything would change. It was the final splinter's cracking across his soul as it broke from the weight of his own darkness.

He looked up at Joel, "Don't speak a word of this." He said turning to Kyle, "Please."

Kyle shook his head, knowing all too well the suffering of secrets inside one's soul. Joel shook his head, "I won't say anything."

"Jessie is a good person, she doesn't need any more trouble in her life." Said Michael wiping his face, "I know what you must think of me. And I'm sorry you had to be here for this."

Joel sighed heavily, looking down at his wrist watch – 22h49. "Shit Kyle, you're late!"

"Are you going to be alright?" Kyle asked turning to Michael who lit a smoke, the first since he stopped in front of the Lloyd residence. Michael nod with dire regret that he had released everything to two strangers he barely knew. He looked up at Kyle, and he knew there was a darkness inside of him that would keep his mouth closed and when he turned to Joel, the shock riddled over his spoilt face made the blade of regret in his heart twist.

"My father…" said Joel softly, almost breathlessly, "He has a temper and my family is completely broke."

Kyle turned to him curiously as Michael frowned.

"We all have something deep and secret about us Mike." Joel said stepping forward, "At least now you have said it out loud and we have your back Harper."

Michael felt tears welling in his eyes again but he grit his teeth and smiled. Joel held out his fist and a smile crossed Michael's face as he fist-bumped him.

"We better go." Joel said turning to Kyle who shook his head.

"No, first we have to set something straight."

The Cortina eased to a stop in front of the Lloyd residence and the Evoque pulled up behind it. Kyle got out and immediately head towards the porch.

Michael limped out of the car in alarm, "Wait!"

Kyle slammed his hand against the front door and Joel nervously got out of the car, looking to Michael in anticipation.

"What the hell is he going to do exactly?"

The door opened and Kyle grabbed the tall thin man by his shirt and plucked him out onto the front porch, tossing him down the stairs and onto the grass.

"Oh shit." Said Joel rushing towards him when the broken daughter stepped to the door crying out for Kyle to stop. She looked up at him, then at Michael and then continued to holler at Kyle to leave her father alone. Seeing her arms and chest covered in the same red markings as Michael, Joel stopped shaking his head as he watched Kyle pummel her father into the ground. Michael limped up beside Joel, resting against him.

Kyle punched at him over and over again, everywhere but in the face. He aimed at the sides, the stomach and shoulders until Mr. Lloyd gasped on the grass. Pressing his foot down on his chest, Kyle leaned downward to ensure that his ribs had broke.

"Listen up shit head. You have issues, and you need help. Stop fucking up your kid's life up."

Reaching down, Kyle grabbed hold of his crotch and crushed and twisted it as hard as he could, his other hand covering his mouth. Joel and Michael stood wide eyed watching as Kyle tore and wriggled at it as Mr. Lloyd's muffled screams echoed behind his hand. After a moment the thin man lay curled up on the grass unable to breath or move, whimpering and crying.

"Or she'll turn out like me. Do you want that Mr. Dickhead?" said Kyle in a whisper as he lowered to face. He nod, his face ravaged in tears. A coldness befell Joel and Michael and they turned to each other in alarm, the gravity of Kyle's tone evident.

"If anyone asks how you broke your cock, you tell them you did this instead of diddling with your daughter. Got me?"

"Please…please…get off of me." Mr. Lloyd gasped and again Kyle put his foot's pressure down onto the man's chest.

"Did you hear what I said you fuck-pie?"

"Yes…please..."

"If I so much as hear that you even raise your hand at a fly hovering around that girl I'm going to be back." Warned Kyle angrily, "Now dig in your wallet dick head and get me the money you owe my friend."

As Joel slowly neared the Evans residence, Kyle relished the silence in the neighborhood as he could again return his thoughts to the warmth of Liz's smile and her company during dinner. It was nice to just be and not think about a darkness or pain. He felt for Michael but it dampened the most amazing night he had ever had. He couldn't help but smile and relish the warmth inside, for the first time feeling something other than destroyed.

His thoughts were lost in her smile, her eyes and the way she made him feel better without even realizing she was. As the Evoque glistened in a brilliant metallic red as it slowed under the street lamps, Kyle turned to Joel.

"Thank you for taking me. I appreciate it."

"No problem." He said shaking off the chaos of the night, "What are friends for right?"

Kyle smiled nodding, "I haven't been able to call anyone a friend in a very long time. Thank you."

Joel looked down to his extended hand and smiled shaking it.

"About what happened back there...?" Kyle said softly.

"No, you did a good thing. I think it's something most people want to do in that situation but never get the chance." Joel sighed, "Disturbing how quickly my life just pan-caked."

Kyle shrugged shaking his head, "It's a sick world we live in."

"Oh seems your parents threw a party in your absence." Joel nod looking up into the Evans driveway.

Kyle frowned turning his attention to the front and in seconds, everything inside of him came crashing down. Beside the red sedan stood the same golden Jeep Cherokee his father had driven the last time he saw him.

"Any idea who that is?" asked Joel.

He felt Joel's hand on his arm and he swung around in fright.

"Dude, are you ok?" gasped Joel worriedly, "You just kinda blanked out on me there."

Kyle nod nervously, "I'm fine, thank you. I have to go."

"Who is that?" asked Joel as Kyle stepped out of the Range Rover Evoque looking back at him.

"My father."

Inside at the dining table, laughing over a glass of wine while little Bennie watched TV in the lounge, Claire, Edward and Jimmy sat visiting.

Jimmy had dark brown eyes, beady even. His hair line was fast receding and his thinning golden brown hair was brushed backwards. He had a slight stubble around his chin and mouth.

Kyle stood still in the entrance hall, cautious to enter because the last time they had spoken ended in a screaming match. Instead he listened to feel the room before entering.

"Bennie's getting real big now." Said Jimmy, "You sure have done a good job Edward."

Kyle carefully walked into the dining room.

"What are you doing here?" he said with a soft but determined adamancy in his voice, "I thought you cancelled?"

His father rose up to face him with a smile, the suit in which he stood thrived with money.

"Well hello son." He nod grinning, "I've missed you."

Kyle nod cautiously and Jimmy smiled.

"Can I give you a hug?"

"No."

"Handshake then?"

Kyle smiled awkwardly, relieved that whatever hatred they had parted on seemed to be subdued. They shook hands.

Jimmy's face was lit up, and he motioned Kyle to join them at the table. Claire quickly made space.

"Kyle, he called just after you left." Claire explained, "I think it's time you get a cell phone, I could have called you earlier."

Jimmy smiled shaking his head, "You look great Kyle, healthy."

"He's a fitness fanatic." Edward teased.

"I look forward to spending time with you, catching up."

"You still expect me to spend the weekend with you?"

Jimmy shrugged, "I know I should've been here yesterday, but circumstances were unforeseen. I was hoping you would be more eager to spend time with me."

Is HE the face from behind the window?

Jimmy sighed and placed his glass on the table, "I've booked us a stay in Sabie. We're leaving in the morning son."

Kyle managed a smile.

"Jimmy's taking us to the lake!" said Bennie excitedly rushing in.

"Yes." Jimmy smirked, his hand running through Bennie's golden hair.

Kyle shook his head, "What about your wife to be? Is she coming with us?"

Jimmy laughed, "Nice of you to think of her. No Linda will be with her folks all weekend. I might not return to South Africa after the wedding so there isn't much time to really see you."

"So are we written off because you are marrying her?"

"Kyle don't do this." Urged Claire sincerely.

"No it's true. Where have you been Jimmy?" His voice was harsh.

"Look son I realize I've not seen you in a long time but…"

"Four years!" Kyle asserted, "You came once and never again. Nothing I asked you was answered, and now you come back thinking I want to spend time catching up with you? Who the hell do you think you are?"

"Kyle!" Edward said hitting the table. Kyle turned to Jimmy angrily, "I don't owe you my time for anything. As far as I'm concerned my suspicions about you are true."

"What suspicions?" Claire asked worriedly as Kyle arose from the table angrily.

"Ask him."

Kyle turned and head out, slamming the back door.

"I'm sorry. It's my fault…" Jimmy turned to Claire, "I should have made more effort to come back but I got caught up in my own life that side. I have a lot of fixing to do."

"Yes you do." Said Edward, "What is Kyle talking about Jim?"

"What suspicions?" Claire said more adamantly. Jimmy sighed and shook his head, "He thinks I'm part of the reason he was taken."

"What? Why?" Claire gasped, "Why on earth would he reach that conclusion Jim?"

"When I first went to see him at that facility, he was adamant that I was able to save him but didn't. He says he saw me and I did nothing to save him."

Claire shook her head, "Did you?"

"God no!" Jimmy said hitting the table, "Christ Claire you know me better than that. I just…I don't know how to convince him otherwise. I tried but I think he's just angry at me in general, blames me for everything."

"He has no reason to blame you." Edward frowned confused.

"Think about it Eddie…" he explained, "Things were bad between me and his momma just before he was…taken. Things were rough. I think he might hate me because if I had just taken control of my household maybe I could have stopped it all."

Tears filled his eyes and he dropped his head onto his fists.

"God knows I would do anything to take back a lot of my life."

Edward turned to Claire, his nice-guy act with him growing weak and he stood up.

"You should have made an effort."

Claire looked up at Edward nervously.

"You should have tried to be a better father to your son, to Claire. You were nowhere in all of it."

Jimmy looked up, his cheeks wet with tears.

"I spoke to Doctor Naidu yesterday afternoon." Edward turned to his wife, "She thinks it would be good for Kyle to mend bridges with Jim and close off the things plaguing him."

"She's right." nod Jimmy looking down solemnly, "I just want a chance to make things right. Truth be told…I don't think I'll ever come back to SA again. This is my last chance to show him that I'm not the monster here."

Jimmy turned to his ex wife and smiled, "Even though I was sometimes."

She smiled and stood up, "Kyle comes first. If he doesn't want to do this, I'm with him. I didn't realize how turbulent things were between you. I mean, I knew he was angry but I never knew he blamed you or thought you were involved."

Jimmy stood up too, "Let me go have a word with him."

The wind carried an icy chill, and Kyle himself frozen with it already. Standing in the deep blackness of the vine, he had just lit a cigarette as the voices inside his mind screamed out.

Was he there? Could he be there? Why were YOU there? Are you really here? Maybe this is your hell? Why are you so paranoid?

Just then his father rounded the corner with his hands casually in his pockets.

"Still smoking?"

"Not that you have a say, but yes."

"Kyle…" said Jimmy looking up at him with a distressing sigh, "I know that the last time we spoke, you hated me. That you blamed me and wanted answers."

"It took you four years to finally conclude that?" he snarled.

"I just wanted a chance to talk about it."

Kyle turned to face him and noticed how his eyes were shadowed by the vine and it made the red memory tear through his mind.

"You're a man already, look at you. How old are you now? Twenty three? Twenty four? I can never remember your birthdays…" Said Jimmy with a sarcastic grin, wiping his hand over his mouth, "So much needs to be said and discussed, things that you might not know or understand. I just need a chance to explain things and…"

"Nothing you say will ever take it away." said Kyle as tears welled in his eyes, "You left me out there."

Jimmy stepped forward again, reaching for the cigarette in Kyle's fingers. Everything froze, his body so tense that it hurt until

Jimmy stepped back and puffed at the cigarette.

"God Kyle why do you insist it was me? Look, I know you think I'm some kind of monster Kyle, and I don't ever expect you to love or even accept me as your father. But you need to come with me this weekend. We need to close this chapter once and for all."

"Was it you?"

Jimmy exhaled up to the sky, the smoke rushing in the brisk air. "You don't know me boy." He said looking back down at him, "You were gone. Gone without a trace for years! God damn it everyone believed you were dead. I didn't leave you boy, you left us. You left your mother to face it all."

"Not by choice!" Kyle stammered without breath as he rushed past his father.

Jimmy grabbed his arm, "You want to blame me for all of it? Go ahead, but if you think for one second that I'll let you off of coming with me this weekend to straighten out the past then you are very mistaken son."

Kyle shook his head, clenching his teeth as he pulled his arm free, "Don't you ever touch me again."

In a second, Jimmy dropped to his knees clutching Kyle's hand as he burst into tears. "Please! Please just give me this one weekend with you. I'm begging you!" he cried.

Kyle stood shivering with fear, incomprehension and wrath as Jimmy continued to plead and cry on his knees.

"Please son, please I'm begging you with all my life, with all my heart just let me try. Before I never see you again, I beg you just give me a chance!"

"What are you talking about?" asked Kyle with a cold voice.

Jimmy looked up at him, his eyes filled with tears, "Once I'm married I'm permanently leaving South Africa and never coming back!"

"Like you said, I don't know you anyway." Kyle said with cruel blunt snarl, "So what will I be losing right?"

Jimmy shook his head, his hand squeezing his sons and Kyle pulled away stepping back. Jimmy fell forward on his hands and knees in the dirt. Above them, a tear of lighting ripped across the sky, giving light to the dark clouds that hung heavy, waiting for the time to break open and free themselves of the heavy rain and Kyle looked down to his father.

"I don't know who I saw." He said behind a broken voice, "But get in your car and leave and don't ever come near us again. We've managed fine without you."

Jimmy rose up to face him nodding as he wiped the tears from his face. The clouds above broke at the weight of the water and rain began pouring down. They stood staring at each other's faces, each seeing in the glimpses of the lighting, the hurt in each other's eyes and the rain drummed down around them in the silence.

Jimmy face's contorted, and the manipulation was over as a grin crossed his face, reaching out he placed his hand on his son's on the shoulder, "There is no Linda. There is no wedding you idiot! I came all this way out here to this shit-hole town to find you Kyle. So ask yourself, why would Jimmy do that?"

Kyle gasped, "Why?"

Jimmy grabbed him by the shirt, "You will get in the fucking car tomorrow morning! And you will fucking smile about it! I'm not asking, I'm telling you and you will obey. Because if you don't Kyle, if you screw this up for me I swear to god you'll fear more than just the dark."

Lighting tore the sky above them and Kyle fought for his breath that escaped as puke shot up into his throat, his father's hand on his chest crushing every part of him.

"As you can see, we have much to discuss Kyle." Jimmy said circling around him, "So stop treating me like some stranger and put on your game face. Or you'll find that there is more to lose than just a dead beat dad."

Kyle gasped as lighting and thunder roared above and Jimmy walked back to the house. Kyle dropped to his knees in the muddy wetness beneath the vine, breathless and his mind racing in fear.

Trichardt, a small town 5 kilometers east of Secunda was a town much smaller than its neighbor yet with the most suitable medical centre, the Hydro Med. The passageway that led to the morgue at the Trichardt Hydro-Med bore in its eerie cold a calmness and somberness that crawled along detective Eva Jordan's skin.

As she reached the pale white doors, she heaved a deep breath to ready herself for the uncomfortable macabre that engulfed being around a dead bodies.

"Evening Eva nice of you to make it." Underwood teased as he turned from the table beside the mortician Andrew Van Dyk, a pot bellied man with black hair and a doubled chin.

Eva managed a smile as she hurriedly covered her mouth and nose with the white anti bacterial face mask.

"So what have you got Andrew?" she asked stepping beside her partner, looking down at the cold white body of the miner.

"Pretty simple really. Brutal but simple." Said Andrew looking to Underwood to whom he had just explained his findings.

Eva nodded and looked to where Van Dyk lowered as he began to explain.

"Over here you can see a small wound where the skin has been slit as though by a surgical steel blade." He said as he placed his finger above the dark bruising wound on the side of the miner's chest.

"Judging by the tissue and flesh surrounding the wound, it appears that the stab happened fast with much precision."

"Are you saying it wasn't caused by debris?" she asked standing up, looking to Underwood who grinned as he nod back to Van Dyk who continued.

"The precision of the wound makes it highly unlikely that it was caused by a piece of flying debris." Said Andrew Van Dyk lowering beside the body again, "The wound lies directly between two of the deceased's ribs. It penetrated the pleura cavity viciously and thus also ruptured the lung. I found no traces of any rustic metals or remains what so ever. Needless to say, debris tends to only move in one direction, what did this was a quick in and out and filled his lung so quick, he died pretty fast."

Eva looked to Underwood frowning, "Someone stabbed him?"

"There's more." Underwood said looking back to Van Dyk.

Andrew Van Dyk nod and moved lower along the table to the miner's legs, pulling back the white covers and exposing his left hand. As he respectfully turned the hand, he brought to attention an almost paper thin slice to his wrists and he looked up at Eva, "The stab wound to the chest isn't what drained his man of all his blood detective, it was the slice to his artery over here, the volar ulnar carpal. I didn't see it during my initial examination because the body was covered in blood. I figured the hand was holding the chest."

"So this man was murdered is that what you are saying?"

"There is no way a chance shard of metal slit this man. Whatever did this was clean and sharp as hell."

Eva shook her head and stepped back nodding. "Penny for your thoughts?" said Underwood stepping towards her as he pulled off his surgical mask. She shrugged, "Well we have a confirmed murder and strange bombing, seems that old mine shaft just got more interesting than we thought."

The storm above the towns of Secunda, Brendan and Evander raged throughout the night, grumbling thunder roared loudly alongside the flaring lighting.

Liz lay awake late, thinking of her rendezvous with Kyle and the way he made her feel. Laying staring out her windows where the curtains hung drawn back, trying to make sense of the way she felt when she had seen him for the first time and how it grew stronger each time she stood in his presence. She replayed the answers he gave to her questions in her mind, trying to figure out what it was that caused him to carry such a great weight inside his eyes, or why he warned her about himself when all she could see in him was a young man lost and broken, desperate for a way to breathe again. She smiled hugging her pillow, closing her eyes in the hopes that she could dream of the most beautiful man she'd ever seen.

Joel too lay awake on his bed, lying on his arms staring into the storm from his bedroom window, hunting his heart and mind for the voice inside of him. He never could understand why his mother kept staying through the ridicule and abuse. Why couldn't he 'Kyle-it' when his father got violent, crude or mean. They didn't need Raymond as much as he needed them and he couldn't understand why she kept on staying with him. He felt a sense of guilt befall him, feeling such despise for the man who raised him, but it was never worth it. All he was to Raymond was thorn and shame. He rolled onto his back, thinking about their sudden rendezvous with Michael and how he confessed everything to them so randomly, so openly and he knew that Michael would come to regret every word the minute the sun rose. His life had pancaked very quickly and it frightened him because he felt himself slipping down a dark slide – darker than his own which he always thought had the most shadows. There was still Kyle and everything he heard Michael exchange with Claire and Edward. There were questions there, something he knew would send Kyle off the edge if confronted. He heaved a deep breath, closing his eyes to a fast prayer of thanks that as bad as his life was, there was someone out in the storm with far darker torment. At the trailer park, seeing in the black boulder like clouds a great beauty that reminded Jessie of how small and seemingly insignificant her role was in the world, she smiled and stood with her arms spread to her sides at the water's edge as the rain fell around her - feeling as though her soul was being drenched clean of her shame and disgrace. Since she and Michael experienced that connection at Kallie's house, she had been feeling as though there was no reason left to have the weight of her shame break her. She knew what she felt for him, she just forgot in the chaos that ensued the night they brought on Andre Naude's death. Parked facing the old shed where his brother was found hanging four years before, Michael stared into the darkness as the downpour shrouded the area and drummed against the roof of his car. Wondering if he would ever see the world through the eyes he lost the night they murdered Andre Naude, but he couldn't feel anything inside. Something had changed since his soul break along the side of the road, as though he had been drained of everything poisoning his life since that night and before. He felt he had the strength again to pursue more than just the battle to escape the walls closing in on him. He knew the story of Boy X and had the pleasure to see this stranger of darkness defend his income earlier. And the millionaire's heir was open about his demons. Something was fresh in the air and once the rain had past he would again emerge to free himself of the demons plaguing him. For the first time it didn't matter how weak he looked because he knew that in the moment on the side of the road, crying uncontrollably from a place deepest in the core of his being - the shattering of his soul brought back a chance for redemption. And he looked up at the dark shed again as lighting tore above the sky, lighting up the dark open fields outside Kinross. He turned the ignition, ready to discover what his brother had left him and what his father's role was in hiding it.

As his car veered out of the field and hit back onto the tar, the black SUV started up in the distance having followed him at Lee's request since the unnerving revelation about a mysterious package around the time of Lyle's faked suicide.

Standing on the balcony overlooking the Atlantic, General Gondwe sipped on his Scotch pondering about how the Corporation was soon set to unleash a new order beginning in South Africa and nothing could falter this close to the objective or it would falter further secrets hiding in Australia, Russian and eventually the United States of America where the plans had been set in motion over years to achieve on single goal – One united government across the globe. It was clear to him and King that murder, greed and mayhem was loose beneath the dark night skies of South Africa as the secrets of the E shaft slowly began to unfold and the chaos had only just begun. He felt they were losing control and he knew that as per King's wishes, that by day break he have to commence the proverbial 'plan B' just in case any further setbacks were put into motion.

<u>Chapter Ten:</u>
<u>The beginning</u>

The first shimmering rays of sunlight touched the vast horizon. The Jeep was silent from the moment they had pulled away from the driveway and hit the road out of Secunda. Bennie had fallen asleep not long after they reached the highway, but Kyle fought the weight of his heavy eye lids - to distrustful of his father to chance sleep. Jimmy had offered him conversation about his life in Secunda, but the conversation was eerie and callous, the void between them was too vast for idle banter, feeling to both of them pointless and hollow.

Sitting in silence in the back seat beside Bennie, with only the soft drone of the wheels on the tar, he felt the shimmering of a dying flame inside of him – it was hope and he could feel the flame dwindling to a flicker. An incredibly elastic, fragile hope he had braved to hold onto since he first moved with his family to Secunda.

He thought of doctor Andy Morris, her honest smile and truly pure eyes that held in them such a sweet sincerity to know him and befriend him and he felt guilty. He thought about Michael and Joel, two young men from opposite sides of the coin who had taken to him without cause, who gave him a sense of unity which he hadn't shared for thousands of days. He recalled his dinner date with Elizabeth Van Rooyen, sweet and wonderful Liz whose unpresuming eyes sought in him the boy behind the pain. Liz whose smile warmed his heart through to the core of his soul, a feeling he normally fought off any peace and gentleness with iron shields.

He sighed, his heart throbbing with guilt, guilt for blocking everyone's efforts, doing everything he could to shut anyone and everyone out when all they wanted was a chance. For his mother Claire the same, even the man who bore no blood relation to him wanted to care and be in his life but he wouldn't allow himself to step out of the darkest shadows. Constantly alone and trapped by his own rage and self despise every day, and through any means fighting off feeling anything. Allowing the dark demons of his soul to shield him off from others, using anything he could to stop the pain and self despise. If he had to tell them *everything*, open his mouth for the black ooze inside to erupt out of his soul, taking with it his very foundation of being – no one would ever look at him without knowing all he had done and what he was. This was the risk he couldn't find courage to take.

His eyes grew heavy and he yawned behind his hand, looking up at Jimmy in the rear view mirror. He wanted with all his heart to fly forward from the back seat and grab hold of the steering wheel. Tug it as hard as he could and send the car into the nearest tree. He knew something was happening, something dangerous and he wanted to do anything to stop it – even through the dire craving to understand where this was going. But Bennie, little innocent Bennie was with them. He had to focus only on Bennie now, nothing else. Whatever his estranged father was about to reveal was irrelevant to Bennie's safety. As his hope cringed with dire desperation not to be broken, he felt rising in the deepest bowls of his gut, the fear of facing the world another day with the same heart beating in his chest and he thought of Liz again and their conversation repeated inside his mind.

"I don't understand what's happening to me."

"I think you could if you gave yourself the chance."

"You don't know me."

"I want to know you."

He felt his skin crawl as they neared the entrance towards the lake resort because he could only imagine what was coming, and he looked down to Bennie, again the face inside laughing at him.

He was the face behind the glass.

"Here we go." Said Jimmy finally breaking the silence, the Jeep rolled off the tar road and into the long winding stretch of gravel that led towards the homes around the lake.

Around the wide dark blue lake stood thirteen wood built homes, each with decks planted over the water's edge. The grass all around was a pure bright green and the trees encircling the resort stood tall and mighty up into the crisp blue sky. All the homes were occupied and the camp site was filled. As the Jeep head along the narrow road past the pools and water slides, Bennie's face lit up with excitement to join all the other kids running about. The 75 meter super tube stood like a titan as screams and giggles filled the air, and it was love at first sight when Bennie saw the sign 'Raging Rapids'.

He looked to Kyle grabbing his hand eagerly, "This is going to be awesome!"

Inside, the wooden floors smelt of polish, the counters were spotless and the furniture seemed almost brand new but they held a history too.

"Wow…" Bennie gasped still shrugging off the sleep, "It's like a castle!"

Jimmy laughed, "It sure is boy. And it's all yours for the whole weekend." He said dropping the baggage on the sofa.

"There will only be two rules this weekend. One, don't get hurt and two don't break anything that we can't hide away before we leave." He laughed with a wink.

Kyle shook his head in annoyance and Bennie ran towards the big glass sliding doors that over looked the water. "Good to be here isn't it Kyle?" smiled Jimmy.

Kyle shrugged silently, still terrified of the stranger that was his father.

"Kyle?" asked Jimmy again. Kyle turned to him heaving an uncomfortable sigh to hide his trembling legs and nod, seeing the knife block on the counter over his father's shoulder. Jimmy smiled and moved to open the doors for Bennie to step out onto the small wooden deck. Kyle stared at the knife block, reeling with the urge to just grab a blade and take away the reason for his disruption. He turned his attention back to his little brother.

"Where's my room?" asked Bennie rushing back inside.

"Upstairs. Choose which ever one you like most." Jimmy said heading towards the small kitchenette. Bennie gasped with excitement and dashed up the stairs, "Come on Kyle, and help me choose a room!"

Kyle turned to him, "Not now bro. You go ahead ok?"

Bennie ignored him and ran up the stairs joyously.

"It seems we'll have to go into town and buy supplies for the weekend." Sighed Jimmy closing the fridge. Kyle walked towards the deck, the breeze gliding over the water as refreshing as rain. Jimmy huffed lazily and began digging into his large blue suitcase he brought, "Unless it's ok to live off of these?" he said with a smile pulling out a pack of beers.

Kyle sighed, "No. it's not ok. Bennie needs breakfast."

"And he'll get whatever he needs, this isn't about him. He was just a way to get you out here. You worry so much." Said Jimmy with a dismal sigh.

"Tell me why we're here? What did you mean last night?"

"We're here to let off some steam. I'll swing by next door and ask Sue and Greg to go into town for us."

"I didn't come here for a holiday!" Kyle shouted, "So don't patronize me! Tell me what the fuck we are doing here!"

Jimmy sighed and his eyes fell dark, like they had the night before out in the rain when Kyle saw danger in them. Sensing chaos brewing, Kyle looked down and head towards the glass doors. The water on the vast lake seemed cold and dark, like the hollowness he felt within. Jimmy heaved a deep breath, clenching his teeth from allowing words of anger or frustration to bubble from his mouth and walked out onto the deck with two beers in his hand.

"Do you remember that time you wanted to build a big boat, go sailing on the lake with it? You were obsessed with sailing boats."

"What do you want from me?" asked Kyle turning to face him, looking at the beer with a desperate thirst as he knew it would help hide his shivering.

Jimmy smiled and placed the beer into Kyle's hand.

"Relax." Jimmy put his hand on his shoulder, relishing the recoil of his son's body tensing, "We just got here, lets enjoy and we'll talk later."

"What do you expect from me?" asked Kyle looking down at the beer to hide the anxiousness that gleamed in his eyes.

"Well…" said Jimmy slugging down the beer, "Let's start by just talking. I wasn't lying before Kyle, there is lots we need to discuss. We can at least be civil about it."

"Why are you doing this?" asked Kyle still trembling nervously when Bennie rushed down the stairs.

"Can we go swimming now?"

"We'll talk later son." Jimmy smiled with a nod heading back inside, "You boys head to the pool, I need to make a few calls."

Kyle dropped his head, his heart racing and his mind spiraling with chaos and confusion. At the counter, Jimmy took his cell phone from his pants pocket and began typing a text message. Kyle gulped at the warm beer, trying to force control over his thoughts and emotions that ravaged through his head like a hurricane and he head back inside, his eyes meeting Jimmy's who looked up at him – the tension alive with a dangerous personality of it's own.

By 10am, the center of the Secunda town was buzzing with shoppers and street hustlers alike. Claire and Edward walked hand in hand through the crowds, window shopping while enjoying ice cones in the heat of the early morning. Walking out of the shopping center with two bags in his hands, Joel noticed Troy across the square at the book store and he stopped to admire the sight of her long legs peering out from her pink skirt when she suddenly turned to his direction, frowning awkwardly at his deep stare.

He dropped his head shyly before offering a wave and she managed a weak smile before giving a nod back at him. Deciding again to leap, Joel made his way towards her.

"Hey." He greeted smiling shyly.

"Hey McDonald." Troy said with a smile, turning away from his eyes to the book shelf, "Did you get a decent look?"

"At what?" He said still smiling awkwardly.

"I think I still haves traces of your have eye-goop on my legs…"

He dropped his head embarrassed, "You saw that huh?"

She laughed teasingly, "I'm not your type McDonald so don't even go there."

"How would you know my type?"

"I'm intuitive." She said grinning, "Where's your pack?"

"My pack?"

"Doesn't the swim team travel like tuna?" she smiled, "In a big bunch always together?"

"No." He frowned smiling. She nod, her eyes fixed on the book in her hands.

"Where's your pack?"

"Liz is working morning shift at the Hot Spot and I'm here trying to read while you continue attempting to strike up a conversation, in the hopes I'll melt at the knees and sleep with you."

He laughed shaking his head, "You think a lot of yourself."

She sighed turning to face him, "Why did you come over here Joel?"

"To talk." He shrugged, "To say hi."

"I'm not going to have sex with you." She said bluntly, "Just because Kyle and Liz have this weird thing going on, doesn't mean it's a cue for you to step in and claim the best friend. I know how this goes Joel, I've been there before."

"You are so presumptuous, it's scary."

"Am I really now?"

"Yes!" he laughed, "God give a guy a break. Ok, yes I was looking at your legs, but you have nice legs and you know you do, that's why you're wearing the skirt – you want to show them off. And yes, I'm a swimmer for the Delta Caps, and I know they have a reputation, but you can't assume everyone is the same. Besides, I quit the team weeks ago."

She frowned with a grin and he shrugged his shoulders.

"I came to say hi, which is a pretty standard greeting around the world as far as I know, shame on you for being so impolite." He said shaking his head in disgust before turning and heading for the door. Troy shook her head and hurried behind him.

"You call me impolite?" she said walking out beside him, "You are the one who eye molested my legs."

"So what do you want?" He sighed, "Should I apologize for finding you attractive?"

She huffed sarcastically, "Oh please, does this work for you rich boy?"

"What?" he gasped confused, and insulted. Troy shook her head smiling, "I know how you Delta Cap's operate alright. And yes, I know you can't judge a book by its fraternity, but at the end of the day you too have a reputation McDonald so get off your high expensive horse and cut the crap. You came over because you figured you'd flash your cute little smile and turn up your rich boyish charm and I would just fall head over heels in love with you like every other slut you've added to your college wall of shame."

This shit just got real.

"Hey! That's presumptuous." He snarled pretending to be taken aback, "So you admit it, I've got a cute smile? Oh, and I do like the wall of shame idea…"

She laughed shaking her head, "Why am I still talking to you?"

"Don't ask me!" he huffed.

"You are such an arrogant narcissist!"

"Well you Troy, are a presumptuous flirt."

Gasping she laughed, "I am not a flirt!"

"Then why are you still talking to me?"

"Because I was here first!"

"You don't own town square."

"And you do Mr. Money-bags?"

He tilt his head frowning, "Is that why you won't give me the time of day? Because my family has money?"

"No." she said rolling her eyes with a sigh, "I just know guys like you."

"Really?" he frowned, "Please do enlighten me then, since you know me better than I know myself."

"I never said that."

"You didn't have to." he cocked his head up arrogantly. She smiled shaking her head in awe of his assertiveness, "Guy's like you don't know how it is being normal, you live in the clouds where servants do everything for you and you get away being a bully to anyone not in your league. You always belong to some team of champions, the best of the best. You surround yourself with everyone who is just as competitive and overconfident as you because it's the only thing that matters. The cars, the clothes, the money, the plastic girls at your sides and ultimately being masters of the world while sipping tea and bathing in two hundred rand notes. Just like that brunette Barbie you call a girlfriend, I think you are shallow and conceited."

He laughed shaking his head, "First of all, I don't have any servants and secondly I would never bath in any money because I'd be putting myself at risk of sever paper cuts. Oh and tea sucks. Brunette Barbie and I are not together anymore and I am not any more shallow or conceited than you are."

She sighed folding her arms, her eyes glaring him top to bottom.

"What's in the bags anyway?"

"Stuff."

"What stuff? Porn for your collection or some more ridiculously over priced name brand items to show off to your pack of webbed footed fraternity brothers?"

He laughed shyly, "No. If you must know, it's stuff for my mother."

Troy's eyes scolded him and he shrugged his shoulders.

"My mother has flu and didn't want to come into town today, so I came and picked up a few things for the house." He said lowering the bags to the ground, flushing the tops open for her to see as he scrimmaged through the contents.

"See, I have some cheap soup packets – No Name branded, wow what a surprise. Also got some vegetables in here, the lentils were marked reduced because the sell by date is today. Along with this strangely shaped garlic roll that I took because I know my mom loves them and I figured it would help her cheer up."

She smiled watching him from above as he continued to prove her error.

"Oh and here I have some tissues, again No Name branded. Got some salted crackers to go with the soup, they were marked down. And just for kicks I got myself a large chocolate nougat bar because I woke up feeling miserable and I thought I deserved the treat since I don't have any plans what so ever for the whole weekend."

She knelt down and put her hands over the tops of the two bags closing them and he looked up at her sighing.

"I'll help you carry these to your car." Troy smiled shaking her head, "In exchange we go fifty-fifty on the nougat bar."

He smiled, "Sixty-forty."

"So now you're Scrooge?" She said standing up with both the bags in her hands, "Allow me, I owe you an apology."

"Speak only when spoken to servant girl." He said standing up to face her with a grin.

"No, don't over reach." She said flinging her hair as she walked around him and he laughed following her, looking down at her legs again.

"Eye's up top flipper boy."

Standing at the counter of the Secunda post office, face to face with the young and uncouth teller, Michael desperately tried to keep calm.

"Is there no way you can get hold of her?"

"She's not here today." She repeated arrogantly.

"Yes, you said that. I heard you." He said trying to smile, "That is why I'm asking if you can get her number so I can call her."

"We are not allowed to give out staff information, now move aside you're blocking the line."

"How does any place operate without someone in charge?"

"Are you hard of hearing or sir?"

"What about a shift manager or supervisor? I want to speak to him or her right now."

"Sorry sir, there is no senior level on duty today. Shift manager will be back at one to close up. Until then you'll just have to wait in line. Next please." She said ushering him aside with her hand obnoxiously flapping in front of his face.

He sighed shaking his head with frustration and walked out past the line of customers queuing behind him and made his way to the door. He turned looking back at her and as she looked up at him, he raised his childishly middle finger.

He head up the stairs past the public library towards the parking lot, as he waited to cross the road he saw Jessie standing at the side of the Cortina and he smiled.

"I thought I told you that I would pick you up?"

"You sounded upset so I hitched a ride with Gladness." She smiled awkwardly, not expecting to feel so riddled with anxiety facing him, "What's going on?"

Her eyes felt hot against him, and he looked down with his heart starting to run inside. Since his break, he felt naked and exposed in a way that made him feel vulnerable and weak, and having her looking at him as she had the night they made love for the first time, he felt as though she could see more than just his face.

He shrugged shaking his head, "We have a lot to talk about and I have a party to throw. It's a really crazy day."

"Then let me help you." She said reaching for his hand, "We can hang out."

"I have to see Nkosi for the rest of the money."

"What happened to you?" she frowned, softly running the tip of her finger against the redness still present on his forearm, and then noticing it higher up and even against his neck, "Michael what happened?"

He looked up into her eyes and heaved a deep breath, he had

forgotten how her pale skin almost glittered in the sunlight and how her chocolate almond eyes light up like layers of brown marble in the light. He wanted to tell her that he was sorry, he wanted to hold her and tell her that he would spend the rest of his life making up for everything he ever did to add to her suffering. But he still wasn't sure what she wanted to talk about, or how she felt about whatever it was that happened between them at Kallie's house. Her eyes were filled with care and concern and he smiled, unable to keep pushing on a face that had melted the night before. "Get in, I'll tell you on the way."

At the park behind the lake homes, many kids who could not yet swim splashed and laughed in the sun in the shallow waters of the toddler's pool. Kyle lay on his stomach on the grass beneath the tall umbrellas made of thatched grass, smoking a cigarette while watching Bennie who rushed from pool to pool, slide to slide. The afternoon sun was vengeful and laying beneath the shade umbrella he felt a calm inside. Jimmy had gone into town and they hadn't seen him in four hours. He knew there was an emotional storm coming, an F5 tornado waiting to be unleashed the moment Jimmy and he spoke.

Bustling in and around both the Olympic sized pool and children's splash pool were all the resorts day guests and the sounds omitted were a reminder that joy existed in the world he had become isolated from.

The area surrounding the resort was massed with stunning greenery and hills and he found himself wondering who he would have been had he not been found in a pool of blood on the side of the road.

"Come on Kyle!" shouted Bennie excitedly from the side of the pool, "Come play with me please!"

"Not in the mood bro." he said with a weak smile, feeling unable to ever shake off the gloom that clung to his soul.

"Come on! Please!" Bennie urged, his eyes and voice filled with desperation. Kyle inhaled a final pull of the smoke and stood up as Bennie began clapping his little hands excitedly.

Kyle pulled off his sleeveless vest and tossed his sneakers to the side. Others around the pool, especially girls and women, watched with inner grins as they admired him leaving the shade into the light where his perfectly chiseled body glistened golden. His swimming trunks hung low at his waist provoking thoughts in some of the older ladies that made them feel ashamed for thinking it with their children in proximity. He felt that they were staring at the scars and it made his skin crawl, so he focused on his little brother with whom he had never had a chance to swim with.

Bennie smiled brightly, taking much pride in his cool big brother who dominated attention and inadvertently demanded an impressed glance.

Kyle stepped to the side of the pool with a shy smile, "Alright little bro. Let's play."

He reached down, grabbing little Bennie's hands and hoisted him up and out of the pool. "You know what happens to little brothers who nag?" teased Kyle, tossing him playfully over his shoulder as he head towards the big pool. Bennie giggled with immense joy, playfully kicking and wriggling on his brothers' shoulder.

"What Kyle? What happens?" he beamed excitedly. Kyle swung him down into his arms, cradling him across his chest. "They get dunked!"

He raised him up high over his head into the air, Bennie's giggle and squealing roaring through the park and Kyle tossed him forward into the water.

Bennie broke the surface laughing spasmodically and Kyle laughed happily, forgetting in that moment of pure peaceful joy that the storm was still on the horizon.

"Again Kyle! Again!"

Kyle looked around at the parks visitors, a lot of eyes still gawking at him and he blushed shyly, leaping in a dive over Bennie and into the water. It was cool against his skin, the silence beneath the water a welcomed break from the noises up top, from the screaming inside his soul. His broke the surface and he smiled as Bennie paddled towards him giggling with excitement.

That moment of pure happiness struck him and he spun around to face the window of their cottage in the distance, expecting to find Jimmy staring at him. Realizing that his thoughts were nothing more than mere haunting, Kyle splashed under the water and came up beneath his brother, hoisting him up into the air above him.

The water was refreshing to the constant tension his body had been in since seeing Michael the night before, and he dipped his head beneath the water again to wash the long hair backwards and away from his face.

"Kyle that was awesome!" giggled Bennie when suddenly Kyle flung back under the water, coming up beneath him and launched him up onto his shoulders. Bennie laughed as again, his big brother tossed him upwards and into pool. His face had barely broke surface and already he was pleading for more, his giggle almost enough to break the chill that still stung to Kyle since the vine. Kyle dipped under again and repeat the toss, sending Bennie into the water with a splash. There was nothing more amazing to Kyle than watching others in the world laughing and shining with cheerfulness and pleasure, especially the young boy who unknowingly was his rock the entire time he stayed at Crown and Lake. It was the awe of a new life and how the purity in little Bennie's eyes made him feel that someone in the world could see him with innocent eyes and never ever see through the brooding darkness. He laughed happily, hurriedly grabbing his little step brother under his arms as he wade towards the edge of the pool. Planting Bennie on his feet, Kyle heaved up the side of the pool. "Back!" said Bennie shoving him at the legs and like the young twenty one year old that barely came to surface, Kyle playfully wailed and tumbled, waving his arms in the air frantically before plummeting into the water with a big splash. Bennie's giggle was uncontrollable and Kyle heaved up against the side of the pool, sprawling out at his brother's feet as though he had lost consciousness, his tongue hanging out the side of his mouth. Bennie giggled and knelt down beside him, nudging him, "Stand up Kyle! Stand up!"

Kyle roared playfully, purposefully grasping just out of reach as Bennie scurried away in a frantic giggle. Kyle leapt up and gave chase around the pool, through the others, humorously gnawing and roaring like a mummy after his brother. To everyone watching, it was the tip of grace to see a young man playing so freely and so lovingly with his little brother, it was heartwarming and cheerful. For a moment it was all gone, he hadn't once thought about the darkness writhing in loom over his soul and he was just a young guy having fun in the pool.

He grabbed Bennie finally, raising him up and onto his shoulders, tickling him as he made his way back to the pool again, everyone else simply nonexistent but him and his little step brother. At the pool side, he swung Bennie around to face the water, holding him up in front of him.

"Do it mummy or I'm gonna beat you in the ground!" Bennie played laughing.

Kyle turned to the cottage down the lane where Jimmy was standing at the door on the small porch with a beer in his hand watching them.

"Kyle? Throw me!" exclaimed Bennie gleefully, "Kyle?"

Jimmy ushered a nod and turned away, instantly Kyle filled with a cold and he carefully put his brother to the ground on his feet. "Not now ok, I have to go back to the cottage and use the bathroom."

"Pee in the pool!" urged Bennie with a naughty laugh. Kyle managed a weak misleading smile, knelt down to face him and brushed Bennie's blond hair away from his eyes, "Bro you're a twisted kid you know that?"

Bennie giggled and followed as Kyle head back to his towel, shirt and shoes.

"Are you going to hurry back?" asked Bennie worriedly.

"No bro, but you can keep playing with your other friends in the kiddy pool ok? I'll ask someone to keep an eye on you."

"Please come back!" Bennie urged with heaviness in his little chest. Kyle again managed a dreary smile, "I'll be back in a few to get you for lunch, don't overdo it."

Bennie nod with a long face, and head back to the splash pool. Kyle looked back to the cottage, the coldness striking over him again and he sighed turning to face a couple of high school girls who had been tanning near him all day.

"Would you mind keeping an eye on my little brother?" he asked with a nervous frown, wishing they would stop sweltering over him. Without any thought the girls vowed eagerly to be there when he returned. Kyle nod courteously and turned to wave at his brother, but Bennie had already gotten encompassed with other swimming friends.

Kyle smiled, wishing that he had never gone upstairs in search for his candles, wishing that he had never had the party, wishing that he had never been born as the darkness whispered inside of him as he head towards the wooden cottage.

Closing the boot of his car, Joel sighed and turned to Troy who brushed her long hair out of her face. Both of them now enjoying the nougat bar.

"So aren't you going to Harper's party tonight?" she asked with a frown, "You said you had no plans for the weekend?"

"I got the text, but I'm not sure I'm going."

"Why's that?"

He smiled shyly, "The last time I was at a party I got a little out of hand."

"I know, your brunette Barbie couldn't stop talking about what she did to your car. I don't know if you remember this, but I was the one who warned you about the guy puking in your stove?"

He shook his head smiling stupidly.

"So you just crumbled back to Brunette Barbie after what she did to your car?"

"What! No!" he gasped, his teeth brown from chocolate.

Troy laughed, "I overheard her in the bathroom telling everyone that you groveled?"

He shook his head as shame blanketed over him, eager to remove the spotlight beaming down on him.

"I'm guessing no?"

"A big fat no. She's history anyway."

"History? Another notch on ye ol belt then?" Troy teased.

"Let's just say I've recently found a voice that's been gone for awhile. I'm not the guy I was a month ago Troy. I got lost in it all somehow, the money, the girls…life…."

"I sense we need a couch for this session?" she smiled.

Joel laughed, "I'm doing alright though just being Joel for a bit."

"What happens when you are tired of just being Joel?"

He shrugged, "I guess I'll purchase a Ferrari and hire some playgirls."

She shook her head smiling and a short silence hung as they chewed on their bars watching the traffic around them.

"Are you going?"

"Liz said she and Kyle are going, so I was going to tag along and play chaperone." She shrugged. Joel nod in surprise that Kyle hadn't mentioned it and a silence hung between them as they finished off the nougat bar.

"You should come, flipper boy." She insisted playfully, "If you don't I'll be forced to believe you're out spending money on flashy sports cars and bling."

He smiled, "Are you asking me on, like, a date?"

"No! Hell no!" she gasped with a giggle, "But if you do show up I guess I could spend a very tiny portion of my time with you. Maybe you could prove me wrong about you yet Joel, don't think this classifies as you being a nice guy."

He nod grinning with narcissistic pride and she frowned.

"What?"

"I knew you liked you me."

"I knew you were conceited." She smiled shrugging her shoulders, "I just think its sweet you're taking care of your mother. It's rare in a college boy."

He laughed, "I may surprise you yet Troy."

"There we go being conceited again." She sighed teasingly, "Well, this was interesting. See you around flipper boy." She said playfully punching him in the arm before turning away and heading off.

Stepping into the house with still just his shorts on, dried only by dabbing his shirt over his body, Kyle felt the might of tension and unease gripping at his chest and he felt faint as the lack of air to his brain became overwhelming.

"How's the water?" asked Jimmy from the couch with his arms slung over the back, a beer in his hand and his blue suit shirt unbuttoned.

He shrugged morbidly, "its fine."

"You are all muscle now I see." His eyes laced all over his son's body, "Like you stepped out of a magazine or something."

Kyle felt his skin coil and he kept his sight to the ground.

"Come here Kyle." Jimmy said tapping on the seat beside him, "Take a seat with me, we need to talk."

Kyle stepped towards him, his legs fighting each step as his heart beat began condemning through his body. He stepped to the sofa across from Jimmy and finally he looked up, the glare of his father's dark eyes glanced over at his naked wet torso.

"Come on son, I not going to bite you." Jimmy said with a giggle. Mustering as much bravery as he could, he sat down across from him.

"I have something." Jimmy started, trying to hide the frustration bubbling inside of his scrawny slightly hairy chest as he motioned forward to the glass coffee table between them, "Something that I'd like to share with you, that the others took away from you."

Kyle watched with careful anticipation as Jimmy reached for the newspapers that covered the glass top, revealing a syringe with the infamous red liquid that once dominated the world of Boy X. Kyle felt his stomach tighten and his entire mind began to spiral.

A trite grin slid over Jimmy's thin lips as he slumped back into the beige sofa.

"Why are you doing this?" asked Kyle coldly, fighting to keep his eyes off the syringe.

"I'm taking the edge off." Jimmy sipped at his beer, "Go on son, help yourself."

Kyle shook his head, stepping back in alarm.

"Yes, I know what you are thinking. You're thinking you were right about me, about what you saw."

"You son of a bitch!" Kyle said stepping against the wall, "Why?"

Jimmy looked up at him, "Daddy's got big problems."

Kyle's eyes filled with tears of rage and hate as the demons within him struggled violently with each other to overcome the temptation and bitter urge they had so successfully subdued after his stay at Crown Lake. Kneeling down with a one hundred rand note rolled tightly, Jimmy slid a thin white line onto the glass beside the syringe. Kyle watched in awe, his body coiled as though an invisible hand clutched at every muscle inside of him, twisting and wringing each part of his fiber into discomfort.

"This shit is good." He closed his eyes, "Imported from Dubai by yours truly. Right up my ass all the way in. I got some liquid here too if you want that."

Kyle stared at him for awhile, watching as this stranger to him relished the rush that engulfed him.

A knock rapped at the door.

"That would be for you Kyle."

Jimmy snickered, raising his arms up behind his head as Kyle stared at the door.

Another knock rapped.

"Open it."

Kyle turned to him shaking his head, "What is this? What's going on here?"

Another knock sounded, more forced.

Jimmy heaved a sigh, nodding towards the door and Kyle shook his head, heading towards the front door. Before his hand could grab the handle, Jimmy slammed into him and pushed him towards the back door. "Kyle...open the door!"

The small wooden back door slammed loudly and Jimmy pushed him forward. With his heart racing against his chest, Kyle reached for the handle.

Three people stood there - faces from the red world of 'V', one of them aiming a gun at him, but before his air gasped from his lips a muffled shot fired and Kyle flung backwards onto the floor with a crash.

As the cars pulled up on the narrow grassy path towards the old mine shed a few kilometers outside of Kinross, the music blared and laughter and voices could be heard before even getting out of their cars. Like all the region surrounding the Highveld area, everything as far as the eye could see was flat and covered in veld grass.

The party within the old storage shed had been the talk among all teenagers and young adults from the moment Michael sent the first SMS.

The shed was now an enormous empty metal building standing two stories high that was once used to house bulk mining equipment that Leslie mine had loaned to one of the neighboring mine's as a type of depot. It was utilized for the duration that the two mines aided in each other's shut down. This was the shed where Lyle Harper's body was found hanging from the centre walk way four years before, but only a few could remember the story gracing the local papers and the party was a raging success two hours in.

As Kyle lay on the floor struggling to regain his breath from the shot to his chest with the bean-bag sized rubber shell that he recalled all too well, the three men entered and closed the door.
"My debt?" Jimmy asked, "Is it cleared? Are we square?"
"Stay out of the way." A deep voice sounded as Kyle rolled to his stomach, still gasping for air.
At the pool, Bennie still enjoyed splashing about with a bright yellow pool noodle another group of boys had given to him as the three of them floated and played sword fighting. Hungry now, he looked back at the cottage, then turned to his friends and politely excused himself, promising to be back.
The three young boys all bid him a friendly farewell and Bennie hurriedly flipped his pool noodle back to his friends as he scrambled for the side, hurriedly clambering out. He hurried across the side and grabbed his towel and shoes, looking at the cottage again, something inside his chest felt wrongness in the world. After waving again at his friends, he sped up towards the house.
"The others are going to be very surprised when they see you again. Hell you give me a hard on just looking at you. This is going to be fun!"
Kyle could not see through the haze that was 'V' coursing through his veins. They let go of his arm and slid the needle out. He tried effortlessly to roll onto his front and force himself to crawl off the bed as he spoke out in a dry husky voice that only whispered raspy from his mouth.

"Don't do this…"

"This is the perfect setting! When we are done here, the others will think Boy X is dead. And business can continue as usual. Hell I'll even let you do what you've been too scared to do when I'm done with him."

"Help me!" Kyle called out from the floor before being plucked back onto his feet. The blurred figure in front of him barely visible but the voice one he knew all too well.

As Bennie crossed the stoned pathway onto the lawn, he felt a sharp pain strike into his foot and he gasped, falling to his knees. He hurriedly turned over his foot to find the stinger of a bee.

"Now the bee is going to die!" he said forgetting that he was no longer surrounded by his friends from the pool.

Kyle cried out hopelessly, their fists tearing at his ribs and sides before he fell to the ground only inches from the tripod stand where the small camcorder recorded everything.

"Get the knife."

Kyle wanted to cry, he wanted tears to physically fall from his eyes but V had him beat and not even his tear ducts could operate. Even through the mystical fog around his brain, Kyle saw his hopes smashing to the ground, his soul sucked back into the cage of darkness and suffering. He thought of Liz and Joel, Michael, Claire and Andy, Edward and little Bennie.

With hands dug into his hair, they pulled him to his feet again and through the blur of the dark room he could only see the silver blade nearing him.

"No one leave's, no one!"

Flinging the front door open, Bennie frowned nervously at the shattered glass table and the cigarette that lay smoldering on the wooden floor. He hurriedly moved towards it, carefully it picking up with his little fingers and rushing back outside. He knelt down and began to dig a hole in the sand with the intent of burying it, his little mind knowing that it was safest underground where it wouldn't burn the house down.

"Kyle?" Bennie called worriedly from the bottom of the stairs, almost in tears as he thought of them leaving him alone. He listened, there were bumps coming from upstairs.

He looked to the glass doors, but the deck was empty.

"Kyle where are you?" he said as his eyes filled with tears as he started up the stairs. Kyle tried to scream past the large wet hand covering his mouth, but a lash tore at his chest – a leather like whip with a sting he would never forget.

"Kyle!" Bennie called again, more urgently with his voice in distress. He leaned up against the closed bedroom door, his heart racing in his tiny chest and he put his hand on the door handle nervously, every available monster and fear in his mind running with his imagination. Bennie closed his eyes, he had to be brave in case his big brother needed him and he clenched his hand to the door handle, hurriedly memorizing the number his father and mother had taught him to dial in emergencies.

Just then the glass deck door flung open and he fell back with a scream as Jimmy stepped out shutting it.

"Kyle went for ice cream, shall we go find him?"

The air around the giant shed vibrated with music as the evening set in. As Joel head through the knee high grass towards the doors, high school teens were already hammered from the excessive supply in the beer drums. Older college boys were making moves on the high school girls because they were all anxious to be with a college guy and the air was alive with an electrifying vibe. To the far side of the shed, as though hiding around the corner he noticed a man in a suit, but when his eyes reached him the man hurried out of site. The entrance condition was that a token bottle of booze be emptied into a separate 25 liter plastic drum. A drum, that only on Michael's word, would be used by each person still at the party to fill their cups with.

Girls looked great, boys looked suave and the inside of the shed had been decorated with streamers and balloons, even two strobe lights hung from the catwalk. As Joel took in the energy he couldn't help but wonder where Michael, who had just suffered a severe melt down, had found the time to put it all together.

The crowd stood the entire lower level full and even the catwalks on either side that crossed the middle had people standing on them.

Joel nod with an impressed grin, realizing then that this night was bound to be a very big one. After taking a bottle of Richelieu brandy from his back pack and emptying into the drum, he head towards the side admiring the number of attendees dancing in the centre of the wide shed. He noticed Rendani and fellow Delta Cap swimmer Brad in the far corner with a crowd of guys and girls. He motioned towards them when a hand grabbed his shoulder and he spun around.

"To avoid complications should a bust be made, no drugs are allowed inside the shed." Said the staunch boy, "If you need to party hard, everyone is asked to gather outside around the side of the building. Got it?"

Joel turned to where his finger showed. The shed next door was smaller, more dilapidated and ominous in the shadows of the fading sunlight.

Joel sighed nervously as he continued to make his way through the crowd, the beat of the music thumping at the soles of his feet and pulsing in his ears.

"Joel! You made it!" said Bronwyn pressing up against him for a hug as she squeezed his behind. He sighed with a vague smile, "If you touch my car I'm going to sue you."

She laughed running her hand through his hair, "Bygones. I know you'll come around."

"I doubt it." he said with a smirk as he gently shoved her back, "I think it's fair to warn you if you or any of your money hustling tramps come near me or anything of mine, I will ruin you – hard."

"Excuse me?"

"No, you've been excused." He said stepping closer towards her, "We are done, stay away from me and stay away from my friends. Got it, B?"

She stared at him, the priceless expression on her face pressing for him to grin but he remained posed and simply stepped around her.

"This is awesome isn't it?" Brad said shouting over the music.

"Pretty cool yeah." Joel agreed, taking the glass from Brad who blatantly shoved it in his hand as he began to move aside, falling in with others dancing.

"You need something to drink out of?" Rendani frowned.

"No, I'm good thanks, will be sticking to ciders tonight." Joel smiled reaching for a bottle inside his back pack. Rendani smiled and took the back pack from him, turning to the row of industrial nails on the shed wall behind him, hanging his bag beside his.

As he made his way through the crowd, admiring the atmosphere and vibe gyrating off of the people, he failed to notice a pillar that structured the above catwalk in place and he banged into it, bouncing to the side and skidding on the ground – the drink in his hand now less than a quarter full.

"Well, well, well…" said the senior Delta Capital chairman Steve Pienaar with an irate grin as Joel stumbled up to his feet stupidly. Joel looked up with a smile while the tall senior with a long blond pony tail shook his head, "We didn't think you'd show your face here."

"Really, why?" asked Joel as collectively as he could. Hugo Michaels, under chairman, stepped up laughing, "You got some nerve freshman!"

"You turned your back on us man, what the hell do you think you're doing here?"

Joel laughed playfully, "Come on man, you make it sound like the Mafia or something."

"You're damn right!" snarled Steve poking his finger into Joel's chest, "You quit the team! You disgraced the Delta Caps!"

"Alright girls, cool it down." Michael said stepping up beside Joel, casually flinging his arm around his neck with a grin, "Let's not forget that this *is* a party. So cool it and deal with your shit later."

Steve shrugged his hands back, granting a daggering glance at Joel, "He quit the swim team."

"Oh my god!" Michael gasped turning to Joel in alarm, "Now the little mermaids won't win the ocean fair!"

Steve sighed and Michael turned to face him with an arrogant grin, "Who cares? Joel's cool in my book so lay off him ok?"

"You don't have a say in this Harper." Said Hugo angrily, "This is Delta Cap business."

"Ok look, I admit, I quit in a moment of weakness." Said Joel, "I have stuff going on with my family."

"That's not our business." Steve scoffed tipping his head back to sip from his cup.

Joel shook his head.

"You never disgrace the Caps!!" Steve said shoving him backwards. Michael grabbed him and leaned in close to his ear. "Listen Pienaar, I've kicked your ass before and I'll do it again. Cut my friend some slack before I tell everyone on campus who your dad paid for a happy ending. Got it?"

Steve stepped back, his face riddled in upset and Michael turned to Joel with a wink before heading off.

"You're welcome back whenever you've sorted out your family business."

"What?" Hugo gasped, "That's not right man!"

"Shut up Hugo!" Steve snarled, hitting him in the gut as he head off into the crowd.

Joel frowned and head after Michael.

"What was that?"

"Ungrateful now Mac D?" Mike asked scanning the party, "He's not going to bother you again, so let's leave it at that."

"How you holding up?"

"Taking pain killers, skin feels like I played in a coal pit." Mike laughed, "I've seen worse."

"I don't doubt it. Any luck at the post office yet?"

Mike sighed nervously, "This isn't the place…We'll talk about it later. For now just chill and enjoy, we deserve it."

"Is Kyle here?" Joel said also scanning the party.

"Not sure."

"How long have you guys known each other anyway? Old friends?"

Mike frowned, "What do you mean?"

"Well I just figured you guys know each other."

Michael shook his head, "No. Why so many questions Mac D? Enjoy the party ok?"

Joel nod, slightly upset that he still couldn't figure out what was going on without blatantly asking. Across the shed he saw Liz speaking with a crowd of people and when he turned back to Michael, he was gone. Sighing, he made his way through the bustling bodies pulsing to the beat.

"Hey!" he smiled as she turned to him. "Oh hey Joel, how you doing?" she asked over the blaring music, eagerly looking past him for Kyle.

"Good thanks, is Kyle with you?"

"No, I thought he would catch a ride with you." She smiled bravely, her heart already slumping at the thought of him not being there.

"Flipper boy, you made it." Troy smiled rounding behind him sipping the last of her drink. He smiled nervously and holding up her empty paper cup, the beat almost overpowering her soft voice, she instructed him to walk with her to get another.

Left alone, Liz sighed awkwardly and continued to subtly move to the music as she glared around the crowded shed in hopes of finding Kyle. In her life leading to the moment when she first laid eyes on him, she had never felt her stomach quiver with lust, nor the temperature of her body warm with such intense desire. As she stood standing to the side with the beat thumping at the soles of her feet and shuddering in her stomach, she felt almost desperate to see him again, to look into his eyes, hear his voice and touch his skin. All her life, every guy she had liked and dated never gave her such an overwhelming burn inside the way he did, and she had always been cautious of both the boys she dated in high school because she knew boys were dangerous, horny creations who would toss her aside the minute someone else tickled their fancy. She had never allowed herself to feel anything sexual because she never wanted to waste her virginity. She believed in the magic her father spoke of each time he'd tell her stories about meeting her mother. Yet their first conversation in the store, the first glimpse into the pools of vast mystery that lay within his blue eyes she knew something within her soul was shifting and changing. It more than lust for his mouth watering physic and good looks, it was a craving to know more, feel more and experience more of Kyle Evans. At first, each time she felt she was losing herself in him, she would shift focus and remind herself to think, consider, plan and be sure before making any irrational decisions that would alter her. Yet each smile from his face melted her, each time his eyes touched her she felt a craving to be utterly consumed by him in every way – without hesitation fully liberated from sense or plan. Scanning the crowd, she could still not see him.

The playful yet snide banter between Joel and Troy built the entire time they stood talking on the catwalk looking down over the crowd. She realized the more they spoke that he was a sub category to the rich and famous, that behind his arrogant smirk and pretty boy face he was down to earth and not nearly as conceited as the rumors about him insisted. For Joel, just having someone to talk to about things other than fashion, swimming or gossip was enough to feel relaxed and comfortable. He knew each time she laughed that he liked her and would enjoy spending more time with her.

"Oh! Look at what your perfectly constructed friend did to Liz." She sighed pointing down to Liz who stood talking in a group, but her eyes and smile conveying the truth inside her.

Joel laughed, "Kyle?"

"He told her he would be here." Troy shook her head, "Such an ass."

"Can't say I'm surprised. I didn't think Kyle would allow himself to be exposed to such light and joy."

"Yeah he does have that shadow like quality to him, doesn't he?" She agreed laughing, "Spooky but sexy. Like that guy who chased aliens on that show long ago."

Joel laughed nodding, "Kyle's a good guy though."

Liz looked up at them and smiled, carefully starting to move through the party towards the stairway leading to them.

Troy wrapped her arms around Liz, hugging her, "I know sweetie…he's a shit."

"No its ok, something obviously came up." Liz laughed, "It's fine, really."

"He's still a shit, typical man move." Troy said shaking her head as she sipped her drink.

"Maybe he just couldn't get here?" Liz frowned with a vague smile as Michael and Jessie head towards them, greeting others standing on the walk way above the party below.

Michael had opened up to Jessie, they spent all afternoon inside the shed alone setting up for the party, just talking and working. They shared their feelings, their fears and frustrations and most importantly they finally gave each other forgiveness.

"You guys good?" Michael said patting Joel on the shoulder with a wide smile.

"Can I ask you a favor?" asked Joel moving him to the side.

Jessie turned to Liz and Troy with a nervous smile as they introduced themselves.

Michael and Joel returned and with a smile that revealed all his inner peace, Michael took Jessie by the hand and they head off.

"That is one pretty girl." Troy said admiring the color of her red hair as they head down the stairs. Liz smiled politely to hide her burning curiosity, "So what's Kyle like when it's just you guys hanging out?"

"He's cool." Joel shrugged shaking his head looking to Troy, "We don't really hang out as such."

Troy rolled her eyes and continued to sip at her drink through the straw.

"He's very intense around me, is he always like that?"

"Since the first time we met." Joel laughed, tipping back a sip of cider, "He's a good guy though. He has a good heart, I think he's just rough around the edges."

"That's putting it mildly." Troy huffed rolling her eyes again.

"Would you like to dance?" asked Joel turning to Troy, curious to see if there could more of a spark between them than just light-hearted repartee.

Troy looked to Liz smirking, "Shall I indulge in my Pretty Woman fantasy and allow Mr. Gere to dance with me?"

"Depends..." Liz said shrugging her shoulders playfully, "Is he paying you for the night?"

"Every ounce of my attention." Joel said holding out his hand as he lowered to a bow. Troy blushed giggling, "Smooth flipper boy, I'll give you that."

She took his hand and he led her to the stairs. Liz laughed watching as they head down the stairs to join the dancing.

A black Ford Everest SUV rolled to a stop aside the long dark stretch between Kinross and Evander as another Everest pulled up beside it. The door swung open and agent Black stepped out, buttoning his jacket as Mr. Lee stepped out of the other SUV to meet him. "What have you found Mr. Black?"

"Harper was lying. We've accessed all the records listed under the local post service for deliveries done on the day of the boy's funeral. Something was scheduled to be delivered to Michael Harper not even twenty four hours after we left the province."

Lee sighed nervously as Mr. Black continued.

"There is no further record of the parcel being delivered, the files are missing from the day of the funeral. We accessed classified SARS records on UIF payments for the post office but it will take a while for us to pin point the exact staff on duty at the time."

"It seems our friend Harper is not as allied as we originally thought." Lee huffed in annoyance, "I need to know what the parcel was, and it's clearly something Harper went to lengths to keep us from finding, such as video evidence of that night."

"Green was sure he saw a light from a camcorder." Black nod, "But even before his death the boy denied it."

"Whatever it was, Harper kept it as a form of blackmail." Lee said looking through the dark fields to the lights in the distance from the old shed, "As for the son, we can't have him asking questions or bringing this to anyone's attention. We can't be sure of what he already knows. This way we have him out of our way and we divert all E shaft attention onto a singular target."

Agent Black nod and Lee heaved a sigh, "You have everything I asked for?"

"Yes sir."

"Good. Good." Lee nod heading back to the Everest, "Then I leave it to you to handle this as professional as always Black. Do not disappoint me again like your little knife wielding at the mine. Report when it's handled and I'll see you back in Cape Town."

Leaving Jessie with Troy and Liz again, Michael explained to Joel that he had dialed enquires for a land line number and spoke directly to Claire Evans who explained that Kyle had gone with his father for the weekend. Joel nod, the look in Kyle's eyes as he saw the golden Jeep still haunting him.

At the Sabie resort, the moon shone into the lake with a brilliant white as the noises of nature sounded around the homes and tents where families were braai'ing meat on fires and laughing. Bennie had eaten and lay watching a cartoon off of Jimmy's laptop, eagerly waiting for his brother to wake up. But his eyes grew heavier as his little body craved for the energy he had burnt in the pool to rebuild.

Coming from the kitchen, Jimmy sighed stretching, "You still awake kiddo?"

"Yes Uncle Jimmy." He said yawning, "What is wrong with my brother?"

Jimmy sighed clownishly, "Your brother's really not feeling very well, probably from all that playing today at the pool. He'll need to stay in bed for the weekend unfortunately."

Bennie frowned and nod with a tired smile, his eyes reddening.

"Why don't you head upstairs and get in bed, before you know it it'll be morning and you know what? You can chose anything you want for breakfast! How's that?"

Bennie's tired eyes lit up, "Ok!"

"Good night kiddo." Jimmy smiled as Bennie got up and moved in to hug his leg.

"Good night Uncle Jimmy."

Jimmy's smile faded the minute Bennie disappeared into his room upstairs and he sighed exhaustedly, not used to having to cater for a small child. Sitting on the edge of the sofa, he lifted the newspaper he had previously draped over the white lines on the table and briefly considered snorting another line, before standing up and opting for a cold beer from the fridge instead.

Brushing his hair backwards, he entered the main bedroom again, where Kyle now lay on his side beneath the white sheet, moaning and shivering. Jimmy smiled looking down at this son and shook his head.

Kyle wearily raised his head and looked up at his father, his eyes red with pain and tears and he tried to speak but could not muster it. His body's senses slowly began returning to normal as 'V' began wearing off, but images touching his eye sight were still slightly stretching and warping. Beneath the covers, his thighs, legs and feet had been beaten and lashed by the belt and buckle. In the corner of the room lay sheets covered in blood.

His entire upper body had been beaten, the only markings visible to the world after this weekend would be the slight swelling on his cheek and neck. Everything had been filmed as a warning to any of the others that they would be found, regardless of how much time elapsed – they would never escape.

Jimmy raised the single sheet covering Kyle and his stomach sank at the remains of the red stains from the fake blood they had poured over him to make it convincing of his death.

"You are going to have to bath eventually." Jimmy said softly.

"I'm going to kill you." Kyle said behind a broken voice, hoarse from screaming behind a gag.

Jimmy sighed nervously, carefully sitting on the side of the bed as he mustered the courage to speak to the boy who was no longer 8 years old.

"I had no choice. I had too much debt."

"I'm going to kill you."

"No you won't." He sighed, "You heard them, they'll be watching you and I think you know you'll never be free. Killing me won't solve that."

Kyle shut his eyes.

"I know you hate me." Jimmy sighed standing up again, brushing his hands through his oily slick hair, "I should probably explain my part in all of this."

"I don't care…" Kyle said with his broken voice, "I'm going to kill you. All of you."

"I racked up so much debt..." he said shaking his head.

Kyle shook his head, fighting back the tears as his hands clenched the sheet.

"I needed a way out. I had to do this, to save myself don't you see?" Jimmy knelt at the bedside, "I had no idea you were ever going to come back."

"I don't care." His voice broke again, "I'm your son."

"That you are." He said standing up again, "This wasn't about you, this was about the others. It's over now, add this to all the other secrets you have wallowing up inside of you boy and move on."

"I hate you."

"Get in line." Jimmy smiled as he got up towards the door, "This wasn't for you Kyle, so be careful because the next time will be."

The haze grew thick and Kyle closed his eyes.

"This isn't nearly over boy…" the voice said standing over him as he lay covered in bruises, cuts and fake blood as two of them tore the sheets from the bed and tossed them to the corner leaving him to land on the hardwood floor with a thud.

"You shouldn't have left. You shouldn't have." He said kicking Kyle onto his back so that one of the others could easily drag him to the bathroom.

"This is just the beginning. I'll be watching you and when you

350

least expect it, I'll come calling."
They threw him into the bathtub without remorse and opened the taps.
"Nobody leaves, no one. You are ours 'Boy X', you always will be." He said watching as both real and fake blood trickled into the water as Kyle huddled his naked body against the wall – the power of 'V' allowing him a world of distorted chaos.

Joel accompanied Troy and Liz outside to use the porta-pottie, waiting outside for them and staring into the blackness around them. The full moon's light the only hope in the morbid tranquility that hung outside the shed, enveloped in the darkness of the fields. Even through the downing of shooters, ciders and flirting with Troy, the mystery of Kyle Evans and the revelation of Michael Harper held clasp like a shiver he couldn't liberate. And in the silent night with the thumping droning inside, the darkness broken by the pale moon above, he closed his eyes trying to understand it all.

Just then a hand grabbed his shoulder and he turned to face Michael who grinned with a drunken fog in his eyes.

"You look deep in thought." He slurred, unzipping his jeans and releasing urine to the tall grass. "You look like you've tapped into the party drum." Joel smiled stepping to the side, "It's a great party though."

"Fuck yeah!" Michael roared raising one hand into the air.

Joel laughed shaking his head, the sound of the running urine making his own urge materialize. "You don't do the hard stuff right?" frowned Michael turning to him.

"Hard stuff?" Joel frowned releasing a flow of his own to the ground, "Like drugs?"

Michael laughed nodding, "Yes Mac D, drugs. E, A, 'shrooms"

Flipper boy versus Mac D...this needs to stop.

"So you interested?" Michael grinned. Joel shook his head zipping up again, "I'm good thanks."

"The ladies taking a piss?" Asked Michael digging for a joint in the cigarette box.

"Use some tact man." Joel laughed shaking his head, "Yes they are in the portables."

Michael laughed, holding his breath.

"So how you doing now?" asked Joel cautiously.

"Yeah about that man, I know it was like 'wow'! And I appreciate you and Kyle being there, putting up with my bullshit and hearing all the things you heard."

Joel frowned and Michael exhaled into the air, "Life is fucked up man!"

"Yeah it is. But it's cool, so don't stress about it."

"No I have to man." Said Michael grabbing Joel's shoulder, "I've never had that man, my brother died a long time ago and I thought I'd lost a part of me. But the truth is it just took a lot of really nasty shit for me to find myself."

Joel nod, unsure if it was the combination of booze and drugs talking or if it was a heartfelt Michael.

Michael smiled shaking his head, "I'm Mike Harper man, everyone knows my name around here and yet I've always been so fucked up and alone. You guys had no business sticking with me yesterday, and you did, so thank you."

Joel laughed nodding, "We're all in hell Mike. We're just slaves to different demons."

Michael nod, "There anything you wanna tell me Mac D?"

"Nah, this party's too good for my story time." He smiled shyly.

Michael nod with a weak smile, "Yeah, I've got to enjoy this one as much as I can."

"What do you mean?"

"That cop…Nkosi…" Michael lowered his voice, "I'm quitting."

"What do you mean? How?"

Michael's head nod with a solemn admittance.

"Do you realize the charge for murder man?"

"No man, it's over..." Michael said, his face dropping, "Jessie said she'd wait for me and after we'd maybe try and be more than just old friends. If you can just get her out of here please?"

"You're taking the fall alone?" asked Joel in surprise. Michael nod with a brave smile, "I'm done with all this bullshit. I mean sure it's been fun but it's been really fucking twisted too. I wasn't meant for this. At least I don't think I was."

Joel smiled and pat him on the shoulder, "I haven't said I'd do anything yet."

"I think you'll do the right thing when the time is right." Michael laughed nodding, but inside he felt the nervousness rising.

"Your dad used to be mayor right? Maybe he could get them to give you lenience on your sentence?"

Michael scoffed, taking a deep pull at the marijuana stick, "If anything he'd tell them to give me the death penalty…"

Joel sighed shaking his head as they looked out to the darkness again.

"When are you doing it?"

"Next Thursday, there's just something I need to do first."

"The parcel?"

"I have to know what it was."

"Are you sure this is what you want to do?"

"I can't outrun Nkosi man, the guys like Judge Dredd." He joked with a heavy sigh, "I'm done trying to be pretend to forget and ignore everything I've done. I killed a man Joel, and since then I've just gotten caught up in far worse. I've sold my soul already, I have nothing left to lose but Jessie. Talk to her, you'll see she's decent and deserves a chance."

"I'll help you get a good lawyer if I can." Said Joel matter-of-factly and Michael turned to him in surprise.

"You'd do that for me Mac D?"

Joel shrugged, "A few months ago I wouldn't have, but then again a few months ago neither of us would be out here talking."

"Joel, about Jessie… I just need to know she and her mother are safe. I know what I've asked you deserves no reply but…"

"You said Thursday next week, which is enough time for me and you to get to the bottom of this and figure it out. For now Mike, I'll keep thinking about it."

"Please do Mac D!"

"I haven't stopped since you told me." Joel said almost angrily.

"After tonight, you probably won't see me again so I'd appreciate if you don't tell Jessie about this."

"She doesn't know?"

"No."

"Where are you going?"

"Someone's been following me since yesterday." Mike said lowering his voice as the cold around them circled, "I think it's my father's guys I don't know. Guys in black suits."

"Lawyers maybe?"

"I don't know, whatever this thing is that Lyle left me - I don't want it hurting Jessie. I think I…I really like her."

Joel nod with a solemn frown across his face.

Just then Liz, Troy and Jessie finally head towards them from the portable loo's and they turned to face them.

"So is the party outside now?" Liz smiled as Jessie snuggled up against Michael's chest.

Joel smiled when in the corner of his eye he saw a movement, someone in a dark suit rushing in the shadows between the two dilapidated sheds. The man in the black suit stopped, almost alarmed to see that their target was no longer inside the buzzing shed and Joel stepped forward as a cold set in over his skin.

"You ok?" frowned Troy crossing her arms from the chill outside. Turning to Michael who frowned worriedly, Joel turned to Troy with a smile as he began to remove his jacket – choosing to ignore his paranoia and return to feeling peace with the first girl he felt at home with.

"Everything good?" Michael frowned, unable to let go of the panic in Joel's eyes. Joel heaved a deep breath nodding, "For n…"

An explosion roared out to the side of the massive storage shed, erupting the silence of the night with a tearing scream of flames overhead.

The flames ripped up into the sky, curling over the roof of the metal buildings as the ground and air grumbled all around the silent darkness. Screams filled the air as students began rushing out of the shed in a dire panic, trampling and shoving to get as far from the flaming building and students as possible as pillar of dark smoke loomed out of the giant door way.

Rushing to his feet in complete distress, Michael rushed towards the crowds streaming out of the building and Jessie screamed for him to stay but he shoved his way into the shed. Joel helped Liz and Troy to their feet, "Run, get as far away as you can!"

The girls nod in dazed terror and confusion as the screaming party goers stampede their way to cars. "Don't!" Troy said trying to grab Joel's hand as he dart after Michael.

Liz hurried to where a girl had been trampled and plucked her to her feet, "Are you ok?"

There were voices that cried out all around, and Liz wrapped her pull over around her, ushering the girl towards the cars, calling out for anyone to take her to the hospital until finally a student grabbed her around the shoulders and hurried the wailing teen towards his car. Troy hurriedly dialed emergency services as Jessie rushed to aid Liz in getting those injured by the stampede, fire and debris as far from the building as possible. Another explosion ruptured the night sky from inside the shed and for a second everyone turned to face the shed as the flames tore through the grass towards the cars. "We have to get out of here!" Troy said grabbing Liz.

"I can't' leave Michael!" Jessie cried as Liz grabbed her into her arms, the cars now speeding off into the darkness. Liz turned to the side where a group of students were trying to subdue the flames engulfing the grass surrounding four of the cars.

Inside Michael hurried through the smoke with the Delta Cap chairman Steven slung over his shoulders like a sack when he rammed into Joel.

"Is there anyone else?" Joel asked behind a cough as the thick smoke began bouldering lower towards the ground, the ceiling of the shed in a maze of fire.

"I don't know!" Michael gasped, the tear in Steve's leg oozing blood, his wailing drowned by the crackling flames surrounding them. Michael rushing to the door post and Joel knelt down, scanning as best he could through the thick grey smoke as chunks of the ceiling and walls began breaking down around him. Jessie and Troy rushed to Michael as t\he stumbled down onto the ground, slugging Steve onto the floor.

"Where's Joel?" Troy asked worriedly trying to see through the monster smoke escaping up from the doorway as more chunks of the walls began to fall.

"Troy!" Liz gasped rushing to her, "You still remember CPR?" Liz gripped Troy's hand as she tugged her to where one of the students collapsed near the grass around the cars.

"Troy, I need you to help him. Can you do that?"

Troy nod with wide eyes and hurriedly knelt down to the boy who had cuts and burns across his arms and shoulders.

Liz scurried back to where Jessie and Michael dragged Steve further to the side away from the building, in the brief moment passing the door she could see bodies laying burning inside.

As she rushed to the doorway, Joel stammered out with a girl clutching to him, both of them choking from the smoke.

"Take her!" Joel gasped, spinning back to Liz's frightened alarm.

As Liz turned to take the girl beside Steve, Michael sprint past her into the smoke and Jessie screamed rushing after him.

Liz carefully helped the girl to her knees beside Steve who lay clutching his leg, "Dimitri's in there."

Liz flung around, fighting away the tears that broke inside her.

"Move! Everyone, get away from the cars!" Troy screamed, helping those away from the cars that now had tires in flames.

Liz turned to face the road far in the distance where lights and sirens approached when the adjacent shed crumbled to the heat and the metal tearing down ripped through the night.

It's structure slammed into the main shed and the metal crunched, the entire structure leaning towards the side with Joel, Michael and Jessie still inside. She flung around again, rushing into the tall grass waving her arms out and screaming at the emergency vehicles to hurry.

"Are you alright?" Troy asked helping the student to a sitting position when one of the car's erupted.

"Troy!" screamed Liz as the explosion roared outwards, engulfing everything beneath its hellish flames and debris.

"We have to get out of here!" Jessie gasped grabbing onto Michael's arm, "Please!"

Inside, screams sounded from within the flames. Students trapped by debris and fire.

"I have to be sure everyone's out!" he said toppling over rubble, "It's all my fault!"

"No!" she said grabbing his arm, "I can't lose you!"

Joel stumbled to the ground, his eyes burning as he failed to gasp for air, the smoke choking at his throat and lungs when the roar of snapping metal echoed through the loud crackling flames. The catwalk above snapped on the one side, and its entire flaming metal structure swung down, slicing through the smoke and crashed down with a deafening slam. Joel forced himself to his feet as debris began toppling down around him, a heated pole scorching down onto his shoulder and he fell to the ground.

"Jessie!" Michael called in a pungent cough, standing up in the smoke, rushing forward blindly calling for her again before slamming into the scorching metal of the catwalk as the other side still connected up top began to roar and crack at the weight. He dropped to his knees, calling for her.

"Here! Michael!" she screamed and he dropped as low to the ground as he could, rushing around the metal structure and huddling to her side. "Michael! Help me!" she cried in choked screams, "It's got my leg!"

"Hold on!" he said hurriedly ripping off his shirt and wrapping it around his hands and hurriedly grabbing at the iron hot catwalk, lifting with all his might.

"It's not lifting!" she screamed, "You have to go! Get out of here now!"

He forced with all his might, and the heat tore through his shirt and he flinched letting go with a furious scream. "Get out of here Mike, now!" she screamed through her tears.

He fell to her side grabbing her hand, "I'm not leaving you god damned it! I fucking love you!"

He sprung up again, grabbing the metal beams, forcing with all his might but he felt his body surrendering to the power of the smoke and unyielding heat.

Standing on the wooden railings surrounding the deck, Kyle raised his arms up at his sides, wobbling without balance as the pain tore through him. The dark water below was calm and silent, encompassing everything he desperately craved to break his soul once and for all. He struggled to keep his eyes focused through the dreadful numb of 'V' and his body was weak from the wounds, too painful to move.

He closed his eyes and heaved in a final breath of the freshness of the night's air.

As his body slammed through the water, its icy grip tore at his aching body, piercing through his clothes. The calm dark water was black beneath the surface, the moonlight barely breaching its surface as Kyle allowed the water to draw weight on his life, allowing it to carry him down into the depths of the murky dark water without a struggle. The cold was numbing, better than the senselessness of his tormented soul. The moonlight faded from sight, the red world of 'V' no longer in control as he allowed the blackness to encompass him.

The fresher air outside crashed into Joel's lungs as he stumbled out of the flaming building with the younger students on either side of him. Flames engulfed the building and tore a light through the fields. The window glass which hadn't yet shattered popped as the heat tore out through the roof. His ears were ringing, his lungs screaming for air and through the burn in his eyes he tried in vain to search out for any familiar face as the paramedics and fire rescue teams rushed towards them. Moments after hitting the ground gasping for air, he was encompassed immediately by fire teams wrapping them in blankets and ushering them towards the ambulances as teams rushed in with axes and hoses.

The nights darkness, previously only lit by the moon had been torn open by red and blue flashing lights as teams of fire rescue tore across the field surrounding the buildings with hoses.

"Troy…" Said Joel trying to see through the burning of his eyes as the paramedics lay him down on the stretcher inside the ambulance. Liz, draped in a blanket, stood watching as they shut the doors on Joel and she turned back to the flames in utter disbelief and torment.

The black Ford SUV crawled out from behind the brush as the ambulances began veering off the field and onto the road, and agent Black sat grinning at the steering wheel as he and two fellow agents drove off with the flames shining across the darkness onto the dark windows.

Their mission for the evening was absolute. Media attention would be torn between E shaft and route 11 and further delays into the reopening of E shaft would be secured. In a breath of madness the shaft's many lies and multiple deaths, dark cover ups and vile secrets were yet again under rug swept.

As the black car disappeared down the road into the silence of the night, all the secrets powerful enough to tear apart the Corporation and send shock waves around the world from the core of the country, would remain buried beneath the rock falls within the shaft. The shadows of the day were breaking on the horizon and light spread across the fields, as the secrets of the nights fell to silence.

To be continued…

'Soul Break Part Two'

With the events of the fire now sparking a nationwide outrage at the copious amounts of unnecessary deaths surrounding E Shaft, detectives Jordan and Underwood embark on a search for the identity of the man in the black suit that their only witness, Joel McDonald, claims to have seen moments before the blaze.

As the Corporation races to bury all evidence of their secrets within the old mine, Michael Harper too begins the search for the only person who can tell him what the package was.

Leaving behind everything he has lost, Joel follows Michael in search of the truth for the people responsible for the death of their friends. With everything hanging in the balance, the Corporation will stop at nothing to progress with their sinister plans, even if it means creating an even darker distraction to the lives of those left sweeping the ashes….

ISBN: 978-0-9921977-4-2

Acknowledgements:

Firstly, I would like to express my thanks to my two children Hailey and Dylan for supporting and encouraging me throughout this book, who understood the time it took and for believing in me regardless.

The thanks and acknowledgement I give to my wife Soreen will never truly express how grateful I am for everything you did to support me. For your important suggestions, support, time, patience, criticisms, suggestions and passion! My right hand and left, always.

To my mom, dad and brother and sister for believing in me and more importantly - for patiently waiting to read my book!

And my friends Rene, Zander, Jackie, Rohan, Johan, Farhana, Jessie, Kevin and Matt to name a few - who always cared and supported me. I have to thank you to everyone who saw me through this book, all those who provided support, talked things over, read, wrote, offered comments, allowed me to quote their remarks and assisted in the proofreading and creation of these wonderful characters.

To all the generous and wonderful people I've met through the course of researching this book, who gave me their time and assistance to get right the characters, the back stories and the arc of the book – to many to name, you know who you are – thank you!

LC

ISBN: 978-0-9921977-4-2

First Edition 1 April 2016
Second Edition 10 July 2016

Cover Illustration © Lynel Coetzer 2016

For more information on Lynel Coetzer, his works, news, previews and more, visit www.lynelcoetzer.co.za or contact info@lynelcoetzer.co.za.

More from Lynel Coetzer:

SOUL BREAK Part Two	The saga continues as the race to uncover the truth of E Shaft brings forth darkness nobody saw coming.
	While Michael continues his search for the box, the survivors of the fire attempt to rebuild their lives as the loss of friends weighs in on them.
	All the while, the Corporation sets in motion a dangerous attempt to keep their past from surfacing, taking their desperation across country in a hunt for the only person with proof of their Face Operation.
	As everything comes to light, the only way to set themselves free of the darkness tearing at their souls is to push through the darkness.

THE FIELDS OF OBSESSION	Detective Caine has seen it all in his years of service. The disregard for kindness especially, whatever the crime. But this crime scene was different. The young boy's body lay face down on the ground, the putrid smell coming from his tortured corpse was enough to cripple him and everyone in the room. This crime was different, the predator was darker. This was a macabre and savage criminal who had only just gotten started....
	"We are the ordinary folk behind you in the grocery line, or beside you in traffic. We are the folk you hold a door open to or share a booth with in a restaurant. "The killer's eyes were cold, but the grin on his face...it was clear he was a maniac. The axe swung in his bloodied hands and he looked to his twisted partner beside him, "We smile at you in passing but when darkness sets in, we are capturing and torturing our next victim. Keeping them prisoner in a small shed out in the fields far from any escape. We are the ordinary folk your lack of courtesy has truly messed up!"
	As the body count rises around town and more people start vanishing, solving this mystery becomes detective Caine's obsession as he races against time to save his grandson.

www.ingramcontent.com/pod-product-compliance
Lightning Source LLC
Chambersburg PA
CBHW062007170626
46813CB00001B/64